Forever Today

A Love Story

Breck Miller

iUniverse, Inc.
Bloomington

Forever Today
A Love Story

Copyright © 2012 by Breck Miller

All rights reserved. No part of this book may be used or reproduced by any means, graphic, electronic, or mechanical, including photocopying, recording, taping or by any information storage retrieval system without the written permission of the publisher except in the case of brief quotations embodied in critical articles and reviews.

This is a work of fiction. All of the characters, names, incidents, organizations, and dialogue in this novel are either the products of the author's imagination or are used fictitiously.

iUniverse books may be ordered through booksellers or by contacting:

iUniverse
1663 Liberty Drive
Bloomington, IN 47403
www.iuniverse.com
1-800-Authors (1-800-288-4677)

Because of the dynamic nature of the Internet, any web addresses or links contained in this book may have changed since publication and may no longer be valid. The views expressed in this work are solely those of the author and do not necessarily reflect the views of the publisher, and the publisher hereby disclaims any responsibility for them.

Any people depicted in stock imagery provided by Thinkstock are models, and such images are being used for illustrative purposes only.

Certain stock imagery © Thinkstock.

ISBN: 978-1-4759-2770-2 (sc)
ISBN: 978-1-4759-2771-9 (hc)
ISBN: 978-1-4759-2772-6 (e)

Library of Congress Control Number: 2012908795

Printed in the United States of America

iUniverse rev. date: 06/5/2012

Acknowledgements

This book has been on my bucket list for over twenty-five years. It is with the inspiration of my wife, Julie as well as her patience, understanding, support and love that I was able to complete this novel.

I also want to thank my daughters, Kristi, Tricia, Kelley, Staci and Lindsay for the support that I needed to finally put ink to my thoughts.

A special thank you goes out to Stephen Edds and more importantly Jon Hueber, who was my strongest critic but tempered his criticism with thought-provoking guidance in bringing these characters to life. Jon, thank you for the many nights you spent on the phone with me going through the editorial process. You are the best!

Last but not least, I want to thank those individuals who were part of my life through the '60s, '70s and '80s. This book is a tribute to the loves of my life and those who made an ever-lasting impact on me as a person. Thank you.

NOW

I t's time.
The sun is setting in hues of pink and blue behind the trees across the still waters of Lake Whitney on an autumn afternoon in southwestern Indiana. Fall has just arrived after a late burst of warm weather. I'm glad for the cool air. The hot, humid Indiana summer doesn't bother me, but it's been hard getting used it to since I've been back. This is the end of my first summer here in almost 30 years, and I wonder why I spend my adult life anywhere else. Of course I know the answer, my restless nature, my wanderlust has taken me away from here, but since I've been back, I know it's where I'll spend my remaining years. What am I saying? I'm talking as though I have a limited time, but I have no such sentence placed upon me. I'm a year away from 50. I feel young, but not everyone I've journeyed with has made it this far. Hopefully I have a lot of years left. The lake is about 1,200 acres of water, with a sand bottom, and lined with houses whose construction goes back 100 years in some cases, though most of them have been replaced due to wear. During the summer, it's fairly active as people come in from the town and surrounding counties to swim and fish.

On this day, the activity on the lake is fairly quiet; the ripple of the lake provides a peaceful companion. On a typical busy day during the summer, the lake would be full of high school and college kids. But now the kids have gone back to school, and the lure of the water and the warm summer air has been replaced by football games on Saturday, and a cool, almost chilly, autumn breeze. It seems like in this part of the Midwest, everyone is excited about the lake until July 4th, where they have a spectacular fireworks display on the water. After that, the crowds slowly diminish, which is okay with me.

It is a beautiful day to just sit on the edge of the dock with my legs dangling over the edge allowing my feet to just hover above the clear, cool water below. My thoughts are of the past and the various roads in life I took, which have brought me to where I am now.

In my right hand is a sealed envelope that contains a letter, which I've been caressing in my hand like a fine cigar about to be smoked for the better part of the last hour or so. I've decided that today is the day I'm going to open the letter and read it. But not yet. I've spent the past couple of hours--hell all day for that matter--in a haze. The emotions I've suppressed over the years have started to surface. I'm riding every wave of emotion you can imagine, because today is the day I choose to quit stalling.

You would think this would be easy, opening a letter. I mean, it's not made of Teflon and it doesn't have some six-digit combination to open. But I've been putting it off.

Until today.

I've ended up spending time reflecting on my life, something I haven't done nearly enough over the years. I let it happen; I let the memories come flooding back to me. It's sad. I should have done this years ago. It's like looking at a photo album with your friends. They notice the pictures, and you remember the little things about the time the picture was taken: the nuances and the stories, before and after.

I never owned a camera until a couple of years ago, so I've missed out on a lot of those photo opportunities. I'm remembering now, and for the hell I've put my body through, I still have a pretty sharp memory, and those memories have been flooding back like high tide during a full moon.

So much has happened over the years. So much I've missed out on because I didn't have the time or the self-awareness to look around and take everything in. So many people I've hurt or ignored, or didn't appreciate because I lived in the moment and thought everyone else was enjoying the ride. I've teared up several times and laughed out loud on several more.

Thank God the neighbors were not home or they'd thought I'd gone crazy.

I'm absent-mindedly twirling the letter and watching what little action is happening on the lake. There are some kids out there--I speculate that it's either high school graduates that didn't go to college and aren't working, or college kids taking the day off--riding jet skis around the lake. There are also a handful of fishing boats trying to catch some late season catfish. However, I imagine they won't be too successful since the jet skis are riding too close to the boats and scaring the fish away.

"Damn kids," I mutter to myself, "they need to grow up and learn some respect." I chuckle at the thought. I was one of "those kids," reckless and unaware, having the time of their lives. They'll probably grow up and be responsible and it'll happen to them a lot sooner than it happened to me.

I look at the envelope again for probably the thousandth time. For some reason I supposed there might be something I missed, something that would give me a clue of the contents, but it is just a plain business-class envelope with the name "Chad Breckenridge," handwritten, on the front. It's a little worn around the edges from being handled so many times, but the contents hadn't magically fallen out and revealed themselves like I had hoped. Nope, I thought, it's going to be up to me to do this.

I look back over the lake, and over the trees, and picture the area about 10 miles west, past the other side of the lake. That's where the sleepy town of Deer Park resides. It hasn't changed much in the thirty years since I graduated from the now-closed Deer Park High School back in 1969. The town still has about five thousand people, with a mostly agriculture-based economy. There have been some manufacturing plants come and go over the years due to the proximity to I-74, and with this came a couple of strip malls and, of course, a Wal-Mart. Downtown Deer Park has remained the same, fashioning itself as kind of a historic "throwback" to the old country towns where people can come and get away from the hustle and bustle of the city. It's not much, but its home. Again. It was my boyhood home, and now I've come full circle, back to where it all began.

I think about the letter, and how I got to this place. The letter can wait, the memories that are washing over me are so vivid that it's like I'm watching a movie. I lean back on the dock just a little as I start to reflect on my life. The film begins to flutter and then images appear. The story begins with a boy who is about to make a decision that will change his life forever. I can almost smell the popcorn.

THEN

Chapter 1

It was October of 1968, and I was in my senior year at Deer Park High School. It was the only high school in all of Warren County, and it had been built right next to the K-8 school. The big ritual at the end of every school year was the eighth-graders walking across the parking lot to the high school. I remember doing it four years ago, but those days were past me. I was nearing the end of my school career. All of us in the senior class were. For some, we'd go on to college, for others, Vietnam. It was a tight nit community there within the walls of DPHS. With only a total enrollment of 785, everyone knew just about everyone else. Well, almost.

High school for me was all you could ask for. I was six feet tall and 180 pounds with short, curly blond hair and blue eyes. I was an all-conference running back and linebacker for the defending Southwest Conference champion Deer Park Aviators. I knew how to talk my way out of (and into) most situations, and due to my being easily distracted, I was not the best student. Let me put it this way, there is a term called "senioritis," which is where a student loses their focus and motivation for the last part of their last year of school. It is a terrible infliction, and there is no known cure. For me, I suffered from senioritis from the beginning of the first part of my freshman year. I put girls, sports, cars, hanging out with my friends, and just about everything else I could think of above my studies. But I was a good athlete and knew how to charm teachers, administrators, and students alike to get what I needed to get done to stay on course for graduation. And every day that I rolled out of bed meant that graduation was one day closer to happening. I was 18 years old and I ruled the world. This year was going to be the absolute pinnacle of my existence. Life was so good!

It was a Wednesday afternoon, and the bell for the last period had just rung. Since I was on the football team, I was allowed to leave class to go to practice at this point. I walked through the gym to the locker room to get my pads on before heading out to the field for practice. Football was not taken anywhere as seriously as basketball was in Indiana in the 1960s, but we were good enough that we had the respect of the people in town and most of Warren County proper. Usually, since not all the football players could get the last period off, the first half an hour of practice was for stretching and light workouts, which meant that I didn't have to be there on time. And most days I was running late for one reason or another, and this would turn out to be one of those days.

As I walked through the gym, I saw a group of about 20 girls from the junior class all scurrying around all excitedly working to decorate the gym for the homecoming dance that was coming up on Saturday night. It was the junior's responsibility to come up with the dance theme and design, and then decorate the gym for the seniors. And it was a responsibility they took very seriously.

The theme for this years' homecoming dance was "Love is All Around," based on the song by The Troggs. I was pretty sure no one on the prom committee was overly familiar with the song, but one of them had probably heard it once on the radio, and thought the title sounded cute. I didn't worry myself with the details. All I knew was that it was coming up, I had my tux rented (or rented for me), and I had a date, not that it was ever in doubt. I was lucky enough to have dated most of the pretty girls in school at one time or another, and for homecoming, I was going with my current girlfriend, Tricia Baker. She was a perky, stereotypical cheerleader who loved that she was dating the starting running back on the football team. I loved that Tricia was cute. I also loved that she had nice breasts.

Tricia and I had started dating during the summer and through the first month of school, and it was quite obvious in her mind that she had our entire post-grad future planned out. We were going to get married; she was going to be a schoolteacher and I was going to work in management at one of the factories in Batesville, and we were going to have five kids and live in Deer Park near her parents. In her mind, we were going to live the Midwestern American dream.

In the meantime, someone had forgotten to get my approval on these plans.

Don't get me wrong, I liked Tricia, she was very nice and pretty and all, but she wasn't the first girl that I'd dated, and I knew she wasn't going to be the last. I didn't know what I wanted to do after graduation, but I knew what I didn't want to do, and that was what Tricia had planned for us. And besides, as I stood in the gym that day, my eyes were fixated on the most beautiful girl I had ever seen, and it wasn't Tricia. Standing on the third and fourth rungs of a six-foot ladder was what I was convinced had to be an angel from above who, as I watched--mesmerized--worked to hang crepe paper streamers in the DPHS colors of green and gold from the bottom of the basketball backboard.

I stopped dead in my tracks inside the door to the gym and became fixated on the girl on the ladder. The mid-afternoon sun was streaming in through the windows behind her, and surrounded her in a warm glow. In the sunlight's aura, she even looked like an angel. She looked to be tall, about five-foot-seven, I guessed, and she was thin with long, sandy blond hair tied back in a ponytail, and had pale, luminous skin. The thing that struck me was that she looked--I don't know--different than the other girls in the school. She looked like she didn't quite fit in yet. I didn't know much about her other than that she was new to the area. Whether she was from heaven, or Indianapolis, that was a great quality for a girl to have when you've gone through twelve years and twelve grades with the same people day in and day out.

She had started this past semester and I had noticed her in the halls a few times, but never had the opportunity (thanks to Tricia) to talk to her. We didn't have any classes together, but I watched for her in the halls.

And each time I saw her, she became more beautiful to me. And now, as I silently watched her hang a glittering plastic globe that was surrounded by little paper hearts off of the basketball rim, I became convinced that I needed to meet her and know more about her. I'd start with her name.

So, I stood and stared. My feet made no more of a movement towards her than it had before, and I just stood there and continued to stare.

"Hey moron, shouldn't you be outside for football practice?" a voice behind me asked, breaking the spell that she had inadvertently put me under.

That was the voice of my best friend since fifth grade, Marty Green. He stood a little shorter than me and he had curly dark brown hair that was already receding in the front. Marty was my attempted voice of reason when I had a plan, and my co-conspirator when he had failed to convince me not to go through with whatever I had concocted. I think I got him into more trouble than he saved me from, but he never gave up hope. Marty was smarter and funnier than me, but not as outgoing or athletic as I was. Plus, we got along great, and that gets you a long way. I didn't even need to turn around.

"Man, I can be late, it's practice," I explained. "You know what you do at practice? You practice running. How hard is that? I know how to run, so how much practice do I need?"

"Coach'll be pissed," Marty warned.

I shrugged my shoulders. "What's he going to do, keep me out of the homecoming game? It's a big game, he needs me. Besides, I'm involved in something more important."

Marty replied sarcastically, "Well, ending the war in 'Nam or taking pi out to the thousandth digit is a little too complex for you, so fill me in?"

I kept my stare on the ladder under the basketball hoop, and the person standing on it. "First of all, go to hell. Secondly, I'm staring at the love of my life."

"I thought Tricia was the love of your life?"

"That would be a 'no,'" I said, nodding towards the basketball goal. "And as soon as I find out her name and introduce myself to her, I'm going to take her to homecoming."

"Chad, that's not going to happen."

I sighed. "I hate when you doubt me. How can you be so sure?"

Marty returned the sigh, walked directly in front of me, and put both hands on my shoulders like a stern parent, blocking my view. "First of all, her name is Casey Martin, she's a junior and her parents moved here from Indy when her dad was transferred to the transmission plant."

"How in the hell--"

"...because I notice things that go on around me, not just the things that affect me personally."

"Okay, great, now I know her name, I can introduce myself and ask her to the dance."

"You have a date, moron. And secondly, she has a boyfriend."

With those words, my heart sank. It couldn't be possible. We were meant to be together, I just knew it. A boyfriend? How could that have happened to me?

I looked at Marty with a fierce determination. "Who is he? I'll take him out with a few good punches to the body and then he'll gladly let her go." That was my actual plan, nothing else was coming to mind.

"Problem," Marty said, defiant of my genius plan to win this girl. "She's going with Billy Ricketts, and you know how those guys from Lawrenceburg are?"

I did, unfortunately. Lawrenceburg was about halfway between Deer Park and Cincinnati, and we played them every year in football. The running bet every year was whether there would be more points or fights during the game. And almost every year, fights won. This year was no different; we won the game 14-7, and lost in fights. Lawrenceburg guys ran in packs, like wolves, but only half as smart. And if one Lawrenceburg guy had a beef with you, it turned into 30 guys carrying a beef with you real quick. I was crazy and impulsive, but I was not stupid.

It was in situations like this that I had to decide whether to do the logical, safe thing, or the reckless, insane thing. I never chose the safe route.

I had an idea. "He's in Lawrenceburg, right?"

"If he's not hunting elk with his bare hands, or in jail, then yes."

"So, I can just talk to her, right?"

"If you want to torture yourself, go right ahead. I personally don't see the point."

"Of course you don't, you're not a genius like me."

Now, to be fair, Marty was a straight-A student, knew every baseball player and stat for the entire Cincinnati Reds organization, past and present, and could quote Civil War battlefields from memory. But he wasn't crazy and impulsive like me.

Marty sighed again. He sighed a lot around me. "I take it you have a plan?"

I smiled. "Nope."

"I figured," Marty said. "When you wind up in the Ohio River beaten to a pulp, I'll tell Tricia it was to protect her honor."

I patted him on the shoulder. "Marty, that's why we're friends, I act and you think."

And then I explained to my best friend, in the simplest way possible, that I had no idea what I was going to do.

"Don't worry about it, buddy, I know what I'm doing."

Marty shook his head. "Oh, sweet Jesus!"

I patted him on the back and walked him out of the gym into the hallway towards his study hall. Football practice would have to wait. We said our goodbyes and as he walked away, I began to put my plan of "no plan" into place. I looked around, and saw Ellen Brown walking down the hallway towards the gym with a handful of new decorations that they had just made in the Art Department. I quickly ran over to her and reached out my arms.

"Hey Ellen, thanks for bringing those in, I'll take those off your hands."

She smiled. "Thanks, I didn't know you were helping."

I didn't either. "Least I can do, I just want to make sure the gym looks beautiful for Saturday."

"Thanks Chad, you're sweet."

I immediately took the decorations and stepped back into the gym. Casey was now in the visitor's stands hanging cardboard globes and hearts on the rails and rafters above. Even without the benefit of the sun's light, she was still luminous.

I sighed to myself. "Here goes nothing."

I walked up the stairs and over to where Casey was working.

"Here are some more decorations," I said, surprised by my own voice. "You're doing such a great job that I figured you must be the one in charge."

She smiled. "Actually, everyone is working in pairs, and no one really knows me, so they stuck me up here by myself. But thanks."

I held out my hand. "Um, no problem. By the way, my name is Chad Breckenridge."

She took my hand in hers. "I know. Nice to meet you Chad, I'm Casey."

"I know. Nice to meet you Casey." I held her hand for what it seemed like ten minutes, but in actuality was just a second longer than normal, which caused her to pull her hand back awkwardly.

"Sorry," I stammered. Dammit, I was losing control of this. I needed something to regain control and fast.

"So, um, you like decorating for the dance?" Not the control-regaining question I was looking for.

She looked around nervously, as if looking for someone to come rescue her.

"Well, it's my first one," she said. "So I don't really have anything to compare it to."

This had officially turned into the most uncomfortable conversation of my life. I had nothing else. The well was dry. Turns out, having no plan was not a good plan. I was enamored, entranced, illuminated and using words in my head that had no possible way of making it to my mouth. So, all she heard was a stammering idiot. Oh, and I was officially in love.

There was nothing left to do. I'd made a horrible first impression, and I lost the chance to impress her. I was devastated.

I turned to leave before it got worse, as if it could.

"Well, it was nice meeting you, Casey. Have a great time at the dance Saturday."

"I'm not going," she said softly.

I turned back sharply, like I was being jerked by a rope. "You're not? I mean, I just thought, you know, a girl like you…"

She tensed. "Just what do you mean 'a girl like me?'"

Oh Shit, MAYDAY! MAYDAY! Brain, pull me out of this one!

I dropped my head. "You know, you're pretty. Smart. I figured you'd have a boyfriend, or at least a date for the homecoming dance. I mean who wouldn't want to go out with you?" I smiled and looked at her. It worked. Somehow it worked.

She smiled a little and relaxed, "Well, I do," she started. "Well, did, it's--it's hard to explain. The guy I am going with is not going, so I'm not going."

"I'm sorry to hear that." I wasn't.

"It's no big deal, really." It was. To me, at least.

Suddenly, I became clear-headed and focused, and I decided what I was going to do. I went for it like no one had ever gone for anything before in the history of going for things.

"Casey, I'd love to take you out tonight," I said. "Maybe for a burger, or a soda, or something. As friends of course. I mean, this wouldn't be a date or anything. Nothing formal or anything like that. Whaddya say?"

She looked at me coyly. "I dunno, what about your girlfriend?"

Damn! I looked at her, trying to come up with a response. She added, "I'm new, I'm not blind. It's a small school. Tricia wouldn't be happy."

She was smart. I responded the only way I knew how, "Well then, she's not invited."

She laughed. I asked the more important question to my overall physical health, "What about this guy you are dating?"

She responded, slightly surprised that I knew about him, though she did just tell me she was going with someone. "Billy? I'm afraid he would just insist on beating the tar out of you, probably not the best dinner companion."

I smiled, however true that statement was. "So, if we went out--just as friends mind you--and had a burger, just to talk, and didn't have to tell Tricia or Billy, would that work?"

Casey thought it over for a moment, "I guess so, but this doesn't mean anything, you understand that? It's just two people talking, nothing else."

"Nothing else, I swear," I said with confidence.

"So, I'll pick you up at 6:30?"

"Okay, I live out at 3415 Winding Road Lane. It's a bit out in the country, do you need directions?"

"Nope, I know every road in Warren County." I reminded myself to ask Marty where the hell Winding Road Lane was.

"Look, I gotta get to football practice," I explained. "When I'm done, I'll stop back by and help you finish the decorations. That way we can grab dinner sooner."

"Okay, that sounds great."

I shook her hand again and said my goodbye for now. I went down the bleacher stairs three at a time reveling in pure excitement. As I was about to head into the locker room, I heard one girl yelling at another, and a voice on the verge of tears (that I was pretty sure was Ellen Brown) saying that I took the decorations and said that I was helping. Oh well.

I got dressed quickly and I was so lost in my own thoughts of Casey that when I left the locker room and walked outside onto the practice field, I looked up just in time to catch a flying cheerleader.

Literally.

And then I was immediately transported back to reality. It was my girlfriend, Tricia. In addition to her wonderful, athletic body, which stood about five-four, Tricia had shoulder-length brown hair that she tied in braids. Her eyes were brown, like chocolate, and her looks to me were just as sweet. Even before we made eye contact, I was questioning myself for even thinking about going to the homecoming dance with another girl. This was my girl. We were going steady. My thoughts of Casey and taking her to homecoming, well that was crazy. Wasn't it?

"Are you running late again for practice?" Tricia asked. "I thought you'd be on the field already. How lucky for me!"

She gave me a kiss, and I sat her back down on her feet. How was I going to tell her I was going to homecoming with another girl? I mean, was

I really thinking about going with another girl? I tried to get that vision out of my head.

"I got stopped in the gym by a couple juniors who needed some muscles to move some stuff." I wasn't going to mention Ellen's name to Tricia, because Tricia would go ask and who knows what Ellen would tell her.

Tricia grabbed my hands, "Aren't you even more excited now that you've seen the theme of homecoming? I'm so excited to go with you! I just can't wait. You should see my dress; it's beautiful!"

I laughed nervously. "Can't wait."

Tricia looked at me, "Oh Chad, boys are so silly about romantic stuff like school dances. It's our night, one we'll remember 50 years from now when we're sitting with our grandkids at the lake."

Jesus Christ, I thought, *she's thinking about us 50 years from now with kids and grandkids and I'm figuring out how to take another girl to this dance instead. I am a top-rate jerk.* I wasn't sure I could go through with this.

Then my heart stopped as she said: "about tonight..."

I cleared my throat, my mind suddenly focused on this potential romantic Cuban missile crisis that was brewing. Kruschev call Kennedy. Kennedy call Kruschev, somebody? Anybody?

"What about tonight?"

"Well, we're going to go to the Big Boy with Johnny and Kelly, remember?"

"Of course, I remember." I had no idea what she was taking about. It did make sense, though. Since Johnny Hansbrook was the Aviators quarterback, and Kelly Simmons was the cheerleading captain, Tricia was always wanting to do something with them, as being seen in public with Johnny and Kelly would put us on their level in Tricia's eyes. I didn't care, either way. Johnny was cool and he let me cheat off his tests, and Kelly was beautiful, but not a snob about it.

"So, what about tonight?" I inquired with a sense of urgency, trying to figure out if I had to come up with a plan to get out of it. Homecoming may be up in the air, but I was not going to miss tonight with Casey.

"Granny Baker is not feeling well, so my family's all going to go to her house to cheer her up and then go grab something to eat. I already told Kelly to tell Johnny. You're not mad, are you?"

I smiled inside the smile of kings. "No, I'm not mad. Of course I'm disappointed, but you need to spend time with Granny Baker, you're her favorite. Let's just call it off tonight and you go to Granny Baker's with your folks."

Tricia suddenly smiled, "Why don't you come with us?"

SHIT! SHIT! SHIT! SHIT!

I stammered, "No, I can't, this is your family. I'll just--"

"--But you're practically family," she countered. "And will be soon enough. Plus, Granny Baker loves you."

"Well, that she does…" *Dammit, why am I agreeing with her?*

"…but we'll have plenty of time to see Granny Baker. Besides, tonight I just want to rest up for the big weekend."

Tricia looked at me for a moment, "Well, aren't you sweet. I'll tell her you send your best and I'll call Kelly and tell her we'll get together another night."

WHEW!

She then leaned over to kiss me on the cheek, as she loved to do all the time, but I didn't even notice her, or the kiss. My thoughts reverted back to Casey Martin, and how I was going to pull this off without being labeled *The Jerk-of-the-Century*. As with most of my plans, I had no idea.

Chapter 2

I was 20 minutes late for football practice, something Coach Acus pointed out as soon as he saw me.

"Breckenridge, you're late!" Coach yelled. "Where the hell have you been? We've been out here for forty minutes and you're nowhere to be found. Get your butt over with the offense and run some plays." The coach was going over the game plan for Saturday's game with the offense, and with my being the fullback, his plan was to run the ball early and often to open up the passing game. Running the ball was no problem as I was quick and tough and I loved running over people. As I ran one play after another, I found myself thinking of Casey and how I had to move quickly so I could ask her to the dance. These thoughts didn't help my toughness as I was tackled for losses on every play. After about nine attempts, I saw Coach Acus walking towards me.

"What the hell are you *DOING* Breckenridge?" he shouted. "You little panty waste. My fourteen-year-old daughter could get more yards than you have after nine plays! Get your head on straight or you'll be standing next to me during the entire game!"

"Sorry coach," I stammered. "I guess I was thinking about something else." Coach got right up near my facemask, his face so close I could tell he had spaghetti for lunch. With great authority he said, "Well, you better start thinking about running over people and getting ready to kick some ass on Saturday!"

I quickly regained my focus. "Okay coach, let me run a couple more plays and I'll show you that I'm ready."

Well, it wasn't easy but I finally got my mind back on football. After three more plays I had accumulated over thirty yards. "Now that's more like it, son! You have to stay focused," Coach said.

"Okay, Coach, I'm ready for Saturday."

Finally, practice was over and I had time to run back to the locker room, shower, and head off to the gymnasium to see Casey again. The juniors were still decorating, and I assumed that she'd be there. Johnny Hansbrook stepped up to me as I was getting dressed and said "Boy, I've never seen you move so quickly. I mean you'd think you had a date with Raquel Welch!"

I chuckled, "Well, not Raquel Welch, but close. I gotta get going." I think I showered and dressed in about three minutes; at least it seemed that way. I could not wait to see Casey.

I ran out of the locker room and into the gym but didn't see her anywhere. I stood there surveying the entire room. The streamers had been hung, along with crepe-paper balls that reflected light off shiny glitter, and green and gold balloons that were taped to every corner of the entire gymnasium. It was coming along great, but there was no Casey. Did she have second thoughts? Was she just running late? I went into panic mode and started to frantically run from girl to girl asking if they had seen her.

After a couple minutes, I saw Kristi Reynolds coming into the gym. In the few times that I had seen Casey Martin in the hallways, she was always walking with, or talking to Kristi Reynolds. If I had to guess if they were friends, I'd most likely be right, as usual. I immediately ran over to her and inquired about Casey.

"Hey Kristi," I said. "Have you seen Casey? I was supposed to meet her here to help her with the decorations."

"Oh, hi Chad," she said, smiling. "I saw Casey in the parking lot with her boyfriend. I don't know what they were talking about, but it seemed serious."

Boyfriend!? Not now! It couldn't be. Not good timing!

"Do you think she'll be back?" I asked.

"Sure, she's responsible for the flower decorations and those need to be done by tomorrow, so she needs to be here shortly," Kristi replied.

My heart rate slowly started to return to normal.

"I have to go make sure Linda and Pam are taking care of the water fountain display," she said. "I'll see you later."

Although somewhat relieved, I paced the gym floor for what seemed to be an hour before I saw Casey come through the door.

"Casey, over here!" I yelled with excitement. She saw me and we each made our way over to one another. "I thought you might have forgotten!"

"No, I just had to take care of a few things after class and before I got back to work here," she said.

"Well, I'm just glad you're here. I'm ready to start helping you with the decorations," I said. I only had a short amount of time to get to know her so I had to move quickly. My plan was to start with *The Question*.

"So, this guy you have been dating; is he a boyfriend?"

The world suddenly stopped and there was silence. I really didn't want to hear the answer because I knew she had a boyfriend, but I guess I just had to hear her say it.

"Yes, he is my boyfriend but I have been thinking about dating other guys."

What?!, I thought. Could this be a miracle handed down to me from above? I mean, I believe in God, but I haven't been His best work lately. Could He be tempting me? No, that's the other guy! I had to pursue the questioning further.

"How long have you and your boyfriend been going with each other?" I hesitantly inquired.

"Well, about two years now," replied Casey.

Well that's enough time, I thought. *She needs to date a new guy. Where do I apply?*

"So, you're thinking about dating other guys?" I asked quietly.

"Yeah," she admitted. "We've been struggling with some issues between us lately and I'm tired of dealing with his anger and how he puts me down sometimes."

Oh my God, this is music to my ears! Did I just hear what I thought I heard…problems on the home front? I was ready to move in for the kill.

"Have you even thought of going to the dance?" I asked. "I mean you are so pretty and you could have so much fun for a change."

"I have thought about it," she said. "But haven't been asked. And, if asked, I'm not sure I would go anyway."

"What do you mean by 'not sure you would go anyway?'"

"Well, I would feel guilty about going to a dance--much less homecoming--with another guy. Billy would be angry and would probably try to pick a fight with the guy if he found out."

Okay, now my plan had a steep hurdle. Do I chance asking her out, knowing that my life could suddenly end before, during, or after the dance? Could I actually take Billy Rickets out with a few punches to the stomach, or possibly a quick kick to the groin area, and a very quick exit maneuver, such as running like hell? After moments of sheer confusion and terror regarding the thought of being brutally beaten by a Lawrenceburg Neanderthal, I decided it was worth it and proceeded with my questioning.

"Well, what if a guy asked you to go to the dance and didn't care what your boyfriend thought," I laid it out there. "And was willing to take the chance of your boyfriend finding out?"

"I don't know," she replied. "I would have to think about that…if I was asked."

I looked upward to thank the Man upstairs. I now owed Him for this chance of a lifetime. How could I ever even the score with God? Okay, I would go to church every Sunday for, say, the next two years. Well maybe, three years. Okay, let's be real; I will go to church every Sunday for the next six months. Or so. Maybe. and I'll also be nice to my brother for the next two months. Okay, Well that's just not going to happen. Maybe I'll offer up some Hail Marys, or something like that; and I'm not even Catholic. Aww, God's not picky. He'll work with me on this. I'd find some way to make it up to Him.

"Well Casey, would you like to go to the dance with me?" There it was. It rolled right off my tongue. "I mean, I would love to take you and, well, we could just go this once and have fun. I wouldn't really be a date. We would just go as friends who worked together at school on the homecoming decorations."

"Chad, you are so nice and thoughtful," Casey said as she flashed those bright blue eyes at me. "Let me think about it and let you know."

Okay, now I had to put the squeeze on her. Somehow I had to get her to say "yes."

"Fair enough," I said. "As for tonight, let's say instead of me picking you up at your place, why don't we just go after we're done here and head over to the Big Boy for a burger?"

"Okay," she agreed. "But remember, it's not a date. We're just two friends getting a bite to eat."

Although we had another forty-five minutes of decorating work to do, I just wanted to think of an excuse to leave with her now. But I didn't want to appear too pushy, so we worked on the decorations until they were all done and then we were finally able to leave. After a long day of school, football practice, and then decorating for the dance, I had developed quite an appetite and I was ready to eat.

I suggested to Casey that instead of going to Big Boy, that we head over to a nice little place over in Reading, about twenty miles away, so we wouldn't be interrupted and we could get to know each other. Actually, it was so that we would not be seen by anyone we knew, especially one of Tricia's friends, but Casey didn't need to know that.

She reluctantly agreed to the new plans and we took my car, leaving hers in the student parking lot. We soon found ourselves heading toward Reading and to a little restaurant called Skyline Chili. It seems I couldn't go a week, or much less a few days without eating Skyline Chili. It was the perfect blend of everything good that God had put on this earth, served over spaghetti noodles or a hot dog, and then covered in shredded cheese. In a word, it was heavenly.

We had a nice drive through the countryside talking about the homecoming and the big game and we both enjoyed looking at the different shades of leaves falling from the trees. To me, this was the most romantic time of year; but I was sharp enough to know that romance was certainly not on Casey's mind. By the time that we got to the restaurant, I felt that things were going smoothly.

The Reading Skyline had drive-in service so we pulled into a spot and I parked my car. After reviewing the menu, I rolled down my window and placed our order. I was hoping that the service would be slow so that I had more time to get to know Casey before our food arrived. Being the witty person I am, I cracked some jokes and impressed her with my knowledge of absolutely nothing. She was very book smart, but was not very knowledgeable about the things that I talked about. In other words, I just made stuff up about sports and cooking. It turned out that she was not a good cook, so I knew I was safe there. After about twenty minutes, the server delivered our food, which came on a tray that hooked to the side of my car on the driver's side. After handing Casey her food, I finally decided to pop the question. No, not "the question." I meant asking her to the dance.

"Casey, I know we are not really on a date-date," I began, as I shoved a Skyline coney dog into my mouth. "But was wondering if you would like to go to the dance with me? I mean we would go as friends."

"I would love to go Chad," she said, as she reached over to wipe some chili mess off my cheek with a napkin. "But just not sure about what my boyfriend would do, or say."

Here we go with the boyfriend thing. I had to make my case, here and now.

"I really don't care about what your boyfriend would do or say," I proclaimed. "I would love to show you a good time and see you laugh and have fun." I followed this up with: "How about we go out tomorrow night and really get more acquainted with each other. If you don't feel more comfortable with me--as a friend, of course--then I will understand if you don't want to go to the dance with me."

Again with that silence thing. It was as if she was hypnotized and was just waiting for some direction.

"Okay," she said. "What time would you pick me up?"

YES, YES, YES!

"I will pick you up at your house tomorrow night at about six o'clock and we'll just hang out for a few hours."

"That sounds good," she said.

We finished eating and continued our conversation through bites of chili and cheese. When finished, we left Skyline and I took Casey back to her car.

"Thank you for dinner," she said as she slid out of the passenger seat. "It was great!"

"No, thank you," I said. "I'll see you tomorrow at 6:00 pm sharp!"

She got into her car and I waited until she turned the engine over and pulled away. She offered me a little wave as she drove by and I returned it with a smile.

Could this be really happening? I thought. *Did I really just pull this off?*

I got onto the road and headed for home. Then for some reason, my brain and mouth finally connected and out came:

"Oh Shit!"

Reality had sunk back in and I realized that I now have two dates to homecoming. One of those dates being with my girlfriend, Tricia. I immediately sunk so low into my car seat that my view was obscured by the steering wheel. My body seemed to have little energy and I thought I was going to pass out. I quickly pulled over to the side of the road and stopped the car to ponder my dilemma. The engine idled as I just stared into the abyss. Tricia was my girlfriend but then Casey was new and exciting. How was I going to tell Tricia that I was going to homecoming with Casey, especially after she already bought her dress?

After eating two Four-Ways, a couple of coney dogs, and an order of fries I thought if I could just puke my guts out, everything would be much clearer. It would be like puking after drinking too much and then feeling normal. I didn't think that would work this time. So I just sat motionless behind the wheel idling on the side of the road.

My thoughts were all over the place, but then the perfect plan formed in my brain. Yep, that was it! I would take Tricia out later tonight and then get into a fight about something and then tell her that the dance was off. I sat upright in the seat, my mind on fire with the possibilities. I put the car into drive and headed toward home to call Tricia.

I was feeling fine. I took a moment out while driving to once again thank the Man upstairs for the great idea and tell Him I would give some deep thought on how to return the favor. I had already committed to going to church for six months or was it a week, so was not sure what else I could give up. Maybe I *could* be nice to my brother. Maybe not. Anyway, I told God I would get back to Him, and I thanked Him again.

Upon pulling into the driveway at home, I jumped out of my car, ran into the house and upstairs into my room as if I was trying to break a new land speed record. I immediately grabbed the phone and called Marty to disclose my plan before calling Tricia.

"Jesus Christ, Chad do you hear yourself?" Marty exclaimed in total disbelief. "You're telling me you plan on taking another girl to homecoming while Tricia already has her dress and everything? You're a Grade-A jerk!"

He was right. He was always right when it came to my sudden ideas about something.

My mind was going a mile-a-minute with absolutely no thought about what I was going to say or do tonight with Tricia, assuming that she could even go out this late on a school night. I had to convince her to go out tonight. Granny Baker be damned, I had to get out of going to homecoming with my girlfriend.

"Chad, I can't fix this," Marty continued. "You're on your own with this one."

"I understand but I have to do this."

"Your funeral," Marty said sternly.

"Will you say something nice, maybe give the eulogy?" I inquired.

Marty laughed, "I'll tell them what a pain-in-the ass you were and how I had to bail you out of everything, and got nothing in return but pain and suffering."

"Thanks, buddy," I said. "I'd better get this over with. I'll talk to you tomorrow."

We hung up with each other and I sat staring at the phone on my nightstand. It was now time to dial Tricia's number and initiate my plan. I swallowed deeply, picked up the receiver, and began dialing her number on the rotary.

"Hello, Tricia?" I nervously asked the person on the other end of the line.

"Oh, hi Sweetie," Tricia responded with excitement. "We just got home from visiting Granny Baker. She told me to tell you, 'Hello,' by the way. She looks good and she asked about you--"

"Tricia," I interrupted, "I was wondering if we could go out tonight? I know it's kind of late but I wanted to see you." *Damn, I'm good.*

"Sure, what time?" Tricia replied.

"I'll pick you up in an hour, okay?"

"I'll be ready."

"Okay, I'll see you then," I said as I hung up the phone. I now had the second date of the night, and it was just Wednesday.

What was I going to pick the fight about? I wondered.

And then came the guilt.

I never thought about the guilt thing. I hate the guilt thing. Our relationship had been pretty good lately, so I'd have to go back awhile to find something that would be so traumatic as to call off the dance. I just couldn't think of anything. I guess I'd have to wing it.

I knew I was going to feel nauseous after doing this, but I was hoping that the feeling would rapidly pass with the thought of tomorrow night's date with Casey. My heart rate was racing past two hundred and I was starting to sweat. I had to somehow get myself to relax. The last thing I wanted was to show up at Tricia's door already appearing anxious, sweaty, and nervous. If that were the case, she would eventually figure out what I was doing.

So, with less than an hour or so before I had to pick her up, I went for a short jog in my neighborhood. I wasn't really into jogging, as I got enough running in football practice, but off I went. As I ran through the neighborhood I found myself visualizing each of my neighbor's homes as the house where Tricia lived. It was awful. This whole idea of getting a date with Casey and dumping Tricia right before the dance was starting to take its toll. I mean, I thought it would be easy just to dump one girl and then take the other one. Guys do this stuff all the time. I think I saw Eddie Haskell do it on *Leave it to Beaver*. Here I was getting all emotional about it. Wasn't that a girl thing to do? It just didn't make sense to me.

After running for a couple of miles, I finally made it back home, and drenched with sweat and smelling like a used gym sock, I ran upstairs to shower and get dressed for my date with Tricia. I pulled off my smelly clothes and turned on the water. It took a few minutes for it to get warm, and while waiting, I suddenly had another moment of genius.

Tricia hates it when I take her out looking like a slob. Whenever I wear sweat pants and tennis shoes and every once in-awhile don't shower, Tricia goes berserk. She feels that when I dress like that, it doesn't show any respect for her, or that I am going out of my way to be with her and make a good appearance. I love casual dress and sweat pants and tennis shoes are casual dress. This would be a good starting place for a fight! I turned off the water and decided to at least change to a fresh sweatshirt since the one I was wearing was full of sweat. I figured without a shower, my aroma would eventually penetrate the fresh shirt anyway.

Finally, my heart rate started to drop and that nauseous feeling started to disappear. I was finally feeling okay about this, at least for now. I got into my Corvair, cranked up the radio, and started to sing along to some Beach Boys song. Something off of *Pet Sounds*, I thought. It was a cool, fall evening and the sky was perfectly clear for the moment. I drove down my street being serenaded by Brian Wilson and I didn't have a care in the world.

When I was about a mile from Tricia's house everything changed. The temperature dropped about thirty degrees and the sky turned dark and threatening. Oh yeah, that nauseous feeling came back. Came back armed and ready for battle. I pulled into Tricia's driveway and just sat there, idling for a moment or two, listening to The Mamas & the Papas sing about west coast dreams, and I tried to gather up whatever courage I had for what was about to go down. Then, the worst of all things that could have happened, happened. Tricia's father, Bill, a man I had come to know and respect--as well as fear--came to the front door and noticed me as he stepped out to head toward his garage. In his hand he held a machete. A MACHETE!

"Hey Chad," he said, waving. "You here for Tricia?"

Once again, that mouth thing happened. You know where the brain sends a message to the mouth but the mouth doesn't move. My brain worked to say hello, but my mouth had other plans. It seemed like an eternity before I finally spoke.

"Hi, Mr. Baker. Yes, I'm here for Tricia." I finally got the words out, though I couldn't stop staring at the machete in his hand. All I could think about was that I am going to rip his little daughter's heart out and then he is going to track me down and chop me into little Chad bits. Death may even come before I ever get a chance to take Casey out.

"Well you guys have a great time and I'll see you when you get back."

Okay, now this was not in the plans. I was now going to have to see Mr. Baker--an armed Mr. Baker--after I emotionally destroy his daughter. I had to think of a plan. Not only was I *NOT* going to see Mr. Baker--and his machete--tonight, I'd also have to convince my parents we have to move quickly out of town. Before midnight, if at all possible.

A couple of minutes later, Tricia stepped out the front door. She walked to her father.

"Bye, Daddy. I love you," she said. "Eww, you stink."

Can she smell me already? I thought.

"I've been chopping the brush in the back yard since we got home from Granny's," he said, as he raised his arm and sniffed his armpit. "Daylight's a-waistin'. You guys have fun tonight."

Fun? Well, that would not be the operative word I would use.

"Hey Chad," Tricia said as she slid into the passenger seat next to me. "I just couldn't wait for you to get here. We're going to have a great time. Where are we going?"

Yeah, where were we going? I haven't gotten that far in my thinking. Think Chad, where are we going? I had to pick a place where my casual attire would offend not only Tricia, but also everyone around us.

"We're going to The Hollows," I replied as I put the car in reverse and backed out of her driveway. The Hollows was a fine, upscale restaurant that overlooked Lake Whitney. It had been *the* place for dates in Deer Park for years, and they made incredible twice-baked potatoes. Also, It didn't require a coat and tie but did mandate nice casual attire. As we drove down her street the silence between us grew larger until finally, it burst like a perfectly blown bubble of Bazooka Joe.

"The Hollows?" Tricia asked. "Dressed like that?!"

Oh, so she finally noticed. How long before she notices my smell?

"And what is that smell?"

Bingo.

"You look like a slob and smell like you haven't taken a shower in two or three days!"

Boy, she does have a grasp of the obvious.

"Well, I was so busy helping out with the homecoming decorations that I didn't have time to shower," I explained. "But I did change my shirt."

"Chad, you know how much I hate it when you disrespect me like this!" she exclaimed.

"Now honey, don't get so emotional about this," I pleaded with some sincerity. Some. "I wanted to be with you so much that I thought it would be okay this one time."

"You just don't get it. I have to be respected as a girl--as a woman!" she demanded.

Okay, this was my cue to escalate the anger that had started to build.

"Look," I said, raising my own voice to match hers. "I respect you a lot, but I'm not going to be emasculated by you, or any woman."

"What did you say?" she asked, the anger dripping off her words.

"You heard me," I said. "I'm not going to always be told how to dress, how to act, or what I can and cannot do. I'm an adult. I'm eighteen and have been around the block a few times and with a lot of girls...err... women!"

Oops, I think I may have crossed the line of no return. Rubicon be damned, I mentioned "other women." That should just about wrap this up. Thanks folks, drive safely.

"What do you mean, OTHER WOMEN!?" Tricia screamed.

Just as Tricia finished with her screaming, we turned into the parking lot of The Hollows. I was hoping to get out of the car and carry our little spat into the restaurant, but Tricia would have nothing of that. As I opened the driver's side door she reached across the seat and pulled my right arm as to keep me seated in the car for further discussion.

"Where do you think you are going?" she sneered. "I have no intention of going into a nice restaurant to eat with you looking and smelling like that!"

"Okay then," I said, carefully stoking the fire I had started. "Shall we order out?"

Well, I thought. *I must say I was getting pretty good at this breaking up thing. Maybe I should write a book.*

"I suppose you will be dressed like this--and smell like this--for homecoming too?" Tricia asked with a lot of sarcasm in her voice.

"Well, I just might."

Now, to put the final touches of my breakup plan in action. Words that all women hate to hear.

"Tricia," I began. "Why are you getting so emotional about such a little thing like this? Is it that time of the month?"

Fuse meet match.

"You piss me off so much right now, I...I JUST WANT TO GO HOME!" Tricia yelled at the top of her lungs.

And we have liftoff.

"Honey, you are so emotional," I bit back a smile, trying desperately to keep my game face on, even as I emptied the gas can on what was left of my relationship with Tricia Baker.

"Get me out of here," she whimpered. "I want to go home now."

That did it. I was home free.

Now it was time for 'The Threat.' Women who are so enraged by a man's actions or comments do not like to--under any circumstances--be threatened. It is just not acceptable.

"Okay then," I began. "If I take you home the dance is off."

At this point, women usually can't even think straight. They can't see the whole picture thing. As I expected, Tricia didn't even hear the words, "the dance is off."

"I don't care," she said, tears streaming down her cheeks. "I want to go home, now."

Although I had now accomplished my mission, I knew deep down inside that tomorrow Tricia would see the big picture thing and realize that this argument cost her so much more than a dinner at The Hollows. And she'll want nothing more than to go back in time and do it all over again. They always do the day after.

I immediately started the engine and headed back to Tricia's house. The drive was about twenty or thirty minutes of sheer silence. Every once in awhile I would look out of the corner of my right eye to see if she was still crying or just looking out of the window at the scenery we were passing. On the drive back, the sky seemed to clear up and the dark gray clouds gave way to bright starlight and the temperature seemed to rise upwards about thirty degrees. I was feeling pretty good. Of course I was still in the moment of our fight and the adrenaline was having its way with me.

I turned onto Tricia's street and as we got closer to her house, I was hit with terrifying thoughts of torture and death. Her dad was still working in the garage so my immediate thought was to just drop Tricia off while slowly driving by her house. All she would need to do is tuck and roll as she hit the pavement. She'd be okay if she did it right. I'd rather risk her life than to pull into the driveway, dump her off, and then speed away before her dad saw his little girl crying. Well, that was my plan, but my conscience got the better of me so I quickly pulled into the driveway and let her out. I don't recall, however, if she was actually out of the car when I started to back out of the driveway, but pretty sure she was.

On all prior occasions when driving to and from Tricia's home, I was very careful about driving slowly and not squealing any tires. That would not have made points with Mr. Baker. This time however was different. Shifting the car into reverse within a millisecond and then exiting from the driveway at a reasonable rate of speed of thirty miles an hour seemed like the normal thing to do under the circumstances. I mean, undertaking this type of action was to save a life: mine!

Once I had driven a mile or two away, and left a good two inches of rubber on the street in front of her house, I felt safe enough to ease off the gas peddle and slow my speed to the actual speed limit. My left elbow was resting on the driver's side door and I soon started to notice the smell coming from the dark recesses of my body. I must admit, if I were Tricia, I would have been mad at me as well. I felt guilty, but it seemed my life would return to normal in no time. I slowly eased back into the seat and sat upright. I tucked my left arm in, because a man could only take so much of his own smell. I was beginning to feel a little cocky. In just one day I had met the girl of my dreams, ripped the heart out of my girlfriend, and was likely being tracked down at this very moment by a bounty hunter hired by Tricia's father. Mission accomplished; or was it?

The longer I drove, the more I started to actually grasp what had transpired in the last few hours. It seemed as if I actually had a conscience.

Now this conscience thing was new to me. I always thought women had a conscience, but men, no way! I think I heard or read something about men somehow inheriting genes or something from way back in the caveman era that prevented them from having a functioning conscience. I mean we, as men, lie about stuff all the time so we don't have to deal with reality. Or something like that. That's why we don't cry. Nevertheless, I was starting to feel remorseful. I wasn't sure I was using the word correctly, and was shocked that I actually knew a word like that. I must have learned that word a couple of years ago while watching the show *Password* on TV. In any event, I started to come to grips with what I had done to Tricia. The fact that her dad probably had an armed posse and a pack of bloodhounds after me had absolutely nothing to do with it.

As I neared my home, I tried and tried to rid myself of this conscience thing and focus more on Casey. I had to look forward, not back. I turned the corner of my street and pulled into the driveway. I parked the car somewhat in the middle and headed upstairs to my room to call Marty. He had to hear about all of this, and I was sure it couldn't wait until tomorrow.

It was Wednesday night, about nine forty-five when I finally relaxed into my makeshift hammock that was tied off to one side of my bunk bed which I shared with my younger brother, Alex. The other end was tied to a reinforced curtain rod over the window overlooking our side yard. I quickly grabbed the phone off the floor and dialed Marty's number. It was busy. I redialed the number over and over again hoping somehow my redialing would get the person on the phone to hang up. It seemed to work as I dialed for the fourteenth time, I heard the ring.

"Hello, Green residence," said the voice on the other end, Marty's mother, I guessed.

"Hello Mrs. Green, this is Chad," I announced. "Is Marty home?" It was almost ten o'clock, where else would he be?

"Yes, he is, let me get him for you."

I could hear Mrs. Green call out for Marty. It took a few loud yells before a groggy Marty picked up the line.

"Hello?"

"Don't even tell me you're asleep right now," I said. "I just had the craziest night in my life."

"Chad?" he asked. "Seriously, man, this couldn't wait until tomorrow?"

"I took Casey Martin out to dinner, then came home and tricked Tricia into a fight," I regaled, proudly. "Tricia and I are done, and I think Casey's going to go to homecoming with me."

"You know you're an ass, right?"

"And you're the best friend of an ass, so what's the make you?"

"An ass's friend," he said. "Look man, I gotta get back to bed. Can we talk about this tomorrow?"

"Sure," I said. "I just needed to tell someone about Casey."

"Well, you did. Congratulations. Good night." He disconnected the line before I could say another word.

I hung up the phone and just took a big sigh of relief. In less than nine hours, I had met the girl of my dreams, taken her on a date, asked her to the homecoming dance, took my girlfriend on a date, broke up with her, and then told my best friend about it all. Oh, and I went for a jog. It was a busy day, even by my standards.

My mind was still digesting it all when my bedroom door suddenly flew open and my younger brother Alex popped in. Alex was 14 years old, and that was 14 long years annoying the crap out of me any chance he got.

"So, who is this Casey and what about Tricia?" he asked in that annoying little brother way that just made me want to punch him. Hard. In the face.

"What are you talking about, Alex," I feigned. "Who's Casey?"

"You know perfectly well who Casey is," he said. "I heard you talking about her on the phone."

"I just ordered a pizza from a girl named Casey down at La Rosa's," I said, somewhat non-convincingly.

"That's bullshit, Chad!" proclaimed Alex. "La Rosa's isn't open this late, and besides, you know Mom would never let you order something this late on a school night.

"All I know is that you're supposed to be taking Tricia to homecoming Saturday night and now you're talking to some girl named Casey. I want to know what's going on right now, or I'm telling Mom and Dad."

"Okay," I was scrambling. "It's just a girl from school whose dog got hit by a car and she is so distraught over it that she wanted me to pick her up and take her over to the kennel where the poor thing is lying in wake."

Not too bad for a quick lie-on-the-fly.

"I don't believe you," Alex countered. "Where's the kennel and what's the dog's name?"

Shit-Shit-Shit.

"The dog's name is…umm…Bingo," I blurted. I'd seen a flyer on the fridge when I came in for Bingo Night down at the Church. My mom was an avid Bingo player, and her love of grids of assorted numbers and letters and little plastic chits had just saved me.

"I still think you're full of bullshit," he said as he changed from his clothes to his sleeper shorts and tee. "And I'll probably tell Mom and Dad anyway."

"Like I care," I said. "Someday you too will have a date. I just wonder who'll be the lucky guy."

"Ha, ha, jerk face," he said as he climbed into the bunk.

It was close to eleven and I was exhausted. It had been a long day and I just wanted to put it all behind me. Alex was on his bunk pretending to read by the light of the desk lamp. I think he must have changed the light bulb from a 40-watt bulb to a 150-watt bulb, as the light seemed bright enough to give me a tan. Also, he liked to read aloud and it really pissed me off.

"Alex, turn off your light and go to bed," I said. "Besides it's just a magazine and only has pictures of men wrestling with each other."

"No it doesn't," Alex said. "It has pictures of beautiful women wrestlers."

"Whatever, man," I said. "Turn off your light so I can go to sleep." I don't know if he ever complied, because I was out shortly after saying it.

Before I knew it, it was daylight. I rolled over in my hammock and looked at my clock.

7:36 am.

Shit, I was late for school.

I flung myself out of the hammock and pulled on my jeans and found a tee shirt in my drawer that read: *Ripple Wine and 69 are Mighty Fine.* My buddies and I had the shirts made because we always were drinking Ripple wine and, well, we were going to graduate in 1969. I ran to the bathroom and did a quick *gurgle-gurgle* with mouthwash since I didn't have time to brush, which happened most mornings.

"Chad, breakfast!" my mom shouted up the stairs. If only she had shouted twenty minutes earlier I wouldn't be rushing around like a decapitated chicken.

"Sorry Mom, no time to eat," I shouted back. "I'm late for school."

I ran down the steps, taking two at a time, and was out the front door before she could object. I jumped over the driver's door into my front seat, started the car, and backed out of the driveway at about the same speed that I did at Mr. Bakers' house when I dropped/pushed Tricia out of the car. I sped down my street trying to leave that particular memory behind in the dust.

Finally I arrived at school, which was about fifteen minutes away. I checked into the office where I handed Ms. Graves, the school secretary, a note from my mom saying that I was up sick all night. Of course I forged the note two minutes before from the front seat of my car, but my handwriting was the only handwriting that Ms. Graves had ever seen, so she was none the wiser.

"Thanks Chad," she said as she recorded the note in a ledger. "But I must say, your mom sure doesn't have good penmanship. I remember when she was a student here, and I don't remember it being this bad."

"I know Ms. Graves," I explained. "She has leprosy and it has affected her writing."

What the hell did I just say? Leprosy? Where did I get that word from? I've got to stop watching so much *Password*.

With that taken care of, I ran to what was left of my first period class. The rest of my school day was spent trying to see Casey in the hallways between periods, dodging Tricia and any other members of the cheer squad, who were all most likely ready to kill me, and eating lunch with Marty where he got all the juicy details from the night before. All in all, it was a successful school day. Oh, and I may have actually gone to a class or two.

The final bell for school rang at about two forty-five in the afternoon. I sprinted to my locker and dropped off all my books. Once I was 30 pounds lighter, I slammed the locker door and headed out to the parking lot to see if I could find Casey before she left.

All of the upper classman students were running around trying to get to their cars and get out of the student parking lot as quickly as they could, so as you could imagine, it was a circus. Unfortunately, I didn't see her in the mess of people.

Since it was Thursday, the JV football team had a game with Batesville on our practice field, so the varsity team didn't have a full football practice. Coach Acus had other ideas for us when we didn't have full practice. I could either run laps around the track or lift weights. I'm surprised he hadn't been drafted into the marines as a drill sergeant. The man loved to tell people what to do. Needless to say, I spent the next couple of hours in the gym's weight room working on my arms and chest. I wanted them to be big and sexy for my date with Casey. After I was sure that my muscles weren't getting any bigger, I decided to head home and get ready for my night of love.

I trotted to my car and had it started and in drive before the door was even shut. I arrived at my driveway in ten minutes or less and got out of my car as quick as I could. I ran upstairs to shower, change my clothes, and brush my teeth. I never showered after my run last night, and with the workout today mixing with the old musty scent of sweat from last night, the smell was even starting to bother me. Besides, the shower was where I did my best thinking, and I needed to do a lot of thinking to figure out the plans for tonight.

I showered in less than two minutes, which is about twenty minutes shy of what women take. I really worked hard on my teeth too. I brushed until the bristles in my toothbrush were smushed flat and then rinsed with *Colgate 100* mouthwash. I think I used the entire bottle. After all, it was the "Mouthwash for Lovers!"

I stepped out of the steamy bathroom and searched my closet for clothes to impress Casey with. I decided to wear a new pair of jeans along with a short-sleeved white shirt with pinstripes that my mother had ironed some time ago. Although I was going to wear my tennis shoes, I wanted to dress as if I was going to a wedding. I threw on my clothes, looked in the mirror for about ten minutes, and then started to head off to pick up Casey.

Before I could reach my bedroom door, Alex came walking in with an armful of textbooks.

"Hey Chad, where are you going?" he asked, as he set the books down on his bed.

"I am late for the wake of Fido," I said.

"Wait, I thought his name was Bingo?"

"Yeah, Bingo was his name...oh," I said, then laughed at my own joke.

"Okay, let me get this straight," Alex began, ignoring my funny. "You smell good and have nice clothes on--clothes you probably stole from somebody because they look new--and your hair is combed. What gives?"

"I told you, I have to get to a wake for Bingo," I explained--again. And then I saw the clock on my nightstand. It was getting close to 5:30. "I have to go."

I squeezed past Alex who stood in the doorway and ignored what ever else he was saying. In the background I heard him yell:

"I'm going to tell mom and dad that you dumped Tricia and are dating a new girl who's doing LSD." I ignored him and kept walking. "And she's a stripper!"

I wanted to turn around, run upstairs, and flush Alex's head in the toilet for even thinking that way about the love of my life, but decided against it, as I had to get to Casey's by six.

I decided to take Casey out to The Hollows. After getting so close last night, I was in the mood for the excellent food and quiet atmosphere. Also, I could avoid detection by my possible enemies. Deer Park is a small town, and people like to talk. The Hollows was out of the way enough to avoid running into classmates and nosy-bodies like I would at the Big Boy in town, where everyone hangs out. I also figured out my cover story in case we were discovered. I was helping a friend who was having issues with her boyfriend. If anyone--especially Tricia--asks, I would just say I was being a nice guy. And besides, who would want to mess with Billy Rickett's best girl?

I drove out to the outskirts of town based on directions that Marty gave me at lunch. The Martins lived in the new Arbor Hills subdivision that was being built. According to My Man Marty, Casey's house was one of the first ones finished, and one of the first ones that was occupied. It was no wonder I didn't know where it was, because a year ago, it wasn't even here. And also, how did Marty know all of this? The kid seemed to know everything. He was like the Swiss Army Knife of friends.

I found the address and pulled into the driveway of their ranch-style home. Since the house was new, the lawn was still mostly dirt and grass seed that was waiting to grow once spring hit. I immediately thought how lucky they were to not have to mow their lawn every week like I had to.

I got out of my car and casually strolled up the walkway to her front door. I rang the doorbell and waited for almost fifteen seconds before the door swung open. There in front of me was the largest male figure I had ever seen. Now, I was six feet tall and it still took me almost ten seconds to move my eyes from his torso to the top of his head. It was a very large head too. We're talking the size of a small boulder. He wore a full beard, like a mountain man, and his eyes were set deep within his skull, and they were focused solely on me. Immediately, I thought maybe I had the wrong address. Well, I was sure hoping I had the wrong address.

"Excuse me sir, but does Casey Martin live here?" I asked.

Please say no. Please tell me she lives next door.

"Yes, young man, she does live here and I'm her father," he said. Well, it was more like a guttural rumble; like tectonic plates grating against each other. At this point I was almost sure that this guy had killed people in the war. How many Germans had died at his hands? He was probably on parole from jail as well. In any event, I knew I was not going to be ripping the heart out of Casey anytime soon. Of course, I was in love and I would never do that. The only way out of this relationship was for Casey to break it off. It was out of my control now.

"Hello, Mr. Martin, I'm Chad," I said, using every ounce of charm that the Man upstairs had given me. "I'm here to accompany your lovely daughter to dinner, where we will be entertained with fine food and music, followed by a brief G-rated film. Of course the movie theater we will be attending will have a lot of people seated around us at all times."

I had turned into Eddie Haskell from *Leave it to Beaver*. Oh my God, I am going to have to be this person around Casey's father forever. I sure hoped he wouldn't ask what movie theater we're going to, or what movie we are seeing. I had one movie in mind and I didn't think to check what other movies were showing.

"Well Chad, what movie are you taking Casey to and where is it playing?" he inquired.

SHIT, SHIT, SHIT.

Well, I was normally quick to think of a good lie, but I wasn't too sure about lying to Mr. Martin. At least not on the first date.

"Well sir, are you familiar with the movie titled, *Old Yeller*? It's a wonderful tale of a boy and a dog--"

"Yes, I have Chad," he said, cutting me off. "Where's it playing because it came out ten years ago and I don't believe it's still in movie theaters?"

I was sweating bullets. Honest-to-god bullet-sized drops of sweat were beading down my face and that ever-so-familiar odor that Tricia had so loved started to come back, wafting up from my armpits.

"Well sir," I stammered. "I believe the movie is being shown in Hanover at a college theater where students taking language arts are viewing it for class."

I am so full of shit, I even believed myself.

"I will have your daughter home promptly by eleven o'clock sharp, sir."

"Try ten o'clock, champ, how about that?" he countered.

"Why of course, sir," I said. "That was what I was thinking all along. The wrong time just slipped out of my mouth."

Thank God Casey came walking to the front door, ending this little game of cat (big, humungous, man-eating cat) and mouse (me). She pushed herself between her father and the doorframe.

"Hi Chad," she said, offering me a warming smile. "I'm so glad you got to meet my father. Isn't he wonderful?"

"Why yes, he is," I said as I took her hand and helped her out the door. "I have thoroughly enjoyed my conversation with you, Mr. Martin."

The mountain-of-a-man stood in the doorway and continued to stare at me with those deep-set eyes. I actually thought of just making a break for it and running away, abandoning all hopes of ever taking Casey Martin out on a date. I started to release her hand when the mountain spoke.

"Well, you two have a great evening and enjoy *Old Yeller*."

"Are we going to see *Old Yeller*?" Casey asked.

"Why yes," I said as I led her away from the door and to my waiting car. "I thought it would be most enjoyable and educational for both of us."

I said it loud enough for her father to hear. The Eddie Haskell impersonation was beginning to make me tired. I opened the car door for her and she slid in.

"Chad, I have never heard you talk like this," she said. "I also never pegged you for the *Old Yeller* type."

"I'll explain in the car."

I opened my door and climbed into the seat. I looked up at the house and her father was still there, staring. I gave him a wave, and started the car. I had the Corvair backed out and down the road before he ever had a chance to return the wave.

The drive out to the lake took about fifteen minutes, and the conversation was once again light. I quickly realized one thing: I was not the smartest person in this conversation, and my charm was only going to get me so far. Every other girl I'd ever gone out with knew me before we went out, so I didn't have to work to make conversation. I just charmed them and kept things simple and let the magic happen. With Casey, things were different. She was smart, and I knew if I tried to talk about cooking and sports, the only two subjects I knew about, this would go nowhere quickly. I just wanted to really get to know Casey and at the same time build off of last night by trying to be humble, funny, and entertaining. I certainly couldn't be all that at a movie. The Hollows was the perfect atmosphere to accomplish all that.

It was another cool fall Indiana evening with a blue sky that was quickly turning dark, and a little breeze blowing in from the west. We arrived at The Hollows and as soon as we pulled into the parking lot, Casey asked, "Have you ever been here before Chad, it looks lovely?"

"Not really," I hesitated. "I've heard the food is fantastic and the atmosphere is quiet. Plus, we can ask for a table overlooking the lake."

We entered the restaurant and were greeted by a friendly hostess. "Weren't you here last evening?" she asked after I requested a lakeside table.

"Uh, no," I stammered. "You must be mistaken as I'm sure you have a number of Chads that eat here."

"I could swear I saw you out in the parking lot last night," she explained. "Don't you drive an old white, convertible?"

Out of the corner of my eye, I could see Casey following the conversation, and the look on her face told me I might have some explaining to do soon.

"I do drive an older car. It's a white Corvair," I said, omitting the convertible part. "But I was home studying last night."

"Well, I swear I saw you out there having an argument with someone in your car."

Great, a hostess with total recall of every person that has ever been to this restaurant for the past several generations! My immediate thought was to change the conversation and demand that we be seated at a table.

"Do you know the names of everyone in this restaurant," I asked. "And if so, can you name them?"

This was certainly not a friendly inquiry but it did change the subject quickly. The hostess just smiled at me, and stood there motionless save for the batting of her eyes. Since I was so abruptly rude, my only thought now was that the hostess would tell the cooks in the back to do something to my food. Those thoughts would now govern what I would be ordering this evening, because regardless, I felt I was also going to be getting some random body fluids as well.

"Well," she said through a smile that I didn't feel was sincere. "Let me show you two to your table."

We followed her through the maze of occupied tables in the dining room and out onto the patio. There were tables lined up along the short wall with a breathtaking view of Lake Whitney at twilight. There were maybe ten tables total, but only four were being used. Each table was covered with lit candles and settings for two.

"Please enjoy your food, won't you?" the hostess said with cheer. I still wasn't buying it.

As we sat at the table and perused the menu, I could only think of eating bread and water to avoid any unnecessary "secret sauces" that might be on my food. Casey decided to order filet mignon with new potatoes and a side salad.

"What are you having?" she asked.

"Well, I just can't decide since there are so many wonderful items on the menu," I said. I knew I couldn't just have bread and water so I had a plan. "I think I'll have whatever you have." I figured that if I ordered the same thing, the cooks in the back would never do anything to the food of such a lovely girl like Casey, and they wouldn't know which dish I would eat. But just in case, I would switch the food when it arrived so Casey got mine.

During the half-hour wait for our food, Casey and I just got to know each other. She liked my sense of humor, which was dry, and I finally explained why I was talking funny back when I was with her dad. Turns out, her father scares a lot of guys away.

Our food finally came out and before the waitress could put the plates down on the table I reached out and grabbed them as if to assist her. She was somewhat hesitant to allow me to hold onto the plates but I was rather persistent and forceful. I had to make sure I could switch the plates.

"What are you doing?" Casey asked. "Let the waitress serve the food; that's her job!"

"I am just trying to help her." I was finally able to wrestle the plates away from the waitress and switch them as I set them down. I received a funny face from Casey, but she didn't pursue a line of questioning. I could now eat in peace knowing that the cooks hadn't spoiled my meal.

As we ate, we talked about life in Deer Park, and my family and the uncertainty facing all of us after school. I didn't know whether I would go to college or maybe be drafted. I didn't want to be drafted, but I also didn't want to go right into another four years of school. I was trying desperately to just live in the moment, and see what happens.

At one point during our meal, Casey reached over and put her hand on my knee, because it had been nervously bouncing up and down since we had arrived at the restaurant. It was the first time that she had touched me, and the thrill was exhilarating. I bit back a smile and kept talking.

After an enjoyable dinner, we left The Hollows and headed toward the drive-in in Shelbyville where we were going to see a movie called, *Night of the Living Dead*. What a night to relax in my car--with the top up of course--and watch a scary movie. My hopes were that Casey would get so scared, that she'd need me there to comfort her in my big, strong arms. I was a genius.

We pulled up to our space at the drive-in and hooked up the speaker to the passenger-side window so we could hear the movie. My Corvair didn't have a lot of room up front so it allowed me to scoot closer to Casey. She smiled and I slid my arm around her shoulders. Things were going well.

The movie started and the first time an undead monster came onscreen, Casey went rigid in my arms. I don't remember much about the plot of the film, but do recall Casey asking me halfway through why I took her to see this movie of all the movies showing. It was certainly not a girl's movie, but she was nice about it and I of course loved it.

The drive-in was quite crowded for a Thursday night, so I suggested that we leave a little early to avoid the traffic leaving at the end of the movie. Besides, the movie was getting boring as the people in the house were just arguing with each other while the ghouls were just walking around outside. There was just one way in or out of the drive-in, so we started to get ready to leave. I knew Casey wouldn't mind since she never really got into the movie. We each adjusted ourselves in the seats and I started the engine, put the car in reverse, and started to back out of our space. I had got maybe four feet out when I heard a loud BOOM! I looked over and saw Casey completely covered in shards of glass.

"What happened?" I cried out.

"We forgot to remove the speaker!" exclaimed Casey.

Great! My only thought was going home and my dad discovering one less window on my car. I could only imagine what he would say. Or do. Alex knowing also came to mind. Actually, that might have been worse.

We spent the next hour driving around looking for a self-clean car wash where we could vacuum the glass out of the car. It was close to eleven-fifteen when we finally pulled up to Casey's house. As I turned off the car, another horrifying thought came to my mind. This would be the last time I would ever see Casey again. Her father was going to torture me, kill me, and then torture me some more. I wasn't sure if it was best for me to escort Casey to her door or just let her get out and then drive away. Far and fast. After much thought, I decided to walk her to the front door and confront her father. I really had no choice since I was going to take Casey to homecoming in a couple of days.

Oh yeah, like that was going to happen now.

I slowly opened my car door and grabbed my left leg--as if it was paralyzed--picked it up and lifted it out of the car. I then grabbed my right leg and did the same. At that point I stood up, but remained motionless and limp. I walked around and leaned up against the car. She joined me, sliding up by my side. I wanted to escort her up to her door, but my legs were like rubber. I was afraid of what was behind her front door. Torture and death were my only thoughts.

I gathered strength from my memories of being with her for the past few hours; looking at her and listening to her and knowing that being with her gave me this feeling I'd never had before. It was like I was thrown out of my comfort zone, and while I was uneasy, I wasn't afraid, I wasn't trying to impress her or show off, I just enjoyed being there.

Prolonging the walk to her door, and my pending murder, I decided to ask her the question I'd been avoiding all evening: "So, what's the deal between you and Billy?"

She shrugged, "I don't know, we've been having a lot of problems lately. He was one of the first boys I met when I moved here, and we started going out. But now…I don't know."

I shook my head, "Don't take this the wrong way, but Billy…well, he's not good enough for you."

Casey blushed, "Well, that's kind of you to say--"

"No, I'm serious," I blurted out. "You're smart and funny and nice, and he's a Lawrenceburg redneck. You deserve better."

She looked at me, "Well, what can I say? I don't have the best luck when it comes to boys. Billy was nice at first and he treated me kind and all, but when he wasn't getting what he wanted, he started talking down to me and…not being nice."

"What was it he wanted?"

Casey looked down and started subconsciously fiddling with a couple of loose threads in her sweater, "Well, you know…*it*."

"It?"

Casey looked at me in frustration.

"Chad, I'll kiss a boy, but that's it. If you want anything else, you'll have to wait until we get married."

"So, when are we getting married?"

That broke the tension, and we both laughed. Casey playfully slapped my arm, "You know what I mean, silly."

To be honest, I was hoping to do more than kiss her, but I was surprisingly all right with her decision.

"I know, I know," I said. "So, you're…is this a religious thing?"

Her smile faded, and she looked back down and began fiddling with her sweater again, "I have my reasons, and I hope you respect that."

I quickly responded, "Casey, I completely respect that…and you."

She looked up at me and smiled, "Thanks. I've…I've gotta go inside now. My dad is probably wondering where we are; and I'm sure he is waiting for us." She used the word "us," not exactly what I was hoping for.

As she pushed herself off the side of the car, I blurted out, "So, will you go to the dance with me?"

I'd asked her two times now, and each time she had maneuvered out of answering. This was it. I needed an answer. I DEMANDED an answer.

"I…I need to sleep on it," she said.

DAMMIT!

"Come on," she said as she took my hand. "We can explain to my father what happened. It'll be okay."

I was still mad that she hadn't given me an answer, and now she had brought me back into the here and now. Somewhere in the house in front of me there was a man wanting to clean me like a fish. But maybe she was right. Only the truth could save me from execution.

"Okay," I said, speaking clearly and loud enough for neighbors to hear in case the authorities asked them what happened 'that night.' "I'm moving away from the car now and slowly making my way to the walkway leading to your front door, where your father will kill me."

"He won't kill you," she said. "Maybe rough you up a little, but that's all."

The porch light was on and the front door was cracked. I thought I heard the sound of a gun being loaded, but was pretty sure that it was only my mind playing tricks on me. I told Casey to quietly go in first and I would follow. By follow, I meant at a distance of about twenty paces.

She opened the door and pulled me along with her into the house. The first image I had was of a very large shadow of a person sitting in a chair that was obviously too small in a dimly light living room. I positioned myself immediately behind Casey, keeping her between this very large shadow and me. I figured he wouldn't hit her and he'd have to go around her to get to me.

"Come on in and sit down," the shadow said. Instead, I went on the offensive.

"Good evening, Sir, I must apologize for our tardiness." There goes that Eddie Haskell persona again. It was my only defense.

"Where have you two been? I thought I was clear when I said ten o'clock." The voice was getting louder. I felt my bladder about to give way.

"Well, Sir, we--"

"Daddy, it was my fault," Casey said. That was good. I like the part about it being all Casey's fault. Now, what story was she going to tell her father? There are no window-hanging speakers at the theater I had described to him earlier. I would be caught in the lie. Death suddenly became a reality again.

"Daddy, I had such a good time and Chad was such a gentleman that I really wanted to get to know him more," she explained. "You know how I have struggled to meet a great guy since we moved here. One with kindness in his heart and who treats with me with respect. You also know how my relationship with Billy has not been good lately."

I loved this stuff about kindness in my heart and the respect thing. I thought only guys used those lines when they wanted to get a girl in bed.

"Daddy, I know we're late, but I was the one who prolonged the date because I was really enjoying myself and wanted to know more about Chad."

"Well," the shadow began as it rose from the too-small chair. "I guess this one time and one time only, I will let this incident slide. But let me be clear about this Chad, when I give you and my daughter a time to be home, I don't mean any time different than that time, is that understood?"

"Why yes sir," I stammered, as the elation of being pulled back from oblivion washed over me. "I must apologize for my lack of consideration and compliance with your wishes, Sir!"

I could not believe how Casey had maneuvered around the issue of being late and what a great story she had come up with. I think I'm finally starting to get it. Boys are known to lie to get what they want, but girls can just bat their eyes and use the word "Daddy" to get something they want. Maybe I could use this on my mom. Anyway, I had a mission to accomplish, and time was running short.

"Mr. Martin," I began. "If Casey will go with me, I would like your permission to take her to the homecoming dance this weekend." I looked at her, right into her eyes. "*IF* she will go with me."

"I can also prepare a list of things we will be doing, and all the phone numbers of where we will be, and the phone numbers of the parents whose house we will be staying at after the dance and everything.

"Would you please allow me to escort your beautiful daughter to the dance?"

"If my daughter says yes," he said. "Then I will too. But again, let's be clear: don't ever be late again. And I would like that list of numbers. Maybe I will drop by and check up on you."

I had escaped death. The less he knew about Saturday, the greater my chance of surviving until Monday!

Casey walked me to the door and thanked me for a wonderful night. She still hadn't agreed to go to the dance with me, but I wasn't going to push it anymore tonight. The ominous shadow of her father fell over both of us in the doorway, so a good night kiss was completely out of the question. I left the Martin house filled with relief and a greater appreciation for how girls manipulate their fathers. And they do it without lying. They just withhold certain aspects of the truth. That's just amazing.

I finally arrived home, parked my car out in the driveway and headed up to my room for some much needed rest before the big day tomorrow. I had almost forgotten about the football game on Saturday, but with my new lease-on-life, I knew I would run faster than I ever have before, because all I had to do was picture Casey's dad chasing after me trying to kill me!

While lying in my hammock, and just before turning out the light to get some sleep, I grabbed a piece of paper and a pencil and wrote:

Casey,

I had a really great time last night, and it was really cool getting to know you. I hope you decide to go to homecoming with me, I think it would be really cool if you did. Don't worry about Tricia or Billy, they may be mad for a while, but they'll get over it. Maybe they'll even decide to go together, ha ha.

Write me back and let me know you're going to be my date Saturday, and we'll have a great time. I'll meet you after school to discuss details.

Chad

Chapter 3

The next morning I awoke with a fresh outlook on life. I flipped myself out of my hammock and headed for the bathroom for my morning ritual. Within twenty minutes I was out the door and headed to school.

As soon as I walked into school, I immediately began looking for Marty. He was in the lobby talking to a group of people, and I immediately ran over to him.

"Hey man, I need a favor."

Marty looked at me suspiciously. "I'm sorry, I checked with the science lab and they have no available brains. You're on your own."

I applauded. "Bravo, sir, Bravo. You writing for Jack Benny now?" This was typical banter for us, the bigger the insult, the better the burn, the more fun it becomes.

We could have kept going, and obviously nothing was off-limits, but I had a mission for Marty, so I pulled him away from the crowd.

"Seriously, I need for you to do me a favor."

Marty sighed, "What is it?"

I handed over the note with caution, like it was the secret to enriching uranium and Marty was Napoleon Solo, *The Man From U.N.C.L.E.*

"I need you to give this note to Casey Martin as soon as possible."

"Are you serious?" Marty asked, as he gave me an incredulous look. "You've pissed off Tricia--who now hates you, and has every girlfriend of hers in school hating you--and now you want me to do you a favor which will--I'm sure--have them all hating me because for some god-forsaken reason I'm still your best friend--"

"Yeah, yeah," I interrupted. "That may be true, but I'm taking Casey Martin to the dance. I just need her to say "yes.""

Sometimes, when Marty is pushed near the breaking point with me, he starts talking to me like I'm a three-year old, hoping somehow the slowed and deliberate delivery would connect with me.

It never did.

"Chad, we've had this conversation," he began. "Well, at least I have. This was a bad plan--if it could actually be called 'a plan.' I told you that in the gym, and I told you that at lunch yesterday. You know this can only end badly, and as your friend--though I really have to re-evaluate that term--I have to tell you to not go through with this. You need to call Tricia up and beg for her forgiveness."

I grinned like the Cheshire cat. "Oh ye of little faith."

The exacerbation in his face was growing. I had him, because some part of Marty, despite his normally conservative nature, always wanted to see how my ideas played out.

"You can't win this time, I'm telling you."

I looked at him and put both hands on his upper arms like a father looking proudly at his son. I had him. Now, I needed him to help me complete the plan.

"Marty, my plan has been simple," I reiterated, counting down the steps with my fingers. "I pick a fight with Tricia--which I did--and I got out of that date, I took Casey out on not one, but two dates in the last 48 hours, and now all I have to do is get Casey to agree to go to homecoming with me. It's not rocket science."

Marty sighed, like he always did when he knew he was beat and was along for the ride.

"Well, at least it appears you've thought it out inasmuch as you think things out."

I concurred. "So you'll help me?"

Marty suddenly realized, "Will I be hated as much as you?"

"Probably."

Marty looked at me confidently. "Well, I'd rather be hated than ignored."

I grinned broadly, "That's why you're my best friend, Marty. Now, take this note and give it to Casey."

Marty took the note and looked at me. "You know you're crazy, right?"

"Like a loon, man. Like a loon."

Chapter 4

This was seriously the longest school day of my life. As much as I didn't pay attention in class on a normal day, today was worse. All I did was think about Casey, about how much fun we were going to have at the dance, and how Casey was going to make my life complete. All I needed was a note back saying "yes." I didn't--couldn't think about the consequences of her saying "no." I couldn't picture going to the dance with Tricia, knowing that Casey was at home alone, or even worse, out with Billy Ricketts and the Lawrenceburg Redneck Wolf pack. What did she see in him anyway? I wasn't the smartest guy, but I was pretty sure I was a scientist compared to Billy Ricketts.

After each period I hung out in the halls, looking for Casey or Marty, hoping to get a note back to confirm the date. After second period, I saw Marty approaching; I eagerly looked for some sign that he had a note with him. Nothing.

Marty approached his locker, which was next to mine. As he was turning the combination, he spoke to the locker, but loud enough for me to hear.

"Gave her the note. Nothing."

This wasn't the answer I was looking for.

"What do you mean, nothing?"

"I mean," he explained, still to his locker. "I gave her the note, she said 'thanks,' and walked into class. No response, nothing."

I quizzed Marty as intently as Edward R. Murrow attacking Joe McCarthy. "Did she read the note?"

Marty turned to me and spoke in his deliberate voice. "What did I just say, Chad? No, she did not read the note. She did not tell me anything other than 'thanks.'"

I stared at my own locker in deep thought. This didn't make sense. I turned to my friend. "Marty, find her and see if she has a note for me."

Marty brushed me off, "I'm sure when she does, she will let me or you know."

I slammed my locker shut. "Dammit man, just do it! Please?"

Marty drew back, both hands raised in response, as if I was holding him up at gunpoint.

"Calm down, 'Donna Dramatic,' I'll take care of it."

I stomped off to my U.S. History class, deep in thought. If I didn't hear anything back by lunch, I'd have to go find her myself and get an answer. Third period went even slower than the first two, and when the bell finally rang, I raced into the hall to do…something. I had no idea what, but I knew I just needed to be in the hall. I had to admit to myself that I had been avoiding seeing Casey until I got the answer, but it was a small school, and I was going to run into her soon enough. I needed an answer before then.

Then I saw her heading towards me on her way to the cafeteria. She floated past the assorted gaggle of teens that congregated in the hallway, and the world seemed to slow down. I studied her body, looking for clues as to her intentions, and, well, looking at her body. She had on a pink blouse and sweater, and a ruffled skirt. Her hair was up in her customary ponytail, and she was walking deliberately, with her head slightly facing downward. That was typical for someone who didn't have a lot of friends in the school, and wasn't looking for constant validations of their popularity. As I watched her, I realized that this trait made her even more attractive to me. Hell, I was as guilty of the "head-up, looking around for validation" as most, but I was looking for attention. Casey wasn't, and I liked that about her.

As for clues, there were none to be had. But to be honest, I needed Marty for this. Unless she was holding a sign that said, "Yes Chad, I'll go to homecoming with you," I wasn't going to pick up any subtle body language.

As she neared, I nervously looked around for Tricia or any of her cheer squad friends who would immediately report to her any suspicious activities. The coast was clear. Here was my chance, and Casey…walked right past me.

"Hi Chad," she said and shot me a sideward glance.

"Um, hi," I said back, stunned. I stood and watched as she walked down to the hall and rounded the corner to head to the cafeteria.

"What the hell?" I asked out loud when Marty walked back up to his locker.

"Hey, man," he began. "Saw Casey walk by. She didn't give me anything. She give anything to you?"

I looked at him dazed, "No. Nothing. She barely even said 'hi.'"

"Man, that's a bummer. You think you're wrong about her?"

"No," I said. "Maybe she thought Tricia was nearby. You know, Tricia always seems to hover, showing up when you least expect it." My mood brightened. That had to be it. Casey was even smarter than I thought.

"Marty, of course she's not going to stop and talk to me," I explained, as if it were clear as day. "She's waiting for the right moment. It makes perfect sense."

Marty, long-since defeated in this argument, just calmly nodded.

"Of course, man, makes perfect sense. If I were you, I'd wait until after school to talk to her."

I nodded my head, carefully considering my friend's sage advice.

"Yeah, okay, that makes sense," I admitted. "Maybe she'll be working on the decorations again, and I can talk to her before I get dressed for practice."

I closed my locker, said farewell to Marty, and headed to the lunchroom to begin the next phase of my plan.

The lunchroom at Deer Park High School was a large, open space with a kitchen and serving line on one end, and tables spread out through the floor. The food was standard cafeteria food, processed and fried and perfectly acceptable for a still-growing high school kid. Only the nerds brought their own lunch from home, and although my mother was a great cook, and had offered many times to fix my lunch for me, I was way too "cool" to bring my own.

From the other side of the lunchroom I noticed Casey was sitting with her back toward me, eating with Marcy Shonk and Linda Ambury, who were both in the French Club with Casey (and until the previous night, when Casey told me about it over dinner, I had no idea Deer Park High School even had a French Club.).

I saw Casey twice more in the hallways between classes, and both times she said "hi," and kept going. And Marty reported no returned note. I was also trying to avoid Tricia, who I'd heard was on the warpath against me, as if I couldn't have figured it out by the numerous dirty looks I got from all of her girlfriends in and between classes. My plan now hinged on seeing Casey after school, and that was not exactly the way I had wanted this to happen. But that was okay. Nothing like this came easy, I reasoned.

I got to the gym as the bell for last period rang. Since there was football practice, I got out of classes early again. I was dying to see Casey and to get her, once and for all, to agree to go to the dance with me. I walked into the gym, and the junior girls were again working on the decorations, this time decorating the gym floor, as there would be no more gym classes before the dance. I looked for Casey, and couldn't find her anywhere. I decided to go into the locker room and get dressed for practice, and then I'd come back into the gym before calisthenics. Surely, I figured, she would be there by then. I got dressed a lot slower than usual, and then walked back into the gym and looked around. Casey was nowhere to be found. DAMN!

I saw Carol Laswell over by the door, and since Carol wasn't friends with Tricia or any of Tricia's friends, I could ask her about Casey without being unfairly judged. I walked over towards her.

"Um, hey Carol," I whispered. "I'm looking for Casey Martin? She has a message in the office and they told me to let her know since I was heading in this direction."

I then heard the words that stopped my world in its tracks:

"I just saw her in the parking lot, talking to her boyfriend. You want me to give her the message when she comes back?"

SHIT! SHIT! SHIT! SHIT! SHIT!

Oh, great, just great! I've intentionally pissed off my girlfriend two days before homecoming in order to take a girl who won't even go with me because her Cro-Magnon boyfriend decided to connect his two working brain cells and come to his senses and take her to the dance himself. So, now I have to suck up to Tricia and act like I'm on-board with her 50-year plan, all while watching Casey dancing and having fun with a guy who doesn't appreciate her. Damn.

"Cha-ad, hello?" Carol said. "Do you want me to tell Casey she has a message in the office?"

I snapped back to reality. "Umm, no, I'm heading outside for practice, I'll just find her in the parking lot."

Carol went back to what she was doing, "Okay."

I walked out the side door and looked around the parking lot, and there she was, about three rows back on the left side, sitting on the hood of her car. Billy Ricketts was standing in front of her, and his car was parked in the aisle in front of her car. He was wearing his letter jacket, and was obviously upset. Although I couldn't hear them, I could tell by the gestures and body language that it was not a fun conversation. I wanted to feel great, knowing that they were arguing, but I felt bad for Casey. I hated seeing her upset, and I didn't quite know what to do at that point. So, I stood there for a couple of minutes. I was far enough away that neither one of them noticed me. Finally, there seemed to be a point when both of them ran out of energy, and they just appeared to be resigned to whatever fate they had decided. Billy walked around and got into his car and took off. Casey watched him leave, got off the hood, and began walking back to the gym door, directly towards me. I froze.

I didn't want her to know I had been watching, but it was too late. She looked up and saw me there. I quickly reached around and lifted my leg back and grabbed my ankle and began stretching like I just got there and was getting ready for warm-ups. I have no idea if it worked, but I had no other choice. She walked toward me, stopped beside me, and turned her head in my direction.

"Yes."

I looked up, "Yes?"

She replied calmly, "Yes, I'll go to homecoming with you."

I was elated, overjoyed, overwhelmed, and should have just said "okay," but I had to know.

I looked past her shoulder towards the parking lot. "What about Billy?"

Casey looked me squarely in the eye. "We broke up. I don't really want to talk about it. I said I'd go to the dance with you, so don't let me down, okay?"

"I won't let you down, I promise."

She started to turn back to go inside, "Thanks. I've got to go inside and help finish decorating. Let me know the plan for Saturday."

"I will," I said. She walked towards the door. "Wait!"

Casey turned around and gave me a quizzical look.

I smiled, "If Carol tells you that you have a message in the office, don't worry about it."

"Why?"

I smiled, "I made it up. I couldn't find you, and had to think of something."

Casey smiled and laughed a little, "Really? That's fine, I'll just act like I already got the message."

"Thanks."

We held our gaze for a few seconds and then Casey gave me a little wave and turned to go inside. I watched her walk inside the door and slowly fade into the shadows inside the hallway leading to the gym. I took in every part of her. Then I had another realization: Damn, I was late for football practice again. Coach was going to kill me.

Chapter 5

Coach Acus was less accommodating today than he had been on Wednesday, and because our homecoming game was tomorrow afternoon, I had to run some extra wind sprints as punishment. I did a whole lot of running and hitting at practice. "One final full-contact practice before the game," was his excuse, but I think he just wanted us to sweat, and sweat I did.

After practice ended, I skipped the shower like I often did, and went home. Normally, our games were played on Friday nights, and I wasn't used to having a free Friday night. It was going to be nice. I walked in the front door and saw my mother was busy in the kitchen working on dinner. I started to race up the steps to my room when she yelled at me.

"Chad?" she called out. I froze on the mid-step. "Tricia called and wants you to call her. She didn't sound too happy. Please be nice to her, she's such a nice girl and the Bakers are such a nice family and all."

"I'll call her," I yelled back down the stairs. "And she's fine, it's just that time of the month."

"What time of the month is that, dear?" she asked.

Crap. Sometimes I forget that I'm talking to my mother.

"Um, the dance is tomorrow," I explained, still shouting. "That's the time of month I'm talking about."

"Oh, Okay," she said. "Dinner will be ready in a half-hour."

I didn't reply, for I was sure that I'd accidentally say something else to my dear, sweet mother that would keep me up nights. What I did do when I got to my room was to call Tricia, who answered the phone.

"Baker residence."

"Trica, it's Chad."

"Well, I hope you're calling to apologize for being a world-class jerk!"

I was ready for this. "I'm returning your call!"

"Well, after the way you treated me the other night and your continual avoiding of me today, I wasn't sure I wanted to go to homecoming with you after all!"

Huh? I thought. *What did I miss?* She must've finally realized what I said that night during our fight about not taking her to the dance. Talk about a delay. It only took a couple of days to hit her.

"Wait a minute Tricia," I said. "You called the dance off when you told me to take you home from The Hollows. Remember?"

"I don't remember anything other than you being a jerk," she said. "And your taking me to a nice restaurant smelling like you just ran a marathon."

"Well," I began. I understood that this was the moment that would forever define my relationship with Tricia Baker. "After that episode at the restaurant, I thought we were done so I decided to ask someone else."

Silence. I held my breath, expecting the worst. But still silence came from the other end of the phone. I was about to ask if she was still on the line when the silence was broken by a high-pitched scream. I jerked the phone away from my ear and held the receiver in my outstretched hand. After about thirty seconds the yelling on the other end stopped. I slowly brought the receiver to my ear.

"Are you done? Hello? Hel-lo?" But she had disconnected the call. Well, my fate was sealed. Tricia now officially hated me and I was certain that her father would be tracking me down within an hour or so. I prayed he would leave the machete at home.

Chapter 6

I climbed into my hammock and tried to relax until dinner was ready, but just couldn't get my brain to shut off after hanging up with Tricia. I picked up the phone and tried calling Marty, but he wasn't home. His mom asked he if I had a message for him, and I told her that I didn't. I couldn't think of anything to else to say. My mind was going a mile a minute and my body was shaking as if I had suddenly come down with the flu. Even my appetite was gone. That's when I knew something was wrong. I grabbed an extra blanket and wrapped it firmly around me. Thank God Alex was not here to see me like this. I would never hear the end of it. After twenty minutes or so I finally dozed off and slept through the night.

The next morning, I awoke to two phone calls, one from Coach Acus making sure I was awake and ready for the game. The second was from Marty finally returning my call from last night, asking questions about the conversation with Tricia and grateful to hear that I was still alive.

This was the first year that the high school decided to hold the homecoming game on Saturday afternoon, after the parade, with the dance being held later that night. For me it was going to be a busy day. Before I got dressed, I stared through my bedroom window into the glaring sun rising above the trees. Wow, what a crazy past couple of days. And it's all culminated into today with me taking Casey to the homecoming dance. I didn't really think about the game, or what Tricia was going through; I couldn't really. I did what I had to do, and if I thought too much about it, I'd feel bad. A train doesn't stop to look at where it's been; it keeps on going down the track.

I was just about ready to get dressed in my football jersey and head to the team breakfast, when I heard a loud, angry voice coming from downstairs.

"Chad, get your butt down here immediately!" my father yelled. What could make him so mad this early in the morning? It was only seven-thirty.

I've had enough confrontations with my father to last a lifetime. Dad was a Texas-born-and-bred army vet who had worked hard all his life to provide for his family and preached discipline in everything. He worked a route selling parts to factories and had a three state territory that took him away from home several days a month.

Dad wasn't a natural salesman, but he'd been in the business long enough to know how the bullshit game worked. He was successful because he worked harder than everyone else, and his word was his bond. He also had what could only be described as a built-in bullshit detector. He thought everything in the world was bullshit.

Now you get why we clashed so much.

"Yeah Dad, I'll be right down," I responded. Slowly I finished dressing and headed downstairs. Normally I view the stairs as a workout tool by running up and down them, but this morning I was going to take my time. I mean I didn't want to injure myself before the football game, or more importantly, the dance. Plus, I wasn't exactly rushing to find out why my dad was so pissed. Then again, maybe if I accidentally tripped and pretended to injure my ankle, he would forget for a moment what he is so mad about and give me some sympathy. After my night out with Casey, maybe it would be like what girls do with their eyes to their fathers. I immediately shifted gears and ran down the stairs with an apparent fall at the last couple of stairs followed with a scream of pain. Although I didn't really injure myself, I think it did the trick.

Dad looked at me with a combination of concern and annoyance. "Chad, what the hell did you do?"

I acted as though I was shot. "I tripped on the last couple of stairs. I'm in a lot of pain!"

I decided to fall to the floor, reached for my ankle, and just held it as I curled up in a fetal position. I thought I was pretty convincing and would for sure remove any angry thoughts my dad had for me.

"Bullshit," he said. "Don't be such a pansy, you'll live!"

No such luck.

"Hobble outside with me, I have something I want to show you."

Shit.

"Sure thing," I replied. Somehow my plan was not working liked I had hoped.

We walked outside, and I quickly lost interest in hobbling on a bum ankle, so after a few steps, I started walking normally, It was a medical miracle!

When we got to my car, we stopped, and I suddenly remembered what happened as Casey and I left the drive-in.

SHIT! SHIT! SHIT! SHIT!

Dad pointed at the passenger-side window, or lack thereof.

"How many times have I told you when you leave your car, or my car, out in the driveway, you are to lock the doors and roll up the windows? I was taking the garbage out this morning and saw this.

"Son, how many times do we have to have this conversation before you finally listen? You have to show respect for your possessions, especially the ones I worked hard to provide for you."

Maybe he didn't know about the window, I thought.

"But that isn't why we're here, is it son?"

I thought wrong. I didn't know what to say, but dad didn't give me a chance.

"Then I tried rolling up the window and nothing happened! There was no window to roll up, just a crunching sound! What the hell happened? I want the straight story and not the same bullshit you usually give me."

I took a deep breath. "Okay, Dad. The straight, no-bullshit story is…"

There was no way I was going to tell him what really happened because

I would wind up telling him the whole story about Tricia and Casey and how his son was a jerk and I'm not sure that would get me through this. So, telling the truth was out. I had to quickly think of one lie that would do the trick. This definitely was not the time to lower my head and bat my eyes.

"Okay," I began, the mother of all lies on my tongue, ready to roll out into the world. "The truth is I was on my way to the dog kennel to meet Tricia whose dog got hit by a car and was in bad shape. She wanted me there to console her and be with her while they put her dog to sleep.

"Somehow a big, crazy dog got loose from the dog pound truck that had brought a number of dogs in, and in trying to escape it tried to jump through my passenger side window and shattered it."

That may work, I thought. It had all the classic elements: compassion, animals, accidents.

"I just couldn't believe it," I continued. "This happened all because I wanted to be with Tricia while her poor little dog was lying there fighting for his life. A fight it ultimately lost. That's the story Dad."

My dad looked at the car, and then looked back at me. "Well son, what can I say, it appears I was wrong to judge you."

Shit, it worked! One small, little lie and now I'm home free.

Then, he gave an exasperated laugh. "Son, you are so full of bullshit!" he exclaimed.

"Chad, I'm your father, not some poor guy you met on the street. That story may work with strangers, but I was telling better bullshit stories to my dad when you were still a mess in my skivvies."

I didn't really want him to go on, but he continued anyway.

"Son, I swear you're eighteen years old, and sixteen of those years I have heard nothing but bullshit come out of your mouth. And the other two years were spent learning how to talk bullshit. Honestly, I don't want to know what the truth is right now. I would prefer you give serious consideration to just not talking. But you can't do that, so let's stop with the bullshit."

It was clear that I was not going to be able to use my car this evening so I took this father-son bonding moment to ask a favor.

"Dad, is there anyway I could use your car for the homecoming dance tonight since, well, I don't have a window on the passenger side? I wouldn't want my date to catch a cold, you know."

Dad looked at me with a sly, knowing grin. "Well, I certainly understand your wanting it to be special, but why are you going to such trouble when you're just taking a tripped-out stripper?"

I was so going to kill Alex!

"You know," Dad said with a straight face. "I've been pretty upset about this and have wanted to talk to you about this new girl."

Wow, this was actually a time I can be honest with my dad and not have to try and bullshit him.

"Dad, I'm not dating a acid-head stripper," I explained. "I'm taking a nice new girl to the dance because Tricia and I had a terrible fight and she broke it off." I put the blame on Tricia because if it had become public knowledge that I had broken it off, well that would lead to more questions. Now was my chance to set some things right.

"Alex made up that crap to get me in trouble. It upsets me that Alex was so concerned about getting me in trouble that he didn't even care about how such lies would affect you and Mom." I put my hand on dad's shoulder. "I can only imagine how Mom is taking this."

"Thanks son, your mother is concerned as well, but she'll be fine. As for Alex, I will be having a chat with your brother about his bullshit, and how he knows so much about strippers and LSD."

I smiled at Alex's impending doom, and Dad gave me even better news.

"Go ahead and take my car," he offered. "But I would only ask that you detail the car today after the game for me in return. Plus, I want that window fixed before it rains again."

"Done and done," I said as I looked at my watch and realized I was running late to catch the bus for the game.

SHIT!

Chapter 7

I got to the team breakfast in barely enough time, and then participated in the homecoming parade through downtown Deer Park. It was silly, but tradition. After the parade, I went home and wandered around aimlessly for a couple of hours, trying to avoid my brother and dad, and after nearly boring myself to death, I finally headed over early to the school to prepare for the game. Coach Acus was impressed with my dedication, when actually my mind couldn't be any farther away from the game. I walked onto the field and looked in the stands for Casey, not knowing (and forgetting to ask) if she would be there. I did see Tricia, whom I had been able to avoid during the parade, and when she saw me, she and the other cheerleaders gave me dirty looks and turned away. Okay, I expected that. Fortunately, I saw the giant redwood-like form of Mr. Martin blocking portions of the sun with his presence, and Casey sitting right next to him! She came to watch me play. And play I did!

We played Indian Hill High School in a game that the entire county usually shows up to, and this year we exacted revenge for the prior two seasons worth of losses with a 28-7 romp. I finished with a touchdown and 110 yards rushing, and 12 solo tackles and a fumble recovery on defense. I wasn't playing for pride, or for the seniors, I was playing for Casey. I spent a lot of time after the game taking congratulations from parents and coaches alike. It was a good feeling.

After the game, I raced home early to get ready for the dance. I detailed

Dad's brand new, 1969 candy-apple red Pontiac GTO Judge in record time. Holy crap, talk about power. I thought Casey was pretty, but this car was simply gorgeous. Good fortune was truly on my side. In the span of a day, I went from a 1961 Corvair convertible without a passenger window to a high-powered, gorgeous, girl-magnet ride that put the "muscle" in muscle cars. Again, God was good!

After I finished detailing Dad's car, I went by and picked up Marty and together we drove over to *Mr. Tuxedo* to pick up our tuxes for the night. Marty was taking Paula Cramer, who was nice, but not particularly attractive, so I didn't really have to pay much attention to her. Marty was pretty excited about going, so I was happy for him.

When we got to the shop, I tried on my white tux jacket and black slacks. Tricia picked it out, so I knew it would look great. They fit like a charm and knew that Casey would be impressed. I now had the look, the car, and the girl. Now all I needed was some extra cash. Ah, good old Dad. My personal, in-house bank. It was about an hour and a half before I had to pick up Casey so I had to move fast.

I dropped Marty off at his place and when I got home I immediately showed my dad the work I had done to his car. It looked like it just came off the showroom floor. His expression was worth a million bucks, so I figured I could get at least fifty dollars from him.

"Dad, now that I have this beautiful automobile--and of course upon its return, I will again have it washed--I was wondering if I could borrow, say, fifty dollars for tonight?"

Dad sighed. "Chad I know you think I'm your personal bank and I also know you think this bank is open twenty-four-seven, but you'll really need to start looking for another bank soon."

"I could never replace you, Dad," I said, sincerely. "But I really need to borrow this money for tonight. I'll start looking for 'another bank' tomorrow."

My Dad used opportunities like these as what we now call "teaching moments." Unfortunately, I paid as much attention to him as I did my teachers.

"Chad, I also continue to hear you constantly use the word, 'borrow.'

Just to be clear, that when you don't pay any money back, the proper term is *have*."

"Okay, can I *have* fifty dollars?"

"No," he replied. "But you can borrow fifty and pay back twenty."

"Deal!" I blurted out.

With that unpleasantness out of the way, it was time to hurry up and get dressed. I actually took the time to focus on washing my body with soap and shampoo, using a razor to shave, and a toothbrush to clean my teeth. Usually, I just do one of the three. Doing all three at once took a long time...almost 20 minutes! How do people do this daily, I thought?

I put on my tuxedo, which was stiff and uncomfortable and ill-fitting, and headed downstairs. I stopped for a couple of minutes to allow my mother to take pictures of me so she could share them with her family and friends later and show that her boy could clean up well when motivated by love.

I hopped in the car and started to head to Casey's house. I realized that for once, I was early, so I thought since I had a few minutes to spare, I would take my bad-ass car around to show off. I slowly drove past our high school where fellow students were already congregating before the dance and then down the road to the Big Boy restaurant where there are always pretty girls hanging out. As I turned into the parking lot, I traveled through at a speed that challenged stalling the car. I revved the engine a few times and with my window down and my left arm resting on the window frame, I just smiled at all the girls standing around. It was the greatest feeling in the world driving this car. I knew I had to make it last as long as possible. After what seemed to be about thirty minutes of driving through the parking lot, I exited and headed to Casey's house. Upon turning into her driveway I saw her standing at the front door anxiously awaiting my arrival.

I was so excited to see her and couldn't wait to run up and give her a peck on the cheek. As I got out of the car, that idea was out the window. Her dad suddenly appeared placing his left arm around Casey's waist.

"So Chad," he said. "You're here to escort my daughter to a supervised evening of which I know you will be a gentleman and return her safely at a reasonable hour."

Okay, I knew where he was going with this but wasn't sure about the reasonable hour part. I also knew that a kiss on the cheek was not a good idea now. Also, as sure as death and taxes, I knew that my idea of a reasonable hour was far different than his. The last thing I wanted to do was ask him what was reasonable.

"Yes, Mr. Martin," I explained. "We will be attending the dance and then will be staying at my friend John's house for some post-dance refreshments. Casey's return will certainly be at a reasonable time and I can assure you that John's parents will be home." I reached into my coat pocket and produced a piece of folded paper. "As requested, I have provided you with the phone number to John's house, so that, should an emergency occur, we can be contacted."

Now of course Mr. Martin's idea of refreshments was again totally different than my idea of refreshments. But the less he knew, the better we all would be. He smiled and took the note from my hand. Casey replaced it with her hand and I helped her down off the stoop. She stepped down and stood before me. I was completely mesmerized by her. The gown she wore was light blue and frilly, which made the blue in her eyes simple explode out of her head. She wore a necklace that accentuated her neckline, and the necklace's pendant nestled in the slight groove of her ever-blossoming bosom. I took a few seconds to take her in, and for the first time, I didn't care that her behemoth father was towering over me. I was literally lost in the beauty of his daughter. Finally, I was able to break her spell and I lead her to the car. I opened her door for her, and assisted as she sat down into the passenger seat. I closed the door behind her and walked to my side. I was aware that her dad was still watching me, but I didn't care anymore. All I wanted to do was to get inside the car, next to Casey, and drive to the dance.

Throughout our entire drive over to the high school, I couldn't think about the beauty sitting next to me, so I focused on the beauty of the vehicle we were traveling in. I just wanted to, or I should say, felt compelled to show some fellow travelers on the road the power of this GTO. I tried to withhold my desire to drive with moderate acceleration, but just could not hold back any longer when we arrived at the last stoplight before the school.

I did something that I could never have done before in my car: I revved the car with my foot on the brake, and then just let loose on green. The smell coming from outside penetrated my senses which added to my euphoric feeling of power. I must have left at least ten feet of rubber on Cooper Road. During this flexing of vehicular muscle, I failed to notice Casey's eyes popping out of her sockets, and her grip on the inside door handle, as well as her left arm stretched out to the dashboard. Both extremities were flush red and her jaw appeared somewhat tight as if she was grinding her teeth.

"What the hell are you doing, Chad!?" she screamed. "We're going to a dance not a drag race!"

Suddenly, I realized that going sixty in a thirty-five mile zone, coupled with the fact that we were traveling only two hundred feet was maybe a little scary to a girl.

"Sorry," I said as I quickly slowed down. "I kind of zoned out and imagined I was at the Indianapolis 500. I really am sorry and will try to contain my crazy impulses."

"It's okay," she said. "Driving like that is just a little scary to me."

We arrived at the school and I turned into the student parking lot. The car and I immediately started getting stares from the other kids gathered there, including some fantastic looking girls. I took my time driving through the lot and finally parked the car in the back. With the engine off, I looked at Casey.

"Well, here we are," I began. "I've been looking forward to taking you to this dance since I met you."

"Thanks, me too, Chad," she replied.

We strolled into the decorated gymnasium where we were greeted by a couple of the freshmen cheerleaders who were taking pictures of all the couples as they came in. We took some pictures, and then headed over to grab some punch and food. A cheerleader named Cathy was behind the table, and since she was one of Tricia's best friends, the death look she gave me and Casey was not surprising. I immediately thought about Tricia, and hoped she was sick or out of town. Either way, I was expecting a lot of death stares from the other girls tonight, but I didn't really care, and I was hoping Casey didn't notice.

I grabbed her hand gently, and turned her away from the murderous looks that were being sent our way.

"Hey, why don't we head out on the dance floor for a couple of songs then grab a seat by ourselves and watch everyone and enjoy the evening."

"Okay, sounds good."

I figured if we stayed in public, but stayed out of the way, then I could avoid any confrontations with any jilted ex-girlfriends, especially Tricia. I personally just wanted to avoid it completely and leave, but I knew Casey would not be up for that idea. I didn't need to be at the dance, heck, I didn't care what I did as long as I did it with Casey. I pictured Tricia showing up with her dad, which would result in yelling and shouting and punching, mostly by Tricia and her dad. I was also sure Tricia would take the opportunity to tell Casey every bad thing about me, instead of allowing Casey to find out herself, hopefully over the course of weeks and months. So, my plan--entirely devised inside the gymnasium--was to stay discreet, stay on the dance floor and off in the corner, then sneak out without Tricia finding me or Casey suspecting that I was avoiding anything or anyone.

I escorted Casey to the dance floor and the Righteous Brothers' "Unchained Melody" was playing, which was one of my favorites. We were one of three couples on the dance floor, which went against the "discreet" part of my plan, but I didn't care. Holding Casey close was all I needed. After that, the Beach Boys' "Don't Worry Baby" was played, and we kept dancing. How many great songs could they play in a row like this? 10? 100? 500? The answer was two.

They stopped the music for announcements and we headed back to the punch bowl. So far, so good, but my luck this night was about to end.

After filling up our cups with some punch and grabbing some appetizers we headed up into the stands to sit, when out of the corner of my eye I saw Tricia headed toward us and the look on her face told me that she was loaded for bear. I instinctively tightened my grip on Casey's arm as I was escorting her up the stairs.

Casey looked at my hand on her arm, then up at me, "Chad, what's wrong?"

Before I could offer an answer, Tricia confronted us.

"So, you break up with me two days before homecoming to take another girl?" she asked, pointing her finger at me. "You are despicable and not worth my time, or any girl's time!" She looked at Casey as she said it.

"It's just like you, Chad, you'd probably planned to take this girl for some time and were just waiting for the right time to get rid of me! Am I right? Am I right?"

I didn't know what to say. I honestly felt terrible that she was missing homecoming because of me, and if it weren't for Casey, she would be there with me tonight. But there was no way to explain it.

I tried to reassure her. "Tricia, let me explain--"

She wanted nothing of it. "Forget it Chad! It's just sad that she has no idea of what kind of guy you really are!"

Okay, now she had hit my panic button. I felt paralyzed, but I could still make out Casey's reaction, and it was not good. She stood there with her mouth slightly open, and I could visualize her mouthing the words "you bastard…you two-timer…you creep!"

SHIT! SHIT! SHIT! SHIT!

What have I gotten myself into? What made me think I could bring Casey here two days after breaking up with Tricia? What position have I put Casey in? Will she be shunned for the rest of her high school career? Worse off, will she dump me to save her reputation? All I knew was at that point I had to salvage this.

Dammit, where was Marty when I needed him? I knew he was doing the proper thing by bringing the girl that he had asked and was just enjoying his time with her. I needed him now to help bail me out of this, just as he always did. I had to do something now.

"Tricia, please," I said. "Let me explain. Please."

She crossed her arms across her chest. "I don't know why I should."

I took a deep breath and exhaled. "I'm sorry."

That took Tricia by surprise and took enough of the wind out of her sails for me to continue.

"I'm sorry. It's my fault, and I don't blame you for hating me. But don't blame Casey, she had nothing to do with it."

Strategy point one: Acknowledge fault.

Strategy point two: Admit her feelings are correct.

Strategy point three: Make sure you deflect her anger away from Casey while defending her.

Three for three.

"You are a wonderful gal," I continued. "And I know you will find the right man who will treat you great and be a great husband to your kids, because you deserve that. But I'm not that guy. I've never been that guy.

"Tricia, I want a life outside of Deer Park, and I want to see what the world holds, and that makes us different. I should have told you this a while ago, but I didn't and it's my fault"

I was on a roll.

"And the fact is that although the timing of our breakup was awful on my part, if you know me like you say you do, timing hasn't always been my best thing."

I smiled and looked at Tricia, and miracle of miracles, she grinned back at me a little. It was working!

"Now Casey here, she had nothing to do with any of this. She was going through a breakup as well, and it made sense for the both of us to go together. She is a great girl, and I would like to get to know her better, but I don't want you or her friends treating her badly. It's not her fault.

"Tricia, like I said, I don't blame you for hating me, but I don't want to spend the rest of the dance having you tell me why. You are a special person, and I wish you nothing but the best."

Without saying a word, Tricia turned and walked away towards the punch bowl.

It worked. Holy crap it worked. I couldn't wait to tell Marty about this.

I waited a few seconds to make sure she didn't come back, and turned towards Casey.

"Well, that was interesting," I sighed.

"Went better than I expected," she replied.

I was taken aback by her attitude. She wasn't mad at me for putting her in that situation, nor did she now think of me as a creep for what I had done to Tricia. Of course, she had basically done the same thing with Billy Ricketts, but really, who's keeping score.

We went up in the stands and sat and talked. After about twenty minutes of talking we made our way to the floor for a dance, this time to "Tuesday Afternoon" by the Moody Blues, and afterwards we hung out with Marty and his date for a while. This was our night, and I didn't want any more surprises.

Before I knew it, it was 11:30 and the dance was over. I hadn't planned on staying that long, but we were having such a great time that I actually didn't want to leave. We danced every slow dance that they played, and even a couple of fast ones. We talked about what our nights would have been like had we brought our original dates, assuming of course Billy had asked Casey, and breathed a sigh of relief that we didn't. But mostly, we each just probed a little deeper, opened up a little more, became more comfortable with each other. My God, had it only been three days since we met? It seemed like it'd been years.

This was a good sign, even to an emotional idiot like me.

Now that the dance was wrapping up, the real party was beginning. I was so into Casey that I didn't even think of sneaking booze into the dance. Believe me, others had, and it was quite obvious as the night wore on that many of the participants had been drinking, some quite heavily. I think the teachers who were acting as chaperones would have been upset had they not been drinking themselves. Needless to say, everybody had a good time at Deer Park High School's Homecoming Dance of 1968.

Even though we were sober at the dance, that didn't mean there wasn't going to be drinking involved at some point in the evening. My buddy, John Kennedy, was having a post-prom party at his house. John was the self-proclaimed "President of Parties." His parents were the kind of parents that would rather have their kid drinking at their house under supervision than out God knows where doing God knows what, and then driving home. The flaw in their logic was that other kids were coming over and would be driving home. The Kennedy's always allowed for any kid who wanted to, or in most cases, needed to to stay the night. Of course, none of this mattered to me at the time, because I was 18 and immortal.

When we arrived at the Kennedy residence there were already about 60 of my friends there along with a few others we didn't recognize, and the party was definitely in full swing. John and his girlfriend, Sarah, had made a cameo appearance at homecoming; long enough to take pictures and make sure everyone was coming to the house. And from the looks of it, everyone was there.

We had plenty of beer at the party, as John was able to drive over into Ohio and purchase, since the legal drinking age in Ohio was 18. And since he was 18, the only beer he could buy legally was three-two, called that because it only contained 3.2% alcohol. This was lower than the 6% alcohol that was standard in most beers. But to us, it didn't matter. It was beer. It had alcohol.

I grabbed a beer and offered Casey some spiked punch, which was available to the girls, as few of them liked beer. To my surprise, she asked for a beer, then proceeded to match me beer-for-beer for the first few. She may have been able to match me on beers, but I was well ahead of her on the road to inebriation due to the amount of shots of whiskey and tequila that guys kept handing me after John had swiped the key to his father's liquor cabinet. After a few more beers, it was time to head for the basement to play spin the bottle.

Not knowing exactly how she was going to respond to this, I feigned ignorance, all the while hoping that she'd play with us.

"Hey," I said. "I keep seeing people heading downstairs, let's go down and check it out."

Though she maintained her cool, I knew the beers were having their effect.

"Sure, why not," she said with the slightest sway in her voice.

We very slowly made our way down the steep basement stairs, one arm around the other's waist, the other holding on tightly to the rail.

When we reached the bottom, we were greeted with a dark, wood paneled room and a sea of people, a haze of smoke, and sounds of The Beatles' *Magical Mystery Tour* filling the air. We made our way towards the back room, where the game of spin the bottle was going on.

I glanced at Casey and raised my eyebrows. "You wanna do this?"

Fortunately, the alcohol was stripping away her inhibitions. Parties can be so much more fun when you don't think about the consequences.

"Sure, why not," she said with a silly, alcohol-fueled smile.

As with most spin-the-bottle games involving extremely drunk people, there was more drinking and talking than spinning. I was able to spin the bottle close enough to Casey to give her a couple of kisses, which made it worthwhile. It also helped that no other guys had to kiss Casey, or she didn't have to kiss other guys. But that was the risk you took.

After what felt like half an hour of this--sometimes kissing, always drinking--it was obvious Casey was quite drunk. And apparently, we had started to play a new game, called "spin the room." I leaned over to give her a kiss and fell over right behind her. I lay there and the room spun. John Lennon sang I am the walrus, and I could feel Casey next to me. I could smell her. It was intoxicating. I was at peace. Goo goo ga joob.

I decoded that I was just gonna lay there for a few more minutes until I started to feel better.

The next thing I knew, some girl was hovering over me, telling me it was going to be okay. It wasn't Casey. I looked around, and the sun was shining through the basement's windows.

This was not good.

I immediately looked around for Casey, and I saw her a few feet away lying in a makeshift pallet made out of dirty clothes, with a DPHS letterman jacket for a blanket, still in her homecoming dress. Even in that condition, she looked beautiful, and I immediately cursed myself for passing out before her and missing out on the chance to be curled up next to her.

I looked around to see what time it was. I was hoping that it was just daylight and I could get Casey home before her father woke up and meticulously planned what I knew would be the last day of my life. Suddenly, I was feeling very, very mortal.

I looked over and hoped Marty was around to help me out, but Marty wasn't much of a drinker, and way too cautious to stay out all night. It was likely that he was at home in bed. I kept scanning the room for faces I recognized, even though an army of pink elephants were currently building a house in my brain, and saw Eugene Hilliard coming to and shaking the cobwebs out of his head.

"Hey man, what time is it?" I asked with panic in my voice.

Eugene took great pains to look at and focus on the hands on his watch before he gave me a groggy answer that stopped my heart.

"Nine-thirty," he slurred.

SHIT! SHIT! SHIT! SHIT! SHIT!

It's an underreported scientific fact that the rush of adrenalin caused by the sudden fear of your impending death is the best hangover cure there is.

I immediately went over to Casey and gently shook her.

"Casey, Casey, wake up!" I said urgently.

Casey slowly lifted her head, which appeared to be a lot harder task than normal.

"What is it?" she mumbled.

I was in a near panic. "It's 9:30 in the morning, and we're still at John's. We're so dead."

The next words out of Casey's mouth left me stunned.

"Relax, it's okay. Don't worry about it."

Don't worry about it? Don't worry about it? I was going to be ripped apart limb-for-limb by some medieval torture device and she was likely to be grounded until she was 35, and she's telling me it's OKAY!?

I tried to maintain my composure and repeat myself with a calm logic that maybe would register the urgency of the situation.

"Casey, it's not okay. It's morning, and you're not at home, and I'm quite sure your dad is going to kill me."

She looked at me with a steady calm in her eyes. "Everything is okay. I called him last night."

I was stunned. "You did?"

She smiled and said: "Yeah, after you passed out."

"And…what did you tell him?" At this point, I still figured I was dead because I was too drunk to take my date home and she had to sleep on a pile of dirty clothes.

She said with assurance, "I told him you were a perfect gentleman, but had a couple of beers and didn't feel safe driving me home, so we were staying in separate rooms at John's and would be home in the morning. John's mom even got on the phone to assure him it was okay."

My brain could barely process this information, and I responded in the most intelligent way I knew how.

"No shit?"

She lifted her head and looked at me and smiled.

"No shit."

This girl amazed me, and the urgency left my voice. "Okay then, let's get you home before your dad changes his mind and decides to drag me behind his truck for fun."

Casey sat up and laughed. "C'mon now, he hasn't done that to any of my boyfriends in months?"

I laughed, but all I heard was the word "Boyfriend." I liked the sound of that.

We stopped in the Kennedy kitchen and each drank some tomato juice before leaving and then I took Casey home. In the car, I asked her an obvious question with some trepidation.

"Um, we both look like hell and smell like a brewery. How is your dad going to react?"

She replied cautiously. "He won't be thrilled, to be sure, but as long as I'm safe and I had a good time, he trusts me."

Okay, that wasn't *the* obvious question, but I needed to know that one. I hesitated, but asked the question I needed to ask.

"Casey, look, we were both pretty drunk last night. I knew the spin-the-bottle room was downstairs, and I probably shouldn't have taken you there." I paused. "Did I do anything bad, I mean towards you? Because I wouldn't forgive myself if I did."

This "conscience" thing was throwing me for a loop, because drunken groping was practically a first move for me, and I never had a problem with it before. But this was different. I wanted it to be different, so for once it meant something to me that I didn't resort to that with Casey.

She reached over and placed her hand on my forearm.

"Chad, you were fine. You didn't force me to have any of those beers, and you didn't do anything but kiss me, and I remember kissing you back."

"Whew! I'm glad to hear that," I said with relief.

Casey added with some playfulness. "I was worried I was going to have to kiss a couple of boys in the group if the bottle pointed their way, and I wasn't going to kiss anyone but you."

"Same here," I replied.

I relaxed as we drove along to her house. The morning adrenaline rush had faded, and the hangover came on like a freight train being run off the rails. I said a silent prayer that I could get Casey home safe and then get myself home before I puked.

I pulled in front of her house and put the car in park. She leaned over and kissed me.

"It might be best if I do this one alone," she said. Before I could raise a protest (even though I was incredibly relieved) she opened the car door and got out. I watched her make her way to her front door and marveled at how the bright sunlight danced off her blue dress and blond hair. She really was the most beautiful girl I had even seen.

When she got to the door she turned and waved at me before stepping in. I hoped her dad wasn't in there with a firing squad. I hoped it wasn't the last time I'd ever see her.

With Casey dropped off I then drove over to Marty's house. I stopped by the side of the road twice to puke, which did make me feel better. I got to Marty's house around the time Marty's family was coming home from Sunday School. Fortunately, my parents knew I wouldn't be making it to church today, because in my condition, I would be doused in Holy Water and brought up to the pulpit to be pointed out as a perfect example of sin.

As I lay on the hood of my car and got some much needed rest, Marty's family station wagon pulled in the driveway and Marty jumped out and ran over to me. As I was still in my tux, he knew I had some good stories to tell.

"Man, you look like shit!" he said as he approached.

I did, and it showed. "Good thing, because I feel like shit. How come you didn't go to John's?"

Marty shook his head disappointedly. "Man, I had to take Paula home, her parents are really strict. Besides, I didn't want to go without a date."

I sat up slowly. "What do you mean? You go lots of places without a date."

"Eat one, Chad!" he sneered. "So, what happened with you and Casey? You make your move?"

I smiled. "Nope, perfect gentleman."

"You look like you wrestled a pig, and smell like you bathed in beer, and you're telling me you were a perfect gentleman? When have you ever been a perfect gentleman…at least with girls?"

"Yep, that's exactly what I'm telling you."

Marty came to the only logical conclusion. "So, she turned you down, huh?"

"Not really," I said. "Look, it's different with her. I…we just kissed a little, nothing more."

Marty looked at me in disbelief. "I can't believe it. You actually like this girl, don't you?"

"C'mon, you act like this is new."

Marty grew serious. "Chad, I know you. I've known you for years. I've been privy to more Chad Breckenridge hijinks and shenanigans than is legally allowed in the state of Indiana. And I've seen you woo, love, and dump girls like most people move their bowels. With a girl like Casey, you would be looking for the first opportunity to make a move, and the fact you didn't means you hate her or you really like her."

He had a point. "Yeah Marty, I really like her," I said. "In fact, I think I love her." I said it in all sincerity, surprising even myself. And…it felt right.

Marty took a step back from the car and turned in a complete circle.

"Ho-ly crap," he said out loud, as if announcing it for the world to hear. "You're really in love. And it's only been less than a week."

I looked at him and didn't have a response.

Marty shook his head in amazement and I reached out and slapped his upper arm.

"I gotta go home," I said. "Let the old man know his car is still in one piece."

As I very gently got off the hood and opened the door, Marty started to walk away and then yelled back over his shoulder.

"Nice knowing you."

I stopped with one foot in the car and turned back to him.

"What does that mean?" I asked bewildered.

Marty replied like he has many times before, like I was an idiot.

"C'mon, you know exactly what I mean. You'll start spending all your time with her and I won't see you. You fall in love and you don't have time for your friends. Happens all the time."

"It won't happen this time, promise," I quickly replied.

It was obvious that Marty didn't believe me. "We'll see. Take it easy."

I thought about what he'd said as I drove home. I thought about how long Marty and I had been friends, and about how many girls I had dated before and how Marty was always right there. But one thing was nagging at me.

Marty was right, and I knew it.

Chapter 8

I spent the next several months hanging out with Casey, like Marty predicted. It became this weird routine, however, as I would spend my days in school writing notes to Casey, talking about class, talking about us, and not paying a bit of attention to what the teachers were saying. It was my last year, and they couldn't fail me because the teachers surely didn't want me back next year. Between classes, I would see Casey in the halls and would give her the notes, and she would smile and put them in her notebook, or her sweater pocket, but she never had a note for me. I would even ask her questions in the note to get her to respond, but she never did. One time, I asked a question, and when got no response, I had to bring it to her attention.

"Well?" I asked after meeting up with her after my fourth period chemistry class.

"Well, what?" she replied.

"I asked you if you wanted to go see a movie on Friday?"

"Yeah," she shrugged. "That sounds like fun. Who else is going?"

"Everyone's going," I said, knowing that she had missed my point. "But why didn't you write me back?"

"Um, because I'm telling you now," Casey said pointedly.

"I write notes to you all day and you've never responded to one. Why?"

Casey exhaled. "Chad, I told you, I'm not a letter writer. I actually pay attention during class, and I see you after class and after school, so I don't much see the point."

I pouted and lowered my voice.

"Sorry, I just like letters, that's all."

Casey playfully punched my arm. "Hey Mr.-All-State-football-player, don't be such a crybaby. Sheesh!"

I gave her a quick peck and we headed our separate ways off to class. I turned and yelled back.

"Hey Casey!"

She turned back with a playful smile. "Yes?"

"I was all-conference," I shot back. "If you'd read my notes, you'd know that."

We dated exclusively over the last semester of school, and we spent as much time together as possible. The weekend before graduation, it was finally warm enough to take her out to the lake to go sailing. I couldn't think of anything more romantic than to spend time with her on the lake, and I had been bragging about my boating skills pretty much since the day I met her.

It was a Saturday morning, and I woke up early, around eight, which was about two hours earlier than I would normally wake up on the weekend. As I was out in front of the house packing up the Corvair and getting ready to leave, Marty pulled up into our driveway and quickly hopped out of the car.

"Chad, are you trying to get yourself killed?"

I gave him my cockiest grin.

"Always, buddy," I replied. "But can you be more specific?"

"I ran into Casey at the store and she was getting picnic supplies for your sail boating adventure today," he explained. "She said you told her you were quite the yachtsman."

I quickly replied with some caution, "And...what did you tell her?"

Marty crossed his arms across his chest.

"Not the truth, obviously," he said. "Chad, how you keep from drowning in the shower is still beyond me. You've never been sailing in your life. What the hell are you thinking?"

"I'm thinking, my friend, that I will spend all day out on the lake, just me and Casey. How romantic is that?"

Marty shook his head, a look that I've seen and ignored a thousand times.

"You have no idea what you're doing, and your 'romantic cruise' is going to wind up with you capsized and Casey swimming for her life."

I walked over to him and put my hands on his shoulders and gave him the grin he'd seen a thousand times.

"Marty, its sailing," I explained. "You raise a sail, point it to the wind and steer. We're not on the ocean, and this isn't Gilligan's Island. How hard can it be?"

Marty sighed, "Just promise you two will wear your life jackets."

I smiled and said with total conviction, "Absolutely not. It's not romantic?"

Marty turned and went to get back into his car, once again defeated.

"Nice knowing you," he said as he walked away.

"You're not getting rid of me that easily," I laughed.

I drove over to Casey's house and knocked on the door. Her father answered, and despite still being quite fearful of him, he was starting to grow on me. Casey came to the door wearing a pink cardigan sweater and long plaid skirt, carrying a picnic basket. God, she looked cute, and I told her so in as innocent a way as possible with her father right there ready to pounce like a mountain lion.

We drove out to Lake Whitney and I paid the one-dollar fee to get into the park. We then headed towards the dock and parked near the boathouse. We walked into the all-wood structure, which had been originally built in 1953 and obviously had not had one improvement since. At the desk were two middle-aged guys who, by their weathered look, had spent more time outside the boathouse than in.

Both workers looked at us with a combination of suspicion and amusement; they knew we weren't experienced yachtsmen. They had us fill out paperwork and emphasized the part where I had to sign liability forms that said if we capsized the boat and drowned, it was not their fault, which was reassuring. The guys asked me if either of us have sailed before.

As Casey shook her head and I acted like that was an insulting question to ask a guy.

"Sure," I said with authority.

The guy behind the counter eyed me with suspicion, but fortunately didn't blow my cover.

"Well then, I won't go into a lengthy discussion on all the things you need to know about sailing on the lake, since Mr. Breckenridge here has a lot of experience. He knows how tricky the winds can be this time of year."

A chill went up my spine. Oh my God, what am I doing? I wanted to pull the guy aside and tell him that I had no idea how tricky the winds were, or that wind can be "tricky" at all. I was about to set sail towards a watery grave and take Casey with me. I had to say something.

"Ah, it doesn't look too tough out there," I said, still feigning my unlimited knowledge of sailing. "I'm sure I can handle it." I turned to Casey.

"Let's get on the boat and set the sail." I don't know what I said, or why I said it. "Set the sail?" I think I saw that on TV once. Was it from Gilligan's Island?

We were in trouble.

Getting into the boat was relatively easy, and the guy untied us and pushed us away from the dock, and I turned and gave him a confident wave.

Now what?

I turned to Casey. "Sit over here on the left side with me while we turn the sail into the wind and get out onto the lake." She sat down beside me and I moved the sail until the wind caught it and the boat lurched forward.

Suddenly, Casey yelled excitedly. "We're moving! Wow, you do know what you're doing."

I just turned and smiled at her. "I have no idea what to do from this point on," I admitted.

For a while, though, it didn't matter. We were having a great time, and I was impressing Casey (and myself, honestly) with my ability to sail a vessel. However, I did notice after a while that we continued to travel in one direction, and that was away from the boathouse. We were approaching the far end of the lake, so I had to figure something out. I recalled something I read somewhere about shifting your weight in the boat, but couldn't remember exactly where I read it, or if it had anything to do with sailing. But in a moment of crisis a boat captain should act decisively.

I turned to her and spoke like I was an Admiral in the Navy.

"Casey, we need to move over to the other side of the boat to shift the weight so we can head back towards the dock."

She looked at me, and I could tell that she was asking herself why shifting to the other side of the boat was going to make a difference. She looked back towards the dock, and saw how far away it was, and at that moment figured out that my nautical skills weren't exactly as advertised.

Reluctantly, she got up and we both moved to the other side of the boat. As we sat down, the weight shifted so dramatically, that the boat capsized and we both fell into the water.

I immediately came up for air and looked for Casey. She was already holding on to the side of the boat, spitting out water. "What happened?" she asked.

"Must have hit a wave when we shifted weight, fluke accident," I assured her. "Let's get the boat turned over and head back to the dock."

The water was frigid and we struggled to get the boat upright. I was getting pretty nervous, since we were on the far end of the lake, and we were both getting cold in the water. Fortunately, another boat was in the area, and the captain saw us capsize and came over and picked us up. He even went so far as to hop in the water to turn our boat over. He asked if we wanted a tow back to the dock, and before I could answer, Casey quickly interjected.

"Yes, please. Thank you so much."

On the way back, I tried to explain to the guy what happened, and give a completely plausible reason why the boat capsized. The guy in the boat was absolutely no help as he explained the proper way to shift in a boat, as well as dismissing my "rogue tidal wave" theory. I don't think Casey cared either way; she was shivering and just wanted to get ashore.

Once we docked, I tried to explain to the guy at the boat rental the same story about "rogue tidal waves" and "trick winds." Casey decided to head into the restroom to dry off since I had conveniently forgotten to bring towels. It was a natural mistake on my part, since I didn't anticipate us going swimming. After a few minutes, Casey came out of the ladies room still soaked, but in her hands was a wad of dry paper towels.

"Well," she began, her teeth chattering. "I tried wiping myself dry with these towels but they're not working, and I'm through the entire roll."

I felt like an ass.

"Casey, I'm so sorry." I pointed back to the guy behind the counter. "He was right about those tricky winds, they were rougher than I've ever seen." Which was accurate, seeing that I've never known about them until today, and technically since it was my first time, I had never seen it rougher.

Casey gave me a look that let me know in no uncertain terms that she was on to my game and that the game was over.

"Well then, 'Captain,' if it's all the same to you, I'd like to go home and get changed," she said sarcastically.

I turned the heater on during the drive back to Casey's house to warm her up, and hoped the goodwill that I'd built with her father wouldn't just sail away on their own tricky winds after all of this.

When we pulled into her driveway, Casey immediately reached for the door without saying anything. I gently grabbed her arm.

"Hey, hold on a sec."

She turned to me, very annoyed. "What?"

I sighed. "Casey, I'm sorry, I really am. I just wanted to have a romantic day on the lake, and if I told you I wasn't an experienced sailor, then I was afraid you wouldn't go. I screwed up and I'm sorry."

This softened her hard stare a bit.

"Chad, I appreciate the gesture, but you could have gotten us killed. What would have happened if that other boat hadn't come by?"

"I--"

"I'll tell you what, we would have been in big trouble." She placed her hand on my cheek. "Chad, you're a great guy, and I enjoy spending time with you, but you don't think things through, and it's going to get you in trouble. And I don't want to see that happen."

I pulled out my best line. "Casey, I can't help it, when I see you, I just--"

"Chad, just stop!"

"What?"

"That's the sweet-talk you use with everyone because it probably works with everyone."

"No," I argued. "I mean it..."

"I'm sure you do in your own way." She paused and then grabbed my hand. "Look, it's sweet, but I have to know the real Chad if I'm going to trust you. And the thing is...I'm not sure you even know who that is."

I was confused. "I'm not sure what you mean. I mean know who I am."

"If you did," she said calmly. "Then you wouldn't have put me in danger like that."

Those words hit me like a Midwestern tornado. I sat there in stone silence, unable to speak. She was right, I had nearly killed her due to my arrogance. I didn't know what to say, I just wanted to crawl under a rock.

Finally, I looked at her. "God, I'm so sorry," I said with a sincerity I didn't know I had. "I didn't mean--"

"--I know. It's okay. I forgive you."

I gave her a quizzical look. "How?"

She smiled. "Because, I'm a great girl and you're lucky to have me."

This woman, this amazing creature from God who was sitting next to me, still soaked with dirty lake water, had just simultaneously broken me down and built me back up in a matter of seconds. She had touched my soul and given me an honesty that I had never felt before.

"I love you," I blurted out. This wasn't how I had planned to say it, or even if I was ever going to say it, but it was the most honest thing I'd said in my life up to that point.

Casey opened the door and got out of the car, turned and leaned her head back in and winked.

"I know."

Chapter 9

It was early in the morning of the most important day of my life when I woke; the sun was rising and shining in through my bedroom window. I just laid there for a few minutes thinking about the past several months with Casey, and the one word that kept repeating over and over in my head was "magical." This magic was surrounded by a touch of nervousness sprinkled with sheer terror. There was a reason for that terror. Today, I would be graduating from Deer Park High School and heading into the great unknown. I had absolutely no idea of what I was going to do. Seriously, not a clue.

    I had offers to play football at some small colleges around the state, but most of them backed off when they saw my grades. Plus, I knew I wouldn't have survived in a stricter academic setting when the current one was bad enough. I knew that I had to further my educational experience somewhere or I had a very good chance of being drafted. One thing I knew for sure was that I had used up all my good fortune with God so the chance of getting a high draft number was out of the question. I just wasn't ready for more school. I wanted to live some life first. And besides, with Casey a year behind me, if I waited a year, maybe she and I could go off to school together. That was but one of the many thoughts rampaging through my brain that morning.

    I wished I had more choices than just war, a job, or school. And when comparing those three, I always leaned toward school. My parents had even brought it up several times over the past few months, making suggestions like going to community college or vocational school, or in the case of my dad, not making recommendations, but declarations.

"Chad, your freeloading days officially end when you graduate high school," was his usual mantra. "You can go to college, or I can see about getting you a job down at the plant. Either way, you pay your own way."

The future was a blank canvas, and while that provided a sense of freedom without direction, that freedom could become aimless drifting. And at 18 years of age, aimless drifting is what I was good at. But Casey threw a wrench in all of that.

I could have done anything with my life, but I wanted the "anything" I did to involve her. She knew I loved her, and although I never told her that after I had blurted it out in the car that day, I signed my letters (which she still hadn't replied) with "Love, Chad."

I thought of my friends from school, most of which I'd known since first grade. Our history teacher, Mr. Swanson, told us on our last day of class to look around the room, that most of the people we saw today we wouldn't see again.

That's crazy, I thought. *We'll be friends forever. I've known these guys practically all my life.*

So, on the morning of graduation, I found myself climbing out of my hammock thinking about what was about to change in my life. I pulled on my cutoff shorts and a T-shirt and thought about heading downstairs for breakfast. My mind was drifting. I liked the comfort zone I was in. I liked high school (the social part, not the academic part); I loved Casey and I didn't want things to change. I wasn't ready for this.

I made my way downstairs where I seated myself at the breakfast table and after several minutes of sitting there, I felt a presence from behind me, and gentle hands on my shoulders.

"Well, today is certainly a big day for you," my mom said. "And I wanted you to know that your father and I are very proud of you."

"Thanks," I said. She sat a plate of eggs and sausages in front of me, and then crossed the kitchen to pour me a glass of juice. Honestly, I couldn't remember the last time I'd had this kind of service from our kitchen. I moved the eggs around the plate with my fork as I continued playing my own personal version of *This Is Your Life* in my mind.

"Honey, your eggs are getting cold," Mom said. "Is everything okay?"

I was now staring out the window; out at the backyard that I used to play in when school was still a fresh idea in my life. Back when the thought I'd be playing football for Notre Dame and then left field for the Yankees.

"Sorry Mom, I guess I'm just in another world right now. Got a lot on my mind." My mind seemed cluttered with thoughts of the past and that this day would be my final connection to life as I knew it. High school was over for me and I now had to focus on my future, not knowing what that was going to be. Tomorrow would start the first day of the rest of my life without the routine I had so grown to know. All of my friends that I've known since first grade would now be looking to their own futures. We would all be making new friends and some of us would be moving away from Deer Park to make new lives for ourselves. And then there was Casey. What would the future bring for her? For us? For the first time in my life, I was scared of what the future held for me.

"Thanks for breakfast, Mom," I said as I got up from the table. I had barely touched the food, but I appreciated the gesture. "I have to go pick up my cap and gown and run some other errands. See you and Dad at the graduation ceremony." I started to walk out of the kitchen and then stopped.

"I love you guys," I said, and then left before she could make a scene.

It was about a half an hour before the ceremony when I arrived at the school (for the last time). After finding a parking place in the student parking lot (for the last time), I jumped out of my car and ran into the gym (for the last time) where everyone was lining up according to their last names, and of course the smart kids with the Magna and the Cum Lauds, and whatever other titles they had earned in their four years at DPHS, stood at the front of the line. I found myself squarely in the middle of about three hundred and fifty students graduating today. I looked around the gym (for the last time) and just took in the memories of four great years and especially the last few months when I met Casey Martin here in this very location. In just a few moments I would be walking thru the gym doors for the last time.

I heard voices coming from the front of the line telling us all to start walking and stay in a straight line. Of course this was followed with further instructions to not do anything that would embarrass the school, teachers, or our parents. We started to move forward and within moments I was outside and heading toward the football stadium where the ceremony would take place. As I entered the stadium (for the last time), I immediately started to look for my parents and Alex, and then I tried to see if Casey was there in the audience. There were probably close to a thousand people in the stands so finding both my family and Casey seemed impossible.

After about an hour of sitting and listening to speech after speech from teachers and local city officials, I was ready for this graduation thing to be over. As much as I had thoughts of possibly repeating my senior year this morning, I now just wanted to get this ceremony over with.

Just call my name, already, I thought.

I hoped that instead of receiving our diploma and returning to our seats for more drawn-out speeches of how proud everyone was of us and that we were heading into a bright future, we could just get the diploma, cross the stage, and keep walking out of the stadium and were done. It didn't happen that way, but a guy could hope.

It was another hour before I finally heard my name. At first, I wasn't sure I'd heard it correctly.

Were they really calling my name?

Could this really be me?

Didn't they want to talk for another hour or two?

I rose from my chair and felt the blood start to flow once again into my extremities. Although my legs were a little numb from sitting, I slowly maneuvered myself through the row of students until I got to the aisle. From that point I virtually became a speed walker until I reached the podium where I received conformation that I had really graduated. The principal reached out to shake my hand and deliver a wrapped up piece of paper with a ribbon on it to me. I had worked and slaved for four years for this piece of paper with a ribbon on it. Wouldn't a letter of gratitude along with some cash be better?

"Congratulations, Chad and I wish you nothing but the best," Principal Harding said.

"Thank you, sir!" I responded. As I started to walk off the stage, the thoughts of just heading out of the stadium came back. They were pulling me towards the exit gate. Then, in my mind, I heard those words from back in the gymnasium: Don't embarrass your parents.

So I followed the other students in front of me back to my seat and sat down for what I thought would be another two hours of senseless yammering. The ceremony only went for another forty-five minutes, and I used that time to occupy my mind with thoughts of tonight's graduation party. Then (FINALLY) it was time to stand up and turn our tassels. Of course, that led the Deer Park High School Graduating Class of 1969 to throw our mortarboards in the air in celebration. I couldn't believe it! Amidst the applause from the stands (for the last time), I had graduated high school. Tonight I was going to party like there was no tomorrow!

I spent the rest of the afternoon being congratulated by my family, and even Alex had nice things to say. I spent time with Casey but asked her if it would be okay with her if I just hung out with all my friends at John's house for our post graduation party. Casey told me that the juniors--now SENIORS--had their own thing going that night and sent me off with a kiss to the cheek and telling me to have a great time and to be safe. She was the best!

At around six, I bid farewell to my parents and headed over to the Waffle House where I was to meet a couple of buddies before heading over to John Kennedy's house for the party. When I arrived, I parked my dad's car in front of the restaurant and headed in to grab some food to help absorb the large volume of alcohol that I was about to consume in just a few hours. Dad had given me permission to use his GTO again, because today was my special day. I loved his car, and didn't complain. As I stepped into the restaurant, I found that my friends had already been seated.

"Glad you made it Chad, we've been waiting for you," said Brad

Denton, one of the Aviators wide receivers. With him was his brother, Bobby, also a now ex-Aviator. I sat down in the booth across from them and gave the waitress my order. We talked about the ceremony, and the party, and everything else.

While waiting for the food, and listening to Bobby drone on about his visit to Purdue University, I noticed a Chevy Impala slowly pulling through the parking lot, stopping just short of the doorway. A couple of girls got out of the Impala and walked across the parking lot toward my dad's GTO. I initially thought they were impressed with the car, but then I noticed they each had a brown paper bag in their hands. I thought that was strange, but then I saw the two girls each reach into the bags and start tossing eggs at the car. I just sat there dumbfounded--and paralyzed. What the hell was going on? I was so stunned, I couldn't move, but my mind was racing a mile a minute.

As quick as the girls appeared and threw the eggs, they just as quickly ran back to their car and took off. At first, I wasn't focused on who the girls were, I was just stunned and panicked that my dad's car was now covered in raw egg. Then it hit me: Tricia's friends! It made sense, and I even figured out who they were. One of the girls was Sharon McGowan, the daughter of Deer Park's Sheriff, Chester McGowan. The other girl was Julie Watson, who I didn't really even know. But apparently, she knew me well enough to pelt my dad's car with eggs!

SHIT! SHIT! SHIT! SHIT!

I ran out to the car with the entire population of the restaurant staring at me. I could feel their stares, but my only concern was getting the egg off my car before it started eating away at the finish. I went back into the restaurant and asked the waitress for my food to go. Both Bobby and Brad had come together so they drove in Brad's car over to the party. I jumped into my car and decided to try and find a carwash to get the egg off my car. I remembered one over on Sycamore Street so I headed over there. As I drove into the stall and parked I started to feel real angry inside and the thought of getting even became stronger and stronger.

After about forty minutes of scrubbing and rescrubbing, I had finally finished washing the car. By that time I was so angry that the only thought that popped into my mind was getting some eggs of my own and egging Sharon's house.

I traveled over to the nearest grocery store and purchased a carton of eggs and headed over to her house. As I approached her street I turned off my headlights and turned down a side street that was a cul-de-sac about six houses down from the McGowan's. I parked the car and quietly opened the door, the carton of eggs in hand.

I walked quietly behind the row of houses leading to Sharon's backyard. There was a row of bushes that separated her backyard from the backyard of the house behind hers. I quietly set up shop behind those bushes. I noted several lights on in the house, but saw no movement from inside. Without any further thought about what I was doing, I came out from behind the bushes and moved toward the house. I got to within twenty yards and started throwing eggs. I threw them, two and three at a time until I had emptied the carton.

Suddenly I heard voices from within the house calling out, "What the hell?" and "What's that noise coming from the backyard?"

I immediately started to turn and head back to the bushes when out of the corner of my eye I saw the back porch light go on, and a shadowy shape appear at the back door.

"Hey you!" the shape shouted. "What the hell are you doing? Get back here!"

I made it back behind the bushes but then just kept running like hell. I made it back to the car, running behind houses, and dodging bright porch lights.

I started the car and laid a little bit of rubber as I rounded the corner of the cul-de-sac and turned onto the main street leading out of the neighborhood. My only thought was to calm down and hope that no one identified me as the culprit.

I decided to stop by my house and exchange the GTO for my Corvair. Better yet, I figured I would go straight to my mom and ask to use her car. In my mind, an extra car of separation between the get-a-way car and me would offer more protection from Sharon's dad, the sheriff.

I asked and she agreed, only because it was my special day. I wished that I could bottle up this goodwill and use it when I truly needed it, but oh well. I grabbed her keys off the hook by the front door and headed out to her car. It was a 1966 Dodge Satellite convertible. Her car was literally on fumes, so I immediately headed for the first gas station that I could find. I wanted to get to the party as quickly as I could because I was already about an hour late. As I was filling up, I saw a sheriff's car drive by slowly. I gave a gentle wave and the sheriff's car drove on. Take that, Sharon McGowan.

Upon pulling up to the Kennedy house, I could hear the noise and music from street. I pulled over and parked a few houses down and walked since parking was limited on their street.

I walked up to John's house and the front door was wide open as if to invite all graduates. I stepped in and waded through a crowd of people I didn't even know, eventually making my way to the kitchen where aluminum trashcans full of ice and beer were waiting. I grabbed a beer, popped the lid, and started to pour every ounce of that beer down my throat as if I had been wandering the desert for the past few days without water.

"Hey Chad, glad you finally got here!" a friend of mine named Chase exclaimed. "Where have you been? I thought you were following Bob and Brad over from the Waffle House."

"No, I had to stop home for something and got tied up," I explained. "Anyway, where are the guys, and better yet, where are the girls?"

"Everyone is down in the basement playing games and shooting beers."

"Thanks, man. I'm there already," I said with a smile.

I downed the last few drops of the open beer and tossed the can. I grabbed another one in each hand, as if to try and catch up with everyone that had started an hour before me and headed down the stairs to the basement.

"Hey guys, the Chadster is here!" John said as he took a hit off a joint in his hand. He was sitting in a circle on the floor with the guys, and a handful of girls that I barely recognized through the haze of the smoke.

"Mister President," I said as I raised a beer can in his honor, and then tossed back the entirety of one can in one large gulp.

"Glad to finally see you, Chad," Bob said, his eyes glazed over a bit. "It's about time."

"How many beers have you had?" Brad asked, wearing a necklace made of beer can pull tabs around his neck.

"Two," I responded, as I popped open my third.

"Well, then as soon as you get twelve, we'll bring you into the game," he said as he belched low and long. I could see this night was not going to be a night that I would remember later in my life.

I proceeded to drink nine more beers over the course of the next hour or so. I started to feel the room move and my legs felt as if they could no longer support my upper torso. I was now ready to party.

"Okay guys, I'm ready to jump in on spin the bottle," I said with slur in my voice. "Let Chad squeeze in here," Bob said. I was now in the circle but knew I had to quickly see who sat across from me. Although my vision was a little fuzzy I did seem to recognize the girl.

"Oh shit," I said softly. It was Mad Max! Or should I say crazy Maxine Markey, who wore thick bottle cap glasses and had two front teeth the size of headlights held in her mouth by a large fence of wire. I forgot why everyone called her Mad Max, or Crazy Maxine, but it had something to do with kittens, latex paint, and an electric mixer.

Anyway, I could drink twelve more beers and not want to kiss Maxine Markey. Fortunately, the bottle never pointed to me or Maxine. After a few rounds, I stood up and challenged Brad to a game of pool. To be honest, I'm not sure if the words I uttered had anything to do with pool. I just saw this blank stare from Brad, as if he was too drunk to even know what I'd said. Then, John chimed in and suggested we do a rubber challenge.

Right about that time I suggested that we all start pinching our faces to see if we still had any feeling left, which indicated that it was safe to drive. I'm not sure if that rule is in the Indiana Department of Motor Vehicles booklet, but I know I had heard it somewhere. Could've been from the *Soupy Sales Show* I used to watch a few years ago.

Anyway, the four us, Bob, Brad, John and myself, stumbled out to our cars and headed down to Deerfield Avenue, which was known for its lack of traffic this time of night. The idea was to pick a spot somewhere on the road within a two hundred yard area with which to try and lay a patch of rubber. The driver who laid the longest patch would be the winner.

We drew straws to see who would go first, and I was last to go. Bob and Brad each laid a patch of about six feet. John's patch was three feet long, if even that. Even in my drunken state I knew that my mom's car, a 1966 Dodge Satellite two barrel, could beat John. Beating Bob and Brad, well that was a different story.

I remembered that there was a hill leading up to the level portion of Deerfield Avenue that was about at a twenty five percent grade. I figured all I had to do was stop my car at the upper most part of the hill, shift the car into neutral and push the gas pedal to the floor, let the car roll back just a few feet and then push the automatic gear shit forward into drive. That would surely give me some good rubber.

I got up on the hill and placed my left foot on the brake pedal while at the same time I moved the gearshift to the neutral position and pushed the gas pedal forward until the engine couldn't take it anymore. While in a moment of egotistical glory, I listened to the rumble of the engine. I allowed the car to roll backwards just a few feet and then I pushed the gearshift forward and off I went. To my somewhat delayed horror because of my inebriated state, the sound I heard was not that of screeching-tires-on-pavement. It was more like the dropping of a large piece of machinery off a five story building and listening to the sound it made when it hit the ground. I had dropped the transmission on that hill that night. As the realization of what had happened began to cut through the drunken fog of my mind, my vocabulary was limited to two words only:

Oh. And *shit*.

This was going to be a very, very bad moment in the life of my father and mother. I slowly exited the car, conceding my loss to John, Bob, and Brad, and then started to cry. I recall using those two precious words an additional twenty or thirty times that night.

Eventually, we moved the car to the side of the road and made our way to a pay phone where I called my dad. Somehow calling him at two-thirty in the morning, half drunk, was not the greatest idea that a group of newly graduated high school student had ever come up with.

"Dad, I am really sorry I'm calling you at this time of night--"

"Chad, are you in jail or at the hospital? Did something bad happen to you?"

"Well, no, Dad," I tried to explain. "I'm not in jail, but that certainly could be a future possibility."

"What the hell are you talking about?"

"Well, Dad, I need you to come out to Deerfield Avenue and get me," I started to cry again. My sobs were met with silence.

"Are you okay?" he asked. "I'll tell you about it when you get here."

"Okay, I'm on my way."

I soon felt like somebody had kicked the wind out of me. I fell to the ground in a sitting position and I grabbed me legs, curling up like a little kid. I just sat there and pondered life in general and what it would be like in jail after my father got here and saw my mom's transmission lying on the street.

"So much for the party," I said.

My father arrived forty-five minutes later. The guys had already gone back to John's place, and I was alone. As he exited his car, I saw him look over at mom's car as if to try and figure out what the problem was, then he noticed the transmission lying on the street.

"What the hell is that, Chad?" he asked.

"Well," I said. "That's...uh...mom's transmission. It just fell out when I was driving up the hill."

I got a blank stare for what felt like seven minutes and then he spoke.

"Bullshit, Chad! I want to know exactly what happened."

There was no way I was going to confess to exactly what I did. Or so I thought.

"Dad, it really doesn't matter," I said. "It was my fault. I was just trying to lay some rubber with the guys. I'll pay for the damages."

My dad looked at me and then motioned for me to get in his car and we headed home. Not word was spoken until we got in the front door of our house. That was when my mom, who was sitting on the living room couch waiting to hear what had happened, bounced up and embraced me.

"Are you okay?" she asked. "I was so worried about you."

"Chad, head up to your room," my dad said with authority. "We'll talk about this tomorrow morning."

While I was walking up stairs I heard my dad fill my mom in on what his version of what happened was. Surprisingly, his version matched my first version, the one he called bullshit on.

Over the next several weeks, things started to get back to normal as I was paying back my dad for the repair of the transmission. Casey and I continued to date throughout the summer by going on picnics, and walks in the country where we would just talk about what the future would hold for us, and over to Dayton, Ohio to see the air show at Wright Patterson Air force base. It was the best summer of my life. The more Casey and I continued to date, the more I got to know her as a person. She was very smart and I knew she would be very successful in whatever she did. It was late June and Casey would be starting her senior year of high school in just a little over two months. I knew she would be very busy with studies and French club and student council. I couldn't care less about anything like that during my last year, but she was different. And I loved her for it.

Our relationship became more serious as summer was starting to draw to a close. But just as Casey was preparing to start her last year of high school, I found myself facing the biggest dilemma--and fear--of my life. Was I really ready to go to college after four long and grueling years in high school? Besides, if I went away to college, then I wouldn't be able to see Casey as often as I wanted. The fear of my life was that if I didn't enroll in college somewhere, I will be taking a chance of being drafted and then most assuredly I'd be heading over to Vietnam. That was one fear that haunted me, and every boy my age, everyday.

One day, I got a call from Marty, who was unnaturally quiet.

"What's wrong?" I asked. "Your mom find your skin mags?"

"You need to come over here, man."

I immediately knew something was very wrong.

"Marty, what's wrong?" I asked, this time seriously. I thought I heard him whimper on the line. "Dammit, tell me what's wrong?"

I ran out of the house and hopped in the car and made the short drive over to his house. I didn't even bother knocking as I flew through the front door and upstairs toward Marty's room. When I walked into the room, Marty was sitting on the edge of the bed, holding a piece of paper in his left hand.

"Jesus, Marty, you scared the hell out of me! What's going on?"

Marty slowly raised his left hand with the letter in my direction. I took it and started to read. It was his Order to Report For Induction. Marty had been drafted.

SHIT!

Chapter 10

It was a hot Tuesday evening when Marty and I decided to head over to Timken's Bar and Grill to talk about what was in store for Marty now that he had been drafted. All he wanted to do was drink until somehow all of the beer and alcohol in his system would magically transform his number from 17 to a number like 206, which would have greatly reduced his chances at being drafted. We knew that the legal age to drink was twenty one, but we also knew that Ed Major, the bartender would serve us beer once Marty showed him the draft notice. Ed's father was a marine who served in World War II and was very sympathetic to those who were being drafted.

When we arrived that Tuesday evening it was just past seven and the bar was pretty empty. We pulled ourselves up to the bar and asked Ed to start each of us out with three beers each. Ed gave us a look, and Marty simply held the draft letter up, which he had been holding in his hand every second since the day I had ran into his bedroom after his terrified phone call to me. Ed didn't even read it, he knew. He just nodded his head and got us our beers. I'm sure Ed had seen this several times, draftees trying to drink until their draft letter said they didn't have to go to Vietnam.

Before Ed could fill the peanut bowl and shove it down to us at the end of the bar, we had finished two beers each. I had a feeling that this night was going to go into the early morning hours. As Marty and I sat at the bar, eating peanuts and drinking one beer after the other, we recalled the stories we had heard about the war from those that had come back earlier in the year, while avoiding talking about the guys who didn't. We also talked about the news stories that Walter Cronkite showed on television when he was over there as a war correspondent. Marty just kept saying that there was absolutely no way he was going to Vietnam.

"There's no way," he said, his voice low and without conviction. "There's no way I can do it, man." Over and over.

Then, before I had finished enough beers to actually forget who I was with and where I was; I remembered someone telling me that if you enlist in the navy, your chances of going to Vietnam were one in a million. In fact, I'd heard that the navy was delaying enlistment for new recruits up to four months before they had to report to basic training. That meant if Marty enlisted by the end of the week, not only would he not likely go to Vietnam, he wouldn't have to go to basic until October. Immediately, Marty, who was half-slumped over the bar and slowly sliding off his stool, grabbed my left arm to help pull himself back up onto the barstool.

"That's it, man!" he exclaimed. "I'm going to go enlist in the navy tomorrow! There will not be any Vietnam for me. Besides, when you join the navy you get to see the world, and the furthest I've ever been out of this hole of a town was watching Reds games at Crosley Field."

"Okay, Marty, good," I assured him. "We'll keep you out of 'Nam, and you'll go boating for a few years."

Marty then got one of those really drunk ideas that sound great at the time.

"Hey, wait a minute, man," he slurred. "Why don't you join up with me? We can go in on the buddy plan."

"What the hell is the buddy plan?" I asked.

"I'm not sure but I think it's where you and a buddy can join the navy and be together in basic, and beyond."

Okay, although I was now a high school graduate and knew everything there was to know about everything, I wasn't too sure about this idea of me enlisting, even if there was such a thing as the buddy plan.

"Marty," I said, breaking his beer-soaked train of thought. "Let's head back to your house and sleep this off. I'm sure in the morning this idea about enlisting will become clearer then." Before he could respond, Marty fell off the barstool and onto the floor. I couldn't help but laugh. Ed came from around the bar to help me pick Marty up and escort him outside where together we placed him in my car.

"Thanks Ed, I'll take it from here," I said. I slowly maneuvered myself around the car toward the driver's side and then realized that I was not in any condition to drive us back to his house. Nonetheless, I opened the car door, got in and started the engine.

That's the last thing I remember.

I awoke the next morning slouched over, leaning on the driver's side door with my legs stretched across the front floor area. I had a very bad taste in my mouth, and quite honestly I felt like shit. I had grown a beard overnight and my entire body ached with pain as I tried to pull myself upright in the driver's seat. I slowly looked over to the passenger's side and saw Marty still passed out from the night's activities. The car was still running, and had apparently drifted into a relatively large tree in the back of Timken's parking lot. Surely Ed would have seen this last night, and must have decided to let us sleep it off.

I continued to let Marty sleep as I drove us both to his house. I pulled into his driveway and reached over and to shake him as if he was in an earthquake. Slowly he started to come to and then snapped awake.

"Man, are we just now getting home," he asked, trying to get his bearings. "Or are we going somewhere else?"

"No, Marty," I replied, my voice hoarse from drink. "We spent the night in Timken's parking lot and now we're here at your place."

Marty turned his head towards me. "Am I still drafted?"

I shrugged my shoulders. "I'm afraid so, man."

Marty visibly shrunk in his seat. "Oh man, what are we going to do?"

I didn't know.

"No idea, man," I said. "Let's get cleaned up then we can figure something out." We got some breakfast from Mrs. Green and some aspirin from the good folks at Bayer, and then I ran back to my house to take a shower. I went back to his place later that afternoon and Marty and I spent the rest of the day on his back porch discussing his options. Whatever he decided to do, he had to act quickly.

We had just sat down on the porch steps, each with a bottle of RC Cola in our hands when Marty told me he had a plan. He always had a plan.

"Hear me out," he began, which told me from the start that I should stop listening. "You said you were going to start college in the fall, but is that really what you want to do?"

I wasn't sure. The thought of going back to school didn't really appeal to me, and that would mean leaving Casey.

"Well, that is my intention, unless I have something better to do. I mean, I'm just not really into college right now but that's what I should be doing. I just don't want to leave Casey here."

Marty took a deep breath.

"Chad, we can do this, we can go in on the buddy plan," he explained. "Join the navy with me and we can see the world together. If you're not going to college, then your draft number will come up eventually. It's only for four years, and Casey will be here when you get back. Then you can go to college and they'll even give you the GI bill to help pay for it. Think about it, man."

The thing is, I had thought about it. These were tough times and I had to make a decision quickly. If I was to enroll in college I would have to do it quickly, or else I would have to wait until spring semester, and of course that may have been too late. But a little voice in the back of my head kept saying: "four years of college is a long time and you need to take a break and have fun!" Then another voice would say: "you better enroll in college so that you don't have to worry about being drafted." I just didn't know what to do.

As much as I wanted to share my thoughts with Casey, I wasn't sure how she would take it. I knew she would push me to go to college because she knew that college was the pathway to success. To take a chance on being drafted and having your world being turned upside down by going to Vietnam; well, Casey couldn't even relate to such a concept. Besides, if I was to be shipped over to Vietnam for four years or so, what would become of Casey and I? She would probably forget about me and move on with her life by meeting some muscle-bound jock at college. And of course she would be just about to graduate college and move on with the rest of her life by the time I got back to the states; assuming I made it back.

All of these thoughts kept flashing through my mind, almost on a daily basis. I couldn't make a decision, but I knew that I had to and quickly. College seemed like the only choice because it took the fear factor of losing Casey to some college jock out of the picture.

So yes, Marty, I thought. *I was thinking about this. Every waking moment of my life.*

I knew that Marty was going to keep pushing the idea until either I agreed, or he fled to Canada to start a life of fur trapping and beer making. His argument made sense. But I had Casey to think about. She was an important part of my life, and she did have a say. And he was probably right; my draft number would be called sooner or later. But I was still so unsure of my own plans to suddenly throw in with his...scheme.

And then it hit me.

For most of our lives together, I had been the one with the crazy schemes, the dangerous idea, and the precarious plans. And he had always been there for me. He was my accomplice, my confidant, and my best friend in the entire world. The more I thought about it, everything became crystal clear. There was no way in hell that I would let him do this alone.

"Okay," I said. "Let's be sailors."

He looked at me, and for the first time since he'd received that letter, I saw relief on his face.

"Thanks, man," he said. I could tell that he wanted to say more, but that was enough.

The next day Marty and I went down to the Navy enlistment office. We spent a good amount of time talking to the enlistment officer, and inquiring about the buddy plan, and finding out where we would be going. We were told that only those who are drafted or are already in the army or marines would be sent to Vietnam. Also, upon graduation from boot camp, we could select whether we wanted to be stationed on the west coast or east coast. Our enlistment was only for four years and that we would get to see a lot of the world. It was sounding better and better as the guy rambled on.

After completing the necessary paperwork and undergoing the testing and physical examinations, we were formally inducted into the United States Navy. We were then told that we would be reporting to the Great Lakes Naval Base in Chicago in the latter part of January. I had never been to Chicago and heard it was a great town to party in.

As I left the enlistment office, it suddenly dawned on me that I hadn't discussed my decision with Casey or my parents, especially my dad. I wasn't sure how he was going to react but figured since he was in the Air Force in World War II, he would be okay with it. Boy, was I wrong! Upon arriving home and telling mom and dad what we just did, mom started to cry and my dad laid into me like I just stole from an orphanage.

"Son, what the hell were you thinking?" he asked. "You joined the navy to see the world? The world is three quarters water!"

"Yeah, Dad," I tried to explain, "But you keep pushing me to get out on my own and I'm not ready for college yet. And besides, when I get out I will have the GI Bill to pay for my education. You and mom won't have to worry about that."

"Chad, what are you going to do in the navy?" he asked. "You have no idea what you've gotten yourself into. You're in for four long years. And that's no bullshit."

I really didn't have any good excuses for doing what I did, other than helping out a buddy, so I had to hit my dad where it hurt the most.

"Dad, I want to serve my country just as you did," I said, laying it on thick. "I'm proud of my country and I want you to be proud of me." Okay, although all of that was true, it wasn't the real reason that I joined the navy. I couldn't tell them it was just a spur of the moment decision to finally pay back my best friend for sticking by me for years. Or a calculated gamble to avoid my eventual conscription into the U.S. Armed Forces, and the war in Vietnam. Plus, I figured: what's four years? I mean, if I could spend four years in high school; well, I could do anything.

I tried to explain to them that it was a sign of maturity, that I was trying to be a better son and a better boyfriend--and maybe husband--to Casey, and I was doing the right thing. None of it was true; I made an impulsive decision because Marty needed me. That and I didn't know what to do next with my life. Regardless, Dad listened to my argument, and for the first time in as long as I can remember, he didn't call bullshit on me.

By the end of the evening, my mom had stopped crying and my dad, well, he started asking me questions about where I was going to boot camp and then where would I be stationed. I was pretty sure everything was going to be okay from here on out.

Life got back to normal soon after, Marty and I started to look forward to a double date where we would be taking Casey and Paula Cramer, a new girl in Marty's life, to the upcoming Fourth of July fair on Lake Whitney. This was going to be one of the last great hurrahs for Marty and I before we headed off to Chicago.

Casey and I would be spending time together for the rest of the summer, but it would only be a date here and there because of Casey going into her senior year and all her extra curricular activities at school and my job trying to do absolutely nothing while waiting for January.

We did manage to actually get away for an entire day together in late June. We headed off to a place called, Speed Freeks, who advertised "Nothing but Speed." It was a small go-cart and mini-golf place about a half hour outside Deer Park. It was a half-mile track laid out with crazy turns and smooth straight-a-ways. We spent about two hours there racing our cars around the track like a couple of fourteen-year-olds so excited about driving a car. It was so neat to see Casey actually drive irresponsibly around the track. At first she was a little...stiff. In other words, she drove the car like an elderly woman pushing a shopping cart. But then I saw this other side of her. It was like watching a flower bloom right before my eyes. I was leading one race by a few car lengths margin. I was so far ahead, that I started to enjoy myself and take in the scenery of people playing putt-putt and kids eating colorful cotton candy spun onto sticks. But as she completed her fifth lap and went into the first turn, she seemed to push the accelerator to the floor. The car started to slide out of control but she was determined to bring the car out of the slide and suddenly she was closing the gap between my car and hers. Before I could try to cut her off, she zipped past me and took the checkered flag. I was dumbstruck at her move, and I think I fell in love with her all over again. I was so happy that I didn't want this time to end. But hunger got the best of us so we left the park and headed over to La Rosas' pizzeria. There we enjoyed a great Italian dinner and reflected back on our racing skills. I also made several inquiries into this "other" person I saw on the racetrack, the speed demon version of my girlfriend. Oh, don't get me wrong; I love the studious and proper Casey, but I found myself more and more drawn to the wild side that just showed itself for a short time. I wondered if there was more of that person inside Casey.

We laughed as we sat eating our dinner and talked on about the day's activities. Before we left the restaurant, Casey turned to me as we were exiting the door and said, "Today was a perfect day with the perfect guy." Those words just about caused me to get down on one knee and propose.

"Casey, today I saw a side of you that I've never seen before," I explained. "You thrilled me." As I drove Casey home that evening, we talked about how our lives were going to be once school started.

I realized that I would eventually have to tell Casey that I enlisted with Marty in the navy. Suddenly, the possibility of four long years overseas without her seemed impossible to bear. Each day that passed was one day fewer that I had to embrace the love of my life. I decided that throughout the next six months, July through December, I would take ever opportunity to be with her. I planned on attending every Friday night football game to sit next to her in the stands rooting on the Aviators. Then on Saturdays we would spend time just being together at Sharon Woods where we would picnic and skip rocks across a creek that ran through the woods. I was committing to her lock, stock and barrel and I hoped that the gesture would be returned.

As we reached her driveway and pulled in, I stopped the car and shifted it into park. I reached over and gently placed my right arm around her shoulders and, as I ever so gently stroked the hair in her ponytail, I looked into her bright blue eyes.

"I love you," I said. She looked at me and smiled. I have no idea why she would never say those words back to me. I tried to let it go, to not dwell on it. But that was not my style. Then, before I could inquire as to why she never said it back, she changed the subject.

"We're going to have great time at the Fourth of July Fair down at the lake," she said. I knew we would have fun with Marty and Paula Cramer, but I really just wanted to be with Casey.

July fourth came quickly and the four of us, Marty, Paula, Casey and I arrived at the lake. You could see the fair from over three miles away. There were tall rides covered in twinkling lights and side shows and booths with all kinds of games going on and an open area where people could dance to the sounds of the Beach Boys, Turtles, and other top 40 bands. It was one of the highlights of the Deer Park year.

No sooner than we handed our ticket stubs to the attendant and entered the park, we saw most of our high school friends and even some of our teachers. It was kind of neat to see some of the teachers outside their element. As we walked through the park and argued about what rides we were going on first, I saw out of the corner of my eye Tricia Baker with some guy who seemed just a little bit older than someone who should have just graduated from high school. To my surprise, Tricia locked her eyes on me and gave me one of those looks that would derail a train traveling full-speed down the track. I guess she still held a grudge. To make things worse, her boyfriend--or the guy she was with--also gave me the stare. There were four eyes staring at me with murderous intent! I just kept moving, arm in arm with Casey; however I started to pick up the pace a bit which in turn caused Marty to yell out.

"Chad, slow down, we have all night to get where we need to be!" At the same time, Casey started to slow down, which anchored my speed and slowed me down as well. She didn't say anything, just looked at me and smiled. While it did ease my tension, I still felt this urgency to get to the other side of the park.

It was not more than maybe five or six minutes since exchanging glances with Tricia and her boyfriend that the four of us reached the dance area. Finally my heart rate started to slow down and those muscle spasms brought on by Tricia started to relax. I looked at Casey and asked her to dance. As we walked onto the dance floor, Marty and Paula followed and before long, we were all cutting the rug without a care in the world. It was maybe four or five songs before we got to a slow dance. All I wanted to do was grab Casey and pull her close. I was in heaven. I held her tightly against my body and rested my head on her shoulder as she rested hers on mine. I didn't want this dance to end. Everybody else on the dance floor vanished and it felt as if we were all alone.

Then suddenly, without warning, I felt a rather hard tap on my right shoulder followed by a grunting sound.

"Do you mind if I cut in?"

At first I thought I was hearing things, but then there came a second tap. "Hey, buddy, do you mind if I cut in?"

I started to turn. "Marty, back off. You have a date!" As I completed my turn, I saw the guy that Tricia was with standing there.

"As I said, do you mind if I cut in?" he grunted again.

Okay now this was an uncomfortable setting. My brain quickly broke the situation down into two options. The first one was to tell the guy to go to hell. The second was to run. Now the first option would most certainly get me killed, as this guy was four inches taller and fifty pounds heavier. And it wasn't fifty pounds of fat, either. I mean the guy looked like a cigar store Indian. One punch to his midsection would most likely break my hand into hundreds of pieces. The second option would most likely make Casey ashamed to be with me, and my world would end slowly and sadly as I would forever lament that time that I ran out on my girlfriend and she had dumped me for it.

"Why yes I do mind!" I said with phantom conviction. Those words just came out. My body had already started to adjust to the running like hell option. For a reason only God knows, I reached out my hand.

"Hey, you're with Tricia Baker. Lovely girl, lovely girl," I began. "I'm Chad, what's your name?"

Silence.

"Come on now, I know you have a name." My immediate thought at this time was that this guy is so consumed with hatred toward me that he just can't get any words out. Just at that moment he spoke.

"My name's J.C. and I'm Tricia's *NEW* boyfriend," he began, "and I'm here to hurt you just like you hurt Tricia." Well, I didn't really hear all he said but I did catch the word *HURT*. Now I was really opting for option number two (in more ways than one). I really liked that option!

"Okay, look, before you get yourself hurt, why don't we step over there and talk about this. You need to understand what actually happened between Tricia and me." "Okay Chief, lets go."

As we walked over to the other side of the dance floor where it was quieter and away from the blaring music, I noticed Marty and Paula watching us. I was hoping that Marty would realize something was up and come save me. He didn't. Instead, I asked Casey to excuse us for a few minutes and ushered her toward Marty and Paula. It was just me and the big guy now.

As we approached the other side of the dance floor I started to tell JC exactly--well not exactly, but close to exactly what happened.

"Look J.C., you look like somebody that is a magnet for chicks and I can tell that you've been around the block like me. Guys like us; we fall in and out of love all the time.

"I really cared for Tricia and still do, but I was never in love with her. Yeah, I cancelled our date to the homecoming dance, and looking back probably shouldn't have done it in that way. But, look at it this way; if Tricia and I were still an item, where would that leave you? You wouldn't even be in the picture. But you are, my friend. You have a great girl. Because of me, you now have a date to this festive evening on the lake. You don't have to thank me, just treat her right and have a really good time. By the way, how did you two meet?"

Time out. Where was this stuff coming from? The words just seemed to flow off the tip of my tongue. He looked at me with steely eyes (and by that, I meant his eyes looked to be made of solid steel).

"I'm a sophomore at the University of Cincinnati," he answered. "And we met at a bar over in Mount Adams one night. She was with some girl friends and I asked her to dance."

Did he actually answer me? Was I actually pulling this off?

"And aren't you glad you did," I said. "She is such a great girl. Listen, are we okay now because I too have a great girl that I really need to get back to?" At that very moment Tricia approached us looking as if she was loaded for bear and I was her target.

"What the hell are you doing here, Chad? You have the nerve to bring that bitch to a fair that I'm at?

"I see you've met my boyfriend, who right about now should be about to beat you into pulp."

"Hold on, Tricia," I said. "J.C. and I have had a great talk and I told him that you are a wonderful girl and a great catch. It's all about you kiddo." To punctuate my point, I tapped her on the nose with my finger. That seemed to slow Tricia the Hunter down in her quest to mount the head of one Chad Breckinridge to the wall of her study.

"Chad seems like a good guy," J.C. interjected, "and besides if things had worked out between you two, I never would have met you." Those words actually disarmed Tricia the Hunter. I'd stopped her, and he'd disarmed her. The crisis was over. Finally, I could breathe.

"Listen, why don't we all just enjoy ourselves and dance the night away? You two kids have a great time, I gotta get back to my group." Before anything else could be said, we parted company and I returned to Casey, grabbing her and slowly moving her to the center of the dance floor where we did in fact dance the night away.

It was about nine o'clock when Marty came up to me on the dance floor. I hoped that he didn't want to dance, because that would have been weird.

"C'mon man, let's go play some games."

"Okay," I turned to Casey and Paula, both of which I had been dancing with. "Are you two ready to go?" They nodded but then advised us that they needed to use the little ladies room. As they sauntered off toward the restrooms, Marty grabbed me by the arm and led me away from the dance floor and toward the midway.

"Have you told her yet?" he asked. I knew instantly what he meant.

"No Marty, I have not told Casey anything about enlisting in the navy. And I certainly don't want you saying anything, either. I will tell her in my own time."

"This is a bad game you're playing, man. She really needs to know sooner than later. You are gonna break her heart if you wait too long."

"Let me be the judge of that. I'm going to wait for--well, I don't know how long, because I'm not sure how she'll take it. I didn't talk to her first. I let you talk me into enlisting without even asking her for an opinion. So I'd appreciate you not giving me any crap as I deal with this in my own way, you dig?

"It's going to be hard on her, just as it is on me."

Marty just looked at me with this face that conveyed to me that he was itching to tell Casey what we did, but he also understood that I had done him a solid, and that meant more to him at that moment.

"I mean it Marty, I don't want a word spilled to her about this." Just as I had said it, Paula and Casey came up from behind. "What don't you want spilled to me?"

Shit!

"Uh...what did you say, hon?" I asked, trying to play it off.

"What don't you want spilled to me?"

I looked at Marty, who resembled a deer in headlights. "I was talking to Marty about your birthday and didn't want him to spill the beans about what I was going to get you." Casey looked at me somewhat puzzled, and deep down I thought that she knew that I was lying. Heck, I wasn't even sure I knew when her birthday was. Had it passed already? I was thrown into a state of mass confusion.

"Oh, okay," she said with a smile.

Wow, I had dodged another bullet this evening. That was two in one night. I was living on the edge but knew it wouldn't last forever.

We played a few carnival games (Marty won an oversized stuffed duck for Paula, I won Casey the right to tell her friends that her boyfriend was terrible at carnival games) and then ended the night by taking everybody home.

Summer came to an end and Casey was back in school at Deer Park High and I decided to take a part time job as a pizza cook at La Rosas. Casey would come by every Saturday night to have dinner and wait for my shift to end. We would then spend time with each other either going to her house and watching television or going to see a movie. It didn't matter what we did as long as we were together. As expected, she was very busy at school and had little time for me during the week, so we lived for the weekends.

The summer was gone and fall was slowly turning to winter. We were now closing in on Thanksgiving and Christmas. Time was moving much too fast. Soon I would be off to Chicago. I had to find the right time to tell Casey what I had done, but the right time never seemed be truly right. When we did talk, it was about our future together and my career after college.

Yes. College. If she only knew.

Chapter 11

I had made it through the holidays and I was about a week away from my departure date when I finally decided to tell Casey. With my enlistment date approaching, I was starting to get cold feet. About everything. Suddenly the idea of leaving Deer Park and seeing the world and leaving Casey wasn't such a great idea after all. She and I had spent every possible day together and started to plan for our future together. Although we didn't use the word "marriage," we did talk about taking our relationship to another level. I decided to plan a romantic date with just the two of us where I would share with her my decision to enlist in the navy and to put off going to college for a few years.

I called Casey and told her I would be picking her up at about six o'clock and for her to dress warmly. I decided to do something romantic so that the mood of the evening would temper her immediate reaction of sheer shock. Upon arriving at her house, I told her to bring her ice skates as we would be going over to Kenwood Lake and we would build a nice fire and ice skate under the moonlight. Kenwood Lake was a very small lake on the outskirts of Deer Park where I often played ice hockey with my buddies from school when the weather was cold enough and the ice thick enough.

The weather had been unseasonably cold for the past four weeks so I knew it would be perfect for ice-skating. When we got there, we walked to the edge of the lake where I started to build a small bonfire to roast hot dogs and marshmallows. I had also brought some blankets for us to wrap ourselves in. After starting the fire, I sat down next to her and wrapped a blanket around us both, leaving just enough room for me to extend my right arm out holding the hot dogs on a stick over the fire. The evening air was cold but calm. The frozen lake had about a quarter inch of fresh snow on it, which glistened in the moonlight. After finishing our hot dogs and a few marshmallows, I decided to tell her what I had done. We held each other closely with one of my arms around her shoulders and the other arm pulling the blanket snuggly around us.

"Casey, I have to tell you something I have struggled with for the past couple of months. I've wanted to share this with you but just didn't know how to tell you." The words started to come up my throat and out my mouth but my conscience and my fear of how she would react kept trying to push them back down. Marty had been right, I had waited too long. This was going to be bad. I decided to bite the bullet. I was soon to be a military man. It was best for me to grow a pair now than on the high seas somewhere halfway around the world. I grasped Casey's hand under the blanket and pulled her even closer.

"Marty and I enlisted in the navy right after graduation," I began, "and we're scheduled to leave for Chicago at the end of this week." For the next few moments, Casey sat quietly in stunned silence. I could see tears welling up in her eyes. I continued to embrace her, but somehow during those few moments, I felt her distancing herself from me. I felt her body disconnect from mine. She quickly moved about five or six inches from where she was sitting, pulling the blanket from around me.

She spoke while wiping tears away. "I'm not sure what to say. I mean, I don't understand why you enlisted and why you didn't talk to me about it? What were you thinking? Why would you put yourself in danger half a world away? What about us?"

That was the million-dollar question. I didn't have any answers for her. I tried to pull her back close to me, but she held her ground. "Marty had been drafted and needed my help--"

"Marty doesn't need your help!" she shot back.

"He's done so much for me," I explained. "And he's my best friend. I had to do something. He's scared. I admit it sounded good at the time and besides I just wasn't into going to college right now. I wasn't sure what I wanted to do."

"But why didn't you tell me or talk to me about it before you decided to do it?" she asked through her tears. "I thought that I mattered enough to you for at least a consultation."

I didn't have an answer. I started to feel I was losing her. What did I do? What was I thinking? The cold air started to penetrate that part of my body that was not covered by the blanket. "I should have and am so sorry that I didn't. All I know is that I love you and want to spend the rest of my life with you. That won't change." At least I hoped it wouldn't change.

For the next couple of minutes we just continued to sit there without any words being spoken. Casey was gently sobbing, and my heart was breaking.

"Come on, " I said. "Let's skate for a bit." She looked at me like I was crazy for suggesting that we skate together after dropping my equivalent to the Fat Man bomb on her. But after a few seconds, she stirred enough to pull her skates out from underneath the blanket. I watched as she slowly slipped both skates on and then she began to lace them up. Halfway to the top, she stopped and just held her head staring at the ground. I watched her, unsure if I should say anything to comfort her or to just let her be. Honestly, I couldn't think of any words that would ease her worries, her fears, or her sadness. She finished lacing her skates and I reached my hand out grabbing hers ever so gently to pull her up and onto the ice.

The night sky was clear and filled with stars and moonlight that gave each small snowflake a glistening appearance as they fell listlessly to the earth. As we walked onto the lake we didn't say a word. We stopped for a moment and just took in the beauty of how the moonlight seemed to bring the snow covered lake to life. Like millions of tiny flashbulbs going off as we stood there; it was if a stage had been set for Casey and I to dance beneath the star-covered sky. Slowly, I began to pull Casey towards me until we were in a full embrace. As we stared into each other's eyes, I slowly started moving backward further onto the lake as we began to dance under the moonlight in silence. The only sound was that of the blades cutting into the ice.

As we danced, she looked at me, as if wanting to say something. That pregnant pause was driving me crazy. Finally she spoke.

"I'm going to miss you holding me."

A tear started to slide down my cheek, growing colder as it trekked its way downward. I had hurt this girl that I loved. And she was right. I should have talked to her. At least told her soon after, not a week before I was to ship out. Sometimes, I just didn't understand myself. I lived life in the moment, but sometimes, that kind of lifestyle can backfire on you. This was one of those times. I had enlisted to help out my friend, and had sacrificed my girlfriend in the process. I felt an overwhelming rush of coldness. I felt empty and alone, even though I was ice dancing with Casey under the glow of the moonlight.

"I'm going to be so worried," she said. "What happens if you don't come home?"

"I'm joining the navy precisely so I can come home," I explained. "My number would have come up sooner or later. By enlisting, at least I have some control in my future." Those words were for her. Inside, I began to doubt myself and my decision and my future. No matter what I said anymore, I wasn't sure I could convince myself, much less Casey. For the first time in my life, I was genuinely worried. Luckily, I could play it off well. "And you know me, I'll write you every day. Will you actually write me back this time?"

"I...I don't know," she stammered. "You know me and letters. I'm a reader, not a writer. I wouldn't know what to say."

I smiled. "Say, I love you and I'm waiting for you, that's all I need to read."

We continued to embrace each other as we danced beneath the moonlight.

"It's getting colder, let's get back to our fire." Casey just stared and nodded her head. Once again, we snuggled in each other's arms with the blanket wrapped tightly around us in front of the fire. It was as if we were the only two people on earth this night. There was no war, no death, no fear, nothing but us. The only sound was the crackling of the fire and a slight howl of wind that gently moved the trees back and forth. I knew it was getting late and that we needed to pack up and head back to her house; but for just a moment or two I wanted to embrace the moment in my mind that we would stay here for all eternity. Then, I looked at my watch and that brought me back to the reality of the moment. I gently leaned over and kissed her cheek.

"We have to go." She nodded at me and we stood up, folded the blankets, and gathered what food remained. As she packed up, I stamped out the fire.

I drove her back to the house, and told her I wanted to remember her like this, and I asked her to not to see me off when we left as it would be too emotional. With tears in her eyes she agreed, we embraced and shared a deep, long kiss.

This was the last time I saw Casey before I left for Chicago and to boot camp.

Chapter 12

It was just after three on a Sunday afternoon when my dad and I left our house for the airport to catch our flight to Chicago. It was frigid cold with a strong wind that churned the snowdrifts that had accumulated overnight. It took us almost two hours to get to the Indianapolis airport and dad and I really didn't talk much on the trip. My thoughts seemed to be very random, and all over the place. But one thought in particular took center stage: What I had got myself into this time?

The idea of giving up four long years of my young life and being told what to do and when to do it didn't really register in my mind. I was also comforted with the thought that my best friend, Marty, would be there with me and together we would get through the next four years. How bad could that be?

As we drove up on I-74 and with Deer Park far in the rearview and Indianapolis just ahead, Dad turned to me and broke the silence.

"Son, I know I haven't said this too much to you," he began. "But I love you and am proud of you. Although your mother and I feel this is just another one of your impulsive decisions, you will learn very valuable life lessons to prepare you for a great future if you let it.

"You've struggled with seeing the big picture in life and have lived each moment of your eighteen years without giving thought to any ramifications. It's the joy of childhood, but the time for bullshit is over and you're about to become an adult real quick. Be open to what awaits you in the navy."

As I sat there listening and looking at my dad, I saw and felt something I had never seen or felt from him before. All throughout my childhood and into high school, my dad was always giving me directions and criticizing me when I failed to do a chore when he wanted it done, as opposed to my time schedule when I wanted to do it. He had always been the disciplinarian, the dictator, and a self-declared living, breathing bullshit detector. But now, the words he spoke were different. They were soft, heartfelt, and meaningful. I also heard something in his voice I've never heard before or after. Fear.

For the next twenty minutes or so he didn't say another word. During that time I just leaned against the passenger side door staring out at the snow covered scenery lining the highway.

We soon arrived at the airport and found a parking space nearby. We pulled into the spot and my dad turned off the engine and opened his door where we proceeded to get out. For just an instance, I remained in place; just sitting in the car thinking about the words my dad said to me. Who was I really? He was right, I am a "in the moment" kind of person, and I didn't always see the "big picture." Yet, here I was, getting ready to leave for the navy for four years, when just a few months ago I was looking at college, and my life with Casey Martin.

Four long years.

It suddenly started to hit me that this was the same long four years as I just had gone through in high school. From one prison to another. Except this time, it would be without Casey. Or Tricia. Or any girls.

SHIT! SHIT! SHIT!

What have I done? I came back to reality and opened the car door, slowly getting out and shutting the door behind me. My dad was standing there waiting for me. I wonder if he had the same thoughts--doubts--before he went off to fight the Germans in World War II. I took my suitcase and we started walking toward the terminal. No words were spoken but I suddenly felt his arm around my shoulders with a slight hug. It felt good.

When we reached the terminal, we saw Marty with his dad, and then I felt okay. This was going to be a great adventure.

"Hey Marty!" I said. "Hey Mr. Green!"

"Hi Chad. Mr. Breckenridge," replied Marty.

Marty and I greeted each other as if we were Tom Sawyer and Huckleberry Finn starting out on another adventure. Both of our dads were reserved, and were just trying to take in the fact that their sons were leaving for the navy. Before we knew it we reached our gate and they were already starting to board passengers.

As I started to head towards the gate I turned back to my father one last time and he reached out to shake my hand goodbye. I leaned forward and threw my arms around him, embracing him and telling him thanks and that I loved him. For a moment, I felt him hold me as if to keep me from going. Then it was done. My dad disappeared and the bullshit detector from Texas was back.

"Give 'em hell, son." I smiled and turned toward the gate.

Marty was already just inside the entry way to the plane.

"C'mon man, lets get this trip going!" he shouted. I headed toward Marty and the plane and when I got to him we both turned and yelled back to our dads: "See you in thirteen weeks!"

Boy, were we wrong.

Chapter 13

The flight to Chicago was just over and hour. Marty sat in the aisle seat and I took the window seat with the middle seat empty. Marty spent the entire flight talking about what a great adventure this is going to be. We would be seeing the world and would be free from our parents dictating what we had to do and when we had to do it. It was going to be a great ride. I wasn't sure if he was trying to convince me or convince himself. For me, I just sat there, somewhat incoherent, leaning up against the window and staring out over the landscape below. For the first time in my life, I actually started to think about the decision I had made and how it was going to affect me. I wasn't sure what to really expect, or what I was headed for, but I felt uneasy about the situation.

We touched down in Chicago and departed the plane. We were directed, like cattle, down to the terminal where we picked up our luggage and then we were greeted by what appeared to be a navy officer who had our names on a card.

"Excuse me sir, I'm Marty Green and this is Chad Breckenridge, are you looking for us?" Marty asked.

"Welcome gentlemen, I'm First Petty Officer Jordan and I'm here to take you and a few other men to Great Lakes Naval Base."

"Well, we sure are glad to get this show on the road," Marty said with a mixture of nervousness and excitement.

I extended my hand. "Officer Jordan, nice to meet you." I found it funny, here I was the quiet one trying to make sense of this whole ordeal and Marty was the one acting like a kid at his own birthday party. Soon several other individuals showed up and Mr. Jordan escorted us all out of the terminal and into a navy van where we headed off to the base where we would spend our next thirteen weeks. We drove for about two hours until we reached the base. As we turned onto the road leading to what, at first glance, looked to be a prison camp with several buildings surrounded by a very high chain-linked fence with barbed wire on top. We all just stared out the window with our mouths frozen in a somewhat opened position. This wasn't in the brochure. We must have taken a wrong turn or something.

"Uh, Officer Jordan, I think you may have made a wrong turn or something," one of the other guys said. "Shouldn't we be going to a nice hotel resort place or something like that?"

Officer Jordan thought it was a lot funnier than we did.

"No sir," he said. "This is your home for the next thirteen weeks!"

It was after ten at night when we finally arrived. We slowly traveled down the road and soon reached a guard shack where we were greeted with large smiles from the sailors inside. It was if they knew something we didn't. I thought, we were supposed to see the world and this certainly was nothing like I had ever seen in my world. Within minutes we were inside the camp and heading towards a very large half-domed building with a metal roof. The van suddenly came to an abrupt stop. The next thing I knew, nice guy Mr. Jordon starting yelling at the top of his lungs.

"OKAY, PUKES, GET OUT OF MY VAN AND GO INSIDE WHERE YOU WILL START THE INDUCTION PROCESS."

Pukes? What happened to the pleasantries and just enjoying ourselves? There were eleven of us in the van and we grabbed our luggage and started to head into the building. As we entered the door, I saw it was a huge open building filled with lines of guys, some standing around, others being handed clothing, and others getting haircuts and the sort. It was like being in the twilight zone. Instantly I was told to remove my toiletry kit from my suitcase and then pack my coat in its place. I was then herded along with the other guys from one station to another until I had been given a couple of uniforms, shoes, a duffle bag, a haircut which I was certain would stunt any future hair growth for the rest of my life, dog tags, and a full compliment of shots. By the time we had completed this so-called induction ceremony, the sun was starting to rise. We were all exhausted and just wanted to get some sleep.

Out of some God forsaken place came an awful sound that sent shivers through my exhausted body. It was what was soon to be known as the "5:30 wake up call." It was reveille. It couldn't be. It just couldn't be. How can you have a wake up call when you haven't even slept? Next came the screeching voice of our company commander, First Petty Officer Michaels, with whom we were introduced to sometime between arriving at the base and after our haircuts.

"Alright you recruits, you have twenty minutes to get dressed and form a single line!" There were now about twenty of us who fought through the exhaustion only to realize we weren't dreaming. We scurried around looking for our clothes, but discovered they had all been packed and shipped home. After putting on our fresh new uniforms that had been handed out to us just a few hours earlier, we collectively realized that we were officially in the Navy.

Half asleep, we were directed to march in a single line outside into what felt like a temperature of fifty below zero towards what we hoped was breakfast. After walking about ten minutes, we arrived, half-frozen, to a building they called the mess hall. We stood outside for what seemed like an hour or so, but in reality was only six or seven minutes. I have to tell you, navy pea coats aren't the proper attire for winter in Chicago.

"Excuse me, Officer Michaels? Um, does the navy have anything warmer in their wardrobe department other than these pea coats?" I inquired.

Without a word being said, I had my answer as Officer Michaels's nose came within maybe a quarter inch from mine. His eyes just stared. A vein the size of a Burmese python popped out of his forehead. Then came this voice from the bowls of hell.

"RECRUITS DON'T TALK," he screamed, his breath equal parts sulfur and brimstone and…garlic? "THEY LISTEN. THEY MARCH.

THEY DO WHAT THEY ARE TOLD, WHEN THEY ARE TOLD, AND THEY DO IT WITH A SMILE. DO YOU UNDERSTAND THAT, SHITBAG?"

I didn't know whether to answer or not, so I nodded my head yes. That seemed to work. He was still in my face, and his eyes were still penetrating not only my soul, but the souls of my unborn children, and their unborn children. But at least he had stopped screaming.

Okay, I figured. This wasn't exactly like being at home. This navy thing? Well, I just wasn't sure it was going to work out. As we finally started to march into the mess hall, I felt a swift kick to my backside.

"Man, what the hell were you thinking?" whispered Marty. I was cold, I asked for a warmer coat. No thinking needed for that.

Upon entering the mess hall and going through the chow line, we were told to hold out our tray and keep moving. As I surveyed the food line, it didn't appear there were many choices to choose from. We moved through the line quickly and were told to take a seat next to the person in front of us until we filled the chairs at the table. Before we could even sit down, a rather large black man, weighing at least 280 pounds started yelling at us.

"Do not start eating until given the order to do so. You will sit erect in your chair with your arms and hands to your side. When given the order to eat you will have twenty minutes to complete your meal. When finished, you will remain seated until you are directed by your company commander to start exiting the mess hall."

I thought this wasn't so bad. Twenty minutes? Usually, I either skipped breakfast all together or maybe took five minutes to eat at the most. Here I had an extra fifteen minutes to just relax.

We finished our breakfast and were then led out by FPO Michaels. I wondered what would happen next.

"Hey Marty, where'd you think we're going now?" I whispered quietly, so Officer Michaels wouldn't hear.

"I have no idea," he whispered back. "But I'm sure we won't be going on a field trip!"

We soon found out that our daily activities included several hours of physical exercise, classroom study on various topics, such as the "Navy way" and the different kinds of ships that we could expect to be assigned to upon completion of basic training. All of this included Officer Michael's theatrical voice, or in layman's terms, loud yelling accompanied by various hand gestures. We also learned how to clean floors, toilets, sinks, and of course how to make our beds. The toilet and sink thing really enlightened me because I didn't know people used a toothbrush for anything other than teeth. I wondered if my mom did it that way, and if so, whose toothbrush did she use?

Aside from the frigid cold weather, getting up at 5:30 and being told what to do all day and then having to turn out the lights at 9:30, it wasn't so bad. The thirteen weeks went relatively quick and we soon found ourselves graduating. When our orders came, both Marty and I received assignment to the West Coast, or in naval terms, West Pac. We were ordered to report to Naval Base Coronado, just across the bay from San Diego, California where the Naval Amphibious Base was located.

It was a Friday afternoon when we arrived at Coronado. Upon our arrival we were immediately directed to Barracks 69, a drab, very dark looking building with windows so small that sunlight barely penetrated the inside of the building. Upon entering the building I noticed a small space heater surrounded by two lines of double bunks on each side that lined the length of the rectangular building. At the end of each bunk was a footlocker where we placed the contents of our sea bags. Across the way was another gray building which we discovered was the head; lined with toilets and urinals on one wall and sinks along the other. This was going to be my home for the foreseeable future.

Marty and I took adjoining bunks and I began to unload my sea bag. Even though Marty was here, I couldn't help thinking about my real home in Deer Park. I wondered what my parents were doing, and I even gave two shakes to what Alex was doing. I finished unpacking and I stowed my bag. Marty finished shortly after and saw the look on my face.

"What's wrong?" he asked.

"I don't know," I said. "I guess, well, I guess I'm finally starting to miss them."

"Who?"

"My family. Deer Park. Casey." Technically, I was missing Casey every day I had been gone, but boot camp had been so taxing on me mentally and physically that I never had a free second to think about anything other than 5:30 reveille and 9:30 taps. The U.S. Military had done its best to turn me into a robot, like the one on *Lost in Space*. Danger Will Robinson, indeed.

"Why don't you write her or something," Mary suggested.

"Maybe I will," I said. "Maybe I will." I didn't tell him that I had written her a letter almost everyday since we left. And she had never written back.

Chapter 14

Classes were to begin on a Monday so we spent the weekend driving around San Diego taking in the sites of this beautiful coastal city. Everywhere we turned we saw sailors in their white dress uniforms. It was if San Diego was at the epicenter of the entire Naval universe. The weather was a brisk seventy degrees and sunny. This was of course a welcome sight coming from the frigid cold of Chicago in the middle of winter.

Monday morning arrived much too soon and after morning mess, we were mustered in front of our barracks and introduced to our instructor, Sgt. Robert "Speedway" McGuire. He was bald with a sharp, protruding jaw line. He was the poster child for physical fitness as he stood about six feet six inches tall and weighed in at about two hundred and twenty five pounds.

As we stood at attention, he paced back and forth spewing navy rhetoric and explaining to us "how things were gonna be." We listened; some of us even paid attention. I began to drift off, thinking about home and Casey when Sgt. McGuire began reassuring us that we were going to be part of the Naval river war in Vietnam and that the current swift boat divisions were experiencing high casualty rates and they were expected to continue. Hey--wait, what did he just say? For the first time in my life, someone had my undivided attention.

SHIT!

Suddenly, the newfound joy of being in warm, sunny California was overshadowed by a tightening of the muscles located throughout my lower and upper extremities. I looked at Marty, ready to use my new military skills to thoroughly kick his ass! I thought we joined the navy specifically to NOT go to Vietnam. I was having an anxiety attack, and as much as I wanted to choke Marty, when I looked at him, I saw the blood had completely drained from his face and that he was completely terrified, and I knew we were in this together.

Our instructor had just come back from Vietnam and continued his speech by telling stories of what he experienced and how it has affected him and would continue to affect him for the rest of his life. There were pauses throughout his speech where it appeared he was trying to temper the dangers that lay ahead for us as a swift boat crew.

Sgt. McGuire told us that we were going to learn everything there was to learn about maintaining the swift boat, from guns to the engine.

"These boats are your life," Sgt. McGuire began. "They have no armor to protect you! Their only asset is speed. The Patrol Craft Fast, or PCF, or better yet, "swift" boat is 50 feet long and made of welded aluminum alloy about one-quarter of an inch thick. That is one-quarter inch of aluminum between you and Charlie's bullets! Do not forget that.

"While they are supposed to hit a top speed of 24 knots, they will probably top out at 20 or so. In any event they will move on the water." He continued telling us all about the boats. Each swift boat was crewed by six people. Each boat was equipped with a .50 caliber machine gun and an 81 mm mortar. There was a cabin forward of the engine hatches, and inside there was a small table that housed five M-16s, three .38 caliber revolvers, one Ithaca 12-gauge shotgun, two M-79 grenade launchers and foul weather and flak gear.

"That is how you will take the fight to Charlie," he explained.

Seeing as how Marty and I did not even expect to be fighting at all, this was too much to hear. Soon--too soon--we would be shipped half a world a way to fight a war that we thought we would be avoiding.

I needed a drink.

Since training was only Monday through Friday, Marty and I often found ourselves wandering the streets of San Diego. There was a place near Broadway where we could drink and watch attractive, bare-breasted ladies who wore nothing but high heels and G-strings while they danced the night away. As often as we went there for entertainment, I often found myself thinking of Casey and I really yearned to go home.

I had continued to write her almost daily, but still had yet to receive a return letter from her. I would think about what that could mean, even as some dancer rubbed my face between her bare breasts.

Before Marty and I knew it, training was over and we headed for the airport where we would catch a flight to San Francisco. From there we flew to Seattle where we then caught a civilian airliner to Vietnam.

We sat in our seats on a plane on the tarmac of Seattle/Tacoma Airport thinking about what was happening and where we are going. As the passenger door was shut and sealed, both Marty and I flinched and then stared at each other as if we were both on a doomed flight. There was no turning back. We sat back in our seats as the plane rumbled down the runway and then lifted into the sky. I was sitting next to the window, so I took what I believed to be my last look at American soil and wondered what Casey was doing right at that moment.

After what seemed to be only a few hours of flying time due to our apprehension of arriving in Vietnam, I looked out the window and saw a dark blue sea lined with white sands that I later found out were the beaches around Cam Ranh Bay. As the plane circled toward the landing strip below, the sound of the landing gear being lowered sent a chill up my body.

We had arrived in Vietnam.

It was late June and when Marty and I stepped off the plane, we were met with a heat so intense with humidity that we both started to sweat profusely.

We immediately reported in and were assigned to a crew at Cat Lo. Cat Lo was in the northern delta where we would pick up our boat, call sign designated, PCF2041. Upon arriving, we would also learn who our other crewmembers were. Marty and I both remembered our first day in training school when Sgt. McGuire told us all that the casualty rate for swift boat crews was high and getting higher. Once again, my thoughts fell back to the time Marty had talked me into enlisting in the navy. What the Hell was I thinking? Buddy program my ass. Now we were both going to be killed. Maybe they'd bury us together too.

We spent the night at Cam Ranh Bay and in the morning both Marty and I, along with several other new recruits caught a flight to Saigon and then onto Vung Tau. Vung Tau is about 50 to 60 miles southeast of Saigon. From there we traveled by vehicle to Cat Lo.

Upon arriving, we found the base wasn't as bad as we had envisioned. My vision of Vietnam was from the John Wayne movie, *The Green Berets*. The base was made up of tents and was surrounded by barbed wire out in the middle of the combat zone. As we began to settle into what would be our new home for the next few months, our Commanding Officer, gave us a brief tour. And by brief, I mean we were shown the mess and our barracks. Marty and I lingered around the barracks as we tried to figure out which bunks were the best. I couldn't speak for Marty, but I wanted a bunk close to the head, but not too close as so I wouldn't have to listen to every guy take a piss. I also saw the barracks had a television but I was certain it wasn't color and I doubted that it picked up NBC or CBS.

Cat Lo was located on an inlet leading to adjoining rivers and canals where the water was a murky brown color. The rivers were surrounded by lush green vegetation that always looked mangled and twisted. It was a far cry from Lake Whitney back in Indiana. Vietnam was a different world, a different planet.

Life around the base was very depressing so we would go into town as much as we could, but that wasn't much better. The Vietnam civilians lived in weathered shacks and makeshift huts, and I could see families of seven, eight, and nine people living in one-room housing. We would buy beer and eat strange foods; all the while the Vietnamese children would beg us for money. Though we were off base, the scene was still very depressing. When I got depressed, I would think of home and of Casey.

The letters to Casey took on an air of desperation as I was trying to hang on to some aspect of Deer Park, of my former life. She still hadn't written me back, and I tried not to think about it. When I left, she was still finishing up high school. Now, she would be graduated and probably working. Her silence scared me a bit, as I would constantly think about our relationship, and my mind would remind me that I could be her new Billy Ricketts. The guy she just casually walked away from for someone new and exciting. It broke my heart to think that, so I tried to keep my thoughts on the up and up.

One day, Marty and I were walking by the docks, and I was having a particularly tough day thinking about Casey. Marty may have picked up on it, and tried to keep my mind on the here and now, and less on what was left behind.

"Chad, look over there," he said, pointing. "Those are the swift boats we'll be cruising around in." I chuckled at the thought of cruising around, as if we were in the Caribbean, drinking fruity drinks and checking out the girls in their bikinis.

As we walked along the dock just taking in the sight of the actual PCF boats that had seen action. There were bullet holes and deep scratches in the hulls. And one boat even had what looked like dried blood on its deck. It was not a very reassuring sight. As we continued our inspection, we were interrupted by a sharply dressed Ensign Officer who introduced himself to us.

"Good morning, sailors," he said, shaking our hands after we saluted. "My name is Ensign James Hueber, but the guys call me 'Midnight.'"

"Good morning, sir," Marty said. "We're just checking out the swift boat we've been assigned to."

"And which one is that?" he asked.

"PCF2041, sir," Marty said.

"Well, 2041 is my boat," he said. "And you can cut the 'sirs' and call me 'Midnight' like everyone else under my command. Besides, we don't want Charlie knowing which one of us calls the shots."

"Excuse me sir, but how did you get the name 'Midnight?'" I asked.

He smiled and answered. "Well, during officer training, I found myself so sexually energized that I was constantly seeking out women for sex.

And because I was so...energized, afterwards, I always asked *them* for a tip for *my* services. So, my fellow officers gave me the name after the movie, *Midnight Cowboy*."

I remembered the movie, as Marty and I caught it playing while we were training in San Diego. I laughed at the reference. "Well, it is a pleasure to serve with you...Midnight, sir."

Marty just stood there shaking his head in disbelief.

Officer Midnight led Marty and I over to PCF2041, the boat we were assigned to and stepped aboard. We had been given orders for a recon mission at 0530 the next morning, and Marty and I were the first to learn about it. Midnight appeared anxious to look over the boat to make sure it was ready to for action in the rivers and canals. As luck would have it, two other guys from our crew, Roger Miles and Stan King, came by, and after a quick introduction, we all decided to get a bite to eat.

After a quick lunch Midnight directed Roger, Stan and I to start loading the boat with ammunition and food, and he tasked Marty with testing the radar, the engines, and the mounting of all the weapons aboard. Finally, our boat was ready for action. I just stood there staring off into the inlet where the rivers and canals started. Thoughts of bullets, blood, and mangled bodies as well as seeing myself being zipped up into a body bag flooded my mind. The thought of the unknown and the uncertainty of combat felt like anchors around my legs. I couldn't move. This couldn't be reality. It was all a dream. I felt a swift kick to my backside, which broke my train of horrible thought.

"Isn't this just peachy!" Marty exclaimed.

I turned back to face him. "Not the part of the world I was looking forward to seeing," I said sarcastically.

The next morning at 0530 we gathered at the docks. The last member of our crew, Eddie Stephens, met Midnight for the first time, and after exchanging pleasantries (and another explanation as to how Midnight got his name) we headed down to the dock and boarded our boat to begin our first combat mission. We shipped off and headed out to the canals where the enemy would be found. It was about thirty minutes into our first run up the canals when we started to receive heavy fire to our port side of the boat. Eddie was driving and Midnight barked out orders. Marty was stationed on the M-79 grenade launcher and Roger Miles manned the twin .50s located just left of the bow. Bullets were flying both ways, some penetrating the boat's hull, some ricocheting off the boat and the surrounding water. Stan and I manned the M-16s, firing repeatedly into the vegetation that surrounded the banks of the river. I had absolutely no idea if I was hitting anything; I just kept firing until my rifle's magazine was empty. Within maybe ten minutes, the engagement with the enemy was over. We all looked at each other, just staring and each one of us with a slight look of confusion on our faces. We had just gone from high school kids from the Midwest to men shooting at--and hopefully killing--an unseen enemy who was, in turn, trying to kill us. We were just trying to survive in a hostile jungle that was filled with uncertainty. It was a game of life, death and the daily actions of killing other human beings.

Upon our return to base, I didn't want to talk to anyone. I just wanted to be by myself. I needed to try to take what just happened and make sense of it all. My mind was filled with thoughts of home. I though about Casey, my mom and dad, even Alex. I could close my eyes and feel myself physically returning to Deer Park where I could actually see and talk to Casey and my high school friends. It was so vivid in my mind. For just a moment, I could disengage my mind from reality. I wanted to write Casey so badly, but was afraid to share with her what I had just experienced and would continue to experience for the time of my tour. What would I say to her? How could I minimize the reality of my situation?

I sat on my bunk with a pad of paper and pencil and stared at the page for a moment. Finally, I started to write.

Dear Casey,
I finally made it over here and find the people to be very nice and supportive of American service men.

I continued to write about countryside and the weather, as well as other non-important events. I didn't tell her about the fact that I had likely just killed people, soldiers, and maybe some civilians--by accident. I ended the letter by telling her how much I loved and missed her. I told her I would be home soon. I was sure I was trying to convince myself as much as her.

For my greater peace of mind, I got back to writing her every day. And every day I looked for a card or letter back from her when I heard mail call, but none ever came. Underneath my pillow I kept a picture of Casey that we took on the night of the homecoming dance. I kept that picture with me to remind me of just how beautiful Casey is and how at peace she was that night.

For the next several months, we went out on patrol on a daily basis, and more often than not, we would have to engage in firefights with the enemy. The heat in country was unbearable and the food and living conditions started to take its toll on me. I could feel myself starting to change. I became callous to life in general and felt hardened as to not allow anyone to penetrate my outer shell. I became a robot for hire.

Every day was the same. The only difference was finding out who would return to base alive after missions. I saw killing as an "us or them" situation, and the more I killed, the less that could kill me. Casualties became the norm, in our platoon and throughout Vietnam. Death was no longer a distant enemy. Death permeated the base bringing hardness to life, as we once knew it. I would write Casey daily, but on each occasion I shielded her from our reality; of the death, the destruction, and leaving her with hope for a future with us together again.

As I distanced myself from everything, Marty was pulled further into it. He cried when he heard about the casualties, he became close to other soldiers, some of whom died in battle. Marty had spent his entire life protecting people, and for the first time, he couldn't protect them. He kept apologizing for getting us into this, and when we had leave, would drink harder than usual and became a mess. I should have stepped in and done something to protect him, but I was doing that on the boat, I was doing my job. Hell, we were all trying to survive, and survival changes people in different ways. I had my coping mechanisms, and Marty had his. Time would tell which one was best.

It was, I believe a Saturday morning when Lt. Roger Danby called me into his office to tell me I had been discharged and was going home. I say

I believe it was Saturday because each day was the same. In country, we couldn't differentiate between a weekday and the weekend. We had times when we could go into Saigon, but the toll of combat reduced life to a one-day-at-a-time theme: get up, eat, load and equip your swift boat and head into the rivers and canals, return (if we were lucky), go to bed. Lather, rinse and repeat. Life and death were at our doorsteps each day. People around us died. Death became a way of life. The question at a certain point became, when would I die?

Not if, when.

Lt. Danby's statement to me that I was going home just didn't register at the beginning.

"Excuse me sir," I asked. "What did you say? I'm going home?"

"Yes, sailor," he said, not even bothering to make eye contact. He just sat at his desk, signing page after page of letters. Letters that I realized were condolences to surviving family, courtesy of the United States Navy. "You have received orders to return to the mainland. You are shipping out!"

I just stood there trying to access what this meant. Thoughts of my life this past year, and how it had hardened my very soul were mixed with thoughts of the limited memories of my former life. At that point, I couldn't even recall all of the events that made up my life through high school. They were all overshadowed by the war and death and survival. I tried to quickly collect my thoughts, but just couldn't focus on what my life had been before coming to Vietnam, or what my life would be like going home.

My thoughts of Casey were a blur. I couldn't even picture what she looked like anymore. If I didn't have that photo of her, she would have become just a face in the crowd of my, now-spotty memory. I tried to feel the love inside that I had carried for her over here, a love that had driven me when we first got to the jungle. But they were gone. Replaced by the desire to keep myself, and my crew, alive day-in and day-out. Would I get those deep feelings of love and passion towards Casey Martin back? What was I going to do? What was my life going to be like? Then I thought of Marty. Did he get orders to go home too?

"Excuse me sir, could I inquire as to whether Gunner Green received orders to return home as well?"

"Mr. Green received his orders as well."

Thank God. I needed to hear that. Suddenly I allowed myself to feel relieved about going home. My best friend, who had experienced all that I have experienced, would be going home too.

"Thank you sir!" I saluted and turning about face, exited Lt. Danby's office as quickly as one could without sprinting. Once outside I ran like the wind towards the barracks to see Marty. He had received his discharge orders before me and was already packing. He turned to greet me as I ran through the door into the barracks. We ran towards each other until we just hugged and slapped each other on the backs as if we were two little kids at Christmas. We couldn't believe our tour had come to an end.

Our flight back to the mainland was not leaving for another forty-eight hours so we decided to head into Saigon for a celebratory evening of drinking, and of trying to take in the fact that we are going home. Even though we were officially on short time, those next forty-eight hours were like an eternity to us. We could not drink away the experience (though we tried, oh how we tried) and as we saw other soldiers--ones who we knew were heading back into action--we felt a combination of guilt and relief. Getting back to the world did not come quick enough. Soon we were on a "Freedom Bird" headed home.

Marty and I were both so anxious to get home to see our families that each of the flights home seemed like we were flying at speeds of 10 miles per hour. While the flight to Vietnam seemed like four hours, the flight home lasted for days. We didn't care. We weren't on a swift boat patrolling the rivers of Cat Lo any longer, and that was fine by us.

After two days of near constant flights, we found ourselves preparing for landing at Los Angeles International Airport. Shortly after landing and arriving at the gate, Marty and I moved from our seats into the aisle pushing forward as to try and be the first to deplane. Finally free of the confines of the plane, Marty and I stood in the passenger area outside the arrival gate and just embraced each other. Marty was to catch another flight that would take him home to Deer Park. I, on the other hand, was going to take a taxi to my parent's place in Huntington Beach where they had moved while I was in the service. I didn't tell them I was coming home because I didn't want to give anyone false hopes until I was absolutely certain I was standing on American soil again.

"So, this is it then," Marty said. "I finally get to wake up and not see your ugly face for the first time in ages."

"Ha-Ha, jackass," I said. "If it weren't for me, you'd probably still be in country, scrubbing the head with your toothbrush and singing 'Swing Low, Sweet Chariot.'"

"I don't sing," he said. "You know that from that night at the Troung Minh Giang."

"Yeah, you and rice wine should never have met," I said laughing. The laughter faded and I got serious again. "Take care of yourself, man."

"Will do," he said. "Do you want me to say anything to Casey if I see her?"

"Tell her that I'm alive, and I'll be seeing you both real soon."

"Okay," he said. He grabbed his sea bag and slung it over his shoulder. I reached out my hand to shake his, but instead he grabbed me and pulled me into an embrace. "Thanks, man. For everything."

I knew what he meant. And I felt I didn't need to say anything more on the subject. "Have a safe flight." We hugged once more then I turned and walked away.

I headed to the baggage area to retrieve my sea bag and catch a taxi home. The taxi ride to my parent's place took about ninety minutes and I was anxious to walk up the driveway and ring the doorbell. Mom had sent pictures of the new house, so I had an idea of what to look for when the taxi pulled into their street.

As I stood at the front door, I just stared for a moment to collect my thoughts and let the reality of being home sink in. I rang the doorbell and through the door, I heard footsteps approaching. Slowly the door opened and there stood my mother. That was when I finally realized that I was home.

"Chad!?" she nearly screamed. Before I could say anything, she reached out and gave me a huge hug. "Oh my God, my son is home safe!" She yelled back in the house, "Donald, come quick, Chad is home!!"

Mom just held on to me, sobbing with joy and looking at me to check and see if I was okay. "Why didn't you tell us you were coming home? We were so worried about you!"

"Sorry mom," I said. "I've been at sea for a very long time. I know I haven't written much over the past year but now I'm home and just want to be with family."

I wasn't sure Mom was going to let go. "I'm so happy to see you, son."

She finally let go and led me through the door and down the hallway. I saw my father actually getting up out of his chair to give me a hug.

He looked at me sternly. "Son, where the hell have you been? We received several letters saying you were at sea, but you weren't really specific on where you were."

"Well, it's a long story," I said. "Basically, I traveled the world. And, as you know, the world is three quarters water." We both chuckled.

Dad continued to ask me questions about my experiences. I tried to avoid specifics on my duties, giving general details about being at sea, mostly from stories I had heard from other navy personnel. I did not want my parents to know where I'd been or what I went through.

For the next few days I just tried to put my life back in order. I tried to look forward, not backward. Thoughts of Casey started to come back to me. Actual feelings started to reappear. Whatever the war had done to me, being home with family had restored.

I decided to call Casey a few days later, as I needed time to re-acclimate back to the world. I picked up the phone and hesitated to dial her number. I tried to think about what I was going to say. I mean I really hadn't spoken to her since our ice dancing date on the lake. I wrote her almost everyday, but never received a letter from her in return. Also, I wasn't sure that I wanted to tell her about my time in Vietnam. How do you tell someone that you killed people? It was haunting enough living with it myself. Why would I share that with others? I had missed her badly and I just wanted her to know that I was going to get in a car and drive across the country to be with her very soon. I was going to take the next couple of weeks to bond with my family again and then I planned to head back to Indiana. That was what we would talk about.

I started to slowly dial Casey's number. I continued to rehearse what I was going to say as the phone rang in my ear.

"Hello?" Casey answered. Her voice was like a drug. As soon as I heard it, my entire speech evaporated. One word from her and I had turned into a high school kid again. She was magic.

"Hello Casey, it's me."

"Chad?" she asked. "Is that really you? Are you home? Where are you?" The questions fired off like machine gun. I could hear the excitement in her voice.

"I just got back to the states a few days ago," I explained. "I'm home with my parents in California." Then came the most wonderful words I had ever heard.

"Chad, I have missed you so much," she said. "I thought about you every day. I know I didn't write and you know me about that stuff, but I read everyone of your letters." Talk about music to my ears! Those words were a symphony.

"Casey, I want to see you so badly that it hurts inside. I plan to stay at my parents for few weeks to catch up on everything. Mom is so excited that I'm home and safe that I'll have to slowly break the news that I am leaving to come back to you."

"You're coming back here?" she asked.

"Of course," I said. "They knew before I left for boot camp that you and I were serious. We are still serious, right?" There was a pause. It was brief, but I picked up on it.

"Of course we are," she said. "I'm just so...so glad you're home."

We continued to exchange pleasantries and did our best to catch up on the lost time. I think we both knew that this was a conversation best suited once we were face to face once again. Instead of talking about feelings, we talked about what had gone on in the lost time of our lives together. She had graduated second in her class from DPHS and was in her first year at Miami College. I knew she had to have met some guys by now and I'm sure she had dated, though I wasn't ready to ask that question. The more I thought about it the more my insecurity grew and my desire to leave California to go home, my real home, exploded. After an all too brief talk, we said our goodbyes and I told her that I would call her the following weekend.

"I'm so glad you're safe," she said. "Come home to me."

"I will," I said. And then the call ended. I didn't even get to tell her that I loved her.

I was so exhausted the first couple of nights I could have slept through a tornado or for that matter artillery fire (which is not an easy thing to do, from experience). However, my third night home brought on nightmares, which seemed to distort reality as I knew it. These nightmares came unannounced and brought despair and mood swings that I had never experienced before. I found out this was quite normal for soldiers returning from Vietnam. I was beginning to wonder if I would ever have a normal life again. I had no answers but knew I had to leave California and get back to Casey as soon as possible. My desire to see her became paramount.

Things had changed; there was no denying it. My feelings of love and intimacy didn't have any depth to them. They were feelings I had, but they weren't born out of emotion. I think they were born from memories. Memories of a life long ago, a life that no longer existed. Although I felt the feelings, they seemed to be just out of reach at times. Nonetheless, I had to go. I had to see her again. But I had to get myself right first.

The next couple of weeks were spent just walking on the beach and hanging out with my mom and dad and of course, Alex.

Alex was older now but still remained a thorn in my side when the opportunity presented itself. At first, he was glad that I was home, but then the ribbing started up again. What I found interesting was that although Alex had been my enemy when I was in high school, now he was going through the same things that I was back then. So I ribbed him back. It was delicious payback. It was how we showed affection to one another. We stayed up to all hours of the night those first couple of days I was home, and just talked about Deer Park and our lives, both then and now. Alex was growing up. I was already there.

As the days turned to weeks, I could tell that my mom knew I was going to leave soon. Call it mother's intuition, if you believe that sort of thing. She didn't say much but her level of smothering went up a couple of notches.

My dad on the other hand, just took each day as a day with his son. He and I compared war stories, his from the Air Force, mine from the Navy. We talked about procedures, and training, and for once, I don't think he said the word, "bullshit" at all. Although we talked about my childhood and times gone by, he stayed in the moment, and I knew that he was proud of me. Each evening of my stay, he would relax in his recliner and I would sit on the couch and we would watch television while my mom cleaned the dishes and prepared for the next day. Alex would be off doing whatever it was that Alex did. It was nice to be home.

Chapter 15

It actually took me a good month to finally get my bearings. California was great; warm weather, beaches, and beautiful girls in bikinis. But Deer Park was calling me back. Casey was calling me back. We'd spoken on the phone a few times since that first call, and it felt as if we were getting to know one another all over again. I think she had finally come to grips that I was back in the states, and desperately trying to get back into her life.

I made the decision to go home--my home--after six weeks back in the world. Dad and I were out driving one day on the Pacific Coast Highway, and we came across a car that I simply fell in love with. Dad had sold my Corvair shortly before they moved out here, and put the money in a savings account for me for when I was discharged. That, coupled with the money that I had accrued in Vietnam, allowed me to walk onto a car lot and pay cash for a brand new car. My first. It was a 1972 Chevy Camaro and it was the most beautiful thing I had ever seen. Something had happened while I was overseas to American car designs. The bulky muscle car had been replaced with a sleeker, stylish motif. I fell in love with it that day on the PCH, and now that I had my own, I decided I was going to drive it cross-country to Deer Park, and to use it to reclaim my love for Casey Martin.

A few days before my intended leave date, I broke the news to my parents.

"You sure about this, Chad?" Dad asked.

"More sure than anything ever," I said. "No bullshit."

My mom started to sob. She had grown accustomed to my being around, and with Alex busy with school extra-curriculars like yearbook and the student newspaper, me being there made us feel like family and this place feel like home.

"Mom, I'm going to ask Casey to marry me," I said, hoping to erase her tears. If I had learned one thing in life is that women loved the sappy stuff. I mean, it wasn't true. Well, not entirely true. I wanted to spend the rest of my life with Casey, but I wasn't driving back to jump out of my car and get down on my knee in front of her just like that. I just wanted my mom to know that this was a seriously thought out decision.

"Chad, that's wonderful," she said through the sobs. "Does she know?" I watched my mother shoot a glance toward my father, and both then deflected the look. Like they knew something I didn't. I made the decision right there and right then to not ask them to clarify. I wasn't sure I wanted to know what was behind that look.

"No, she doesn't," I said. "But if I don't do this, I will forever wonder what if. It's time for me to find out what my future is going to hold. And if Casey is going to be a part of that future."

"Go to it, Son," Dad said. He reached over and took my mom's hand. It was rare for him to show any affection toward my mom, and frankly it freaked me out a little bit. "And you are always welcome back here. With us."

Finally, the time had come to depart. I packed the car with as many of my belongings that would fit. The Camaro didn't have much room in the back seat. But somehow, I was able to squeeze in my new Pioneer stereo system, all my clothes, and some small pieces of furniture that had been in my room growing up. It was going to be a real tight fit.

I had planned the quickest route, which was about twenty-one hundred miles along Interstate 40, and three very long days of driving. I didn't let any of that scare me. I was so focused on seeing Casey again that I would have driven the circumference of the earth if need be.

With the car packed up, my parents stood in the drive way watching as I slammed the Camaro's trunk shut for the last time. Seeing as all of my clothes were packed in there like sardines in a can, I hoped I didn't get a flat tire on the drive, as getting to the spare would be comical. Mom started to sob again.

"I guess that's that," I said. "It's all packed up."

"Give us a call when you get there to let us know you are okay," Dad said.

"I can do that," I said.

"Where are you going to stay?" Mom asked.

"I haven't got that far yet," I said. "Maybe with Marty until I find a place, maybe with Casey and her dad. She mentioned that a couple of nights ago."

"Just be careful, honey," she said.

I didn't want this to get any more emotional than it already was. "I'll see you guys soon," I said.

"Be careful," Dad said. My mom gave me a hug, and my dad gave me a handshake that would have dropped a lesser man to his knees. I returned the squeeze, and he smiled. His boy was now a man.

"I love you guys," I said as a climbed into my car. "I'll call you in a few days."

I turned the engine over and listened to her rumble. My parents waved as I backed out of the driveway and got on my way. I spied them in my rearview still waving as I drove down their street, and when I turned at the stop sign, they were gone. All that was left was 2100 miles of driving. I turned on the radio, tuned it to the clearest rock station, and The Guess Who were singing the first few verses of "American Woman." Perfect. I gunned the engine and headed east.

I'd mapped out my trip a few nights ago. To get back to Deer Park, I'd be driving through Flagstaff, Arizona, and on to Albuquerque, Oklahoma City, St. Louis, Missouri, and finally back into Indiana. I'd joined the navy in part to see the world, and while I did get a round trip to Vietnam, I would see most of this great country on this drive.

I'd been going purely on beef jerky and Mountain Dew, and after nearly fourteen hours on the road, I was just outside of Amarillo, Texas. Through most of the mountains of northern New Mexico, I had not been able to pick up any radio stations, so I had switched to the eight-track. The Beach Boys were singing about California girls, and while I would agree that the west coast girls get all nice and tanned, It was one Midwest girl in particular that I was thinking about. And she wasn't a farmer's daughter, though she did make me feel all right.

It was late and the road was dark. I was having trouble keeping my eyes open, so I decided to pull over for a quick rest. I figured I could nap for half an hour or so and get back on the road to keep my schedule. I pulled into a rest stop and I saw there were other cars with the same idea. I pulled into a space at the end, near the exit and cracked the window, locked the doors and closed my eyes. When I opened them again, the sun was shining and the car was like an oven. I looked at my watch and saw that I had been asleep for almost five hours.

"Shit!" I said aloud. I got out of the car to stretch my legs and to hit the head to empty my bladder.

I got back on the road and other than quick stops for gas, snacks and the occasional piss, I did not stop again until I reached Terre Haute, Indiana. I crossed over the state line between Illinois and Indiana, and at once felt I was back where I belonged. Unfortunately, it was after midnight and once again, I was driving purely on fumes, both in the gas tank and in my very being. I pulled over at another rest stop and rolled the window down. The smell was atrocious, but I didn't want to drive any further that night. I needed a rest. I didn't even kid myself that this would be a quick nap. I knew this was going to be a full-on sleep. Besides, I didn't want to pull into Deer Park in the middle of the night. If I could sleep for a few hours, I would roll into town in the daylight, and in my mind's eye, I saw a parade waiting for me. Marty was there, as was Casey. Tricia was even there, congratulating me on my service in Vietnam, and for successfully driving across the country. The mayor handed me the key to the city, and even gave me a house that was across the street from where my parents had lived. Casey told me she was pregnant, and that I was the father, so we got married, and Tricia was her maid of honor, and Marty was my best man. My son was born soon after and was a quarterback at DPHS. He had the NFL scouts watching him play every week, but he didn't want to play football. He told me that he wanted to go to Vietnam to kill people. To kill people. To kill--

I woke with a jolt and saw that once again, the sun was climbing high in the sky and while the smell was still there, it wasn't as strong as it had been the night before. I realized that I had been dreaming, but it didn't soothe my heartbreak of what my dream son had said to me. I tried to forget about it as I hit the facilities and got back on the road. I'd been driving for over 40 hours, well, driving for 33, sleeping for about 10, and all I wanted to do was to get to Deer Park and see Casey.

Two hours later I reached the Warren county line and was hit with a wave of nostalgia. Although it had only been two years, it honestly felt it had been closer to ten. I drove into town, and there wasn't a parade waiting for me, as I had dreamed. Deer Park seemed to be going about its day with or without me. I drove past the high school and was hit with the memories of football games, and cute girls, and the shenanigans that Marty and I used to pull. I hadn't thought much about my high school life in my time in 'Nam, but now, here, driving past the school, all of those memories came back.

I drove past my old house. Another family lived there now, and I didn't linger too long as that would have just been creepy. I kept going. I drove out to where Casey lived. The Arbor Hills subdivision had grown exponentially since I was last here. In fact, there were so many houses, I got lost trying to find Casey's street. Finally, I saw a house that looked familiar and turned onto the street. Casey's street. I slowed down and when I got to her house I pulled into her driveway, sitting there for a minute, collecting my thoughts as to how this was going to be played out.

"Keep cool, big guy," I said to myself. "It's only been two years. What could have happened in two years?" I don't know what it was; fear, dread, exhaustion, and even though I had spoken to her a few days ago, I wondered if she would be happy to see me. It's easy to fake enthusiasm over the phone, wasn't it? What if she didn't really miss me at all?

Suddenly, her front door burst open and Casey came running out towards me with a huge smile on her face. I jumped out of the car and caught her as she leapt into my arms. I don't think I ever embraced anyone for as long and as hard as I did her that day. No words were spoken for the first couple of minutes. I set her down and looked at her.

"I have dreamed and waited for this moment for almost two years," I said, emotion driving me further and faster than I had planned. "And no matter how beautiful I pictured you in my dreams, and no matter how beautiful you were in the pictures, you've never been more beautiful than you are right now."

Casey's eyes refilled with tears, and as she wiped them away, she whispered: "I'm so glad you're alive."

Casey's dad walked out of the house, looked me square in the eye, and shook my hand firmly. "Welcome home, son. Welcome home!"

This man who had intimidated me two years ago now called me son.

"Thank you, sir."

It sure was a long way from our first meeting. I guess being trained to use an M-16 rifle changes a person. I used to be terrified of this mountain of a man, and now, now was just glad to see him.

"We've got you set up in our basement," he said. "I'll help you get unpacked and set up, and hopefully it'll be just like home until you find a place of your own."

"Thank you, sir," I said, then looked at Casey. "I already feel like I am home."

Once we had unloaded my car, Casey joined me in the basement and began unpacking and organizing my clothes. I would turn and catch her staring at me like I was a mirage. I wanted to hold her and tell her that I was real, and that I wasn't going away again. But we didn't talk very much while unpacking. I was too exhausted, and I think she sensed that, so she just kept it to small talk about where she was putting my clothes or positioning my stereo near an electrical outlet, which I could barely answer anyway.

After my belongings were settled, we went upstairs to grab a bite to eat, which was great because I was starving. At that point, my hunger overcame my exhaustion, and the food brought back some energy. So as we ate, we talked. It had been nearly two years since we had last seen each other, and although I had written her almost continually, she had remained consistent and not written back. I had received brief updates from my mom, but I wanted to know everything that had happened after the night on the frozen lake.

I didn't think it was possible, but we talked for three hours and yet, barely felt like we started the conversation. There was no talk of "us" or what she had been doing since she finished high school. And neither of us mentioned the phone conversation that first night back at my parents place. I think we both were just enjoying the long reunion. We laughed together, and I tried to hold her hand, but she seemed reluctant. I wasn't sure what that meant, but the elation of being back in her presence was enough for me at that point.

After dinner, we went down into the basement while her dad watched TV upstairs. There was one thing I had to tell her, something I didn't tell my parents or anyone else, but she needed to know.

"Casey, there's something I have to tell you," I began. "Something bad, and I have to know you're okay with it before we move on."

She looked at me as if she too held a secret that she wanted to tell me, but swallowed it in deference to what I wanted to say. "I'm here, you can tell me."

"In Vietnam, my job was to man a gun on a boat and shoot the enemy. Sometimes it was hard to tell who was the enemy and who was a farmer or a fisherman. I didn't have time to think, I had to protect my unit and myself.

"I killed a lot of people over there, and I don't know how many of them were innocent civilians. But I know that some were. I--I think I killed innocent people." I broke down sobbing for the first time since I left Vietnam. I had to tell someone, or else it would have continued to eat me alive.

Over my own sobbing, I heard Casey's soothing voice.

"It's war, Chad," she said. "You were only doing your job. It's the government that should be ashamed. It's the government that is killing babies. The government holds the gun and pulls the trigger. You were just the bullet.

"I don't blame you. I don't think anybody would blame you. You were just doing what you were told."

Over the course of several minutes, as I continued to sob, I kept hearing her last words: *"you were just doing what you were told."*

She held my head in her arms and I was slowly succumbing to my exhaustion. Just as I was slipping away into sleep, all I could think of was what she had said, and how I had heard that somewhere else before. It was what the captured Nazi's said during the Nuremburg trials.

Chapter 16

Morning came quickly and as exhausted as I was, even after a full night's sleep, I felt the fog from the trip, and from the last two years begin to lift. I probably could have stayed in bed all day, but I could smell bacon cooking, and I heard Casey's voice call out from the top of the stairs.

"Chad? Chad, are you awake? It's eleven-thirty and I made some breakfast for you."

I threw off the covers and bounced out of bed. Yeah, I could have slept all day, but there was bacon cooking, and some things take precedent over others. "Yep, I'm awake. I'll be up in a minute."

I couldn't wait to start this new phase of my life. I sat down at the kitchen table, and Casey served me a plate full of scrambled eggs, toast, and crispy bacon. As I buttered a piece of toast, I imagined that this could be the rest of my life. A beautiful woman, one I loved so deeply, making me breakfast every morning before I went off to work. I could really get used to this. I ate all of my bacon first, as was my custom, and by the time Casey sat down to join me, I was halfway through the pile of eggs. After three long days of snack cakes and beef jerky, this meal ranked as one of the greatest of all time.

After we finished eating, I cleaned up a bit while Casey did the dishes. I got dressed and rummaged through Mr. Martin's newspaper to find the classified page. It was time to start looking for a place of my own. It wasn't that I didn't appreciate the courtesy of the rent-free basement apartment, but Casey would be going back to school in a few weeks, and I just couldn't see myself living here alone with her father. In fact, the mere thought sent a shiver down my spine.

Casey and I headed into town to look for a place for me to live. I scoured over each listing in the classified section from the Deer Park Sentinel, and there were several available apartments in and around town. We drove by and looked at several units, and in the apartments where the landlord was on-site or available we stopped and were given a walkthrough tour.

Although they were all adequate--I mean I wasn't exactly looking for luxury at this point in my life--none of them really struck us as "the one." So, when we got back to Casey's house, I made a few phone calls to some old friends who I knew still lived in Deer Park to just let them know I was back in town and to see if any of them knew of anyplace that I could live. But the first call that I made was to Marty. Unfortunately, his mom answered and told me that he and his dad were in Cincinnati for a few days. She was happy to hear that I was back from Vietnam safely, and promised to tell Marty that I had called as soon as he got home.

After calling Marty, I rummaged through my sea bag to find my old notebook of phone numbers. In high school, this book held the key to my dating life. It contained the phone numbers to girls in a three county radius. As I flipped through it, I saw names of girls that I didn't recognize, that belonged to faces that I would never see again. Oh, and Tricia. She was in there too. Her name had a heart drawn beside it. I was a different person in high school. The Chad of today wouldn't draw a heart next to a girl's phone number. Heck, I'm not even sure I did it back then. I set that mystery aside and flipped to the very back of the book where I kept the numbers of my friends. These were my teammates, my study partners, guys that I hung out with at the Big Boy on Saturday nights when I didn't have a date. I didn't know who still lived in town, but I was about to find out.

The first name listed was Bill Skelley (I alphabetized by first names), who I'd known since first grade. I called the number listed, and whoever answered told me that he didn't live there anymore. I remembered that

Bill had been dating Kathy Woods during senior year, so I flipped back to the "girls" section of the book and gave her a call. As luck would have it, they were in fact still dating, and Kathy gave me his number, but only after trying to catch up on two years over the phone. I tried to act like I cared, but I didn't. I was never a friend of Kathy Woods, and that is why a little skull was drawn next to her name. I still don't remember drawing these things next to people's names. Weird. Anyway, I got off the phone with Kathy and I gave Bill a call.

"Hey Bill, it's Chad Breckenridge," I announced. "How've you been?"

"Man, it's good to hear your voice," Bill said. "I'd heard you joined the navy and went to 'Nam."

"Yeah, but I'm back in town now and staying at Casey Martin's house until I find a place to live."

"Wow, are you like *staying* at her house?" he asked, putting emphasis on the word as if it was a double entendre. "Does her dad allow that to happen under his roof?"

"I live in her basement," I explained. "That's all. They put me up until I can get on my feet and get my own place."

"Man, what perfect timing," Bill said excitedly. "I live in this boarding house over in Manchester and my lease runs out at the end of the week. I'm packing right now to move. I've got an apartment with Ricky Wilson until the end of summer, then I'm going back to Bloomington when school starts back up.

"If you're interested in coming over here, I'll talk to the owner, and maybe you can just move in."

Manchester was only about 10 miles east of Deer Park, so that would work out great.

"Hell yeah, I'm interested," I said. "How much do you pay each month?"

"That's the beauty of it all, man. It's only a hundred dollars a month!" Bill exclaimed.

That was a number I could afford. "Fantastic! Give me the address and Casey and I will head over there now. Are you going to be there?"

"Yep," he said. "I'm knee deep in packing up my junk. Come on over."

He gave me the address, which I scribbled down in my phonebook under Kathy Woods' name. Then I scratched her name, and the little drawing of a skull, out of my book. I told Bill I'd see him soon, and hung up. I had expected the hunt for a place to last a few weeks, not a few hours. I guess the luck of Chad Breckenridge had returned once I crossed back into Warren County. Oh how I had missed it!

I ran upstairs and excitedly told Casey about my conversation with Bill, and we both felt better that we knew who had lived in the place prior. We got back in my car and made the short drive over to Manchester.

The boarding house was a two-story brick house on a quiet tree-lined street in the middle of town, and while it was a little run-down with age, structurally it was well kept and nice. Casey and I walked up the front walk and Bill came down to meet us both.

He had changed since high school. His hair, which had always been high and tight, was now long and unkempt, and his t-shirt was stained and his jeans were riddled with holes. He embraced each of us with a big hug. I suspect he gave me a hug because he was glad to see I made it back from 'Nam. I also suspect he gave Casey a hug because she was wearing a tight-fitting Miami College T-shirt and short-shorts that really showed off her long, tan legs. And I didn't blame him a bit. But then the hug seemed to drag on a bit longer than it should have.

"Wow, you look great," he said.

"Thanks," I said, mock posing, like a model in a magazine. "Two years in the jungle will do that to a guy."

"No, I meant Casey," he said, staring at her burgeoning chest and pointing. "How's school going?" I was about ready to slug him in his jaw when I realized that he was pointing to the *Miami College* print on her shirt, and not her breasts.

"Good," she replied. "How's Kathy?"

That's my girl.

"She's, uhh, good," Bill said, blushing. He tore his eyes away from Casey's chest. "C'mon, let me show you the place."

With the catching up part of our visit apparently concluded, Bill escorted both of us upstairs to the room. As we entered, I noticed the dark, weathered walnut flooring lined by a rather dark hallway leading up to his room. The hallway had one light that was so dim that the illumination was barely strong enough to cast shadows on us as we walked up the stairs. I gave Casey a quick glance, to see if she was as spooked out by the lack of light as I was, and then I turned around to make sure Norman Bates, in his crazy wig and carving knife, wasn't following us.

At the top of the stairs we passed a small bathroom, which Bill explained was shared by all eight tenants. As we entered Bill's room, I saw four walls with one small window that opened up to an alley and a very small closet. There was only enough room for a bed, possibly a small table, and an equally small television set. My mind immediately started to calculate the size of this room and determined it to be about twelve feet by twelve feet. It certainly wasn't my idea of home, but it was something I could afford until I got a job. But then again, sharing a bathroom with eight other people wasn't the greatest situation to be in. It was still better than living with Casey's dad.

"Tell me a little about the other people who rent here?" I asked. Bill thought for a moment before responding.

"Well, there are six guys and two women," he replied. "All in their early seventies, but very nice."

Oh great, I thought. I'm going to be living with eight people who are one step from death's door. It wasn't quite the party house I was expecting, but then again, I couldn't afford to be picky.

I looked at Casey and she shrugged. That one act told me that this would be my decision.

"Well, Bill, I guess I'll take it," I said. "Is the owner here? I'll sign the papers and come back this weekend and move my stuff in."

"Great, man," Bill said. "You'll really dig it." We walked downstairs and met the owner, a man named Mr. Reynolds. Bill gave me a glowing recommendation and more importantly, I gave Mr. Reynolds a hundred dollars, and he was happy to have me.

When we got back in the car, I looked over at Casey. "Well, what do you think?"

She laughed. "Well, it's dry."

I was a bit taken aback. "What do you mean?"

She counted out on her fingers, "Well, it's old, dark, and depressing. And your roommates were alive during the Civil War, and you will be sharing the only bathroom with all of them."

"Yeah, but it's *my* place," I said, having warmed to the idea and beaming. "And I won't be here that much once I find a job." Though I had started to enjoy the idea that I had a place of my own, I didn't anticipate Casey spending many romantic nights at the old boarding house with me. Not with half the Old Testament as roommates.

The next day, I woke up at a more reasonable time (nine-thirty, which was still late for the new post-navy Chad Breckenridge), and once again ate a breakfast that Casey had prepared. This time it was thick sausage gravy over warm, fresh-baked biscuits and freshly squeezed orange juice to wash it all down. If I'd had a ring, I would have got down on one knee at that very moment, but then a ring was something that I couldn't afford, so I finished eating, got cleaned up, and headed out to find a job.

The first place I went to was Anderson's Department Store, which had been a fixture in downtown Deer Park for as long as I could remember, and a place that my brother, Alex, had worked at before my parents had moved out west. I used to frequent Anderson's while in high school, as they were the only place in town that sold hit vinyl LP record albums. I mean, if you wanted the newest pressing of Beethoven's Ninth Symphony, or something by Bach, you could get it at Carter's Music Emporium, but old Bob Carter refused to stock the popular stuff like The Beach Boys and The Beatles. If you wanted good music, you had to go to Anderson's. Besides, It would be a short drive from my new place, and since it was downtown, there were a number of restaurants and other places to hang out in while on lunch breaks.

I went directly to the second floor, bypassing the army of mannequins dressed up in the latest fashion trends, and the smaller army of shoppers looking for those trends, and I found the hiring department. I approached the counter and found an elderly woman sitting at a desk. She looked to be filing some paperwork.

"Excuse me, ma'am," I said. "My name is Chad Breckenridge and I just got back from Vietnam and would like to apply for a job. Are you, by any chance, hiring today?"

She kept on working on her piles of papers. I wasn't sure if she'd heard me or not. I cleared my throat not once, but twice. Still she focused all of her attention on the pile of paper.

"HELLO!" I nearly shouted. "MA'AM?" She looked up and I saw the biggest hearing aid ever attached to the side of her head. It looked like a transistor radio had been half-inserted into her skull.

"Can I help you?" she asked, oblivious that I had been standing there unattended for a few minutes.

"I'm looking for a job," I said, and then repeated myself, only louder. "I'M LOOKING FOR WORK."

"You don't have to shout, young man," she said. She stood up from her desk and I could barely tell that she had. She stood only about four feet tall, even with sensible pump-heeled shoes under her flower-print dress. She walked to the counter and handed me an application.

"I have an opening in our Shoe Department if you're interested," she said. "I was about to call the Sentinel and post the opening in the paper. You're a lucky man, mister--"

"Breckenridge," I said. "Chad, ma'am. And I'll take that job if you are offering it." I didn't care what it involved or how much it paid, it was a job indoors and I wanted it. And again, my luck looked to be paying off. Sometimes I loved being me. The receptionist handed me a pen.

"Well then, fill this out, and call me when you're finished."

Great, another game of shouting at the deaf lady. "Will do, ma'am."

"Please, call me Mrs. Jablowski," she said. Honestly, her name was a mouthful. I think I preferred calling her "ma'am."

"Mr. Anderson is a veteran himself," she said. "Berlin, 1945. He always tries to look out for fellow soldiers. We would be honored to have you come to work for us. Personally, I think it's just sick that all those hippies and commies are giving you grief for fighting for our country."

I haven't got much grief from hippies, and don't know if I've ever met a communist on U.S. soil, but I wasn't going to tell her that.

"Why, thank you so much," I said. "I really need a job and can start immediately."

"Well great," she responded. She then put her old, wrinkled hand on mine, patting it gently. "Why don't you fill out the paperwork then come in tomorrow morning at nine and we'll get you started." I think I was just hired on the spot.

"Are you saying--?"

"Mr. Anderson would definitely approve of your hire," she said. I was excited to know I had a job, no matter what it was.

"Then I'll finish this application and see you tomorrow morning," I said. I took the application and folded it once, in half. "Thank you Ms. Jablon--Jablew--ma'am."

I ran down the stairwell and walked briskly through the sales floor until I got outside the store. Relief washed over me and I exhaled. Things were starting to look up for me. I walked back to my car with a spring in my step, and the natural high that came with the feeling of new possibilities. I couldn't wait to get back to the Martin's and tell Casey the good news.

The next morning I appeared promptly at 9:00 a.m. in front of the same counter in the hiring department on the second floor. For the first time since being back, I wasn't greeted with a huge breakfast courtesy of Casey, so I had to make due with a cold bowl of corn flakes. It would be enough to hold me over until lunch.

After a few minutes, I was greeted by Mrs. Jablowski, who took me over to the Budget Shoe Department and introduced me to the manager, Mr. Graves. He was a rather tall man, standing well over six feet (of course, next to Mrs. Jablowski, he looked to be about nine feet tall) with a thin build and he wore what appeared to be a hairpiece. That, or a raccoon was sleeping on his head. Either way, it was quite mesmerizing to look at and I couldn't quite take my eyes off of it.

"Mr. Graves, this is Chad and he'll be working with you," she announced. Mr. Graves walked over and reached out his hand.

"Hi Chad, glad to have you," he said. "Have you ever sold shoes before?"

I not only hadn't sold shoes before, but I hadn't sold anything since hawking candles to raise money for a class trip in the fifth grade, and even then, I think my mom sold or bought most of the candles. Looking at Mr. Graves, I thought, it couldn't be that difficult. "No sir, but I'm a fast learner."

"Then let's start teaching you the fine art of selling shoes." I laughed, as if he'd made a joke, but then his reaction told me that it was no joke. I was embarrassed and the dead raccoon on his head mocked me for it.

After spending the rest of the morning training with Mr. Graves, I was getting close to actually selling. Mr. Graves showed me the backroom, and went over the cataloging system for the literally seven million different pairs of shoes that were piled back there. He told me how to rotate stock, making sure the most expensive shoe was the one that was easiest for the customer to see and to get to. He instructed me on how to do inventory when new shipments of shoes came in on a truck, and how to differentiate between this year's and last year's styles. It was a good three solid hours of training, and while Mr. Graves loved talking about shoes, I wasn't retaining any of it. Shoes were shoes.

"Okay, Chad, you now know everything I know about selling shoes," he said. "After lunch, you will be on your own. Make me proud."

After lunch, I came in and surveyed the entire shoe department. There was six or seven customers fondling the product, opening up the boxes and trying to play matchmaker with the shoes on the display racks on the wall. To a seasoned shoe salesman, six or seven people were a piece of cake. But to me, on my first day on the job, I was terrified. I stood there trying to recall everything Mr. Graves had told me, and kept drawing blanks. When I clocked in after lunch, Mrs. Jablowski had informed me that I would be on my own for the afternoon as Mr. Graves was called to assist in another department. This was all up to me. These people needed shoes, and I was the only person in the entire world that could help them. I swallowed hard as beads of sweat ran down my face. It was go time! I stepped into the department and tried to look busy, hoping that the customers wouldn't see me, and if they did, would think I'm too busy to ask for help. It didn't work. A couple of elderly women came up to me and waited for me to acknowledge them. I ignored them as best I could, going so far as to start whistling to try and show them that I was terribly busy.

"Excuse me, young man," one of them said. "Can you help us?"

"Oh, good afternoon ladies," I said. "I didn't see you there. How can I help you?" "Well, my friend is looking for a pair of shoes that are comfortable when walking. We were looking at the gray ones over there with the open toe. Do you have any in gray, size 7-wide?" she asked.

I stood there like a deer trapped in the beams of powerful headlights. And the vehicle that was about to smash into me was a gray, open-toed shoe driven by two old women that could easily be my roommates in the boarding house that I was about to move into.

"I can check on that," I said, though really I couldn't. Everything that Mr. Graves had taught me was gone from my brain, *IF* it was ever in there in the first place.

"I'll be right back ladies," I said. "Why don't you two have a seat while I check our stock in the back?" I headed into the back room and started to look at the skyscraper-like towers of shoes. It was an entire city made up of shoeboxes. I started checking tags, but the words had no meaning. They might as well have been printed in hieroglyphics. I started to panic. How long had the customers been waiting? What if I got lost back here and never made my way out? Would they find my body years from now, mummified and dusty, next to a palette of last year's style of wedge sandal? And then I saw something I recognized. A familiar box, with a familiar tag and I saw the words GRAY and WIDE in large block letters. And then I saw the final piece of the puzzle, SIZE 7, illuminated by a mysterious beam of light, as if the Man upstairs was showing me the way in this deadly maze of shoeboxes. I felt like Allan Quartermain finding King Solomon's mines. I grabbed the box in question and yanked, and the entire tower collapsed around me. But I didn't care, as I had my treasure!

With great excitement, I started to dash for the sales floor where the ladies were seated, but gathered myself enough to slow to a walk upon reaching the back room's door. I collected myself, and with box in hand, I stepped through and greeted my customers with a big smile and the strong confidence of a seasoned salesman.

"Well ladies," I said, beaming. "I apologize for the wait, but I found the pair you were looking for."

I got down on my knees and extended my hand to grab the left foot of the lady in question, to assist her in trying on the shoe. I pulled off her beaten, brown leather flat and to my surprise, a puff of smoke exploded off her foot. I gagged, as the smell was atrocious. My eyes began to water, and I tried to blink away the tears, but through the haze, I could see her pale, white foot. It wasn't smoke, but foot powder. An ungodly amount of foot powder. The plume of reeking powder settled all over my clothes, and I held back the urge to vomit. This old woman's foot odor was now going to be with me for the rest of my shift. I had survived the rivers and canals of Vietnam, but was about to be taken out by the gnarled, smelly feet of a woman who most likely helped Martha Washington sew up the American flag. Both ladies acted like there was nothing wrong, even though I was green in the face and had just let all of the world's evil out of Pandora's shoe. I tried to play along, I tried to act as if nothing was amiss, and luckily for me, the shoe fit!

"Perfect," I muttered, trying to hold in my breath. "It looks good on you." As the woman stood up to walk around, I wondered what I had gotten myself into. This was my first customer and I felt that no matter what happened from this point on, it could never be any worse than it was with these two ladies.

"I'll take them!" she said. And I exhaled, which caused the foot powder that had settled onto my face to dance again. I'd made my first sale. And it was one that I'd never forget.

My second day went much better than my first, and even I was surprised at how quick I had taken to selling shoes. When my shift ended, I drove back over to the Martin's for dinner. Casey was home, working on some project in her room, even though school was still a few weeks away. I walked into the kitchen to get a bottle of soda and saw a hand-written note on the table telling me that Marty had called.

I forgot about the drink and picked up the receiver and began dialing the number to the Green residence.

"Hello?" Marty asked.

"Well, well," I said. "Look who finally decided to call me back."

"Hey, man! How've you been? How was the drive?"

"Good, good," I said. "Uneventful, at least. How was Cincy?"

"It was great," he said. "Dad and I went to the new Reds stadium and saw a couple of series against the Padres and Giants."

"How're they looking this year?"

"Man, they got this new second baseman named Joe Morgan," he explained. "The guy's a wizard. I think they're gonna go all the way this year."

I'd heard Marty say those words every season since we were too young to even know what baseball was. Even when the Reds lost over 80 games and finished dead last in the league, Marty had always kept the faith.

"That's great, man," I said. "So, how're you adjusting back to civilian life?"

"Pretty good, I guess. I'm looking to move out of my parents place..." I was about to tell him about my place out at Manchester, and how Bill Skelley had done me a solid, when I heard him say something peculiar.

"...and I was wondering if you wanted to get a place together and share an apartment."

I didn't even think about it. In my patented way of living life, I just jumped at the opportunity, not thinking it through.

"Hell yes," I said. It didn't matter that I had signed a lease to live in the boarding house of the dead. It didn't matter that Bill Skelley was, at this very moment, moving out so I could move in in a couple of days. What did matter is that I wouldn't have to share a toilet with eight other people, most of who came over on the Mayflower. I also recalled Casey's comment when she and I walked the place. She had called it "dry" and "dark and depressing." I didn't want my girl exposed to a place like that... and that brought me to my last point: I just couldn't see me and Casey hanging out together in a house occupied by the living dead. It would be difficult to be romantic amidst the smells of Geritol tonic, and that waxy, musty scent that old people gave off. At least if I lived with Marty, I could have my alone time when needed. Just in case Casey changed her mind about waiting until she was married. That was probably the biggest justification.

"Count me in." Things were still working out quite nicely.

Two days later, I had my first day off and Marty and I started looking for a place. We eventually found a large one-bedroom apartment in a building just off of Main Street, south of downtown. The building belonged to Wrightson's Pharmacy, and the apartment was situated upstairs, over the store. It was a nice place with new carpeting, freshly painted walls, a large living room and a nice kitchen area. We saw that the ceiling had wooden beams that ran the length of the place, so we thought of putting up a piece of wallboard to divide the living room into two smaller rooms. We both agreed that this place was perfect and that partitioning the living area was a great idea.

I called Mr. Reynolds at the boarding house and told him that something better had come along, and that I wouldn't be moving into Bill Skelley's old room. He was initially upset, and told me that I would not get the hundred dollars I had paid in advance back, but if that was the cost of breaking a signed lease, I accepted it.

The following weekend Marty and I moved into our new place. We both brought all of our personal belongings, which collectively consisted of clothes, two mattresses, a beanbag chair and a nine-inch black and white television set. Seeing as how meager our things looked mixed together in our own place, we made a list of what we needed and then headed out to make some purchases. Most of my things had been sold at garage sales, or had been moved across the country. Marty's parents had tossed most of his things the day he and left for boot camp. The Green's weren't big on nostalgia. So, after all this time, it was just like starting over.

Marty and I purchased another mattress, a wallboard, a package of bed sheet linens, a black light, some colored dyes, and some things for the kitchen, namely pots and pans and eating utensils.

Upon our return to the apartment, we immediately hung up the wallboard by nailing it to one of the ceiling beams. This created an enclosed ten-foot-by-ten-foot section of the living area. We then put the new mattress in that room, along with the black light. Voila! We had created what we imaginatively and subtlety called our "get laid room" or "sex room."

Marty proceeded to tie-dye one of the sheets a dark purple color, and then cut it into several long, four-inch pieces which we also nailed into one of the ceiling beams thereby providing for a colorful entry into what we hoped would be the room of love.

While he was finishing up the touches on the sex room, I looked around the apartment for any additional ways to enhance our bachelor pad. I was rummaging through some musty boxes that had been in Marty's garage when I found the mother load of love! Throughout high school, Marty had collected a number of issues of Playboy Magazine and, though I had, at times, visited his house and read some of the finer articles, I had totally forgotten about the stash, and honestly had expected them to have been thrown out when we went into the navy. Thank god, they hadn't.

I found one issue in particular that I had enjoyed and turned to the layout that I had remembered. I laughed out loud as an idea formed in my head. Marty was busy hanging the strips of bed sheet over the sex room's doorway, so I grabbed the pair of scissors and cut out a picture of a cute blond girl who was situated in a provocative, if not inviting pose. The picture would fit nicely over the peephole in the apartment's front door. I carefully trimmed the picture, keeping only the part I wanted, letting the rest fall away to the floor as I worked diligently. Once I had the perfect image I taped it to the door, around the peephole. I just stood there admiring my work, and then broke out into laughter. Marty popped his head out of the sex room.

"What's so funny?" he asked.

"Someone's at the door, come check out who it is." He stepped out of the room and gave me a look that said he didn't have time for this. Then he saw what I had done. Around the peephole was a picture of a beautiful young girl with her legs spread open and her vagina WAS the peephole. He looked at me, stunned, and then he began to laugh. Even with the creation of our sex room, this action was the first that really said that this was our place.

I would admit that it wasn't such a good idea, since we had hoped to be entertaining girls in our new place, and the peephole was tasteless. Heck, the purpose of the sex room was to get laid, or at least to invite girls over to be romanced into having sex. But then I thought to myself that they probably wouldn't even see the peephole until they were leaving, and by then, it would be okay if they never wanted to see us again. Besides, as impulsive twenty-year-olds, we thought it was extremely funny.

Together, we declared the apartment was now ready for occupancy. And guests.

The next day, our phone was installed so I immediately called Casey to plan a romantic evening at our new place. Even though she wasn't due to go back to college for a few weeks, she had been slowly moving her stuff back to her dormitory, and staying on campus working on different projects. She had told me all about what she was doing one night after I had got off work, but I was so exhausted that I hadn't retained anything that she'd said. It was something to do with the war, and President Nixon, and Kent State, but I was just too tired to pay attention.

I wasn't too sure of her schedule (another thing she'd told me that I couldn't remember), so I hoped that I could get hold of her before she headed back up to school. I dialed her number hoping she was home.

"Hello?" an angel's voice asked.

"Hey beautiful," I said. "I'm so glad I got you before you headed back up to school. I was wondering if you'd like to spend sometime together today and come and see our new apartment."

"I would love to, Chad," she said. "But I can't stay long. I have to get back up to campus tonight."

"Oh, so you're going back to school already?" I asked.

"Well, not for classes, but yes, I'm going back to campus until classes start in a few weeks." I didn't have anything to say so I didn't bother. She picked up on my silence. "I told you all of this last week."

"I know." *I didn't. I had no clue as to what she was talking about.*

"So why don't I come over around four or so?"

"I'll make you an early dinner," I said. I was hoping for a night of romance, instead, I felt that I was just an appointment on her busy calendar.

"I'll see you then," she said. "Miss you."

"I love--" I tried to tell her but she had hung up.

Without thinking too much about it I hung up the receiver and got to work making sure the place was in order for Casey's visit. Actually, there was little to do, as the only furniture we had was the one beanbag chair in the living room and the mattress in the sex room. We used a small cooler for drinks and our nine-inch black and white television set sat on top a stack of boxes filled with books. Looking at it through the eyes of a guy trying to impress a girl, the place wasn't as impressive as I originally thought. But it sure was a lot better than the room I would have had at the boarding house.

It was just after one in the afternoon, so I ran down to the grocery for the ingredients to make a nice early dinner for us. I decided on my famous beef stroganoff with a side of fresh boiled spinach, finished off with a fruit dish topped with whipped cream. We had a bottle of cheap wine in the cooler, but even I thought it was nasty, and I knew Casey wouldn't touch a drop once she smelled it.

When I returned from the store, I put away the food and swept the floor and cleaned up the back bedroom, which Marty and I shared. It was a disaster already. Although we had a closet, we never seemed to use it. It was just easier to throw our dirty clothes in a pile on the floor, or what was really a series of piles all over the floor. You would think the military discipline would have helped us organize our belongings, but I think it was our rebellion in not being organized. If Petty Officer Jordan, our training officer in boot camp, were here right now, he would have stomped Marty and I into paste. I sure didn't miss the navy.

I tried kicking the piles of dirty clothes into bigger piles, but I couldn't even tell what was clean and what was dirty. I didn't have the time to give each garment the smell test, so for now, it was all dirty. I used my foot and guided all of the piles into our closet. Why we had all of our clothes all over the floor when we had a perfectly good closet (and a dresser) was beyond my comprehension. I kicked all of the clothes into the closet and had to shove hard to get the door closed. I thought about trying to make the beds, but of course our beds were nothing more than two mattresses lying on the floor, and we didn't even have sheets. We each had a scratchy wool blanket and that was it. The bedroom was looking as good as it ever would, so I went into the kitchen to start making dinner.

It was about ten to four when I heard a knock at the door. I figured it was Casey, but Marty and I decided that before opening the door, we would always look through the peephole to see who it was. We felt we owed it to the beautiful girl in the photo.

I opened the door and there stood Casey, dressed in a pair of tight white shorts and a frilly burgundy blouse. She was absolutely beautiful.

"Hi honey," I said. "You look beautiful! Come on in." As she stepped through the doorway, she seemed to slow her pace while just surveying the layout. She stopped and stared, somewhat curiously at the sex room. I could see her mind trying to figure out as to what was behind the wood façade with the dark purple tie-dyed sheets.

She chose her words carefully. "Well, this is certainly much better than the room you had over at the boarding house," she said. "Can I see the rest of the apartment, or is this it?"

"I'd be honored to give you the grand tour," I said. "If you'd follow me, let me take you down the hall into the kitchen." I waved my arm in the direction of the sink and stove. "And then over to the dining area." I used my other arm to show the cooler/table with the flatware set out in two settings. "And back into our bedroom." This actually took a few steps, and as she walked through the door I could tell she was surprised that it was clean and in order. The entire tour of our apartment only took about six seconds. Despite that fact, Casey appeared impressed.

"This place is quite cute!" she said, and gave me a quick hug of accomplishment. "And I can't believe the bedroom is clean and organized."

"Well, Marty and I are neat freaks," I said boastfully. Just as I finished my sentence, Casey walked over to the closet and started to slowly open the door, and time went into slow motion. I tried to speak, I tried to stop her, but it was too late. As she opened the door, the massive pile of clothes spilled out onto the bedroom floor.

SHIT! SHIT! SHIT!

I heard a quiet laugh, and then she turned to me. "Well, I can certainly see why your room is so clean."

"Wow, will you look at that," I said. "Looks like all of those are

Marty's. That kid is a slob, I tell you. I took all mine to the Laundromat and I was going to go get them out after dinner." I spoke with mock confidence, like I had never seen those clothes before, even though Casey had seen me wearing most of them in our time of dating.

"Let me show you what we did in the living room," I said, changing the subject--and the location.

"Okay," she said, ignoring the pile of clothes and walking with me back to the front room. "I think I saw you added a room when I first came in." We entered the living room and Casey parted the tie-dyed sheets that made up the entrance into the extra room. As she looked in the room, she just stood there silently.

"Exactly what is the purpose of this room?" she asked. "All I see is a mattress, a few boxes covered with bed linens, and a radio."

It was all you needed for love, I thought. But would never tell her that out loud.

Nor was I going to tell her that it was our "get laid" room. Not if I ever wanted to be in that room with her. So, I took the high road.

"This is an extra room for when we have guests over."

She turned back to look at the mattress, then back to me with some bitterness in her voice.

"Guests? What kind of guests?"

This wasn't the direction I wanted to be heading in.

"Guy friends," I explained. "Navy buddies, people we know, stuff like that." I quickly tried to redirect her. "How about we go into the kitchen while I finish dinner? It will be ready soon and I bet you're hungry."

"Fine," she said, though I knew she wasn't. If we kept on this path, we would have started a conversation that I wasn't sure we were ready to have. I didn't want to talk about the fact that we hadn't consummated our relationship, and I didn't want to talk any further about this room, or what it was used for. To be safe, I think we both just wanted to move away from this topic.

I finished dinner and we sat on the floor to eat, using the cooler as a table. I offered her the nasty cheap wine, but she settled for water and I followed her lead. I lit a candle and sat it between us on the cooler as we ate. The dinner conversation was light. I wanted to ask her about what she was doing on campus, even though classes hadn't started, but that would mean that I was a terrible boyfriend who didn't listen (which I was), so I tried to talk about something else. And then it all took a strange turn.

"Why didn't you ever write me?" I asked between mouthfuls of stroganoff.

She swallowed hard by the abruptness of the question. "Huh?"

"When I was gone, in the navy," I explained. "I wrote you almost every day, sometimes even twice a day. And I never once got a letter back. Why didn't you write me back?" Honestly, I had no idea where this conversation was coming from. I mean, I had wanted to ask her ever since I got back in the world, but the cross-country drive, and the chaos of apartment and job hunting had left no time. And I guess now I needed to know.

"I told you," she said, carefully selecting her words. "I'm not much of a writer. I prefer to talk, person-to-person."

"I was half a world away," I reasoned. "I could have been killed. And all the while, I was thinking of you and had no idea if you were thinking of me in return. Not even one letter. I just needed to ask why."

"I was thinking of you," she said. "But I was also living my life. It was my senior year of high school. I had to get into a good college, there were so many things going on, that all I could afford was to *think* of you." I wasn't sure how to take what she was telling me. Was she telling me that I was third, or fourth in her list of priorities? If so, how was I supposed to take that?

"I did read each letter, and I still have most of them," she explained. "But I told you when we first started dating that I didn't write letters. It wasn't fair that you would expect me to change, to become something I wasn't--a letter writer--just because you decided to enlist." Now, that one stung a bit.

"I'm sorry," she said. "That didn't come out right."

"No, it didn't," I said. "If I didn't enlist, I probably would've been drafted, with no say as to what I did or where I went. I enlisted to maintain some control of my life."

"That's bullshit," she said. "You enlisted because of Marty. You've never cared about the direction of your life. That's the problem with you."

A pregnant silence formed in the air between us. Neither of us wanted to say anything else that would hurt the other. But enough had been said, and I felt each word, like a diamond-edged dagger skewering my very soul.

"Maybe you should take up writing," I said. "Because when you talk to someone 'person-to-person,' you say some really mean things."

Again, she was quiet, eating small bites of stroganoff and avoiding eye contact.

"I'm sorry," she said. "I'm just thinking about school, and moving back to the dorm, and my fall classes, and everything else. I didn't mean to say anything to upset you. I love you."

"I love you too," I said.

"Once I get settled at school, why don't you come visit me?" she asked. "Maybe you'll see the value of higher education, and start taking classes yourself."

"How long will it take you to get settled?" I asked. Any thoughts I had about entertaining Casey in the sex room tonight had all but evaporated, but her olive branch sounded like an invitation to revisit the thought once classes started. Suddenly, the anger--and the hurt--of the whole argument was wiped away upon orders from my groin, which admittedly made too many of my life's decisions.

"Shouldn't be more than a few weeks," she said, and gave me that smile that I loved so much. And just like that, the conversation was over, as was dinner. The rest of the evening turned out great, as we were able to just spend time together.

At eight-thirty, she announced that she had to go. As she walked toward the door to leave, she stopped and gazed at the picture taped over the peephole. Damn it! I had honestly hoped that she wouldn't see it. And I had almost made it.

My next thought was that she'd never come back here again. I mean we had no furniture, had massive piles of clothes in the closet, a room that--no matter how hard I tried to explain otherwise--had a distinct purpose, and now a picture of a beautiful woman with the peephole as her vagina.

"Who's your friend?" she asked.

"Miss November, 1970," I said. "But she means nothing to me. I swear." We both shared a laugh and the weight of whatever that was that happened over dinner lifted.

She stepped into my arms and I enveloped her. I inhaled her scent and kissed her neck, then her chin, and finally her lips. She smiled and broke the embrace.

"I gotta go," she said.

"Okay," I said. "I'll call you later this week. I love you very much!"

She smiled and blew me a kiss as she walked away. She was down the hallway before I realized that she hadn't told me she loved me back. But I knew she did, in a "Casey" sort of way. Whatever the hell that was, it was all I had.

Chapter 17

Three weeks went by and I was still working in the shoe department of Anderson's Department Store. Somehow, I just felt I had to get another job. Selling shoes was not the career path I had anticipated for myself. About the only thing I had learned from this job was that there were over seven thousand types of women's shoe, and that it was always better to breathe through my mouth. Not exactly the life lessons I needed to survive. And most of the customers were elderly women, so it wasn't even that I got to meet and talk to pretty girls. In fact, the cons of the job far outweighed any of the pros.

That morning, as I sat in the break room waiting for my shift to begin, I saw an ad in the paper stating that Wyndall's Grocery was hiring. I thought I would go and check it out over my lunch break. I'd rather bag groceries or stock canned goods on shelves than spend one more day whiffing sweaty feet while trying to shove a shoe that was two sizes too small onto a foot of a woman who just would not admit that she was part ogre below the ankles. Lunch couldn't come quick enough.

The morning was spent pulling some fifty pairs of shoes out of the backroom for customers to try on and then having to turn around and restock them. Twenty of those pairs were for only one customer, Mrs. Paschal. She was a nice lady, but she had to be well over a hundred and twenty years old. She had severe arthritis, coupled with a foot odor that meant death and rigor mortis had probably already started in her feet and was slowly working its way up throughout her body. I couldn't even breathe through my mouth, because the smell was so bad I could taste it! After an hour of trying on shoe after shoe with Mrs. Paschal, I wasn't hungry for lunch anymore. That would make my visit to Wyndall's that much easier.

At twelve o'clock, I clocked out and headed over to the grocery store as quickly as I could. I pulled into the parking lot and started to get out of my car while trying to turn off the ignition at the same time. I was almost completely out of the car when I noticed the car was still running. Quickly, I sat back down and slowly turned off the ignition. This time, I moved a bit slower as I stepped out and started for the front door. As I entered the store I noticed several people to my left filling out applications. I walked over and asked one guy where he got the application and he just pointed to a gentleman standing outside a small office talking to a young and very attractive girl.

Now, in a town like Deer Park, everyone knew everyone else. Most of us grew up together, generation by generation. But this girl was new to me. She looked to be in her early twenties, with long blond hair and gorgeous blue eyes. She stood about five feet, six inches with a slight build, but well developed. She could stop traffic, and she certainly stopped me. I walked over to the gentleman and waited until they had finished their conversation.

"Excuse me sir," I said. "I am here for the position advertised in the newspaper. I was told to see you."

I wasn't sure what he thought of me at that very moment because my eyes were solely focused on the beautiful girl standing next to him. He didn't seem to notice or care as he reached down to the table behind him and grabbed a packet and handed it to me. "Here is an application for you to fill out," he explained in a monotone voice, as if he'd been saying the same thing all morning. "You can go over there and fill it out, then return it to me. I will call your name."

I took the application. "Okay, thank you," I said, more to the beautiful girl. Again, I don't even think the man noticed.

I walked over to the area he had directed me to and took a seat. I took a quick glance over at the cute girl to see where she going to be directed to sit to fill out her application. She was still talking to the man, so I began to fill in my information. A couple of minutes later, the girl sat down in the empty chair next to me.

I love my life, I thought. *Thank you, God!*

I saw that she was also carrying an application.

"Oh, are you filling out an application?" I asked, striking up a perfectly innocent conversation. "I thought you worked here already."

"Hopefully," she said.

"I'm Chad Breckenridge."

"My name is Staci," she said. "With an 'I'."

I looked down at her application and saw that she has put her name down as "Eustace." Staci-with-an-I was so much more fitting for a girl of her beauty.

"Glad to meet you, Chad," she continued. "Say, did you use to play football? I think I remember you."

I was surprised she would have remembered me, because I was sure I had never seen her before. I searched my memory banks for any recollection of any girl I ever knew named Stacey, Stacy, Staci, or even Eustace. I came up blank in every instance. "I did, but I graduated back in '69. How'd you know?"

She smiled a little. "My brother, Gary, played for Walker County and you guys beat us pretty bad in '68. He was a linebacker and I think you got the better of him that night. He was cussing your name for weeks after."

I beamed a little with pride. "I had one of my better games against Walker County," I explained, though it was mostly a lie, as I didn't recall the game at all. "But they were a good team."

I admit that this girl had my complete attention. She was beautiful and knew how to play to my ego. I had to find out more about her.

"Hey, after we finish up here," I said. "If you haven't eaten lunch already, would you like to grab some food?"

Staci smiled. "I'd love to."

I couldn't help myself. If there was one thing that defined me as a person, it was that I lived for the moment, and in this moment there was a beautiful girl talking to me and willing to go out to lunch with me. Besides, it was just lunch. It wasn't like I was going to whisk her away to The Hollows for steaks over the lake.

We both got to work on our applications. After a few minutes, Staci finished hers and handed it in. With her looks, I was certain she would get the job. I, on the other hand, would probably have to beg, barter and maybe shed a tear or two. Only then would I have a chance. I finished mine and handed it to the gentleman. He casually set it down and called out Staci's name. I sat down and waited. After about twenty minutes she stepped out of his office and came back over to where I was sitting.

"Well Chad, he wants to see you now."

"How'd it go?" I asked.

"I don't know."

"Well, wish me luck," I said. "We'll get some lunch when I'm done, and hopefully we'll have something to celebrate."

Hell, I had something to celebrate already, but the job would be nice too.

I threw back my shoulders, lifted my head and walked with my usual naïve confidence over to the store manager's office where I greeted him with a smile and my outstretched hand. He took it in his, and I gave him a firm, hearty handshake, like my dad taught me back when I was in high school.

"Thank you, sir, for taking time to meet me today," I said. "And for your consideration. Although I recognize you have several top candidates for this position, I believe my work ethic is demonstrated through both my academic and athletic commitments throughout my four years of high school, plus in my service to this country in the military." This was of course absolutely one hundred percent bullshit. The only thing I was dedicated to in high school was girls, football, and girls, and the navy had taught me to make my bed and to destroy things and kill people. But I always reverted to Eddie Haskell when talking to people in authority, and today was no different.

"Thank you, Mr. Breckenridge," the manager said. "Let me look over your application and I will make a decision shortly." He pointed out towards the snack area where the other applicants were. "Go ahead and wait over there with the other folks. This shouldn't take long."

At this point I was concerned because he spent twenty minutes interviewing Staci but had just accepted my application and sent me on my way. I didn't even get a question asked of me. Damn my rampant Eddie Haskell-ness!

I took my seat next to Staci.

"That was fast," she said.

"Yeah," I agreed. "We can wait around a bit to see if you get hired, but I obviously will need to get back to my other job, as it is the only one I have."

Staci and I sat at the table with the others and made uncomfortable small talk while waiting. What had started out as a group of eleven people began to dwindle. After about thirty minutes, the store manager approached the five of us who remained and advised them that I was being offered the job. I wasn't sure I heard that right. *I* got the job? I didn't even get a proper interview, and now I was being offered a job. Staci and I looked at each other in disbelief. Thank God I no longer had to sell shoes to the elderly. No more dead, smelly feet. No more backaches from kneeling all day long. No more being covered in foot powder. I was free--but...wait. That meant that Staci didn't get the job. I turned to her and offered what condolences I could.

"I'm so sorry, Staci," I said. "I don't know what to say. I'm happy for me but sad for you." That seemed to work, because she didn't look too heartbroken.

"That's okay," she said, smiling. "Let's go get some lunch."

After a quick meal with Staci, I ran back to my car, as I was already almost 40 minutes late in getting back to work. I didn't think I'd have to worry too much about quitting as they were probably going to fire me as soon as I got back. I gunned the engine of the Camaro and left a good two inches of rubber on the road as I tore off towards Anderson's.

During the drive, I couldn't help but think of how cute Staci was. Her blond hair was like spun gold, and her face was symmetrically perfect. And I won't even mention her body, which was tight where it needed to be, and curvy everywhere else. My heart palpitated in my chest when I thought about her. I don't think I'd felt that overwhelming feeling of love since that day in high school, right before homecoming, when I met--

SCREEEEEEEEECH!

I stomped on the brakes, again, leaving another couple of inches of rubber on the pavement. The car came to a stop right in the middle of Euclid Street. I looked up at the rearview mirror and saw my own ghost staring back at me. Well, it wasn't my ghost, but I was pale enough to be confused with one. For some reason, I had completely forgotten about Casey! When I saw Staci in Wyndall's, the world had stopped and she was all that had mattered. But there was a girl who I was already in love with, and normally couldn't keep my mind off of.

I don't know why I do these things. I mean, even I can admit that what I did to Tricia ranks up high there in the Asshole Hall of Fame, but I was just following my heart. Tricia had our entire futures mapped out, down to the names of our children, and the patterns on our china. The good china. I wasn't ready for that. Any of that. Casey was the anti-Tricia. She represented new and fresh. She represented a way out of that possible future with Tricia. And I had made my choice. But here I am, doing it all over again. Casey doesn't have our future planned out. She doesn't wait on my beck and call. She's a strong independent woman, and I think that's what drives me so crazy about her. Other than she being somewhat distant, her inability to ever write me a letter, and the lack of a physical component to our relationship, I am still madly in love with her. Hell, I couldn't wait to go up to visit her at school. *What the hell is wrong with me?*

I realized that I was still in the middle of the street as I pondered the intricacies of my love life. There was now a line of cars behind me, honking their disapproval of my tactics. I snapped out of it and took my foot off the brake. I drove the rest of the way back to work unsure of myself. I didn't like that feeling. It was not the Chad Breckenridge way.

I didn't get in any trouble for being late. Mr. Graves had covered my absence, and so I spent the rest of the day lamenting on how much I wasn't going to miss this place. As soon as I finished my work for the day, I handed in my notice on the second floor and headed home. My time at

Anderson's Department Store had come to an end. There was no parade, no parting gifts. Just a guy with a sore back walking to his car to rush home and wash the acrid smell of feet off for the last time.

After I was clean, I decided to call Casey and arrange for a trip up to see her. The thing with Staci had shaken me at my core, and I needed to recharge with Casey quickly, or I wouldn't, or couldn't be responsible for my actions.

"Hello?" a female voice asked over the phone. It didn't sound like Casey.

"Hi, umm, is Casey Martin available?" I asked.

"It's me, Chad," Casey said.

Great, thanks to my lunch date with Staci, I couldn't even recognize my girlfriend's voice anymore.

"Wow, it doesn't sound like you," I said. "Hey, I just quit Anderson's, and start a new job next week at Wyndall's. Now that I have some time off, I was hoping to be able to come up and see you."

"When?" she asked.

"Well, I was thinking tomorrow," I said. "I really miss you."

"I have class until noon, but after that I'm free."

"Great maybe we could have lunch together," I said. I don't know what it was with me and lunch dates all of the sudden. "Then I could drive back in the evening."

She gave me directions to campus and I told her that I'd see her tomorrow. We hung up and a wave of excitement washed over me. I couldn't wait to see Casey again. I tried to picture her in my mind, imagining a picnic lunch on the quad, while people around us tossed Frisbees and played acoustic music on their guitars, but all my brain could came up with was Staci's gorgeous blue eyes. I shook it off and tried again. I pictured Casey's long legs, and her perfect tan, but then that changed to Staci's sexy curves, and the way her smile made her whole face shine.

I was in trouble.

Miami College was a small liberal arts school located about thirty miles north of Deer Park in Miami, Indiana and the campus was set in a rural area surrounded by rolling hills and forests. The trees were just starting to turn, and the color was breathtaking. I figured that Casey and I could just enjoy the outdoors and then maybe take in a movie, or go to one of the local bars for a drink and maybe see a band play.

I had packed up the car and checked and double-checked to make sure that I had remembered everything. You would think I was taking a two-week vacation somewhere, not just traveling up the road some thirty miles. Hell, I wasn't even going to spend the night.

After a boring forty-five minute drive, which was basically straight north, and a few twists and turns when I actually got to campus, I turned into the parking lot across from Casey's dorm. I got out of my car and ran through the parking lot, hurtling a few bushes that separated the sidewalk from the front lawn that led up to the dorm. You would think I was training for the Olympics, and not just here to see my girlfriend.

I threw open the front doors of her dormitory and headed to one of the phone booths located just off the lobby. I dialed Casey's room and waited for while the phone continued to ring. Finally, she picked up.

"Hey good-looking," I said, doing a terrible Hank Williams impersonation. "What you got cooking?"

"Hey, sweety," she said. "I'm just changing my clothes, I'll be down in a second."

"Or," I said, playfully. "I can come up and help you, you know, change your clothes."

"This is an all-girls dorm."

I liked where this was going.

"You'd need an escort."

Definitely liked where this was going.

"I'm sure I can convince one of your lovely neighbors to escort me up," I said.

"By the time you found one, I'd be dressed," she said. "I'll be down in a sec." She hung up the phone before I could continue the banter. And so I would wait.

Fifteen minutes crawled by and as I sat on a hard wooden bench in the lobby and watched her dorm mates come and go, each giving a judging glance my way. Any one of these fine, beautiful women could have easily taken me upstairs to Casey's room, but judging by the looks they were giving me, I would be shot down instantly if I even asked. I saw a sign posted at the front desk that read:

No Boys without escort, and No Boys after 9:00 PM

What was this, Gloria Steinem University? This building was one big four-story chastity belt. I wouldn't let the Panty Nazis get me down. I was here to see my girlfriend, and no sign posted on a desk was going to prevent that from happening.

Finally, I saw Casey coming down the stairs and she looked as beautiful as ever. With each step she took, it seemed like she was moving in slow motion. I noticed each strand of hair move as if blown by a light summer breeze. Her blue eyes sparkled as two bright stars in the darkest of nights. She had on a sweatshirt that said, Miami College across her chest and a pair of blue jeans. I could also see her bosom jiggle and dance under the schools logo, it too in slow motion. God, I had missed her.

"You look fantastic," I said, standing up from the hard bench. "I mean absolutely beautiful!" I grabbed her hand and leaned in for a kiss. It was a peck, simple and innocent. After three weeks apart, I was hoping for more.

"Thanks," she said. I reached my hand out to her and she took it in hers. We walked hand-in-hand as she gave me a personalized tour of the campus. I saw the boy's dorms, and the different buildings, for which Casey called them "The School of Something or Another." There was a common area that was called, interestingly enough, the Commons. There was a small bookstore and a coffee shop. I saw plenty of grassy areas, like I had imagined, except nobody was throwing Frisbees, and there was nary a guitar player in sight. Everybody seemed to be hustling off in different directions, books in hand. This was nothing like the movies. This was like...school!?!

We stopped back at her dorm and she ran in to grab a bag of things that she had prepared for us to eat, and then we walked over to a park that was a few blocks away, off-campus. The air was warm for late-September and the sun was shining through the rapidly falling leaves. It was a perfect Indian summer day. We got to the park and Casey pulled a football out of her bag. I was taken aback. I knew that Casey had a "tom boy" quality to her, but I would never have expected her to want to toss a football around. I think this is what heaven is like. Seriously, it's described somewhere in the bible. In the New Testament. Sometime after the whole "love one another," line, or something like that. I just know it.

We began to toss the ball back and forth and that evolved into running passing patterns. I would pretend to take a hike from center, back up about five steps, and then throw the football to Casey who ran forward about ten yards and then did a crossing route. She had great hands as she caught every ball I threw to her. On occasion, the warm fall breeze would gently blow the ball out of Casey's reach, but she would make the necessary adjustment to still make the catch. I was falling in love with her all over again.

I continued to watch her gracefully run different routes and then pretend to score a touchdown as if she had just won the game. I just stood there observing her crossing an imaginary line and then jumping up and down holding the ball high into the air and yelling, "I'm the greatest of all time!" At that point, I couldn't agree with her more.

After about an hour or so of throwing the football, we decided to explore the little park a bit more. The trees were shedding their leaves with each push of breeze, and it was almost like walking through a storm of orange, red, green, and brown. We came upon a trench that sat below a line of sycamore trees. It was a few feet deep and over ten feet wide. Without saying a word to each other, we looked around and started to pick up the fallen leaves and toss them into the trench. It took us about twenty minutes but we gathered enough leaves to fill it up.

Casey and I just looked at each other as we slowly took about thirty paces back. We held hands, took a deep breath, smiled, and started running toward the tree line and the pit of leaves that we had created. We both leaped into the air, screaming like children, and then we crashed down into the pool of dead leaves. The impact caused them to explode out of the trench and scatter and we started anew, gathering and jumping, gathering and jumping. We must have jumped into the leaves a hundred times that day, and as other people walked by and saw us, they must have thought we were crazy. We probably were, but we didn't care.

After our final jump, we remained motionless at the bottom of the trench on a bed of dead leaves and we looked skyward while holding each other's hands. The afternoon had gone by so quickly as the bright fall day had started to turn into a gray sky with the surrounding trees starting to slightly sway back and forth in the cooling afternoon air. It seemed as if life had stopped for just a moment that day. We just held each other's hands and while looking at each other conveyed our love through our eyes and a twinkle of a smile. Not a word was spoken until Casey finally broke the silence.

"Forever, today," she said, not as much to me as to the whole world.

I continued to look into her eyes, and I wondered for a moment what she meant. But then I figured it out; this moment, this place in time, today, the love we had for each other; she wanted this day, this feeling, to last forever. This was Casey loving me "in a Casey sort of way," and it intoxicated my very soul. Her words erased any doubts that I had, any fears that had been gnawing at me ever since she had walked out of my apartment without telling me she loved me back. This was her response, just a few weeks late.

I didn't want to move from this spot. Ever. Forgotten were my jobs, and the apartments, and Marty. Hell, even the memories of Vietnam faded as I lay there next to her. Still, no words were spoken. We just lay there because I knew when we moved, this moment would be gone forever. I liked to say that I always "lived for the moment," but I wanted to live for this moment for the rest of my life.

I don't know how much time had passed before I squeezed her hand, telling her it was time to get her back to her dorm. I leaned over and gently kissed her on the lips. The kiss lasted longer than most, and then I slowly pulled away. We climbed out of the leaves and I leaned against one of the mighty sycamore trees and we immediately embraced each other. I looked her in the eyes.

"Forever, today," I said, echoing her sentiment.

She just smiled and rested her head on my shoulder. The moment was drawing to a close, and I wondered if I would ever feel that much love toward another person. I had what I'd always wanted here in my arms. What's-her-face back in Deer Park wasn't even on my mind. Maybe I was finally growing up. Maybe this was the moment that I would look back on twenty years from now and tell my kids about the day I realized that their mother was the one for me. This made me smile all the more so.

Since we never did have our picnic in the park, I was starving, and when Casey admitted the same, we set out to find a place to eat. North of campus we stumbled upon a place called Banyan's. It was your typical bar-and-grill-type of place, and with it being just after six on a Friday night, it wasn't crowded. Yet.

We grabbed a seat and I ordered a round of drinks and a couple of cheeseburgers with a large order of fries that we could share. Casey was only twenty, but she looked mature enough that she didn't get carded. We sat and talked while waiting for our food. The place was nice. It was foggy from the blue cloud of cigarette smoke that hung endlessly in the air, but there was a jukebox in the corner and three pool tables in the back.

"Do you play pool?" I asked Casey.

"I have," she said. "But I wouldn't say I'm any good at it."

"Good. It'll make it easier for me to beat you."

"Drink up, my friend. I'll just wait you out, and when you are sloppy drunk, I'll whip you. Bad."

I liked her attitude. She was definitely not the same girl that I had met in the gym all those years ago. College had sharpened her wit, and her tongue. Almost to the point that I felt that I had to watch what I said and did when I was around her. I've never had to do that with a girl before. I think I liked it.

The food came and we ate. By the third round of drinks, we started playing pool. The bar was filling up with college kids, and the jukebox was working hard to provide a rocking soundtrack to the night. After the fourth game of pool, and at least the same number of drinks, I glanced at my watch and saw that it was past ten! I still had to take Casey back to her dorm, drive 45 minutes home, and then get up to work my shift at Wyndall's tomorrow.

I paid the tab and we left Banyan's as an even larger crowd of students stood waiting to get in. I guess I figured out where everyone in Miami, Indiana goes for fun on a Friday night.

As we approached Casey's dorm, she turned to me very deliberately and stared for a long second or two.

"Hi," I said, turning to her and smiling.

"Do you want to spend the night with me?" she asked. "You've had a few drinks, and you could always get up early and drive home tomorrow."

I felt warmth in my heart, and a jump below my belt. Casey didn't believe in premarital sex and had been clear about remaining a virgin ever since the day I met her. But that was then and this was now. I didn't want to get ahead of myself. My brain was already swimming a little, so I tried to play it cool.

"Hell yes."

That wasn't cool, I thought.

I wasn't sure what to expect but I decided I would just follow her lead.

She looked at me and grabbed my hand. "I'm concerned about you driving home tonight, especially on the dark roads. I want you to stay with me tonight; my roommate is out of town so I have an extra bed."

I was really starting to absorb the fact that I would be spending the night with Casey Martin. FINALLY! I think I heard a chorus of angels sing praise, and all of the stars in the sky seemed to twinkle that much brighter. It was finally going to happ--

Wait, did she say extra bed?

"We have to figure a way to get you into the dorm and up into my room on the second floor," Casey said.

I dropped the subject of the extra bed and started to look around to see if there were any trees that I could use to climb up to her window, or hell, any window on the second floor. I'm sure I wasn't the first boy to ever try to get into the dorm after hours. And that would possibly explain the lack of trees anywhere near the building.

"I have an idea," she said. "Wait here and I'll be right back." Casey ran toward the building and disappeared through the front door. I stood, waiting, staring at the windows on the second floor. A group of frat guys walked by, talking and laughing.

"Don't even try it, my friend," one said out loud. "The housemother really busts balls." The entire group laughed as they went on their way. I nodded and smiled.

"Kiss my hairy ass," I said under my breath.

Casey burst through the front door carrying a paper grocery sack. She made her way over to me then grabbed my hand and led me around the side of the dorm, into the dark shadows.

"What're you doing?" I inquired.

"My roommate is in the theater department," she explained as she started pulling things out of the sack. "Put these on, and we'll sneak you up as a girl from Jones Hall."

I looked at what she had in her hand and didn't know if I should have laughed or turned around and ran away. She held a long, blond wig and a long, tie-dyed summer skirt. I looked into her eyes and waited for her to say that she was kidding. That she had drugged the housemother, or better yet, had killed her in her sleep. No such luck. If I wanted my night with Casey, I was going to have to do it in drag.

She has to be kidding, I thought.

She's not kidding, I realized.

Before I could finish my thought, Casey pulled the wig over my head and started to adjust it.

"Go put the skirt on," she explained. "I brought some makeup too."

"I'm glad I shaved this morning," I said. "If I hadn't, I would have looked like old Mrs. Taylor back at DPHS." Mrs. Taylor had a beard. Not a few patches of stubble, but a full-on beard. Of course, Mrs. Taylor was also a P.E. instructor who stood well over six feet tall and had more muscle in her arm than I did in my body. Long story short, nobody made fun of the Bearded Lady.

I pulled off my jeans and tried to figure out how to put on a skirt. Instinct told me to pull it up from my feet, like one big pants leg, but I had seen girls shimmy dresses over their heads and body. I checked the tag to see if there were instructions.

"C'mon, Chad," Casey hissed.

I set the skirt on the ground and stepped into the hole. I then pulled it up over my hips and secured it with a hook.

"You look beautiful," Casey mocked. "Now, hurry up with the blouse."

I ripped off my jacket and shirt and pulled on the top. I went to button it up, but the buttons were all wrong. They were on the wrong side. My fingers fumbled with each button, as I tried to snake it through each hole. Maybe this was why women were so hard to understand. All of their clothes were designed to be overly complicated. Which in turn made them overly complicated. Just as I was about to reward myself for solving a mystery that had stumped the world as far back as the time of Adam and Eve, Casey forcefully began to apply makeup to my face. She rubbed something on my cheeks, and then painted lipstick on my lips.

"You look like Faye Dunaway," she said. I didn't think there was any way I could look like Faye Dunaway. I didn't have the cheekbones to pull that off.

What the hell was I saying?

"Okay, that's it!" I exclaimed. "I'm not going through with this. It's embarrassing."

"No, no," Casey said. "Let me fix your hair and you'll be okay to just walk in and hurry up to my room." Somehow those words were not comforting at all, which really should have been the first clue that this wouldn't work. I'd get my balls busted by the housemother, and the cops would come and take me away, and those damn frat boys would be there laughing and pointing at me. But then again, I *was* about to spend the night with the love of my life.

"Okay, let's make this quick." No sooner than I finished my sentence, we ran for the front door and started to walk through the lobby to the main stairwell. As we approached the fire door, we heard a voice from the other end of the lobby calling out.

"Hey, Casey," the voice said. "Here's that book on depression-era economics that I borrowed." Casey stopped at the first step and turned to grab the book from the girl. I tried to turn and look at whoever was speaking, but the long, blond locks of the wig cut off most of my peripheral vision.

How do women do this?

I just kept on walking up the stairs. Upon reaching the second floor, I quickly recognized that I had absolutely no clue which room was Casey's and then noticed a couple of girls walking down the hall towards me. They were dressed in their nighties, and they had their hair pinned up. I stared at their long, beautiful legs as they walked and I just froze in place. This was the forbidden zone. In each of these rooms there were girls in varying states of undress, or better yet, lingerie! This was a smorgasbord of sex. I never wanted to leave this place. I had found my life's calling. I was meant to be here. This was heav--

Suddenly Casey appeared at my side and grabbed my arm, leading me down one hall into another until we rounded a corner and came to her room. The brass plate on the door said 242. She fumbled with the key and I tried to glance around to make sure the coast was clear, but again the damn wig was in the way. All I wanted to do was get inside, take off this ridiculous outfit, and then stay there until the next morning. Oh, and maybe have sex.

The door swung open and I literally jumped into the room. Once inside, I immediately took off the wig and threw it across the room followed by the blouse and skirt. It dawned on me that I was standing there naked with only my underwear, white socks and tennis shoes. Oh, and enough makeup on my face to tour with the Barnum & Bailey Circus. This was not the romantic start I was looking for! Casey appeared even more embarrassed, refusing to look in my direction.

"Which bed is yours?" I asked.

"That one," she said, pointing to the one on the left. I sat down and she handed me a washcloth with a healthy dollop of cold cream already mushed into the fabric. I went to work on my face, and shortly after, Little Miss Breckenridge went back to just being Chad.

While I was working on my face, Casey changed her clothes. I didn't even try to hide the fact that I was checking her out every step of the way. She stripped down to her bra and panties, and then pulled on a pair pajama bottoms and a large, white tee shirt. With the shirt on, she reached under and removed her bra. She did it in one smooth move. It would have taken me a good twenty minutes to navigate that course.

Once she was dressed, she flipped on the television and climbed into her bed. She looked at me and patted the area next to her.

Houston, we have mission Go!

I climbed in next to her and gave her a kiss.

"Thanks for coming up," she said. "I had a really great time."

"Me too," I said. "I love you."

"I know you do," she said and then returned my kiss. I don't think she had ever kissed me that deeply. We continued to make out for good while, and then settled into just lying there together, watching an old black and white movie starring Spencer Tracy. Shortly after the movie started, Casey fell asleep in my arms and I was starting to nod off as well. The entire day had been so perfect and I had spent it with the girl of my dreams. As I reflected on the time we'd spent together, I found myself falling into a deep sleep. I wanted this to be my life. Now and forever. This was love. And the fact that I went through all of that to get to her room and we didn't even have sex told me that this was real. I don't think I had ever been happier as I slid further and further into a deep sleep. A peaceful, wonderful sleep.

I was awakened by a sharp blade of sunlight that shined through Casey's window and stabbed me in the back of my eyeballs. I rolled over and looked at my watch. It was just after eight o'clock in the morning and my head was throbbing due to the alcohol that we'd consumed the night before. It wasn't a full-fledged hangover, thank God. But it still ached in my brain and was mildly uncomfortable. Honestly, that was the least of my worries. The first thing I always have to do when I wake up in the morning is to empty my bladder. And since I was in Casey's room, on Casey's floor, in Casey's dormitory, I didn't know where the restroom was located, and I was a guy in an all-girls residence. I really didn't have time to debate what

I had gotten myself into. I had a gallon of processed beer trying to find its way out of my body and I needed to do something fast!

I slowly slipped out of bed as to not wake her and tried to look for my clothes. The morning fog began to lift and I remembered that I had left my jeans, shirt and jacket in a pile, behind a shrub, on the side of the building! I didn't have time to address that little problem, as there were more immediate needs to be dealt with.

I proceeded to walk to the door. I stopped and listened for anyone on the other side, and then I slowly opened it, sticking my head out to see if the coast was clear. I didn't see anybody in the hallway, nor did I hear anybody stirring on the floor.

GOOD!

I stepped out of her room and quickly made my way down the hallway. I stopped at the corner, and carefully reconnoitered the connecting hallway like Sean Connery in any James Bond film. I turned the corner and nearly ran down the length of the hall until I came to a "T" junction. This time, I didn't even bother to look and just turned the corner and ran. I held myself in my hand, as if subconsciously, it was helping me hold everything in. I finally came across what appeared to be a bathroom. There was no signage outside, and that made sense. Why differentiate between boys and girls if only girls were allowed on the floor. I stepped in and noticed that restrooms for women are like fancy hotel suites! They have soft, comfortable-looking couches with end tables and a long counter with a large mirror in the entry area. I admit I was a little confused. I thought that maybe I was in somebody else's room. I didn't see any stalls or commodes, but I heard what sounded like somebody using the shower. I started to make my way across the entry area where I turned a corner and saw what was the ingress to the shower area. Past the showers were the toilets.

You have to be kidding me, I thought.

I now heard three or four voices coming from the shower area.

"I'm done," a voice said. "I'll see you back at the room."

I heard the water turn off in one of the shower stalls, but others were still being used. That meant there was more than one girl in here with me. Okay now, as many times as I had dreamed of this scenario in my lifetime, this wasn't a dream. This was DefCon One, and things were about to get messy. There were possibly naked girls just a few feet away from me, and here I was, in my underwear and socks, literally holding myself in my hand and doing what my brother Alex had always called the "Indian Pee-Pee Dance."

I couldn't risk trying to cross the showers to the toilets and getting caught, so I did the only thing I could. I jumped into the nearest shower and pulled the curtain closed behind me, just as a girl walked by. I saw her bare backside and that she had her head wrapped in a towel. I wanted to stare, to lose myself in the perfect rear end as it *va-va-voomed* past me, but time was of the essence. I pushed the showerhead away from me and turned on the water. Before one drop of water from the showerhead hit the tiled floor, I was out of my undies and pounding a powerful stream right into the drain. I did everything I could to not moan out load, as the feeling of relief was incredible. I didn't look at my watch when I first started, but guessed that I had been going for at least four minutes. My bladder sighed as it emptied. When I was done and I had shaken off every last drop, I turned off the shower. My socks were soaking wet with a combination of urine and shower water. I peeled them off and left them. Let the maid figure out how a pair of men's socks ended up in the girl's shower. I peeled back the shower curtain and checked both ways before stepping out.

I started back toward the ornate entryway of the restroom when the door swung open and a girl stood there holding a plastic basket in her hand. She was looking down the hall, and just started to turn her head in my direction when I bolted. I had never run so fast in my life. My naked feet slapped at the tiled floor as I ran back to the shower area and past it, and literally jumped into the nearest toilet stall. I slammed the door shut and latched it. I then sat on the toilet, and pulled my legs up to my chest. I could feel my heart pounding on my knee.

"I think I saw someone run past the showers to use the toilet," I heard a girl say.

"Who was it?" another asked.

"I don't know but it was either a really ugly girl or a guy!"

"Go see who it was."

"I'm not coming out until we're sure it wasn't a guy."

I heard footsteps coming towards the toilet area then suddenly the door to my stall was jiggled as if someone was trying to open the door. I froze like a perverted toilet edition of Rodin's, *The Thinker*. My door stopped jiggling and I heard one of the other girls say something.

"Let's get out of here. I don't want to know who's in here."

"Maybe we should call the housemother."

My heart stopped. I heard the girls leave the restroom, as I could hear the door shut behind them and the room got quiet. I allowed myself to take a quick breath and I immediately jumped off the toilet and made my way to the door as fast as I could. The last thing I wanted was to be trapped in an enclosed room with a housemother. Especially one who is publically known to bust balls.

I ran out of the restroom and looked both ways before spilling out into the hallway. I was in full Jim Phelps mode. In fact, I could hear the theme from *Mission: Impossible* in my head as I ran down each hallway and rounded each corner. Then it dawned on me. I had no idea what room was Casey's!

I tried to remember the room number from the night before, but I was a little drunk, and had been under the impression that I was about to have sex. The room number was the furthest thing in my mind at the time. I started to panic, as all of the hallways looked exactly the same.

Just how big was this damn building?

Was the room number 246? I remembered something in the two-forties. I heard voices coming from the stairwell and they were heading my way. I ran to room 246 and I panicked. I turned the handle and the door opened. I jumped in just as the people in the stairwell made it to the second floor. I shut the door and exhaled. I slowly turned around and quickly saw that this was not Casey's room. Lying in bed in front of me was a topless girl who had slowly started to sit up. She rubbed her eyes as if she was trying to wake up and as her eyes adjusted to the morning light, she saw me, naked except for my underwear, standing in her room.

The world stopped turning. Birds stopped flying in mid-flight. Leaves that had dislodged from the trees outside on the quad and had begun to fall to the earth literally froze in mid-air. I literally saw my life roll before my eyes, like a Saturday afternoon nickel movie at the Rivoli Theater. The film wasn't all that great.

"Who the hell are you?" the girl demanded as she bunched the sheets up around her naked figure. I could try and tell her that she was only dreaming, or that I was an angel, sent here to watch over and protect her. Instead, I blurted out, "I'm so sorry, I have the wrong room. I was looking for Casey Martin's room."

She looked at me with shock painted on her face. She finally spoke, and in a very annoyed voice.

"She's in room 242."

"Thank you," I said. "I apologize for bothering you." I turned to leave.

"Hey," she called out, as I was turning the door handle. "What's your name?"

NOW she wants to talk to me?

"Uh...Chad," I responded, then as naturally as I could, the charm turned on like a fountain. "And you are--wait, I'd really love to stay and chat, but I have to go now. Sorry!" I opened the door and jumped back into the hallway. I figured that this young, gorgeous, NAKED, freshman girl woke up and saw a great-looking guy in the peak of physical shape, barely dressed and standing in her room. She must have thought that God had answered her prayers. And under any other circumstance, I probably would have stayed there and engaged in conversation. However, this was definitely not the time to be doing that.

I slipped back into Casey's room without any other problems. As I closed the door behind me, I saw that she was just waking up.

"Sorry, honey," I whispered. "I had to use the restroom."

Casey squinted her eyes and stretched. "Where'd you go? There isn't a boys bathroom in this building?"

"Well, let's just say I've journeyed to a place that I had never journeyed to before, and discovered a world seldom seen by the eyes of men. Yes, friends and neighbors, I have seen the Promised Land!"

I gave her a brief recap of the morning's events, carefully leaving out the naked girls in the shower, and the beautiful set of breasts in the room down the hall. I had to be at work by eleven, so I pulled on the skirt, blouse and the wig and leaned down to give her a kiss.

"I had a great time," I said. "I will call you and come back up as soon as I can." We kissed again, and I gave her a long, heartfelt hug.

"You can pick up these clothes behind the shrub outside," I said as I fixed the wig in the mirror and opened the door.

"Does this skirt make my butt look big?" I asked and Casey laughed. She was still laughing when I shut her door and made straight for my clothes outside and the long drive home.

Chapter 18

After six months of working in a grocery store, I decided that it wasn't the life for me. I liked meeting people, but really, I got paid a few dollars an hour to bag groceries, and stock cans of corn and peas on a shelf. It wasn't exactly rocket science, and I felt I needed more of a challenge.

That was when I decided it was time to use the GI Bill and go to college. I was going to let Uncle Sam take care of me, after risking my life to take care of him.

Marty had also been looking for something more. He was still clearly affected from his time in Vietnam. He had constant bags under his eyes from lack of sleep, and he even took a late-night job as a disc jockey at a local radio station. He had the perfect voice for a career as a record spinner. In fact, his Jewish features were so comically prominent, that he resembled Woody Allen from the film, *Take the Money and Run*, a movie that he and I had watched while in training school at Coronado. A bunch of us caught the film off base, and I truly expected the guys to rag him because of the uncanny resemblance. Luckily for Marty, they either missed it entirely or just didn't care. Though Marty and I had completely different work schedules (me in the day, he at night), we still made time for each other, even though it could get very depressing. Hanging out with Marty was like going to one long funeral. The kind that even Catholics would complain about.

Every time that he and I would get together for beers or dinner, he would constantly bring up guys that we had served with. Guys that didn't make it home. I knew that he was haunted by them. They were our friends, our brothers, and I guess I was able to just move on while Marty carried the burden of their deaths like an open wound that wouldn't heal. I tried my best to forget, but Marty couldn't do that. So, in a weird reversal of roles, I talked him into enrolling with me at Indiana University in Bloomington.

Marty had always been the "smart one," and I thought that an education, along with the constant flow of beer, broads, and bacchanalia would get him back on track. I think we all had high hopes for Marty Green back in high school, and if I didn't do something drastic for my friend now, he wouldn't last much longer. Luckily, he was on-board with my idea (he didn't even refer to it as a "scheme," so I knew I was on to something here.)

Although I had originally wanted to go to Miami College, which was a private school, to be with Casey, I knew my grades and my finances weren't going to allow that to happen. I'd been up to see her a couple of times after that first visit, so as long as I was still geographically close to her, I figured it would work out. Bloomington was a couple of hours south of Indianapolis, and a couple of hours west of Miami. Either way I looked at it, I was two hours from a good time.

I enrolled at Indiana University in the fall of 1973, and immediately got into the swing of things. Marty and I were able to get a dorm room together, because by now, after the navy, and our place in Deer park, he and I living together seemed like the norm. We were like an old married couple. We'd talk about things that happened to us each day while I watched TV and he read the newspaper, and we didn't have sex, just like old married couples.

After a few weeks of classes, I pledged a fraternity, Alpha Phi Omega. I figured it would be a fun way to pass my time in college. I'd heard stories of the craziness that happens at frat houses, and right now I needed some crazy in my life.

Casey came to see me several times during my first semester, and I drove to Miami to see her when I could. I felt that she had put us on hold, and I definitely wasn't doing anything to change that. I was busy with pledging, and my studies, and making time for her became harder and harder. Since I was pledging a fraternity, she in turn had pledged a sorority on her campus at Miami. We were both experiencing the Greek life, which for me meant ridiculous parties that lasted for days, and for her, it meant being invited to those parties. We were together but separate. Together in spirit, but separated by a hundred miles. Such was my college life.

As my pledgeship with Alpha Phi Omega intensified, and Casey's full plate of sorority events and third year coursework began to bog her down, we were relegated to phone calls from community pay phones at odd hours and promises to see each other very soon. I got back to writing her weekly, sometimes twice or three times a week if my classes were boring. But as was the case before, I never received a letter in return. At least she was consistent.

I had taken a part-time job at a grocery store in Bloomington. My boss at Wyndall's had set it up for me. So I was working on top of everything else (still stocking cans of corn and bagging groceries. I had come so far in my life!). So my daily dance card was filled, and there were no signs of it letting up anytime soon. I don't think I had ever really understood the term "stretched too thin" until my first semester in college.

It was the last week in September, and classes were in full swing. It was also the beginning of a time most affectionately called, Hell Week. Now, it wasn't called Hell Week, because it was all wine and roses. Hell Week was the very end of your pledging of a fraternity. This was the time when your brothers pulled out the big guns (sometimes, literally! I'd heard a few years back that a pledge at Purdue had to play "Russian roulette" to get his pin) and the pledges, or "pukes" as we were called behind closed doors, were put through an veritable Olympics of ridiculous stunts and outrageous pranks.

And for the record, the festivities never lasted an entire week. It was called "Hell Week" because all of the campus fraternities wrapped up their pledge initiations during this seven-day period.

Friday was the start of my Hell Week at the Alpha Phi Omega house, so I was not so anxious for the week to be over. Between school and work,

Friday had arrived all too soon and all of the pledges were to be at the house at five o'clock sharp. I wasn't sure what to expect during the next few days, but anticipated being used and abused by the brothers of the fraternity. To be honest, there was nothing these guys could throw at me that would be any worse than what I went through in boot camp or in Vietnam, but I wanted to make them think I was concerned about their hazing rituals, so I faked worry. I mean, drinking pigs blood while standing naked in front of a bunch of guys can't hold a candle to having bullets whiz by your head as you are boating down a river in South East Asia. I wasn't worried at all.

I arrived at the fraternity house about ten minutes early only to find that I was the last pledge to arrive. The other pledges were standing in a line on what was a makeshift stage looking out into the lobby area that was filled with folding chairs. Most of those chairs were filled with members of the fraternity. I was asked to put my belongings in the pile in the foyer of the house. There were already piles from my fellow pledges so I sat my stuff down and took my place in line. Then nothing happened. After waiting for what felt like half an hour, Brian Dillon, our pledge trainer, stormed over to us and started yelling--well, screaming--at the top of his lungs.

"OKAY, ALL OF YOU PUKES GET IN LINE AND STAND AT ATTENTION!"

It didn't matter that we had been in line and we had been standing at attention. Brian, who had been our best friend for the last couple of weeks, was now our enemy. His screaming brought cheers and yelling from the brothers seated in the rows. There were current brothers seated there, as well as legacies that went back centuries judging by the white hair on some of their heads. It was Friday night and they wanted a show.

And we were it.

I tried my best to keep from laughing at Brian's attempt at intimidation. I guess when you are being yelled at by a muscled FPO while doing pushups in the yard, in Chicago, in February, a little shouting by an economics major who stood just over five feet tall and weighed one-twenty wet just couldn't compare. But I remained stern. This wasn't part of a training program to prepare you for combat, but this was a college kid on an ego trip.

We were ordered to strip down to our underwear and told to run outside behind the fraternity house. We did so and were met out back by another brother. We were each given a pot and pan and were told to parade around the house, in our underwear, while banging the pots and pans together and screaming: "We are pledges, the scum of the earth and we love to eat dog poop." We did this parade of humiliation until the sun set behind the tall trees of the Hoosier National Forest.

After the sun was down, we were led to a large black iron kettle that was hung over a fire pit. One of the fraternity brothers, who was dressed in a dark hooded robe, stood next to the kettle, stirring whatever was inside. A crowd of brothers stood around us and I could hear their whispers, asking each other what was in the pot. I was certain that I didn't want to know. The hooded brother made some speech that I didn't even pay attention to, and then each pledge was given an empty bowl. We marched by the kettle and the hooded brother ladled a serving of whatever it was into our bowls.

Now, in Vietnam, I ate some pretty weird stuff. A lot of times, we'd go off base for drinks and then in a drunken challenge to each other, we'd all eat something strange. Vietnam was a whole new world, with new foods, and customs. In fact, I'm not sure, but I think I may have eaten dog testicles sometime while in country.

Vodka makes you do bad things.

Once our bowls were filled, we were commanded to eat the soup. Actually, the exact term used was, "Lick it clean, puke faces." I tipped the bowl into my mouth and held my breath as a swallowed. If I had to guess, I would have said it was dirty dish water, though in the dancing light of the fire, it looked greenish and had a frothy head. It was terrible, by the way.

After our "dinner," we were herded back into the house and led to the showers where we were hosed down with ice-cold water shot at us from fire hoses. It was actually painful as the stream of water tore into my skin. After that initial blast, the cold didn't even bother me. But the pain of impact hurt and I was starting to become annoyed. This exciting evening of sharing and bonding with other like-minded men had become a night of hell. And for the first time, I worried about whatever was coming up next.

After succumbing to the icy cold shower and being constantly yelled at and berated by people my age or younger, we were all marched down to the basement where we found beach towels laid out and lined up on the floor of the kitchen eating area. Each towel had our individual name on it. We were commanded to get to our respective towel, to lie down, and to go to sleep. This was boot camp all over again, except the food from the kettle was probably better. I was used to this, but I felt sorry for my pledge brothers.

The following day brought more of the same torture and humiliation. We were yelled at, publicly humiliated, made to sing songs while marching up and down outside the houses on sorority row, forced to recite historical fraternity information when asked, deprived of all but basic food and water, and that was all before noon. That night, once again, we were fed something, this time from a mop bucket, hosed off and led back to the kitchen to sleep. We were like sheep, each one of us following the other. If boot camp was meant to break a man down so he could be rebuilt to military standards, what the hell is the purpose of fraternal hazing? I pondered that question as I lay on my multicolored beach towel and tried to sleep, all the while continuing to shiver from the freezing shower we had just received. One of my pledge brothers, Nick, had the great idea to use the towel to dry himself off. We all followed his lead.

Nick would go on to become a doctor.

The night was long and uncomfortable, and it was reminding me a little too much of my time in the navy, and of Vietnam. What I had once thought would be my strength in the hazing ritual had become an enemy, as the memories being drudged up weren't always good. And thinking of the bad times just made me angry and scared. When I had originally decided to pledge Alpha Phi Omega, I'd tried to get Marty to pledge with me, but he'd said that he had enough of organizations and declined. If he had been here now, on the towel next to me, he probably would have snapped and pulled a Charles Whitman. I could clearly imagine him perched on top of the clock tower at Franklin Hall, shooting people with his standard issue M16.

I was really worried about my friend.

The next morning, we were awakened by several brothers who poured tomato juice on us. I stood up and gave them a look that made them aware that they were approaching a line with me they may not want to cross. The look I got back made me realize they had gotten my message, and I noticed subtle changes in the way they treated me as opposed to the rest of the pledges for the rest of Hell Week.

As we stood on our towels, drenched in tomato juice, we were told to go upstairs and to get our clothes on that had been collected after we were ordered to strip to our underwear. Thank God, I thought. Now we would get a warm shower and be allowed to put some clothes on. We marched upstairs and saw that our clothes had been neatly folded in respective piles and set on a folding banquet table. We found our piles and before we could do anything further, Brian reappeared to tell us that we were to put our clothes on without showering or cleaning ourselves off. Reluctantly, I slid into my slacks and pulled on my white, starched, button-up shirt. The tomato juice bled through the fabric, literally ruining what had been my best dress shirt. Again, I could feel my anger rising.

After we were dressed, we were subjected to more of the same humiliation, yelling, and menial tasks that took all day. At the end of the day's festivities, we were given an opportunity to take a warm shower. But there was a catch. There was always a catch. We were allowed a hot shower however; it could only be taken in a shower at one of the houses on sorority row. It was late in the afternoon on Sunday, so that meant that in all likelihood the houses would be well populated with sorority girls studying for a new week of classes, and to take a hot shower, we would risk running into wet, naked co-eds, angry housemothers, or worse, the police.

Being twenty-two years old, and standing with a bunch of nineteen year olds, each full of freshman hormones, we all looked at each other and in silent agreement decided to go for it.

It was like a mission, and since I was the older one and had military experience, I was looked upon as a leader. And since this mission involved the possibility of naked girls, I immediately took command. We were broken down into three groups and I grabbed my group of pledges and mapped out a strategy, giving each pledge a job to do. Once everyone knew their role, we immediately headed over to the Delta Pi house, the one house we felt we had the best chance for success. The Delta Pi girls were on the heavy side and were more studious and if a guy got caught in their shower, they would see it as a gift from God. The only downside here was that if we lost a man in the Delta Pi house, he might actually get eaten alive. It was worth the risk.

The tomato juice had long since dried into our clothes, and we looked like complete bloody messes, as if we had just come from a massacre. We quickly and quietly maneuvered behind houses, trees, and bushes until we arrived at the Delta Pi house. We huddled behind some thick bushes at the corner of the house while I updated the mission with new strategies and new assignments. The sun was beginning to set, which would give us limited cover of darkness, but it was also starting to get cold, so we had to act fast. There didn't seem to be much activity in the front of the house so we went around to the back and tried to peek into whatever windows that weren't covered in curtains.

With our limited recon, a decision was made to just run in as fast as we could; strip down, shower, and get the hell out of there. If there were girls in the shower, then we both would have to just share the soap.

"Are we going in as winners, or are we going to be losers?" I asked, trying to rally my troops, but using a very hard whisper. I saw the looks in their eyes and knew that each of these men were ready for the task at hand.

"Okay, let's do it on three," I paused for effect. I was having fun, and what was the worse that could happen? A fat girl would get her prayers answered, and we would get clean. Everybody wins. "One, two, three!" And off we ran.

We hopped over the bushes, and charged up the front porch steps. As leader, I was in front, so I threw open the front door, and the squad poured in. We ran across the lobby and then upstairs to the second floor. Fortunately, no one had seen us. When we reached the second floor, we ran down the hall and found the restroom whereupon we stripped down naked and got into the shower. The water felt amazing. There were six of us in the group, and the shower only had five heads, so we had to move fast for all of us to get clean. A bar of soap was passed around, and since it was already in the shower when we got there, we all had a lovely lavender scent. Whatever the scent, it sure beat the smell of stagnant tomato juice. We were so focused on getting in and out of that shower, and out of that sorority house, that we didn't even notice whether there were any girls in the lobby, the hallway, or even the restroom. So, when we heard a scream, it really shocked us. Then that scream turned into several screams, and I turned to see three very large girls, completely naked, and ready to shower. The screams didn't stop, but we knew our time was up.

"Thank you, ladies," I said as my group collectively exited the shower and ran back the way we came. When we got to the top of the stairs, I heard what sounded like car engine rumbling to life, but realized it was the housemother who was barreling up the stairs. The woman--using the term loosely--looked like she could play linebacker for the Baltimore Colts. Heck, who knows, maybe she had. Regardless, she was intimidating so we needed another plan. Grabbing our clothes with no time to put them on, I led the troops to the window at the end of the hall and I slid it open.

"Go, Go, Go," I encouraged as my soldiers each went through the open window and jumped down to the bushes below. I was last out, but not before the housemother reached for me to grab my arm. She missed the arm, but got a full grip of my wet, naked butt cheek. I jumped and for a second, I honestly thought that she was going to be able to hold me up by my ass. I landed in the bushes below as my troops had already dispersed and making their way back to the Alpha Phi Omega house. I turned to the open window on the second floor and standing at full--albeit naked--attention, saluted the housemother.

"Next time, ma'am," I called up to the window, "I must insist that you buy me dinner first!" Before she could respond, I too ran away into the darkness, clean and naked, and finally having fun.

When I finally arrived back at the house, I regrouped with my squad. We were laughing so hard, and it felt good to be clean, even though most of us were holding our naked selves in our hands. We entered the house and learned that we were the only group to actually get a shower. The other groups of pledge brothers had made their way to various sorority houses, but just couldn't get up enough courage to actually enter and get a shower. As a reward, we were able to put on new underwear. I think they did this as to not stare out our bare asses any longer. A few of the senior year fraternity brothers gave us each a high five and gave us a hand towel to dry off with, even though the sprint through sorority row had pretty much taken care of that. Once the excitement of our success had died down, we went back to being pledge pukes, and that entailed another night of hazing. Once again, after the torture and abuse, we were led down to the basement for what would be another uncomfortable night's sleep. We were told that the final night of Hell Week would be spent interacting with another fraternity, and then the lights went out. Although we were curious as to what that meant, we were so tired we just got on our towels and tried to go to sleep.

The final morning came all too soon as we were awakened by three brothers banging pot lids together as loud as they could. Even though the "alarm" had jarringly pulled me out of a troubled sleep, this was the final day and relief was coming soon. I did have a fear that one of the fatties at the Delta Pi house would have recognized me, and called the cops. What would Marty say when they beat down the door of our dorm looking for me? I stayed with this thought for the rest of the morning, even as we were forced to eat "Butt Waffles," which were frozen waffles that we had to warm up to eat by pulling our pants down and sitting on them, and then we had to perform a play about the history of the fraternity, while dressed in drag, and on our knees. It was called, "Conquests." The rest of the day progressed with the usual threats, beatings, and other fun male bonding exercises.

At five-thirty we were once again lined up in front of the entire house of brothers. Our final task was about to be revealed. All week we were told to prepare for this one special undertaking, one that would bring pride and respect to not only ourselves, but our fellow fraternity brothers, their children, and their children's children. We all stood in line waiting with bated breath. Finally, Brian Dillon reappeared and in his hand, he held a scroll. The house went quiet as he unrolled the paper scroll and began to read.

"Hear ye, Hear ye," he said. "Pledge Pukes, we have but one more sacred mission to be performed by each of you as a group; one body. This mission will be at great personal risk, but will earn each of you the right to call yourselves brothers of Alpha Phi Omega. Should you not return from this mission, we will ceremoniously bury your remains in the backyard, next to the tree that Clyde, our beloved house dog, has urinated on for the past ten years.

"At the stroke of six o'clock you all are to go over to the Sigma Alpha Pi house. There, in their front yard, you will find expensive, woodcarvings of their letters proudly presented. Your mission is to burn those letters to the ground!"

The house erupted in cheers and huzzahs. Brian held up his hands to bring the room under control.

"This is your last mission, pukes, and failure is not an option. To fail is to bring shame to this house. To fail is to ensure that you never, ever wear the sacred pin of Alpha Phi Omega. In fact, if you fail, do not even bother coming back here. We will mail your belongings back to you, or your next of kin."

I stood there and listened to Brian go on and on. Of all the misdemeanors I had performed during these last few days, arson would be a real crime. A felony. As that thought began to set in, I looked around and saw that my pledge brothers must have been thinking the same thing. They collectively stood with mouths wide open and their heads listing to one side, as if trying to comprehend what they had heard. Then Stan Markey, our pledge class president, stepped forward.

"Let's do it!" he shouted. "Let's burn it to the ground!" That got the house up in arms again. I wasn't shocked. I'd gotten to know Stan during the pledgeship, and he was probably the one person who you'd figure to drop out of school, enlist in the marines, and hit the frontlines running and gunning, while enemy fire whizzed by his head. His favorite line to say when given a task was "Let's do it!" I'd personally heard him say it six times, at least, during our time together pledging Alpha Phi Omega. And unlike me, he relished the military, and since this mission didn't involve naked girls--fat or otherwise--I let him assume the leadership role.

So, we were allowed to dress (finally) and at six o'clock sharp the doors of the house flew open and off we went, like a pack of wolves searching for food. We arrived at the Sigma Alpha Pi house and saw our objective: the letters SAP (which was appropriate for our little band of idiots when you think about it) were right in the front yard. Each letter stood approximately five feet tall with a width of about four feet and a depth of about one foot. I think that all of us in the pledge group, save for Stan, started to question the risk of life in prison versus a life of APO brotherhood. Before it could even be debated, Stan pulled out a can of lighter fluid from his pocket.

"You carry that with you?" I asked incredulously.

"Yeah, doesn't everybody?" he said as he smiled at me. It sent a chill down my spine. Then without any thought or hesitancy, Stan walked right up to the letters and began dowsing them with the lighter fluid. There was no plan, no recon, no scouting. At any time, the SAP guys could come bursting out of their house and then there would be hell to pay. I stared at the front of the house, praying that nobody would come out. In my peripheral vision, I saw Stan light a match (which apparently he also carried with him at all times) and then the SAP erupted in a bright ball of flame. I didn't wait to see what happened. As night turned to day at the SAP house, I turned and bolted back to our house. For a second, I actually though of just running back to my dorm. I could explain to Marty what had happened, then wait for my belongings to be mailed to me. Luckily, other pledges were running with me, and I could already hear the screaming of the fire engine sirens.

We finally made our way back to the Alpha Phi Omega house and as we stood on the porch, sucking in air to catch our breaths, things started to calm down and the joy of the completion of Hell Week began to set in. Bobby Porter, another pledge brother, tapped me on the shoulder.

"Where's Stan?" he asked. "Has anybody seen Stan?" We all looked around and couldn't find Stan. My immediate thought was that he got caught, so I grabbed another pledge and headed back towards the Sigma Alpha Pi house to see what was going on. I learned in the navy that you never leave a man behind.

As we came within sight of the SAP house, we saw Stan working to help the firemen put out the burning letters. I didn't know what to think.

Five minutes ago I would have pegged Stan Markey as an arsonist, but here he was working to put out a fire. A fire that he himself had started. I was so confused. Whatever was happening on the SAP lawn, I wasn't going to hang around and wait to be discovered. We returned to the Alpha Phi Omega house and I told everyone what we had seen. A few minutes later, Stan arrived, smelling like a cookout, and with ruined, sooty clothes.

"What the hell was that about?" I asked.

"I've always wanted to be a fireman," he said. In my mind's eye, I could clearly see Stan sitting in a firehouse years later screaming, "Let's do it!" every time an alarm went off. Stan would, in fact, go on to have a career as a firefighter, stationed in Atlanta, Georgia. He put out fires until he retired at 55. No word if he started any of them.

We were all exhausted after Hell Week, and I for one couldn't wait for the pinning ceremony. We were no longer pledge pukes, but seasoned veterans of ridiculous hazing and now, equal Alpha Phi Omega Brothers. After the pinning ceremony, we did some hardcore drinking and celebrating with our new fraternity brothers and the white-haired alumni that had come into town for the ceremony. Two days later, I finally woke up, took the hottest shower on record, got dressed, and then called Casey. After all of that, all I wanted to do was to see my girlfriend. If a man could truly crave a woman, I was craving Casey.

"I can't," she said over the phone. "I've got mid-terms coming up, and next weekend, a bunch of us are going to Indy to protest President Nixon at the capital building." Her protesting started while I was in Vietnam and when the war ended, she struggled to find other things to protest. Luckily, something the press called "Watergate" happened, and she had her new pet cause. And honestly, I hadn't minded. Her activism hadn't interfered with "us" before, but it was starting to now. I was disappointed, but that was how our relationship had gone lately, with not much time to see each other. I would be lying if I said that it didn't bother me.

"Maybe the weekend after?" I bargained. I really needed to see her.

"I have sorority stuff," she said. I swallowed the anger that was rising in my being.

"Well, let me know if you find some time for me this year," I snapped.

"I gotta go to work." I hung up the phone and went back to my room to finish getting ready. I headed off to work for the first time in a week stressed and angry. When I got back home after my shift, I found a message that Staci had called. The timing couldn't have been more perfect.

Chapter 19

Staci had started at Indiana University the same time that I did, and we had stayed in touch. Nothing beyond a friendship had happened to this point, and I was fine with it. My feelings for Casey seemed real, and in what I can only describe as me growing up, I decided to pursue those feelings, and not just run off with every cute blonde that gave me the time of day. But a man has his limits, and my "girlfriend" never had time for me, or for us. That left a void in my life, and I was never a big fan of voids.

One day after my conversation with Casey, during a break at the grocery store, I picked up the phone and gave Staci a call. I thought since I'd had a rather interesting, and exhausting weekend, I deserved a break. I called the number to her sorority house, and after a few exchanges with random female voices, where the phone's receiver was just passed around to almost every girl in that house, Staci eventually got on the line.

"Hey Staci," I said. "It's Chad. I just got your message that you called. How've you been?"

"Hey, Chad," she said. "I would have expected to hear from you long before now." It was almost as if she had followed me to school in the hopes that we would begin dating. That was crazy, right?

"I thought that if I came to IU, we'd see so much more of each other."

Do what now?

"I'm just kidding," she said. "How're things?"

"Just working and going to class," I said. We carried on with the small talk for a little while longer, and my mind began to think in what I have since referred to as "The Old Chad Way." Casey was a hundred miles away, doing who knows what, and I was here, celebrating my survival of Hell Week, and my new life as a fraternal brother of the Alpha Phi Omega house.

I deserve to have some fun, I thought. *And if it wasn't going to be with Casey, then Staci would do.*

"Well, how'd you like to go out Saturday night and maybe catch a movie or something?" I was getting sick of waiting on Casey. I was getting sick of waiting for her to love me like I loved her. We'd never had sex, and I had written her a novel's worth of letters, only to have never received a reply. Not one letter back to me. If this was a horse race, then my relationship with Casey Martin was the one pony last out of the gate, the one who stumbled around each turn, and ended up not even finishing. At the end, that horse would be taken out back and dealt with. It may have just been the exhaustion of pledging, work, and classes, but maybe my relationship should be taken out back...and be dealt with.

"I would love to," she replied quickly. Too quickly, I thought. "Can you pick me up at my sorority house?"

"Sure," I said. "I'll stop by around six o'clock."

"Okay then, it's a date."

And it was a date. Seeing it any other way, or even trying to justify it any other way was wrong. This man was sick of waiting. It was time to bet on a new horse. I finished my lunch and headed back to work with a new spring in my step. The rest of the week was spent attending classes and hanging out at the fraternity house with the brothers as I waited for the weekend, and for my new life, to arrive.

Saturday morning came in like a lark, and I rose from my bed refreshed and ready for a great day, and hopefully better evening. It had been an exhausting week and I was looking forward to just relaxing and catching a football game on television until it was time to pick up Staci. It was nice to just sit and do absolutely nothing but watch football with my brothers. Yeah, I had spent three grueling days in hell for the right to sit on a couch eating potato chips while watching guys try to move an inflated pig carcass up and down a field of grass. This was the life. Before I knew it, it was five o'clock and I had to start getting ready for my date.

I arrived at the Gamma house and the place looked like it was packed with what looked like an official sorority function. Maybe a dance, or social, or something. There were girls on the porch, and I could see them through the front windows. For Staci to forego a sorority event to go out with me made me feel special. More special than Casey had ever made me feel. Tonight was going to be a great night.

I pulled up in front of the house, and even though cars lined the street on both sides, I found a parking space immediately in front. The campus fraternities called this spot in front of a sorority house "the loading and unloading zone." I guess I was here to load.

I got out of my car and I started to walk up on the curb towards the sidewalk. I smoothed out my clothes, and did a quick breath check by cupping my hand over my mouth for a quick blow and sniff.

It was showtime!

I walked up the sidewalk and I heard one of the girls inside the house yell. "Hey Staci, your date's here!" I loved it when my arrival was announced. Now I would have an audience, and the entire house could see the guy that Staci was going out with. I was feeling cocky and confident. I walked up the sidewalk towards the porch area of the house and I saw Staci step out through the front door. Holy Smokes, she looked beautiful. Her long blonde hair was slightly curled, and was gently blowing in the breeze. She wore a skirt that showed off her legs and her well-proportioned body was causing my heart rate to rise. My thoughts became increasingly non-gentlemanly. She looked great, I felt great, there was nothing that was going to affect this evening, and whatever happened with Staci, I was ready for it. It was time, and damn it, I deserved it.

Staci met me at the bottom of the porch steps and enveloped me in a hug. She smelled wonderful and I inhaled her deeply and closed my eyes. This is what I had wanted. This is what I had needed. I opened my eyes to tell her that she looked beautiful, and I saw Casey standing in the doorway of the house, a clear plastic cup of punch in her hand. Was my mind playing tricks on me? Was I feeling guilty for thinking impure thoughts about Staci while supposedly in a relationship with Casey, who was studying a couple of hours away? There was no reason that she would be here. It was all in my mind. I mean, why would Casey be down here at this campus, in this sorority house? I held the embrace and I continued to stare at the girl in the doorway. The girl dropped her drink and turned away, back into the house. And that is when I knew that it wasn't my mind playing tricks.

SHIT! SHIT! SHIT! SHIT SHIT!

Staci had no idea what was going on. "Let's go Chad," she said. "Before any of the other girls try to steal you from me."

For a brief moment I couldn't move or respond. I had no idea of what to do. I was frozen in time and although my mind was going a mile a minute, I couldn't make a decision. I had flashes of Casey severing our relationship without ever speaking to me again. In that moment, I realized that there was a path for me to take, and that path had come to a crossroads. A fork in the road that led off in opposite directions. I'd spent so long on one path, that now as I stood at the crossroads, I just couldn't commit to either path. All of these thoughts came within a millisecond as I was still standing, with Staci in my arms, looking at the front door. My heart was pounding in my chest and I felt like I was having an anxiety attack. It was getting hard to breathe. I could see little dots appear and disappear before my eyes. I hadn't felt like that since Vietnam.

I remembered a story my Alpha Phi Omega brother Mark Ryerson had told me about when he was in high school. His dad was a car dealer in town and let Mark use a burgundy, 1955 Rolls-Royce convertible for the football homecoming parade. When his dad had given him the keys, he let him know that in no uncertain terms that the car had to come back perfect. As his dad had put it, "Son, if you dent it, go ahead and total it." At this point, I may have only dented my relationship with Casey, because nothing had happened with Staci, and maybe I could explain it away using every last ounce of my charm. But then I just said screw it, and I decided to total it.

So, without any rhyme or reason, I planted a kiss on her lips. Our mouths held together, and her tongue began to explore mine. It was the most passionate kiss that I could muster. I opened my eyes and looked up at the house. I thought I saw Casey's silhouette at the window. I don't think I even cared any more. I slowly turned around towards my car and grabbed Staci's hand, leading her to the passenger door. I had started to rationalize my actions. What had just been a simple dent, a simple scratch in the paint, had now become the end result of a four-car pile up on the interstate.

I opened the door and held Staci's hand while she entered and sat in the passenger seat. I shut the door and looked one last time up at the Gamma house. The silhouette in the window was gone. And just like that, it was over.

I got behind the steering wheel and drove off. Staci was talking to me, but I wasn't listening. It was at that moment in time when my flawed relationship philosophy finally caught up with me. I had lived my life "in the moment," for as far back as I could remember. I would make emotional, sometimes life-changing decisions "in the moment" without thinking through any of the repercussions or consequences. And I never really dealt with any of those repercussions. I just moved on unfazed, or had Marty figure ways to get out of them. I had always thought that living in the moment defined who I was, so it was okay. It was my character flaw. I never stopped to think about how others felt.

How did Tricia feel when I dumped her the day before homecoming for Casey? How did Casey feel when I up and enlisted without even discussing it with her? And now, what was she thinking having seen Staci and I on the front lawn of the Gamma house? I had felt her heart break, because mine had broken as well. It had broken long before I saw her standing in that doorway. It had been breaking for months.

In my mind, I pictured the Tin Man from the *Wizard of Oz* receiving his heart. All of my interactions and decisions had been without heart or any substantive feeling. I had been okay with that, as it had always meant nothing to me. I just kept moving on. But this was different. I felt remorse. I felt sorry for Casey, even though I was lonely, and empty, and I needed someone in my life, I still felt bad for what had happened. I wanted to just move on. I wanted to have a nice night with Staci, and I wanted to end the night in bed next to her. But my heart said otherwise. My heart said that the wrong person was in this car next to me. My mind told me that Casey had always been there for me. That she had waited for me for two years, and I couldn't do the same for her in return. The only reason I was with Staci at that very moment was for sex. But sex didn't equal love, no matter how many times I did the math. And that is when I saw it clearly. For once in my life, my heart, my brain, and my penis were all on the same page. Now, all I could think about was Casey and how was I going to save a relationship that I now, for the first time in my life, so desperately wanted to save. I was no longer living "in the moment." I think I had just learned the meaning of the word, *consequence*. This feeling was certainly new to me and I wasn't sure how or what to do with it.

At this point, I was glad we were going to a movie, since I wasn't really in a talkative mood. Staci never picked up on it, I just told her early on that I was tired, and she understood, though she had no idea. After the movie I used the tired excuse to end the evening early and take her back to her house. The walk up to the door was as stressful as being on patrol in Vietnam. I was nervous and on edge, and checked all of the windows and the shadows for a sign of Casey. I gave Staci a quick kiss on the cheek and quickly retreated to my car and sped off.

Back in my room, in my bed, alone, I tossed and turned as my brain punished me for my transgressions. I lay there wondering if the ache in my heart was just a temporary feeling. Had I really been in love? Did I even know what love was? If I was in love, why was I so quick to go out with other girls? Did I love Casey because I loved *HER*, or because I loved the idea of a relationship? I mean, it was me that always broke up with girls, it was me that always initiated physical contact, and it was me that always controlled my emotional involvement. I had always used the fishing term "Catch and Release" to do describe my relationships.

But with Casey, she controlled all of this. It wasn't a relationship on my terms, it was on hers. So, using that reasoning, I couldn't have been in love with just the relationship. I had to be in love with the girl. I had to be in love with Casey Martin!

I continued to lie there thinking about all of this, my brain going on and on analyzing every relationship that I had ever been in. I don't remember actually sleeping at all that night, but I do remember coming up with a plan of attack.

This time, if I was going to save this relationship, I would have to make a commitment to both myself and to Casey. I didn't know, or wasn't smart enough to know the answers, but I did know that I had to get Casey back. I knew it wouldn't be easy, but I had no idea how hard it would be.

Chapter 20

It was Tuesday afternoon, and I had not been out of my apartment since returning from my date with Staci on Saturday night. I was depressed and didn't feel like moving. I had called into work, telling them I had the flu and skipped Monday and Tuesday classes. I hadn't even changed out of my sweats or showered since Saturday and I had the smell to prove it. I didn't have an appetite at all, but ate White Castles that Marty brought home for us. That and Hostess Cupcakes and Dryers Ice Cream; you know, the major food groups. Our dorm was quickly filling up with food wrappers and empty ice cream cartons. I was too depressed to even take out the trash.

I just sat on my bare mattress all day, every day, having pulled off the sheets to use as cover to block out the daylight, Marty, and life in general. When I wasn't sulking on my bed, I was pacing the small dorm room, having long, heartfelt conversations with my head. Most times, I was oblivious to things going on around me. Marty would show up, ask how I was doing, leave me some food and disappear. For three days, this had been my existence. But on Tuesday afternoon, things began to change. I woke up a little bit. My heart ached, and my mind would not shut up about Casey, and Staci, and me (for whom my brain called, "the asshole.")

It was just after two when I sat up from my linen-less mattress and started to open my eyes again, literally and figuratively. I surveyed the room and noticed that there were several open bottles of cheap wine and a few premixed bottles of vodka and orange juice scattered here and there around the dorm. I also noticed an odor that was coming from somewhere, but couldn't quite make what it was exactly or where it was coming from. The smell was like old dirty shoes, soaked through with urine and worn by pigs. I looked in the mirror and saw a guy that had aged some fifteen years and looked to have been living on the streets for the last five. I was alone, in just about every way.

Marty had tried to be there for me, but mostly he just went about his business, going to classes and, like a good hunter-gatherer, he brought home food for us both. He never once asked about what had happened, probably because he knew me, knew how I handled things, knew how I "lived in the moment," and he had been preparing for this contingency since the fourth grade. Good friend or not, for the most part, Marty stayed out of it.

It was time for me to get ahold of myself. I couldn't rely on Marty to carry me any longer, nor could I expect Casey to just show up at my door and demand an apology. No, this was all on me, and only I could fix this.

I pulled the telephone off the table next to my bed and set it on my lap, one hand gently caressing the receiver, as if unsure on how to use it. One part of me wanted to shower, shave, and get into some clean, fresh clothes and then call Casey, another part was just content to wither away and die a lonely, broken man.

After a few more hours of just sitting and thinking and trying to gather enough courage to pick up the phone and call Casey, I finally started to move. I stood up off my bare bed and sat the phone back on the table. I picked up my shower caddy and a towel and for the first time in days, I left my dorm room. I hit the showers and scrubbed every bit of self-loathing off my body. I shaved off my four-day stubble, and actually ran a comb through my hair. The person staring back at me in the mirror looked familiar again. It was that guy who was going to pick up the phone and make that call. It was that guy who was going to fix this and make it all better. It was the man in the mirror who would be my savior. And luckily, that man was me.

Now that I was cleaned up and ready for the world again, I went back to my dorm and sat down, not on the bed, but on the chair at Marty's desk. For the next thirty minutes I could not think of what to do or even what to say to Casey, assuming I got the nerve to call her. And then what if she refused to talk to me? Could I handle that sheer rejection? Finally, I decided to just forego the whole phone call idea. I had done some serious soul-searching since Saturday night, and even while out on a date with a beautiful woman like Staci, all I could think about was Casey, because she was my true love. It was this great epiphany that I felt I had to share with her. And I just couldn't see me doing that over the phone.

I decided I would just drive to Miami and share this great bit of news. She would have to forgive me now that I had found out the truth of my feelings. I would just drive up and somehow make my way to her room and talk to her. I didn't think it was something that I could do alone. I needed some support so I decided to wait until Marty got home to see if he could come with me.

At just after four, Marty walked into the room and saw me dressed and looking at him expectedly. He sighed.

"Marty, I know what I have to do," I said confidently.

"Let me guess," he said. "Keep dating the girls in Casey's sorority until she takes you back?" I was undeterred.

"I have to drive out to Miami and tell her that I love her and want to be with her forever," I said. "I have to do this today, and I would like you to come with me?"

His answer was simple. "No."

"C'mon, man," I pleaded. "I need your help. I need your support."

"All I've ever given you is my support," he said, "only to watch you squander it each and every time. Back in high school, it was fun, but this is real life. Things don't always end up in favor of Chad Breckinridge. Sometimes, you have to take one for the team, and move on. You screwed this up. It's time that you paid for it."

"I have to try," I said, ignoring his lecture. "You don't even have to go with me to her dorm, we could get into town and hit one of the bars and you can stay there while I talk to her and then we come home. I'll even get your beers."

"You haven't heard a single word that I've said," Marty countered. "Since you simply refuse to see the forest through the trees, I'll go with you. Because once she levels you with her truth, someone will need to be there to help pick you up. And at least I'll get a few beers out of it."

It was a two-hour drive from Bloomington to Miami, and Marty and I had barely said two words to each other during the entire trip. We arrived and I parked the car in the parking lot across from Casey's dorm. I sat in the driver's seat and tried to pump myself up. Marty gave me the look that he knew I had lied to him about going to the bar first, but just shook his head like he had done a thousand times before. We both sat there for a few seconds just staring out the front window.

"Well, are you gonna do it?" he asked.

"Yeah," I said. "I may take a little longer than usual but it shouldn't take more than an hour."

"Take your time," Marty said, his voice dripping with sarcasm. "I'll just sit here or maybe walk around campus and stare into the girls' dorm windows. You can get your heart broken while I play 'Peeping Marty.' Maybe I'll get a nice shot of boob for my troubles."

As I started to get out of the door, Marty grabbed my arm.

"Wait." I eased back in the seat and closed the door. Marty looked at me sternly. The sarcastic tone was gone. He was back to being serious. "Chad, you can't fix this, I can't fix this, and there is likely nothing you will say to her that will change the fact that it's over between the two of you."

"Seriously, you need to work on your Vince Lombardi inspirational speeches there, buddy," I said. Marty didn't even smile.

"Chad, you're my best friend and I adore Casey, but this day was coming. You've been reckless with this relationship as you've been with all of your relationships, and this time it has come back on you in spades, and we both know she isn't going to take you back."

I was taken aback, but forged ahead with my usual mix of swagger and naiveté. "You're right that I screwed up, but I've learned the error of my ways, and as soon as Casey sees that, she'll understand. I love her, that's all that matters."

"You hurt her and you embarrassed her, and *THAT* is all that matters to her. Look, this isn't getting us anywhere. Go, do your thing so we can get those beers."

"Good luck, I'll be here when you get back."

As I excited the car and shut the door, I found myself still searching for a plan on how I was going to approach Casey and what I was going to say. I was out of my comfort zone with this "feeling" thing. I had this pit in my chest that seemed to keep pushing to get out. It just wouldn't go away. It had been there since that moment I turned around and didn't see Casey standing in the doorway at the Gamma house.

I continued my walk from the parking lot to a phone booth located near the sidewalk on the side of the dorm building where Casey lived. I dropped a dime in the slot and dialed her number from memory.

"Hello, Shermer Hall, how can I help you?"

I responded quietly, "I would like Casey in room 242, please." My heart was pounding out of my chest as I heard the phone ring once, then twice, and a third time before I heard Casey's voice on the other end.

"Hello?"

I hesitated. I couldn't speak. My mind was all over the place with so many confusing thoughts. The moment had finally come and I couldn't think of a single word to say. Then, finally I spoke.

"Casey? It's Chad--" I heard a click and silence on the other end.

I paused for a second. Maybe she'd hung up thinking there wasn't anybody on the other end because it took so long for me to say anything. I reached into my pocket and grabbed another dime and slipped it into the slot once again.

"Hello, Shermer Hall, how can help you?"

Again, I said, "I would like Casey in room 242, please." I listened for the phone to connect and expected Casey to answer on the first or second ring. The phone continued to ring and ring and ring, maybe twelve times before I finally hung up. I just stood there confirming the one thought that I had feared the most. Casey had answered the phone and once she knew it was me, she'd hung up and would not answer the phone again knowing I was on the other end. Marty was right. It was over.

The realization of losing Casey was overwhelming to me. I dropped to my knees letting the receiver fall from my hand and just dangle from the cord attached to the phone. I looked downward at the ground with thoughts of hopelessness. For the first time in my life I was lost. I didn't know what to do. I had these feelings inside me that were emotionally gut wrenching.

No, I thought, *it's not ending this easily; I'm not giving up*. I loved her and I was going to let her know, and even if she hit me, and threw things at me, and screamed at me, I was going to let her know she was the love of my life, and that I was stupid and selfish for just now figuring it out.

I knew she was in her room so I picked myself up off the floor of the phone booth and started to look around for a few small pebbles to toss at her window. Her room was just on the second floor. Within a minute or two I had gathered enough pebbles to throw at about five windows. I maneuvered myself beneath her window and threw the first pebble which struck the window with enough force the she would hear it. Within a second or two I threw the second pebble followed by four more. They all hit their mark but failed to produce any response. I had one pebble left so I decided to just throw it at the window in the room next door. Suddenly, a girl with dark, short hair came to the window and peered out. I instantly recognized her. It was the window of that girl whose room I accidentally went into the first time I had ever visited.

"Sorry!" I waved and made a hasty getaway. I ran back to the car and found Marty reclined with the seat back and listening to the Chambers Brothers sing about time on the radio. I had a plan that was equal parts brilliant and stupid. It was the Chad Breckinridge way. I jumped in the car and started it up quickly.

"So, as expected, it didn't work," Marty said.

"Don't count this dog out of the race just yet," I said. "I need to go into town real quick. I swear, when this is done, we'll get those beers."

"Famous last words," Marty said and then he turned up the radio and started to sing along as I sped off toward downtown, and the Woolworth's Department Store that I had seen the last time I was here.

As I approached room 242, my heart rate speed up and my palms started to sweat. I reached the door and just stood there trying to think what to say. This was insane. I had been rejected twice within the last forty-five minutes so what could I really expect this time? I faced the door, took a deep breath and slowly and hesitantly raised my right arm and lightly knocked on the door. I didn't hear any movement or noise from inside so I knocked once again, this time with a little more authority. I could hear footsteps heading toward the door. The door opened and there stood Casey. She was absolutely beautiful, and I felt like the biggest jerk in the world. I suddenly felt every muscle in my body start to tighten and my mouth suddenly became dry as a desert. She stared for a second, but it felt more like an hour.

"Chad?" she asked. "What're you doing here in that ridiculous outfit?"

I had gone to Woolworth's and picked out a skirt and blouse in my size, and then I'd found a wig and some makeup. The cashier looked at me funny as I paid at the register, but a man in love would do some crazy things. Marty drove us back to campus as I sat in the back seat changing into my new outfit, and then he helped me apply the makeup while trying desperately not to burst out laughing. Luckily, my plan worked to get me past the front desk, and here I was, staring at the true love of my life, and hoping like hell that I could fix this thing.

"What more could you possibly want?" Casey continued. "Haven't you hurt me enough already?" I tried to speak but she continued, pointing her finger right into my chest as she punctuated each word.

"You hurt me and embarrassed me."

"Can I come inside and talk to you?" I asked. I felt vulnerable standing in her hallway dressed in drag.

"There's nothing to say," she said. "We're through. You made your choice."

"Now wait a minute--"

"It's always been about you, it's always been about what you wanted and needed, and you never cared about anybody else."

"That's not true," I began. " I--"

"In high school, we always did things on your schedule. You never asked me what I wanted to do. I was just some person that you dragged around, and used when you needed companionship."

"What are you even talking about?" I asked. The floodgates were open and years of anger were pouring out. Pandora's Box was open and all hell was breaking loose. I felt the skirt begin to slip off my hips so I pulled it back up. I had never felt more ridiculous in all my life.

"You enlisted in the navy without even talking to me first," she said. "I still have never forgiven you for that. This has always been about you, and never about us. I see that now. It took me years, but I see that now."

"Casey, let me--" That's all I got out.

"Let you what? Explain why you were with someone else? There is no explanation needed. I saw you. You saw me see you, and still you carried on. You're an asshole, Chad Breckinridge, and I know that now."

"You never made time for me," I shot back, anger rising in my voice. If I was going to stand here in a skirt, wig and makeup getting berated, I was going to get my words in as well. "A relationship is two people, but with you, it was me and you when you had time. You put your stupid protest stuff before me. You put your classes before me, you put everything in your life before me. You aren't innocent here. You did the exact same thing that you accuse me of doing."

"So, if 'little 'ol Chad' doesn't get his way, it's okay to cheat on your girlfriend? You're pathetic. You are...You're a child. Grow the hell up."

"I wrote you everyday when I was in Vietnam, and you never once wrote me back," I said. "People died, my friends died, and I needed you more than ever, and you were never there."

"I was there, Chad," she said. "But in my way, not yours. And because of that, it was wrong. Because it's always been 'your way or the highway.' You think the entire world revolves around you. But guess what, it doesn't. Other people have lives. Other people have feelings.

"I thought of you everyday, but it was never enough for you. You put our entire relationship on the backs of letters and sex. It was just that black and white with you. If I didn't write you, I didn't care. If we didn't have sex, I didn't care. Can't you see how ridiculous that is?"

Other girls were starting to peek out of their doors at our conversation. I had never felt more uncomfortable in my life.

"I'm standing here in a dress," I said. "Can we please go inside to discuss this?"

"And how dare you come here with your bullshit and try to think this little stunt would work? Was I supposed to forgive you because you dressed in drag to sneak in here? This is what I'm talking about, Chad. You never think things through. You never even consider the step after.

"For the last several days, I've sat here crying over you. Ever since I saw you with that girl. I waited. I waited three days for you to call and give me your patented excuse. But then nothing. Not even a phone call. I think you knew it was over. I think maybe even you had figured it out."

At this point, this wasn't a conversation to try and reconcile our relationship, it was a war. And I would be damned if I was going to take it without giving back.

"What were you even doing there?" I asked. "You were on my campus and you didn't even call and tell me you were there."

"First of all, it was a sorority event, something I had to do. And secondly, what does that matter? This is not the issue here. Did you want me to call you to what, give you notice so you could cancel your other date?"

"No, Casey," I responded firmly. "I wanted to see my girlfriend, and the woman I love, and you were on *MY* campus without letting *ME* know. Even after I had called asking to see you. You said you had things to do. I guess I wasn't on that list.

"I'm sorry I went out with Staci, but she was just a friend. I would have much rather spent time with you."

"Bullshit," she said. "That's why after you saw me, you left with her? I don't believe a word you're saying. You blew it, and you hurt me and I never want to see you again." She exhaled and looked me square in my eyes. "It's time you leave before I call the house mother to have you escorted out. Goodbye, Chad."

Before I could say anything more, the door shut. I just stood there feeling angry, sad, heartbroken, and guilty and all while wearing a cheap dress and wig. By now, the other girls had figured out what was going on and they hovered by their doors giving me the evil eye, waiting for me to leave. I felt as if I was going to faint. I wanted to knock on the door. I wanted this conversation to continue, because even an argument was better than nothing. But then it slowly dawned on me that I had truly screwed up here. And maybe there was no repairing this. We both had some deep anger toward each other, and we were both guilty. And neither of us wanted to admit that.

I walked down the hallway dejected. I couldn't believe that I had lost her. It didn't seem real. The girls on her floor stood in their respective doorways and called me an "ass" and a "jerk" as I made my way to the stairwell. They were right.

I finally made my way back to the car where I slowly opened the door and just slumped into the seat with my left leg dangling outside and resting on the pavement. "I take it that it didn't go well?" Marty asked.

"Man, I lost her," I said. "I lost the love of my life and I'll never get her back!" I recapped the conversation to Marty and he sat there for a moment before putting his hand on my shoulder.

"Hey man, you did your best. It was a helluva effort if I do say so myself." He teasingly ran his hands through my wig. "Give it some time, and maybe she'll take you back." I knew Marty was lying, and Marty knew he was lying, but somehow, I still felt better.

Marty clapped his hands. "Okay buddy, time to drown your sorrows. Let's head over to that bar you were telling me about. I think we both need some drinks and chow, as I'm officially starving."

I just nodded my head and climbed into the backseat to change back into my clothes. I did my best to wipe off the makeup and then I got back into the driver's seat and drove, lacking the energy for any more talk of Casey and I. We arrived at Banyan's Bar and Grille and we got out of the car. I'd come here with Casey a few times, and I hoped that being here wouldn't stir up too many memories.

Marty pushed me towards the bar and ordered four beers to start off. No sooner than the bartender put the drinks down in front of us, I was downing one after another, including one of Marty's. I immediately ordered five more and told Marty I owed him an extra one. They arrived one after another, and once again, I had downed all three of mine simultaneously. Slowly I was easing out of my state of depression and into a state of walking unconsciousness. Marty ordered a couple of burgers, but I was more interested in tying one on and trying to forget about Casey Martin for a night.

The beers continued coming, and to be honest, I'd lost count. It was now past midnight and I was pretty sure that I had more beer in my body than blood. Marty finished his last beer and set the bottle on the bar.

"Come on, Chad, let's go," he said. "It's been a long day for me and I want to go home." Marty continued to harass me about going home, but I continued to ignore him. Since I had obviously had too many, I was depending on him to get me home. Marty only had a few beers and had eaten some food so he was fine to drive home. I was afraid that if I stopped drinking the depression would wash over me like a wave and I didn't want to break down crying in a bar called Banyan's.

"Marty, I'm not ready to go back yet," I slurred. "I want a couple more beers!"

"Look man, I gotta get back," he explained. "The world doesn't revolve around you."

"Funny," I said. "Casey said the same thing."

"Then maybe you need to stop and ask yourself why we both think that."

"I just want another beer or two," I said. "Quit being a girl about it."

"Fuck you, man," Marty said. "I've covered for you most of our lives, even after you screwed this up with Casey. I still tried to take care of you, to make it better for you. But why? You don't care. You don't give a shit about anyone but yourself."

"That's bullshit, " I said. "I joined the navy for you. I tried to be there for you."

"Well, lotta good that did," Marty said. "You know damn well that your number would have come up sooner or later. You were too damn stupid to stay in school, so your time was coming. I just gave you an out. I gave you an option. Don't you ever think yourself the hero for enlisting with me.

"You're a piece of work," he continued. "Maybe one day you will realize that you have friends, and then you'll treat us like equals, and not the supporting cast in the TV show that is your life.

"Now, I'm leaving, are you coming?"

"No."

"Fine, good luck getting home." He calmly got up off his bar stool and walked toward what I thought was the men's room. I continued to sit there at the bar and drink my last two beers. After finishing the last drop of the last beer I started to look around the bar for Marty. I didn't see him anywhere so I got up off the bar stool and headed into the men's room to get him. He wasn't there. I slowly stumbled over to a few stalls and didn't find him there either. I went back into the bar and walked all around but still couldn't find him. Marty had left me, Casey had left me; everyone had left me!

As drunk as I was, my only thought was to try to make my way over to Casey's dorm and try one more time to talk to her. In my drunken state, I believe it took me almost an hour to walk a half-a-mile. In fact I wasn't even sure that I was at the right dormitory. They all looked the same sober, so while drunk it was impossible to differentiate. After falling several times in my attempt to pick up some pebbles, I finally gained enough strength to throw a handful at a window on the second floor. This time, I used a little more strength in my throw and the window shattered. A light went on from inside and a frat guy leaned out the window and told me he was coming down to kick my ass. I immediately asked him if he had any beer up there. The guy quickly withdrew from the window, and I figured that I had better quickly move on and find Casey's dorm. I wandered her campus for an hour or two. I had virtually no clue where I was so I just started walking down a street that led to a dark and lonely stretch of a two-lane road with only the light from a half-moon to guide my way. After about a half hour of walking I came to a road sign that confirmed that I was on the road towards Deer Park, but nowhere near Bloomington. I was drunk, and confused, and a little scared. I had no idea what to do, so I kept walking.

Within fifteen minutes I heard a car approaching from behind me so I turned and stared waiving like a prostitute on a main strip in Las Vegas. It was the only car that I had seen all night. I was tired and could barely move one foot in front of the other. As quickly as I saw the car approach, it started to slow down and eventually stopped next to me. The passenger window slowly lowered to where I could see an Asian man who appeared to be in his mid-forties. I saw his mouth move and heard words come out, but had absolutely no clue what he was saying. I wasn't sure if he was speaking Chinese, Japanese, or possibly even Vietnamese. God, I hope it wasn't Vietnamese.

"You need ride?" he asked in broken English.

"Yes, to Bloomington."

"I go to Muncie."

"No, Bloomington."

"I go to Muncie." Muncie was over a hundred miles away from Bloomington, and over a hundred and fifty away from where I figured I was right now. This guy wouldn't be of any help to me.

"Muncie? You get in. We go to Muncie."

"I need to go to Bloomington, man."

"I go to Muncie."

It was useless. I was so tired, and the world was starting to spin, and I just wanted to be home. I was pissed at Marty for abandoning me, and I was mad at Casey for causing me to get into this mess. I was pretty mad at the entire world, and the man in the car spewing broken English wasn't helping. I turned to keep walking and then buckled over and vomited. I collapsed onto my knees on the side of the road and kept puking. All that beer and a handful of partially-digested fries shot out of my mouth with a force of a hurricane. This night couldn't get any better.

"Okay, we go Bloomington," the man in the car said. I wiped my mouth off with the back of my arm and got in the car. I was asleep within minutes. He woke me up once we got to Bloomington and I directed him to my dorm. My long strange trip had finally come to an end.

The next few weeks I tried constantly to contact Casey without any luck. I wrote over a hundred letters; short letters and long letters, pouring out my heart and apologizing for everything, but she never responded. Everyday I went to the mailbox looking and hoping for a letter, but each time I walked away empty handed. Those weeks became months, and at least once a month I drove to Miami and tried to contact her, but it was obvious she did not want to see me. It was clear that she had told her sorority sisters that if I came around they were not to tell me where she was, or what she was doing. I had no idea if she even still lived in the dorm. Finally, I stopped driving to Miami.

In June of 1977, I graduated from Indiana University. I knew that Casey had graduated a couple of years before me, and when her letters started coming back as undeliverable, I knew that she had moved on. I didn't know where she was or even if she was okay. I think it was then (and only then) that I realized it was over. What can I say; I'm a stubborn fool.

It had been years since I last saw her, but the pain I felt inside was still there. I just couldn't shake the memories that were so imbedded in my mind of our time together. But I knew I had to somehow move on. Too much of everything around me reminded me of Casey. Of us. I decided that I would move back to the west coast where my family was and try to find a job. It was finally time for me to move on as well.

Chapter 21

I asked Marty to move out to California with me, more so as a courtesy, and less of as a friend helping another friend. Regardless of the reason, he chose to stay home in Deer Park and to continue working for the radio station.

I had confronted him about leaving me that night at the bar shortly after it had happened, and he told me that I was being a self-serving asshole who was more interested in feeling sorry for myself than being thankful that he had been there to support me. He had also said that I should have honored his wish to leave. In sober hindsight, he had been right, and I apologized for it. The thought that couldn't escape me was that Marty had never left me behind, not in high school, not in Vietnam, not ever. I had been heartbroken and drunk and needed a friend that night more than ever, and he had left to prove a point. I don't know, maybe we were finally growing up and growing apart. I've said countless times that Vietnam changed Marty Green, and that night had proved it beyond all doubt. I loved Marty like a brother. We'd lived together for most of our adult lives, and finally, because of Casey, because of me, it was time for us to split. It was time for me to move on. Marty was still sinking deeper and deeper into his post-traumatic stress disorder, and as he became more and more withdrawn, I had to be the one to make the change. I offered to let him come with me to California, and he had declined. And that's how my friendship with Marty ended.

During a ridiculously hot July in the summer of 1977 I loaded up my Camaro again and returned to Southern California without any specific objective in mind. I wanted to see the beach. I wanted to see beautiful girls, girls that didn't remind me of Casey. Huntington Beach would be the polar opposite of the Midwestern ideals of Indiana. Hell, I was ready to just live on the beach if need be. I felt that I'd earned it.

My vacation from life didn't last too long. Boredom set in and by the fall, I had enrolled in classes at UCLA to pursue a law degree. As to not burden my parents, I even moved into the Alpha Phi house on campus. I dove into fraternity life and was actively involved in their pledge drive as well as intramural sports. I found a job at a local department store, which allowed me to once again enjoy the fruits of being back in school and the fraternity life as well as being able to support myself. I'd traveled two thousand miles to do exactly what I had done in Indiana. But at least in California, I had a beach to go to when I needed time for myself.

I enjoyed UCLA girls as well, and I dated my fair share and enjoyed the atmosphere of being a single, older guy in a fraternity house. Honestly, most guys would be envious of the situation I was in, but I still had Casey on my mind. She was like a ghost that haunted me day and night. I'd see her face, or feel her presence almost every day. I started writing her weekly, sending them to her house in Deer Park. These letters weren't returned, so a small part of me believed that she was getting them and reading them, and that one day, she would call me out of the blue and ask me to pick her up at LAX and we would begin our lives together in the great state of California. I even started checking the mailbox for her letters back to me. I thought that after all these years, maybe, just maybe she would take the time to write me a letter back. She never did.

Because of Casey's spell over me, I wasn't interested in dating anyone seriously until Gary Sheppard, a fraternity brother of mine set me up on a blind date with a former UCLA cheerleader who he had known since grade school and who he had thought would be a great match for me. I honestly wasn't interested. With cheerleaders, it was a "been there, done that" mentality thanks to Tricia and her gang of cronies and the way they had terrorized me after our breakup. And most of the cheerleaders that

I had met both in Indiana and in California were airheads that couldn't even keep me interested, no matter how gorgeous they looked. Blonde hair and tall, tanned legs could only go so far. But Gary had been persistent, even after I told him about Casey and how I could never fully give my heart to another girl. Gary had assured me that this girl was different, and if it didn't work out, that would be fine; at least I had given it a try. So I reluctantly agreed, and that is how I met my wife.

Gary had arranged for us to meet at the Holiday Inn Lounge on Sunset Avenue adjacent to UCLA and the Alpha Phi house on a Saturday evening for drinks. I had walked into the restaurant and saw Gary sitting next to this absolutely breathtaking petite brunette with penetrating green eyes and feisty little smile. She introduced herself as Julie Watson and I immediately knew this woman was different than anyone I had ever met--other than Casey. She immediately broke the mold of what I believed was the typical cheerleader when I found out she had a biology degree and was in her first year of medical school.

I knew immediately I was over my head on an intellectual level, but she never talked down to me, or made me feel uncomfortable. She was supremely confident in who she was, and we connected in our passion for living for the moment. Julie was a native southern California girl who grew up in Beverly Hills and was smart, athletic and fearless. She was a cheerleader who didn't know anything about football, because, as she explained, her back was facing the field the whole game. She asked me about my military service and about my time in Vietnam, and for the first time, I felt comfortable talking about it. She told me I wasn't what she had pictured as a Vietnam Vet, and I told her she wasn't the average cheerleader, and we both laughed at the dispelled stereotypes. We never even noticed that Gary had left the bar.

We talked for several hours before the manager asked us to leave. We exchanged phone numbers and we went out for our first date a couple days later. For the first time since Casey, I felt connected to someone, and I couldn't get enough of Julie. She was different than Casey, Julie had a zest for life that I appreciated, and while Casey was more low-key and deliberate, Julie was energetic and driven. Julie appreciated my "live for the moment" mentality, especially as it had evolved a bit over the years to not be quite as thoughtless. I still wrote to Casey, but the letters were shorter and less involved. I had turned Casey into a fictional being who served only to hear my thoughts and hopes. Hell, at that point, the letters I wrote to her were more like episodic diary entries. Casey Martin was no longer a person to me and I quit checking my mailbox expecting anything in return.

For the next six months, Julie and I spent every moment together that we could when she wasn't studying or I wasn't working. It made our time together more exciting, as we felt like we were stealing the time away from life. I was constantly on my toes with her intoxicating appetite for living and she relished in my "in the now" attitude. We were perfect for each other.

In April of 1978, we decided to get engaged and planned to marry in June of 1979, after Julie had graduated from medical school. I had bugged out of law school and had obtained a job working for a major consumer products company in their regional sales office. We continued working our personal schedules around her school and my job, but now our free time had been spent planning a wedding. I admit that I had my doubts about the whole thing. Casey was still on my mind. She didn't dominate my thoughts as she had in the past, but she was still there. I wasn't sure if that was normal. Should I have been thinking of another woman all the while planning to marry Julie? I had been constantly wondering if I was actually marrying Julie the person, or the ghost of Casey. Was I just marrying her to try and get rid of the ghost of Casey once and for all? These were questions that I wasn't sure I should be asking as time went on.

I loved Julie with all of my being, but from the moment we first starting dating, I consciously compared her to Casey in every way possible. Her looks, her smile, the way she laughed, the way she held a conversation, the way she ate popcorn, the way she walked, danced, and slept. It was obsessive how much I compared the two. It was as if Casey was some magical litmus test that all women would have to go through before I could give them my heart.

And for the record, yes, I knew how ludicrous that sounded.

I loved Julie for her spirit and zest for life. Like Casey, Julie was compassionate, loving and committed to a relationship. Julie was the type of person who, like Casey, thought more about others than themselves. It wasn't fair to Julie that she was being compared to Casey, and Julie was so driven and fast-paced that she should have slowed down to see who she was marrying, because I obviously had a problem that wasn't apparent from the start. And it led to issues later on.

In June of 1979, Julie and I got married in a beautiful wedding chapel in Beverly Hills followed by a reception at the exclusive Rolling Gates Country Club. Marty had flown out to be my best man, and my brother Alex was a groomsman. Marty and I had a long talk over beers one night after he landed in LA, and we got a lot of stuff out. He was now a station manager for the radio station back in Indiana, and was being courted by a station in Ft. Lauderdale to come down and run not only that station, but also a few others along the Florida coast. Marty sure was making something of himself.

It had been nice to sit and talk again, and I think we both missed it. By the time he stood next to me at the ceremony, we were back to being like brothers. And speaking of, Alex, my real brother, had just graduated from the University of Kentucky with a degree in journalism when I called and asked him to stand with me. I guess all those nights "reading" those magazines actually amounted to something. The childish animosity that we had once held for one another was gone, and it was nice visiting with him, and I really appreciated him standing with me. And I think my parents enjoyed it the most, as they sat in the audience and watched their firstborn son take a wife. My mom cried the entire time, and if I had to swear, I'd say I thought my dad cried a little too. No bullshit.

Our marriage was challenging from the beginning. Julie took over as the responsible adult of the house, and I was on the road for work, which required me to travel up and down the pacific coast selling my company's wares. I was providing for my family, but I also took too many opportunities to have fun. I stayed out late with my friends, or spent too much time on the golf course, or watching football with my buddies. Julie buried herself in her residency and her boards, and when we would actually have free time together, we would spend it rehashing our days or hanging out with our friends. On the surface, we were a young, successful, happy couple. And although Julie loved me and I loved her, there were some nasty cracks forming in the foundation.

I loved Julie, but it was difficult for me to concentrate on the needs of someone else. Even as married life was taking off, I would find myself caught up in thoughts of Casey and wondering where she was and what she was doing. Oh, I loved Julie very much, but something inside me kept triggering thoughts of Casey every so often. I couldn't explain why or when the thoughts would occur, but they tugged at my heart quite often throughout my marriage.

After a year, we decided to start a family. It didn't take long for Julie to announce that she was pregnant, and nine months later, our wonderful daughter, Jennifer, was born. When I saw her I cried. She became my life, but like everything else, it was on my terms. I was taking care of my family, but was away when I should have been there, and I spent more time bragging about my daughter to my friends and co-workers than actually taking care of her. It wasn't intentional, and hopefully she didn't feel that I wasn't a part of her life, but I was still the old selfish Chad. Somewhere in Florida, Marty Green was patting himself on the back for correctly labeling me all those years before in a townie bar in Miami, Indiana. Jerk.

Fortunately, even with her incredible work schedule and obligations, Julie was an incredible mother to Jenny. She spent every possible moment with her, and when she was working and I was off doing something or another, Julie's parents stepped in to help. This increased the already tense relationship between my in-laws and me. I thought they didn't think I deserved their daughter, and they didn't understand how I could spend time away from my family. They were right, of course, but I was too flippant to realize they had the best interest of their daughter at hand.

The next few years we settled into a routine, with Julie buried in her work and motherhood, and with a group of friends that gave her the connection I couldn't give her due to being on the road selling or studying. I had my friends and my work, and had gone back to UCLA to finish my law degree. We loved full plates in our household. It was a routine many couples settle into, not out of a lack of love, but of necessity. Julie and I loved each other, and we both loved Jenny, but sometimes life gets in the way, and old ghosts come back to haunt you.

Chapter 22

Julie and I both noticed the rut that our marriage had found itself in, so we began talking more, and spending more time together, with and without Jenny; and I once again discovered this amazing person that had come into my life. I was embarrassed that I had not taken the time to fully appreciate her, even under the stress of work, classes, and everything. I had rediscovered the promises that I'd made on our wedding day.

To love and cherish, in good times and bad, on this day and everyday, for as long as we both lived.

About this time, I also started to write short letters to Casey again. I knew Julie would be furious if she found out, but I saw this as a mode of therapy. Casey to me wasn't a person any longer. She was a distant memory. A face and name that I could imagine as I wrote my deepest feelings down on paper (always by hand) and sent them to her address in Deer Park. They never came back, so in my mind's eye, she was still getting them. I would tell her all about Julie, and of Jenny, and about my life in general. It was such a therapeutic exercise that I risked the rage of my wife--and the sanctity of my marriage--to write and send these letters. In hindsight, it was stupid. But at the time, it made perfect sense. I couldn't explain it.

One rather cool day in January of 1989, I received an announcement that would change my life forever.

*The classes of 1968, 1969, and 1970 cordially invite you to the
Deer Park High School Class Reunion
Friday, June 23 and Saturday, June 24, 1989
Details to follow.
RSVP*

They say time flies with age, and I couldn't have agreed more. Had it really been 20 years? I had missed our ten-year high school reunion because of the wedding, but I wasn't going to miss this one. It was bad enough that they were already combining years, which signaled that people were either dead or indifferent. In a small school like Deer Park, where graduating classes of a hundred kids was common, sometimes the organizers had to group years together to make sure it was worth it for those who attended. At this rate, by the fortieth reunion, the entire decade of the 70s would be in one grouping.

Julie found the invitation on my desk a few days after it had arrived, and, as expected, the can of worms split open.

"Are you going to this?" she asked.

"I'd really like to," I said. "I'd really like to see how my friends turned out."

"It sounds like fun," Julie said. "I'd like to see Deer Park and see where you grew up."

"It's not the Waltons," I explained. "But it is very Midwestern. Nothing like the hustle and bustle of Beverly Hills. In fact, I think the town charter of Deer Park prohibits any hustling and/or bustling."

"I can ask my parents to watch Jenny," she offered. "Go ahead and RSVP."

I didn't need her approval. My mind was set the moment I had opened the envelope. But it would be nice to show Julie my roots. It could be a nice romantic weekend with my wife in the tiny town I grew up in.

"Will *she* be there?" Julie asked. Immediately, all the goodwill I was feeling evaporated like morning mist at noon. I knew who she was asking about. And I didn't want this to turn into an argument.

"She graduated in '70," I said. "She could be. I haven't heard anything about her since college." In the back of my mind I was truly hoping that Casey would be there. Hoping isn't a strong enough word. I was *Yearning* for her to be there. I began to wonder what would happen if she were there. I knew it would be awkward, and I wasn't even sure how I would feel or react when I saw Casey after all these years. I didn't know if she was married, or had kids, or if she even ever thought of me. And how would my wife respond if she met this girl that I spoke about too often, wrote to (secretly, now) weekly, and thought about more times than I was comfortable to admit?

I thought through every possible outcome of that possible meeting and I was equal parts afraid and excited. The reunion was still months away, and already my mind was going over a laundry list of things to do, up to and including a thousand sit ups every day between now and June.

"You still think about her?" Julie asked.

"I do," I admitted. "I'm curious to see who she married, how many kids she has, where she was living now." I expected a haymaker to my jaw, or worse. What I got was unexpected.

"I don't blame you," she said. "You two had something special, and she obviously held a spell over you. I can't wait to meet her."

What?!

In the beginning of our relationship, I had often spoken to Julie about Casey and discussed how much they both were alike in so many ways. At a certain point, I knew it was having a negative effect on Julie and was beginning to make her feel inferior, so I quit bringing it up. However, the comparisons continued in my mind. Julie must have wondered how hard it was to compete with a ghost, and now that she could stand and talk to Casey as a person, I could see why she was so intrigued.

As for me, my mind was cluttered with inner feelings that were in serious conflict. One of my thoughts was to go back to the reunion by myself, but I knew that Julie would never allow that. Maybe by them meeting and talking, then Julie would understand why I still thought of Casey, and maybe then *I* would understand why I still thought of her.

Right then and there, I pulled out a blank piece of paper from my stationary and wrote the words, "Dear Ca--" Julie watched me, with a puzzled look on her face. Normally, when I begin a hand-written letter on this particular stationary that is how I started. I acted quickly to cover it up.

"What am I doing?" I said, chuckling, as I took the sheet of paper and wadded it up. "All this talk of Casey has got her back on my mind."

She was always on my mind.

I took another sheet and started again, this time addressing the greeting to Mike Dixon, the chair of the reunion committee. I RSVP'd for Julie and myself and sent it out the next day.

In the next few weeks, I sent Mike Dixon several additional letters asking if he knew who else had RSVP'd. I got one letter back stating that it would be a surprise as to who showed, and asking me to stop sending letters requesting that info.

I downplayed the reunion as much as I could leading up to it, but up until the day we were to leave California, my mind was filled with thoughts of Casey Martin. I was becoming very anxious about the possibility of seeing her and wondered if the thoughts I had about her throughout the years would trigger deep emotional feelings once I saw her face, heard her laugh, and took in her very essence.

I began to worry.

Then my mind would shift to Julie; and the thought of being married to a woman whom I loved and was sharing a life and family. These thoughts became ever so present in my daily life, that I used them as best I could to beat back the ghost. I don't know what it was that I felt for Casey, but those feelings disappeared when I held Julie at night, or looked into the eyes of my daughter. I was at war with myself, and I wasn't sure there could ever be a victor. I couldn't even share this conflict within my head with anyone close to me. This is the stuff that I used to share with Marty, but not anymore. None of my friends in California knew what I was going through, and I wasn't about to bring them into this. I was alone.

When Julie began packing for the trip in mid-June, I acted like I had forgotten about it, but in fact, had been waiting for this, counting down the seconds until the flight left LAX and landed in Indianapolis. My in-laws came by to pick up Jenny, and acted like their usual icy selves to me.

They had never fully accepted me, and I was okay with that because they loved their daughter and granddaughter more than anything else in this world. I'm sure Julie told her mom about Casey and the reunion, so they were more dismissive of me than normal, and for once, I couldn't blame them.

We kissed our daughter off and drove to the airport. Finally, after everything, we sat, my lovely wife and I, side-by-side on the airplane, and my excitement was beyond palpable. Julie picked up on it instantly.

"You really *are* looking forward to seeing Casey?"

Finally! I knew the question would eventually be asked, but I never gave any thought as to how I would respond, or what I would say. I exhaled a sigh and looked my wife in the eye.

"You know I am," I said. "But she's just one person. I'm just as interested in seeing all those people I have lost contact with. My friends. My teammates. It's been 20 years.

"I don't even know if Casey will be there. Besides, even if she is, I'm a married man. I'm off the market. I'm unattainable. Whatever would my wife think?"

Julie smiled and thought for a moment. "Am I a bad person to hope that she's fat and old and ugly with twelve kids and breasts that sag down past her belly?" We both laughed, and the release calmed the mood. I took her hand in mind and squeezed it for assurance.

"No, you're not a bad person. I would feel the same way if I were in your shoes. I admit that I'm somewhat anxious about seeing her, but I don't even know for sure if she'll be there. If she is, great, if not, great too." I lied. Inside, my guts were turning to ropes, and I was doing everything I could to keep my breathing calm and under control.

My entire adult life had been leading up to this reunion. I had turned the idea of Casey into some mythical goddess, and there was no way that she could ever live up to what I had created in my mind. If she wasn't at this reunion, I would be crestfallen. But, to keep the peace, I lied to my wife. She asked her probing questions, like a good doctor should, and I answered as best as I could without coming out and saying what I was truly feeling. And I felt I was doing okay with my answers. However, I knew deep down that Julie was as anxious as I was. She suspected that I was still in love with Casey and that I really never lost some of those feelings for her. And she was probably right. My wife felt threatened, and she needed to mark her territory with Casey and size her up. She was probably right to do that as well. Although the mood was lightened with the joke, the weight of what was coming was almost too unbearable. As the plane lifted off the ground and into the sky toward my destiny, I leaned back, kissed Julie's hand, and closed my eyes. We didn't talk for the remainder of the flight.

We landed in Indianapolis and rented a car for the drive out to Deer Park. We went directly to the hotel to check in and freshen up before we were to attend a mixer later that evening that officially opened the reunion weekend festivities. Upon entering our room, Julie immediately walked over to the bed, turned and fell backward, Nestea-style--like the commercial--onto the mattress. She was both physically and emotionally exhausted from the non-stop, cross-country flight. She closed her eyes and for the next two hours she remained motionless, slipping into a deep sleep.

As Julie lay on the bed, I slowly paced the hotel room as my mind filled with anticipation and a level of nervousness that I hadn't felt since trolling the rivers of Vietnam. I kept thinking that somewhere in this town--hell maybe in this hotel--Casey Martin was there, possibly thinking about me the way I was thinking about her. To get those thoughts out of my mind, I would ever so often just stare at my sleeping Julie and be overcome with thoughts of thankfulness, love, and appreciation--and apprehension--for her being here with me. I felt an incredible rush of guilt for putting her through all of this. A good husband would not have even had these issues. A good husband would have loved, unconditionally, the woman he had asked to spend the rest of her life with, and not waste a single second lamenting on some past flame. Especially a flame that he hadn't seen, nor heard from, in decades.

"I'm an idiot," I said aloud. I ran my hand through my hair and sat down in a chair. I kept hoping for the best, but the realization crept in that the best scenario was for Casey to not be there at all. But then again, I would still be saddled with "what ifs" and would constantly wonder what had become of her. I couldn't help it. I wanted and needed to see Casey. I had to know, one way or another, what had happened, and to know if what I felt in my heart was just some phantom longing, or the embers of something just waiting to ignite. I began to feel guilty with those thoughts, but somehow they felt so right. For the moment. I was tearing myself up inside, and I didn't even know why.

Julie finally woke up, and sat up, rubbing her eyes and yawning.

"How long did I sleep?"

I tried to make a joke, "You missed a helluva reunion." She smiled weakly, so I gave her a serious answer. "About two hours, and you didn't move a muscle. How do you feel?"

"Ask me Sunday," she responded.

I looked at her, "Please know that I love you more than anything. I wanted to come to this reunion to see all those people I have lost contact with, people that I once cared enough to call my friends. And, I want to show off my hot doctor wife."

She smiled at that.

"I don't even know if Casey will be here," I continued. "Or even if she is, if she's married, has kids, or even what she will do if we see each other. Remember, when we broke up, I wrote hundreds of letters to her and tried calling her without any response. It's not as if this is going to be a tearful, Hallmark card reunion." Then I said something I didn't expect to say, or that it would hit me like it did. "I'm sure she still hates my guts."

Julie just sat there on the edge of the bed staring at the floor listening. Somehow, I felt my words were giving her some comfort but didn't fill *all* of the emotional holes that she had within her. Holes that I had created, one way or another. Her demeanor was quiet, reserved and somewhat distant. I grabbed her hand and pulled her up off the bed and embraced her tightly. In that moment, I forgot all about Casey, and the reunion. Julie returned the embrace, and I inhaled her essence. In my mind and my heart, she had finally taken her place as my world, my being, and my soul mate. I loved this woman. Really loved her. This revelation was something that should have happened 10 years ago, and now my guilt for wanting to see Casey so bad had become guilt for not treating Julie better, or with more attention. I decided at that point that I didn't care if Casey was there or not, that whether or not I even saw her this weekend, Julie was my wife and she was the one that I loved. I didn't need to confront some old flame to know that anymore. I loved my wife for richer or poorer, in sickness and in health, for as long as be both shall live. That vow, as with all my vows to her, meant everything to me.

We cleaned up and went to the evening mixer at the Deer Park Country Club. About 30 people attended, mostly classmates that still lived in town. The rest were coming in tomorrow. To my surprise my old Aviator quarterback, Johnny Hansbrook was there. He'd never left Deer Park. I was shocked at how different he looked. His full head of blond hair had been replaced with thin wisps of gray, and widow's peaks that reached well into the stratosphere. His once athletic frame was gone, and his midsection was expanded greatly. In fact, he looked as if he was trying to smuggle in a basketball under his shirt. Johnny--well, John, now--and I talked for a good half-hour, all the while I kept on eye on the door. John ran a Ford dealership in Greensburg, and was doing quite well for himself. I asked him whatever happened to Kelly Simmons, and he had no idea who I was talking about. So much for the DPHS Power Couple of 1969.

I fluttered around to various groups in and around the banquet hall, injecting myself into conversations, reliving old tales, and introducing my wife to whoever would listen. I was having a great time, and for the first time since the reunion announcement had arrived in January, I wasn't thinking about Casey Martin. Julie was having a great time as well, and each time I introduced her, she rose to the occasion. Having a hot doctor wife is pure gold at a high school reunion. We were king and queen of the mixer, and we both knew it.

Several times throughout the evening, I was pulled aside by guys and told how lucky I was to have such a beautiful wife, and by girls who told me how lucky I was to find such a beautiful wife that would put up with me. I agreed with them all, I was lucky. I won the lottery 10 years ago, and was just now realizing the extent of my winnings. I was lucky to have her, and lucky that she had decided to stay with me, even when I was being stupid and selfish, which was 90% of the time.

As the mixer began to thin out, we went back to the hotel and as soon as we stepped through the door of our room, we attacked each other like teenagers. We made love with a passion and intensity that had been absent for years. I was never more in love with Julie than I was that night. After the fact, we collapsed, exhausted, into each other's arms and slept as one. It was the best night of my life.

The next morning I signed up to participate in a golf outing, and Julie was going to catch up on some paperwork in the hotel and relax. At half-past nine, there was a knock on our door. I opened it and Gary Bartner, my old friend, stood there in his garish golf outfit holding a bottle of Ripple wine and wearing a smile that told me that he might have already started drinking it.

"Gary, please tell me that's not Ripple?" I pleaded, smiling.

Gary grinned broadly, "You know it. I brought it over to celebrate."

"Oh, sweet Jesus," I replied.

"Remember those tee shirts that we had made?" he asked. "'Ripple Wine and Class of '69 are mighty fine?'"

"Yeah, but that was a few years ago, and we were broke then," I said. "I can afford better wine these days."

"I know you can," he said. "But today is for the cheap stuff."

Julie was still in bed, not having adjusted to the time change, so I kissed her on the cheek and then Gary and I headed to the golf course. What I didn't count on was that Gary had three more bottles of Ripple wine with him, and by the time we finished the round and hung out at the clubhouse with the rest of the group, I was pretty drunk. I don't even remember my score, or even if we kept score. At this rate, I wasn't even going to make it to the dinner and dance.

I got back to the hotel room, and I told Julie I would have to take a nap to be ready for tonight. I asked her to wake me up at six in order to give me time to get ready. That was the last thing I remembered before I passed out, still wearing my golf shoes and everything. I woke up with a horrible headache and decided I wouldn't drink that night. Hell, I wasn't too sure I would drink ever again. I downed some aspirin and took a long, hot shower, and although I felt better, the mere thought of alcohol turned my stomach.

I stepped out of the shower, and Julie stood in the doorway of the bathroom looking like an angel.

"How do I look?" she asked.

"Like the most beautiful woman to ever be in Deer Park," I said. I pulled the towel away from my midsection and showed her how beautiful she was. "Look at what you do to me." She smiled.

"Keep that thought for later," she said, smiling.

I wrapped the towel around me and started to get ready. I stared at Julie through the reflection in the mirror, and admired her stunning beauty. In fact, I don't think she had ever looked more beautiful to me than at that moment. I got dressed and we left our room. Like newly minted lovers, we held hands as we walked out of the hotel to the car and made our way to the high school for the reunion.

As we walked into the gymnasium, I started to survey the people that were there and tried to match names with faces, plus twenty years of time. Thankfully, the nametags helped. There were about one hundred and fifty people already there, all drinking and engaging in conversation. For the first hour or so, Julie and I just seemed to linger around the peripheral boundaries of the gymnasium, or we stayed at our table greeting people as they came by. Although I was excited to see many of my classmates, I was somewhat reluctant to engage in any conversations. I really couldn't explain it but there was this desire to keep my distance from these people. Julie was seated at the table and I had just finished meeting the wife of Jimmy Miller, the Aviators kicker when I felt a presence behind me that sent a chill down my spine.

"Chad Breckinridge!" a female voice said aloud from my rear. My heart stopped, literally stopped in my chest. I saw spots dance before my eyes. The room's temperature went up to one-twenty, and a sweat broke out on my forehead. I slowly turned to see who had called my name, and saw Tricia Baker standing there, hands on her hips. Her wide, wide hips.

"Tricia?" I asked, though I knew the answer. "Tricia Baker?"

She smiled and threw her flabby arms around my shoulders. I looked over at our table and saw Julie sitting there, with a smile so big it lit up the entire gymnasium. I saw her mouth: "is that her?" I shook my head, and Julie's smile faded a bit. Only a bit.

"How are you?" Tricia asked and she pulled away, but still kept me at arm's length.

"I'm good," I said. "How're you?"

"I'm great," she said. "I'm married to Doug McGary, you remember Doug?"

I didn't, but nodded anyway.

"We have six kids," she said. "My oldest just got into IU. You went to IU, didn't you, Chad?"

I nodded, and looked over at the table begging Julie for help. She was enjoying this. "I did, for my undergrad. I got my law degree from UCLA. My wife and I live in southern California." I hoped that mentioning my wife would somehow help me out of this. I stared at Julie, wanting so much to be there with her, talking to her, and not Tricia Baker--err--McGary, or whatever. Suddenly, in the middle of all of this, I saw Casey Martin walk into the gymnasium alone. Julie saw the look on my face, and whipped her head around faster than I had ever seen it go toward the entrance. My breath left me. Tricia became non-existent, having once again been replaced by Casey. The irony was delicious. Immediately my thoughts started to fluctuate and become somewhat erratic. My heart started to pound, and once again I saw spots and I felt an ever-increasing pressure in my chest. I couldn't take my eyes off Casey. I don't think I even excused myself from Tricia; I just walked away. I absently made my way back to our table, staring at Casey the whole time, hoping that she wouldn't notice me. I had to gather my thoughts and get past this anxiety attack before I could decide what to do. Instead, I just stood there watching her move throughout the gymnasium talking with various people. I knew I wanted to go up and talk to her, but for some reason, I held myself back. I finally got back to the table and I sat down to compose myself before I went over and spoke to her.

I needed a drink, but didn't want one.

"So, that's her?" Julie asked. I had completely forgotten that she was there. This was going to end badly. I turned and looked at my wife and weakly offered her a smile.

"How'd you know?" I asked.

She kept looking at Casey, "It was so obvious, you stopped in your tracks. Hell, you look like you've seen a ghost."

I had. That was the problem. I was staring at a ghost from my past. A ghost that was alive, and was still as beautiful as I remembered. I didn't know what to say next. My mouth was dry, and my palms were drenched. I could feel Julie watching me closely, but I'm not sure I cared.

"Go talk to her," she finally said. "Sitting here is not going to help."

I tried to respond, "No, I don't need to do that--"

"Chad, don't make this more awkward than it is already. Please." I gathered myself. Julie was right, it wasn't going to make things better to sit there. The only way I would ever get past this, and get on with my life was to confront the ghost. I stood up, still staring at Casey from across the room.

"You want to go with me?" I asked, both out of courtesy, and as a cry for assistance.

"No," Julie said, with icicles hanging off the word. I could tell that she was pissed. I could tell that regardless of what happened in the next few minutes, our lives were going to be different. Forever.

I stood up, took a deep breath, and strolled confidently over to where Casey was standing and talking to a group of girls that I vaguely remembered was the French club. They were over by the bar.

"Hey, Casey," I said, shocked at the sound of my own voice. "Long time no see." Sixteen years I had waited to talk to this woman again, sixteen years and that is what came out? That sure wasn't the line I had intended to use. As usual, she had cast a spell over me.

Casey smiled, as the recognition of who I was crept over her face.

"Oh, hi Chad," Casey said with a voice that sounded...fake. She kept her distance, and didn't even offer a hug. I thought about offering my hand to shake, but decided against it. This was a train wreck.

"You look great," I said. "How have you been?"

"I've been just fine." Again, a monotone response. I was quickly losing the already fake confidence I had walked over with. I tried again.

"It's been a long time." For some reason, my heart rate continued to increase and that pressure in my chest would not go away. The conversation with Casey wasn't anything like I had envisioned it would be. There weren't birds singing, nor were there rainbows hanging in the sky. It was very matter of fact and it was clear she was keeping her distance from me. After a few more awkward exchanges, she gently placed her hand on my arm and said, "Well Chad, it sure was nice seeing you again, I'm going to mingle for a bit. Maybe we can talk later." I stood there, stunned. Before I could say anything, she started to walk away.

"Nice seeing you again too, Casey," I said under my breath. And there it was. Sixteen years of wondering dissipated into the ether. This woman that I had loved practically at first sight, who had been there for me during the war, and after was truly gone from me. I had wasted so much of my life on a ghost. And as she floated away, the realization set in. Now I knew. Now I could get on with my life. I could be the husband my wife deserved, and the father my daughter needed. Now I knew.

I stood there for several minutes after she left, and greeted several people who stopped by to talk. I wasn't up for telling old stories with people I haven't seen in 20 years. I'd got what I had come for. I felt a mixture of relief that I finally saw her again, but also felt somewhat depressed by her demeanor and her apparent lack of interest in me. Sixteen years later and I finally realized that Casey was over me.

Unfortunately, Julie hadn't seen it that way. She saw Casey's hand on my arm, the look in my eye, the across-the-room tenderness that in reality was a gentle, but harsh letdown. I was having my life's greatest epiphany at that moment, but to her, all she saw was confirmation that I had never been fully in love with her. It was a stupid thing to let her sit there and confirm her worst fears, and allow her anger and anxiety to build. I should have asked Casey to come meet Julie, I should have taken Julie with me, I should have just turned around and went back to the table like nothing had happened. Instead, I took an awkward situation and made it worse.

When I finally did get back to the table, Julie was distant and cold.

Every bit of renewed intimacy we'd had over the past couple of days was gone. Although the party was just getting started, she just said one thing to me. "Let's go."

I didn't argue, didn't make my goodbyes, I took her arm and led her out and to the car, neither one of us saying a word. When we got into the car, any remaining composure Julie had was gone, and she broke down into hysterical tears.

"Honey--" I tried to assure her.

"*DON'T* 'honey' me!"

"Julie, I'm sorry for losing my composure, but she--"

"She *WHAT*?"

I lowered my voice to a near whisper. "She wanted nothing to do with me."

"So *THAT's* what this was all about? You wanted to see if she still had feelings for you? What if she had? What then? Would you leave me sitting at that table? Would I even get a courtesy wave before you and her ran off? You stood there, practically worshiping her, and I watched *MY* husband in love with another woman."

"Julie, I was nervous."

"You were like a damn teenager! If you *EVER* showed half that much affection towards me, I could at least appreciate it. You have spent most of your life wondering if the grass was greener on the other side, but you neglected your own grass in the process. You're an asshole."

"Julie, that wasn't--"

"You *STILL* love her! I watched the whole thing. When she walked into the room, the world stopped. *YOUR* world stopped." She broke down sobbing again. "I'm supposed to be your world," she said, under her breath, between sobs.

I was embarrassed, mad, ashamed, and confused. I decided to just drive back to the hotel. Arguing now wasn't going to solve anything. I needed Julie to calm down, and I needed to process my own thoughts. What I saw as a positive in my life, Julie saw as a negative.

"Julie, I'm sorry," I tried to explain. "But you weren't there, she wanted nothing to do with me--"

"Chad, stop! Just please stop talking." She leaned forward, head in her hands, sobbing.

As we drove along Highway 141 heading back to our hotel, I was hoping that I would be able to explain what had happened; that Casey had moved on and deep down inside myself, I finally had as well. As soon as Julie calmed down, I would tell her how much I loved her, and how wrong I'd been, and how I would dedicate the rest of my life to her and Jennifer. If she would let me, I would be the man she married; the man who vowed to love her forever. I would be the man she needed. I had finally realized, without a doubt, that I was in love with her. I couldn't wait to tell her that.

I never got the chance.

Chapter 23

According to what I was told, Mary Decker was a 38-year-old mother of four, born and raised in Deer Park, as were several generations of Deckers before her. In fact, I think I played football with her brother. Mary had married Tommy Stevens right out of high school and stayed at home to raise their kids until it became obvious that her husband was not going to stay employed anywhere long enough to keep the bills paid.

She had been working as a certified nursing assistant making ten dollars an hour for the Boucher Nursing Home in Deer Park for the past 10 years. Since her husband left her two years ago, Mary had taken control of her life (as well as taken her name back.) Mary decided to attend nursing school at a local Community College, and had taken a second job as a clerk at the local Stop & Shop convenience store near interstate 74. Her mother had moved in to help take care of the kids, but even with two jobs and her mother's social security, it was barely enough to make ends meet.

Mary told her friends and family that once she got her nursing certification, she would triple her income, and finally leave the more disgusting aspects of caring for the elderly to her current co-workers.

It had been a long week, with Mary taking a couple of extra shifts at the nursing home in addition to her summer school schedule and her late shifts at the Stop & Shop. According to her co-workers, she had been exhausted, having been up for 47 of the last 52 hours, but had the next two days off to catch up with her sleep and spend time with her kids.

She had been on her way home after a double shift, and was heading out of Deer Park on Hwy 164 to her house, which was in a little subdivision about halfway between Deer Park and the lake. It was a drive she had made thousands of times over the years, and she used to joke that she could drive it in her sleep.

On this night, she was mistaken.

There was one winding curve, and according to the Warren County sheriff, Mary had fallen asleep behind the wheel. Not for long--probably about 10 seconds--but her 1981 Chevy Caviler had headed straight where the road curved.

I didn't see her until it was too late.

According to the official police report, based on eyewitness testimony and accident forensics, I hit my brakes and turned the wheel sharply to the left to avoid the oncoming car. Mary's foot must have slipped off the accelerator, and I had hit the brakes, and the angle of impact had prevented a full head-on impact, which would have probably killed us all.

It only killed one of us.

Julie had been bent over forward crying over the events at the reunion, that much I remember. She didn't have her seatbelt on, and the rental car only had driver-side air bags. According to the sheriff, the impact had sent her head-first into the windshield, the downward angle of her head and the force of the impact severing her spine between the third and fourth vertebrae, killing her instantly. The sheriff assured me that it was likely that she hadn't suffered.

I knew otherwise. She had been suffering for years.

Mary and I had both been wearing our seatbelts, which likely saved our lives. Since Mary was in a relaxed state when the impact occurred, she only suffered a concussion, a separated shoulder from the seatbelt shoulder harness, and multiple abrasions and bruises from the impact.

I had a mild concussion from the deployment of the airbag, and a broken wrist, as well as a busted knee and bruised ribs and assorted cuts and abrasions, all which would heal in time. I also had a broken heart, and I wasn't sure that it could ever heal.

Most of this is what I was told by the sheriff and what I had read in the report.

I remember nothing of the accident itself.

I do remember waking up in a hospital room at Deer Park Hospital, a 104-bed acute care hospital which had just gone through a $4 million dollar renovation to upgrade facilities and to encourage patients to stay in town for healthcare instead of making the trip to the larger hospitals in Indianapolis or Cincinnati.

The face I saw when I came around was a familiar one, John Kennedy, who threw the best parties in high school and last night was one of my bright spots at the Deer Park High School reunion, but today he had returned to his duties as medical director of Deer Park Hospital. According to what he told me later, when he was paged about the accident, it was his decision to keep us at Deer Park, instead of transferring us to Methodist Hospital's Trauma Center in Indianapolis. He decided to keep us here, and to act as our primary physician. He was a good friend.

When I opened my eyes, John was standing at the end of the bed, making notes in the medical charts. He looked at me, and gave me a warm smile.

"Hey buddy, how are you feeling?"

I flexed my fingers and toes to make sure they worked, and looked from side to side.

"Fine, I think. What happened?"

"You were in a car accident, pretty bad one," he explained. "You're lucky to be alive."

He walked around to the side of the bed, I expected him to begin to examine me, or ask me questions, but he just stood there, looking at me. Something was wrong.

Instinctively, I again flexed my fingers and toes, and looked down to make sure I wasn't feeling "phantom limbs." Julie had once told me about the sensation that amputees feel when they lose limbs. To them, it felt like there was something there, even though there wasn't. I had to make sure I was intact. Luckily, everything was still there, even though it hurt all over.

I looked at John, "Am I okay?"

"You'll be fine, you just need some time to recuperate, and…"

"There's something you're not telling me." I could sense it. John Kennedy had always had a peculiar tell, which made playing poker in his basement a lucrative thing back in high school. But now, since he was my attending physician, that tell scared the hell out of me.

Even though I was under a haze of the medication and the concussion, it finally dawned on me.

"Julie!" I exclaimed. I tried to sit up, to get out of bed. "Where's Julie? I need to go see her and make sure she's okay."

John gently, but firmly put his hand on my arm, and spoke softly. "Chad, just lay back down," he paused, "there's nothing you can do."

I became agitated. "What are you talking about? Where's Julie? She needs me, I'm her husband."

I turned my head from side to side, and saw that I was in a private room. Why wouldn't they put husband and wife in the same room? It didn't make any sense. I caught John's eyes focused on mine, with a look that I'm sure he's had to hold many times over the years in his career as a physician. He didn't say anything, didn't quickly assure me that Julie was okay, or offer an explanation as to why she wasn't in the room with me. I was hoping he'd tell me that she was outside waiting, or in another part of the hospital being treated. But John offered me nothing but that endearing look of compassion.

And then I knew.

"Oh God."

"I'm so sorry, Chad."

"I…I don't understand…"

"It was a bad accident," he tried to explain. "She wasn't wearing her seatbelt. She was--there was nothing that could have been done."

"Oh my God! Oh my God! Oh my God!" I just repeated it over and over; tears cascading down my face. A nurse stepped into the room and John motioned for her to leave. He kept one hand on my arm, while pulling up a chair with the other hand. He took a seat.

"Chad, I know this is hard, but I'm here for you buddy."

"I…can't believe it. It's my fault. It's my fault."

"Chad, it's not your fault, it was an accident."

He didn't know. There was no way he could know.

Julie was gone.

I sat there for the next hour or so, and John popped in to check on me as much as he could. I was in a level of shock that I could never have previously imagined. I just lay in my bed, repeating the same things over and over. I kept seeing our last conversation in the car as we left the reunion. It was like a film, and I watched two actors argue over something that, as an observer, seemed trivial.

Julie was gone.

My head was swimming in confusion from the concussion, and from the medication, and from the hard reality that my beautiful wife was dead. I finally fell back asleep, hoping that when I woke up, I would be back in the hotel with Julie lying next to me in my arms, and this had all been a horrible nightmare.

It wasn't.

Julie was gone.

I slept in spurts and each time I awoke, I held misguided hope that I was somewhere else, and that this wasn't happening. Instead, I still found myself in the hospital recuperating from injuries sustained in a car accident that had taken the life of my wife. And as my head began to clear, an additional grim reality struck me.

Julie was gone...and it was my fault!

It was my fault that she had been in Deer Park. It was my fault that she had to come to try and let me get Casey Martin out of my system. It was my fault that she had witnessed Casey and I, and my stupid reaction had infuriated her so much that we had to leave the reunion early and that we had to fight in the car.

It was all my fault and it got her killed.

I got her killed.

The next time that John came in after to check on me, I asked him to take a seat. I was more coherent now, and I needed information. "Have you told my family?"

"The sheriff's department called Julie's folks in California last night," he explained. "You were in no shape to make that call. This morning,

I placed a call there myself to explain to your mother-in-law how your progress was coming along."

"I need to talk to my daughter," I said as Jenny's face haunted my thoughts. What would I say to her? How could I tell her that her mother was dead because of me?

"I understand," he said. "If you think you are ready, I would suggest to you to make that call. Your family is worried sick. I told them not to come here, that you'll be released and back on a plane in a day or two."

"Thank you."

"You want me to stay in the room?"

"No, I need to do this alone."

John placed the phone on the tray over my bed, patted my shoulder, and walked out the door. I dialed the number to my in-laws, and it was answered on the first ring.

"Hello?" my father-in-law asked.

"Terry, it's Chad."

"Son, how are you feeling?" I could tell in his demeanor that he was generally concerned. Plus, since I've known him, he's never called me "son."

"I'm so sorry, Terry," I offered, and then I began to break down. "I'm so very sorry."

"Sheriff told me it wasn't your fault," he said, matter-of-factly. "It was an accident. There was nothing you could have done."

"I'm just sorry…for everything." I don't think I had ever felt so lost, so scared, or so sad. As I spoke each word, I felt like tiny parts of me were dying. All I could see in my mind was Jenny's face, and that just made me even more despondent.

"I know," Terry said. "It's okay. You just worry about getting healed and getting back here. Your daughter needs you."

"Can I talk to her?"

"Okay," he said and then he lowered his voice to a near whisper. "I hope you understand that she's really upset."

"I know, but I need to hear her voice."

There was a pause, and I knew that she had been in the room. After a few seconds, I heard her voice. "Daddy?"

"Hi, sweetheart."

"Tell me mommy's okay," she said, and I could hear the anguish in her voice. "Tell me she's coming home."

I tried to be strong, but my voice choked. "I'm sorry honey."

She sniffled for a few seconds, and then her voice got very low and firm, "Why did she even go there with you?"

"Honey--

"If she had stayed home, she would still be alive."

"Honey, it was an accident."

"It should have been you," she said and my heart literally stopped in my chest.

"Honey, don't say--"

I heard her sobbing intensify then lose volume as it moved away from the phone. Then the voice of my father-in-law was back. "I'm sorry, Chad, she's...she's just very upset."

"It's fine, she's--"

"I've made arrangements to have the body flown back," he interrupted, changing the subject. "And I'll be flying into Indianapolis to bring her home. Her mother and I have made the funeral arrangements as well."

"That sounds fine," I said. "Thank you."

"You get your rest, and we'll see you when you get home." The conversation had turned to business; the business of one man burying his daughter, while the other sat in a hospital room two thousand miles away crucifying himself over her death.

Terry had always been distant toward me, and had been very vocal about me not being a part of my family. Both of my in-laws thought very little of me, and something like this would not make any of that better.

"Thanks, Terry." The line went dead.

I hung up the receiver and replayed my daughter's words over and over in my head. She was right. It should have been me. Jenny and Julie were so close, as much as any nine year old and her mother could be. I was just the absent father who worked too much, played too much, and put old ghosts before the living, breathing people in my life.

It should have been me.

Julie would have been able to go on without me. Hell, she'd done so well for the last ten years, that she probably wouldn't even have grieved. Julie would have gone home and her family would have taken care of both she and Jenny, and Chad Breckenridge would have slowly faded from all of their memories.

It should have been me.

My daughter wished that I had died in her mother's place, and now I agreed with her.

I had barely touched my lunch, having lost my appetite when John stopped in to ask me if I was well enough to take visitors. I told him I was. I thought maybe Casey had come by, and I immediately hated myself even more for the thought. Instead, it was a deputy from the Warren County Sheriff's Department to follow up with the accident investigation.

I asked him to tell me what happened, since I didn't remember. He read the accident report with the calm nature his job required, but with a nervous crack in his voice, knowing that the fatality was my wife. He asked me if I had been drinking, since I was at a party with alcohol. I told him I hadn't, but didn't tell him why. He said the blood work would confirm my story, but the accident was obviously the fault of the other driver.

The other driver.

I hadn't even thought about it. I asked the deputy about the other driver, about how she was doing.

"She's pretty banged up," he offered. "And she's an emotional wreck, but she'll recover.

"She's a good lady," he added. "It was an accident, she feels horrible about it."

He then told me all about her. About her life, her history, both past and present, and what had happened that night from her perspective, whether he was supposed to or not. When he was done, I felt I knew more about Mary Decker than I did my own mother. "Don't worry deputy, I don't blame her. It was an accident."

"Well, I'm glad you think that," he said. "I've known her and the family for years, and she'll never forgive herself for this."

I guess neither of us could forgive ourselves for our parts in the play that had killed my wife.

"Do you need anything else from me?" I asked. "I'm pretty tired."

"No, no I'm done here," he said. "We'll get the report to you to submit to the insurance companies."

Companies? Then I realized that he meant both auto insurance and life insurance. It was another in a long line of reminders that Julie was gone. And with each reminder, my heart died a little bit inside.

John came in later that afternoon and told me there were no adverse signs of damage from the concussion, and that I was going to be discharged the following morning. The hotel had delivered our luggage to the hospital and John offered to take me to Indianapolis for the flight back to L.A. I asked if he knew when Julie's body would be flying out and he did not have an answer. I could tell that he probably knew, but didn't want to share. I don't know if it was to protect me, or to protect my father-in-law, who had made all of the arrangements without my input. I just wanted to get home. I needed to see Jenny. I'd missed the chance to act upon my revelations with Julie. But I could still be a good father; I would *HAVE* to be a good father. No more chasing ghosts for me. Not now, not ever again.

Throughout the afternoon, there was a surprising stream of people who visited me in the hospital room. Chuck and Debbie Arnold, who owned the flower shop in town and graduated a couple of years after me, Miles Williams, the pastor from Deer Park Baptist Church, where I attended as a child, but hadn't been back since I was 18, Larry Anderson from Anderson Ford, who offered to give me a free rental can to drive to the airport; people I hadn't seen, nor heard from in years were showing up and offering their support. It's amazing what small town hospitality means to someone who has spent the past few years in Los Angeles, and the majority of his time on this earth focused selfishly on his own life. It meant a lot.

Around 4:30, there was a knock on the door, and it opened before I could say "come in."

It was Casey.

I looked at her and was overcome with an overwhelming sense of guilt and anguish. I remembered my daughters words, "it should have been you."

I remembered all of the years of wasted thought and yearning pursuit and careless wondering what it would have been like to have Casey to myself. I wondered at that moment if maybe I didn't turn the wheel on purpose, if maybe I had wanted this to happen. I doubted that very thought, but did not question why it was there. I am, and have always been an asshole.

Jenny was right, it should have been me.

Casey slowly walked halfway between the door and my bed. I could read an entire novel in her face.

"Chad, I'm so sorry," she offered. "I'm sorry for everything."

"That makes two of us."

"We make our choices," she began, almost as if she had prepared for this speech. "We live with those choices. You and I were something once, and you blew it. And for some reason, it seems like you just can't let it go. You had a wife, a family, and the way you acted with me at the reunion... the fire is still there, it's still in your eyes. I can see it plain as day, and I'm sure your wife did too. After all these years, you are still carrying a torch that was extinguished years ago.

"Casey, I--"

"Let me finish, please," she begged. "I didn't know your wife, but the fact that you had somebody that cared enough to be with you--and from experience, that wasn't easy--to even come across the country for you told me everything I needed to know about the woman. You broke my heart all those years ago. And I still feel the effects of that everyday. So I understand how your wife felt." Casey paused, unsure if she had the courage to continue, to say what she had come to say.

"I was your wife's Staci."

I'm not sure I'd ever been hit like that before. I felt the air leave my lungs, and as quickly as the words had left Casey's mouth, I was crying. Full-on crying.

"I shouldn't have come here," she apologized. "I'm sorry for what happened to your wife, and just wanted to make sure you were okay."

She turned towards the door, "I've...I've gotta go."

"Casey, wait," I sobbed, but I didn't want her to stay. I needed time. I was broken, more so than a concussion and a few bruises. I was broken on the inside. And not even Dr. John Kennedy, the self-proclaimed President of Parties, could heal me.

"No Chad, I shouldn't have come here," she said. Her eyes filled with tears.

"Please..."

"Goodbye, Chad." She walked out of the room, and as the door shut behind her, I closed my eyes and felt every bit of the anger, guilt, rage, and sorrow and I wanted to scream out, but instead I just wept. I wept for me, for Julie, for Jenny. I wept for what was left of my life, which admittedly wasn't much. I loved my wife. I loved my daughter. And--God help me--I loved Casey Martin. But I did not love myself.

It had all fallen apart. Everything in my life was in chaos.

It should have been me.

I laid there in silence for the next couple of hours, thinking and crying. I had nothing left. My wife was dead, my daughter wished I were dead, Casey still hated me. I was broken and had no idea how to get myself fixed.

The night nurse came in to check on me just after eight. As she left the room, I heard a brief conversation in the hall, and then my door swung open and Marty Green stood there in the archway, stoic and serious.

"How you doing, buddy?" he asked.

"I've been better," I said. "Visiting hours are over, how'd you get them to let you in?"

"I told them I was your brother," he said. He stepped into the room and shut the door behind him. He pulled a chair over to my bedside and then sat down. "You know, when I first heard about the reunion, I had no desire to come back. I was just too busy, and these things are always the same. Bad jokes, terrible stories of a time we all hated--and can only now look back on and smile--and catching up with people we barely knew in school, but now we're glad to know them because they represent a time when we were all innocent.

"It's all a game, and no one ever stays in touch. Old girlfriends get fat, and the clique mentality of high school is exasperated by we, as adults, now trying to one up each other with comparisons of wealth, family, and status."

"Well, thanks for your positive attitude," I said sarcastically.

"I couldn't give a shit about the reunion," he continued. "But when John Kennedy calls me up and tells me what happened, I cancel a week's worth of meetings and fly up here.

"So I ask you again, how are you doing, Chad?"

I looked at him. My best man, my best friend, the godfather of my daughter. We'd served together in the jungle, and we'd studied together in college. And then, because I was stupid, we had a fight and our friendship had suffered. We'd patched things up before my wedding, but we both knew that it was never going to be the same between us. He basically was my brother. And I his. And brother's fight and they make up and they do it all over again. Regardless of where our friendship was at that moment, the fact that he sat there, right here, right now in my hospital room in the crappy little town that he and I had grown up in, it hit me hard. And I started crying again.

"I'm not good," I admitted.

Uncharacteristically, he reached down and took my hand in his. He didn't say anything; he just let me cry.

"It's my fault, Marty," I said. "I killed her. I killed Julie."

"That's not true," he said. "It was an accident. John told me the whole story."

"She wouldn't have come if it weren't for--" I stopped myself, then decided to put all my cards on the table. If there was anyone in the world that I could have this conversation with, it was Marty. "--because I still had feelings for Casey Martin."

He exhaled a pronounced sigh.

"I've never stopped thinking of her, and I still write her those damn letters. Julie knew about it, but let me be. I told her it was therapy. Like it was my diary, or journal, or whatever. But in reality, I don't know what I was doing. I used those letters as a way to get away from the life I had.

"When I'm in California, all I do is work, go out and hang out and have drinks with friends, and write those letters. Those three acts make up the life of Chad Breckinridge. I'm not a husband. I'm not a father. I'm just a guy who pays the bills and sleeps in a bed under the roof that I pay for. But Julie still cared. She still loved me. When the reunion came up, Julie wanted to come and see her. She needed to see Casey to understand who she was battling with all this time for my affections. She'd hoped that this weekend would be the catharsis I needed to finally assume my role as husband and father.

"Julie and I fought the night of the reunion. After Casey and I finally met up, after I finally got to confront this person who in my mind I had turned into some kind of mythical creature. Casey barely gave me the time of day, but Julie didn't like the way I acted. She picked up on that still-burning fire in my heart.

"We left the reunion, shouting at each other, and then I woke up here, in this bed. I killed her. I didn't put a gun to her head and pull the trigger, but I broke her heart time and again, and she was in this town, in that car because of me."

"Are you done?"

"No. Because now Jenny is--I don't know. I talked to her, and the last thing she said to me was that she wished it had been me instead of Julie. And I agree with her. It should have been me."

"Now are you done?"

"Why are you even here?" I asked. The floodgates had been opened and everything was pouring out. Everything! "The same shit that I always did to you, I did to Julie. You, better than *ANYBODY* in my life, can understand what Julie went through with me. I'm an asshole to my core, and Jenny is right. It should have been me."

"What you are going through is called survivor's guilt," Marty said. "I go through it day in and day out because of Vietnam. It weighs on your soul, but all you can do is push on and hope that the next day will be better than the last.

"You can sit here and analyze yourself until you're blue in the face, but until you find your center, you will never move forward. It sucks that Julie is gone. I liked her. Of all your 'loves' she was probably my favorite. But this is a golden opportunity for you to rebuild yourself. This accident took your life away, but left you with the pieces to rebuild. I had to do it after 'Nam, and I think I finally got the hang of it. Now it's your turn.

You have to change now, not just for yourself, not just for Jenny, but for everyone in your life.

"You realize that you're an asshole. Good. That is step one. How do you stop being an asshole? How do you stop being so selfish? How do you begin to change? These are questions you will need to ask yourself everyday for the rest of your life. But only if you want to change."

"I do," I said.

"I've spent way too much of my life pulling your ass out of the fire," he said. "My mistake was never teaching you how not to get burned in the first place. So, maybe this tragedy will have some positive come out of it. Only you can figure that out."

I squeezed his hand and then used my other hand, which had a cast on the wrist, to wipe my eyes with the blanket.

"Thanks for coming up," I said. "It means a lot."

"That's what brothers do."

We stayed up and talked more and eventually the tears dried up. He told me about his job in Florida and how the company he works for is looking to expand over the entire southeast. I told him about Jenny, and my job, and southern California. After an hour, we were just two friends catching up. The night nurse checked in on us every hour, never once mentioning that even family had set visiting hours, and that my "brother" should probably go home. She let us be and Marty and I got a lot of stuff out in the open. I don't think I'd ever felt better inside.

I dozed off sometime in the night, probably in the middle of a conversation and Marty had been there until I went under. He was gone when the nurse woke me up for my three a.m. meds.

The next morning I was checked over again by John, and around noon, he came in with a couple of hangers full of clothes and a small suitcase.

"I had them bring your toiletries and I got you an outfit to wear. As soon as you're ready, you're discharged and I can drive you up to Indy. Your flight is at six, so we have plenty of time."

"Thanks, John…for everything."

"Doing my job and helping a friend. Sorry it had to be under these circumstances."

"Yeah, me too."

I was still sore and with a cast on my wrist, basic grooming took a lot longer than normal. After I had shaved and washed my face and hands and felt respectable again. I put on the khakis and golf shirt John had brought me, which also took longer than normal. I felt like I was in a comedy bit on *Laugh-in*. Any second, I expected Goldie Hawn's head to pop out of the closet with a terrible joke. I finished dressing and luckily, John had brought my loafers so I didn't have to worry about tying my shoes.

Finally, I put on my blazer and as was instinct, checked my inside pocket. Julie used to put little notes of encouragement, or "to-do" lists, or grocery lists in there so I wouldn't forget. I didn't expect anything, but checked out of habit.

I felt a piece of paper.

I tried to remember what it could have been, if there were a packing list for the trip I forgot, or a list of groceries from two months ago. But as I opened it, I noticed the stationary was from the hotel here in town, which meant Julie wrote it while we were here. I guessed that she had written it when I was taking my nap before we left for the reunion.

I took a deep breath and opened it up. When the light of the room hit the words, a chill went down my spine. Julie, my wife, was talking to me again.

Dearest Chad,

My life with you these past few years have been the most wonderful years of my life. You've brought sunshine and hope into a life that had been barren for so many years. You gave me unconditional love, in your own way, where I had none. Your sense of humor has given me a reason to smile and laugh when I had none. The times you made fun of me when I became depressed and so serious, caused me to laugh at myself. Your love, and yes, I know it is YOUR love, gave me trust and hope when I had none. Your spirit gave me wings to fly and to embrace life.

I know that I seem distant and this trip has been challenging for you these past few days; but know that I love you, I trust you, and have faith in you. You are the beacon of light, which gives me safe harbor in a restless sea. This is your time; your place and I am here for you.

I love you and regardless of what happens this weekend, I always will!

Your wife forever,
Julie.

I couldn't move. I just sat there grasping the letter and bringing it to my chest as if I was embracing her once again. Tears were flowing down my cheeks like rain sluices. I just kept reading and re-reading that last line:

I love you and regardless of what happens this weekend, I always will!

I felt that she was forgiving me from beyond the grave. Forgiving me for being an asshole. Forgiving me for still holding a candle's flame for a girl that I had known years ago. Julie, in her infinite wisdom, had given me the greatest gift ever. An accident had taken the life of my wife, but I would not let it take mine as well. Julie had made sure of that.

I kissed the letter and folded it up and slid it back into my pocket, close to my heart, where it belonged. After several minutes, a knock on the door broke the silence and John peeked his head into my room.

"Hey buddy, you ready, or do you need a few more minutes?"

It was obvious that he had seen me in the room from the tiny little window and had waited until I was composed. I could see why he was medical director of the hospital, and I couldn't have respected him more.

"No, no, I'm ready," I said. "I'm ready to go home."

Chapter 24

When I got back to California, I was a changed man. Everything that I had promised to do for Jenny and myself, I did. I started working from home two days of every week, and cut down most travel. I knew that this could hurt my chances at partnership with any of the bigger firms, but Jenny needed me, whether she would ever admit it or not. I also ceased going out with my buddies all together. I'm sure the southern California beer and golf industries felt the economic impact of the new Chad Breckinridge. We'd still have occasional get-togethers at my place, or family outings where Jenny could come along, but my days of acting like a perpetual teenager were over.

The biggest change that I had made occurred in my personal life. I refused to date, or to see anyone until Jenny was at least out of the house and in college. This was a personal decision that I had made on the flight back from Indianapolis. I guess fate, or karma, or God, or whatever you wanted to call it had given me my life's "good times" when I was young, and now I was going to pay for it. And to be honest, I also saw this as a penance for what I had done to Julie and to Jenny, and to myself for those years before the accident. No matter how lonely I felt, I stayed away from women. I was dedicated to my daughter and to my home life, and career and relationships ranked far down the list. I stayed true to that promise, even after Jenny eventually left home.

For the first couple of years after the accident, I just seemed to drift through my daily routine to get by. I became interested in scotch and fine wines, but that was just an excuse to drink in excess to numb the fact that I couldn't come to grips with the reality of what life had brought me. I was still dealing with the overwhelming guilt that I had been responsible for Julie's death, and no matter how I tried to convince myself that it hadn't been my fault, taking Marty's words to heart, it still continued to wreck me emotionally. It was probably a good thing that I had refrained from meeting anyone. I had more baggage than a Dutch heiress on an around-the-world cruise. What woman would even want to talk to someone like me?

I had screwed things up with Casey in my twenties, and I had killed Julie in my thirties, so I had to make it right with my daughter in my forties and beyond. I had to show her the love that I felt for her. As Jenny got older, she had become the spitting image of her mother, and it hurt sometimes to look at her. She was a teenage girl who had lost her mother and blamed her father. Though she never came out and said it, she was bitter and angry at me for a long time after the accident, and no matter how hard I tried to talk to her, to explain to her what had happened, she just shrugged it off. She hurt me with her apathy. It was her greatest weapon.

So all I could do in return was give her the best life possible. I tried to be the best father to her I could, I attended every school event and concert, and play, and made sure I was there when I thought she needed me, but she became independent and defiant with each passing year. Had it not been for the influence of Julie's parents, I'm sure Jenny would have spiraled out of control. Fortunately, she had her mother's intelligence and a fierce determination to succeed. She had worked hard in school and earned a scholarship to Cal-Berkley and went on to become a doctor like her mother.

The mutual friends that Julie and I shared had tried hard to incorporate us into their lives after the accident, and I appreciated the gesture. It's not as much that I became a stranger to those people who were trying to help Jenny and I; it's that I was always a stranger to them. It was amazing how much of my life went by without me ever noticing. I used to pride myself on "living in the moment," but this was the furthest thing from that. I had no idea where I was living for all those years, but it definitely wasn't "in the moment." It was more like "outside the moment." Or, as Julie once said in an argument, "living in my own world." Looking back on it, she was 100% right. The trivial things that Julie had hated about me were the things that had defined me. And in retrospect, I hated them too. Why is hindsight always the clearest view?

I realized that after Julie died, she had always been the glue that held our friendships together because she had such an amazing presence. After she died, even though our friends tried to reach out, I just wanted to keep my distance from them all and not allow them to intrude into my emptiness. After all, it was still my penance; it was my cross to bear.

After Jenny went on to Cal-Berkley, I poured myself into my work, becoming a moderately successful labor attorney. I liked the meticulousness of the legal process, and being able to distance myself from my clients was seen as an attribute. With Jenny now in school upstate, I even began to distance myself from everyone in my personal life.

Every so often after Jenny was in college, I would stand quietly as I was getting dressed and just stare into the bathroom mirror above the sink, wondering who the person was that was staring back at me. It couldn't have been me. This person had graying hair, and a face lined with wrinkles. But it was his eyes that spoke the most truth. His eyes were windows to an empty soul. Where had Chad Breckinridge gone? All I ever saw was a hollow shell of a man. There was never any emotion that would have given me hope for signs of life. The person in the mirror was dead, but he just refused to lie down and accept it. And every day was more of the same. Every day the man in the mirror and I would have this melancholic exchange with each other. That emptiness, that feeling of being lost amongst the redwoods of life was so overwhelming. But I wouldn't let it win. Julie would never have wanted that. Jenny--whether she ever admitted it or not--would never have wanted that. I had to somehow quit feeling sorry for myself and find a new purpose in my life. So, fifteen years after I put my wife in the ground, I decided to try and start dating again.

My penance was over.

Chapter 25

I'd been out of the game for a long time. I was a successful attorney, who had aged well, and there were no shortage of woman interested in me, or friends willing to set me up with their friends, but I still found dating to be somewhat challenging. Me, the guy who always had a date lined up--sometimes two. I was the guy who was always wont for female companionship, in high school and beyond. But the game had changed. I felt like I had to be someone else when I was on a date. The women were nice, and moderately attractive, but I was mostly uninterested, no matter how hard I tried, or how much I wanted it to work. When did dating get so hard?

I met a woman through a mutual friend named Lindsay. She was beautiful, and funny, and dare I admit it, sexy. She ran a boutique in the part of old downtown that used to be overrun with prostitutes and drug dealers, but was now cleaned up and respectable. And she did well for herself. Her client list included many well-known celebrities, though she declined to tell me their names. I could have dismissed it as fibs to pad her life resume, but something about her told me that she was legit. And I liked her for it.

I was instantly attracted to her and we started going out. Over the course of several dates with Lindsay, I would find myself drifting off into other dimensions, where I was still engaged in conversation, but didn't hear or comprehend any of the words that were spoken. Lindsay and I would be sitting at a table in a fine restaurant eating dinner and she would be chatting away about something and I would just sit there staring off into space. I'd think of Julie, and of Jenny, and of the things that needed to get done around the house, and about clients, and cases, and Marty in Florida, and damn it all to hell, I thought about Casey. The next thing I knew Lindsay would be shaking my arm and asking if I was okay. I called it "dating Alzheimer's." Every time I tried to focus, my mind would set off on foot over the barren desert of my life, and I would bear witness to the journey without even knowing that Lindsay--or anyone--was there with me.

I wanted to ask Julie if this was an early sign of stroke, or worse. But I couldn't ask Julie. Not anymore. As my personal disconnection with other human beings--namely of the female persuasion--increased, I broke down and asked Jenny about it. She was still in med school, but that didn't mean that she couldn't be a vault of medical knowledge. Of course, any time I did this, I usually got the same response:

"Go see a doctor, Dad."

I have this thing growing on my foot.

"Go see a doctor, Dad."

I haven't had a bowel movement in a week.

"Go see a doctor, Dad."

I get dizzy when I first step out of the shower.

"Go see a doctor, Dad."

I can't stop thinking of your mom, you, my friends, and of a woman named Casey Martin when I'm on a date.

"Go see a doctor, Dad."

Except I never did ask her that last one.

The episodes seemed to reoccur only on dates with women. Eventually, Lindsay saw it as disinterest in her on my part and stopped making time for me. But other women quickly stepped into that void, even though I was realizing that maybe I still wasn't ready to date, or worse, that I never would be. The funny thing is, the more I didn't care, the more I was pursued.

I was getting somewhat concerned about my absenteeism during my brief dating spree, but scared shitless of the fact that I didn't even care about sex. I wondered if this was what was known as the "midlife crisis?" Would I soon go out and buy a sexy, cherry-red convertible car, or worse, a Harley Davidson motorcycle, just to make myself feel manly? Is this what happens in mid life? And even the term, "mid life" means that the pinnacle had been reached and that everything going forward was all downhill. That sad, graying man in the mirror seemed to be winning the battle for my soul. I just wasn't ready to give up the fight.

One evening after returning from a date with a woman named Barb, who was a successful realtor and together we had shared a mutual friend, I found myself sitting on the couch staring at the television set with a scotch and soda, watching reruns of the 70s version of *The Dating Game* on the game show network. *The Dating Game* had always started with host Jim Lange coming out and telling the studio audience--and the audience at home--about three eligible bachelors. I chuckled at the thought, as I had never heard of a bachelor that wasn't eligible. At least until now.

There were three bachelors and a pretty girl (which was always good for TV) who would ask several questions to each of the bachelors and then she'd have to pick one for a date based on their answers. Of course the girl couldn't see the three guys because there was a wall between them. It was mindless entertainment, and watching it took me back to a time where everything made so much more sense in my life.

I wasn't really concentrating on the show, but the idea of the show, when suddenly, my eyes immediately focused on the young, well-proportioned blonde bachelorette. She was absolutely stunning and somehow she looked familiar. She had incredible green eyes, and when she smiled at Jim Lange's terrible jokes, my heart fluttered in my chest. It actually fluttered, like a butterfly in a cage. I had not felt that flutter in over fifteen years.

I knew I had never seen her before, but somehow I felt a connection to her. I watched intently as she played the game. The feeling in my chest spread throughout my body. It was warming, like fresh baked sugar cookies. I felt so much at peace, and I just couldn't understand why. Why was this girl from a 1970s game show rerun making me so excited? Then it finally hit me: the bachelorette looked almost identical to Casey!

I watched the rest of the show, focused on the young girl, whose name was Wendy I think, and just marveled at the resemblance. When the show ended and a *Match Game* rerun started, I turned the TV off, stood up off the couch and paced the room, drink in hand. I began to wonder about Casey, not as a fleeting memory, or as a mental misstep while out on a date, but as a heartfelt inquiry. Even though I had quit writing her after Julie's death and our brief conversation in the hospital, I still wondered about her occasionally.

I began to parade around the living room wondering where she lived now and how she was doing. Was she married? Did she have children? I had successfully exorcised her greater memory from my brain years ago, but seeing that girl on TV had reopened the vault. I kept asking myself questions about her and I decided that I had to have answers to these questions.

I refilled my drink, more soda than scotch this time, and sat down at my writing desk--the same desk that had been the scene for many unanswered letters to this woman. I took out a yellow legal pad and started jotting down ideas and questions that I would need to try and track her down. Where was I going to start? It had been fifteen years since there had been any contact between us (which usually meant that I had written and sent her a letter) including her visiting me in the hospital. We hadn't spoken at all about our personal lives at the reunion, though she obviously knew about Julie. I was positive that she was married and had several children by now. I wrote that down on my pad.

This was crazy!

I jotted down all the things she used to say about where she wanted to go, where she wanted to end up. Deer Park, Indiana was *NEVER* on that list. I'd have to send a cursory inquiry to be sure, but I was confident that she would not still be there. Indy, or Cincy, perhaps, but not Deer Park.

This was crazy!

I reminisced about our time together, and hoped to find clues there. She used to joke with Marty that she was a Red Sox fan, but I think that was only to get him riled up since he was a Reds fan. I wrote that down. She loved fresh fish, and especially lobster, which could have put her in Maine, or Florida. She liked to ski and we had gone to Brown County to snow ski many times when we first started dating. So I wrote down Denver, Colorado. As I poured over everything I knew about her, and made notes of it all, I realized how epic this task was.

This was crazy!

She could literally be living anywhere in the world, and be married to a man who would not take kindly to an old boyfriend looking her up. I could be putting us both in an uncomfortable situation. After all, I couldn't just all of a sudden reappear in her life again. My thoughts were erratic and certainly weren't rational by any stretch of the imagination. Maybe it was the scotch. Maybe it was the fact that I had felt something looking at the girl on TV. Regardless, I pushed forward with my notes, throwing all caution to the wind.

This was REALLY Crazy!

I slowed my frantic pace down and started to think. I started to try and gather my thoughts so that they would make sense. I realized that my feelings for Casey had been buried deep within me over the years since Julie's death. It had been my choice to do that, but now, now I had a shovel in hand and was ready to dig. Feelings of anticipation started to pour out of me. Whether I was rational or not, I had to try and find out where Casey lived, to contact her. But I couldn't do it by letter. Not any more. No, I had to go see her. Any thought of an angry, jealous husband or children was just pushed aside to allow credence for my decision. For the first time since Julie's death, I was "living in the moment" again. I didn't care that that lifestyle had ruined me countless times. I focused on the fact that I was finally *living* again. And that is what drove me. I went to bed that night excited about the possibility, and disregarding any thought of failure. I was going to do this. I was going to find Casey Martin again.

The next day at the office, I asked my secretary, Danielle, to use the Internet to help me find Casey. She was much better at that stuff than I was. My task included contacting our Class Reunion Committee in Deer Park to see if they had a current address. I had not bothered to attend the 25th or 30th reunions. I always found a reason not to attend, but knew the real reason was that I wasn't ready to see Casey, or be reminded of what happened the last time I was in Indiana.

Lisa Schafer, who was in the class of 1970, told me that according to her records, Casey had not attended any of the subsequent reunions either and that they had no current address for her on file. She did say that she thought Casey had moved to Boston a few years ago.

BOSTON! So she WAS a Red Sox fan.

I began to hone my search in Boston, Massachusetts. As it turned out, Boston (and its many suburbs) had a population of over 3 million people, so I turned to a private investigator named Ran Nealy to assist me in my search. Ran was an ex-LAPD detective and a guy that I had used many times in my job as an attorney, and he always got results. I had worked under the assumption that she had married because my searches under her maiden name always came up empty. I had very little information to provide him but he assured me he could locate Casey for me.

Three days later, I received a phone call telling me that he had located a Casey Martin in Boston, Massachusetts. He listed her age as 52 (which was about right, based on my quick mental math) and he said that she'd been born in Indiana (which was also correct, she had been born in Indianapolis). This was as close to a match that I could have hoped for. I just stood there in my office with the phone to my ear trying to grasp what Ran was saying and asking myself if I really wanted to do this. She and I had parted in my hospital room all those years ago with less than kind words. Even though I was heavily medicated at the time, I knew that it had gone badly. What would she think if she found out that I had gone so far as to hire a private investigator to track her down. This was more than an old friend looking up another old friend. This was bordering on obsession.

But I just had to know.

I'd spent way too many of my 53 years on this planet thinking about this woman, and then and there, in my office, on the phone with Ran Nealy, I made myself a promise. If she was married, or if she asked for me to never see her again, then I would acquiesce and never, ever think of her, or look her up, ever again. Making that promise to myself was the only way that I could convince my inner thoughts that this wasn't a bad idea, and to justify what was most assuredly the worst decision I had ever made.

But I just had to know.

Before hanging up, Ran provided me with her address and phone number. After thanking him, I slowly and methodically lowered the receiver back onto the phone rest. I stood there for a few moments trying to map out my thoughts on what I would say after all these years when Casey answered the phone when I called; *IF* she answered the phone. Her husband, or kids could just as easily answer. What then? How would I respond? Who would I say I am? But then I remembered that Ran said the name of the woman he had found was Casey *Martin*. Wouldn't she have changed her name if she were married? I know she was into the anti-war and women's lib movements in college, but she never struck me as a woman who wouldn't change her name.

As I pondered this, I decided to get some air so I left the house and walked around my neighborhood for a couple of miles mentally pouring over the facts as I knew them, and urging myself to make a decision on how to act with the information I had. Ran Nealy hadn't come cheap, and I'd come so far that NOT calling her would be a crime. So I went home, stepped back into my office, and took a leap of incredible faith.

With several deep breaths, I took the receiver from the phone and dialed the number that Ran had given me. As I waited anxiously to hear the first ring, my hands started to shake and could feel my body start to tighten. Then came the second and third ring. My anxiousness increased as the phone kept ringing. After seven rings, I hung up the phone. My entire body exhaled, and I wiped the clamminess of my hands on my pants leg. Again, I asked myself, should I even be trying to contact her after all these years? She'd made it clear fifteen years ago that I had to move on from her.

But I just had to know.

Trying to contact her now was just absurd. She had her life and I had mine. I need to get over this once and for all.

But I just had to know.

I got up from my desk and went into the kitchen to make some lunch and to make a list of things I had to do for the rest of the day. As I was writing a few things down, I found myself starting to sketch a picture of a rose, complete with a thorny stem and leaves. In high school, I used to draw roses just like that at the bottom of all of my letters that I wrote to her. I always thought it classier than drawing hearts, or "XOXO." I looked at the rose that I'd drawn and was inundated with memories of high school. That, coupled with the fact that I hadn't drawn one in years meant something. Finally, my decision became clear. I was now determined to contact her!

Caution, meet wind.

I looked at the phone hanging on the wall in my kitchen and made another decision: I wouldn't try to call her. I would go to Boston to see her. It was classic Chad. This was my moment, and I was living in it. Just like the old days. Any rational reason to not do this went right out the window. For the first time since the reunion, I felt I had a purpose to myself. I'd been the father that Jenny had needed. I'd provided for us as a family, and now she was in school, and I was ready to do something for me. And it felt great to be back.

Before the end of the week, I found myself on the plane approaching Logan International Airport in Boston, Massachusetts. We were on our final descent when my old anxiety began to kick in and I started to hyperventilate and feel light headed. In some weird way, it was a welcome feeling. I closed my eyes and slowly started to take deep breaths. The elderly woman next to me on the plane probably thought I was having an issue with flying--or landing in this case. I gripped the armrests and continued to steady my breathing. I told myself that I was doing the right thing and that everything would be okay. Sure enough, by the time the plane reached the gate, I was feeling okay again and the old woman was happy that I hadn't vomited on her. She even told me as such as we both deplaned.

I grabbed my bag and rented a car. I had already mapped out the directions from the airport to Casey's house before leaving California and had written them down on a 3x5 card. I estimated it would take me about fifty minutes to get to the north suburb where Casey's address was located. I had drilled this down to a science.

During the drive, I rehearsed what I would say (which included various movie lines that I had written down) and prepared myself for what the various scenarios could be. Even though I prepped myself like an attorney before a big trial, I knew when I got there, like always, I would just wing-it. Classic Chad was now in control.

Before I knew it, I had reached the suburb town of Woburn. Even with traffic, it was far less of a drive than the fifty minutes I had figured on. I found Mulberry Street and slowly approached the house where Casey lived. I parked on the curb three houses down and shut the engine off. As I sat there, I once again tried to reassure myself that I was doing the right thing but I also wanted to prepare myself for the possible rejection. Rejection like I had received years ago at the reunion. Back then, I had expected her to be glad to see me, and what I got instead was a bitter reality check. If that happened again, I wanted to be prepared.

I just sat there in the rental car and surveyed the house she lived in, and the surrounding neighborhood, trying to get a sense of Casey's life there. Woburn was a nice, middle class neighborhood, a nice mixture of the working-class older homes and the middle-class newer ones. There was a ton of history in this town, dating back well before the American Revolution. That could be expected from the town built on the mouth of Mystic River. Like many suburbs of bigger metropolitan cities, Woburn was a mini-city upon itself with a big mall, and fast-food places that littered every corner of every busy intersection. Casey's neighborhood was far off the busy path. It was a perfect little place to raise a family. That line of thought triggered more questions (and assumptions) and instead of conjecture, I decided the best way to find out about her life was to just to ask her.

I got out of the car and started to walk up the steps leading to her porch. I now stood in front of her door. I took one final deep breath and swallowed whatever saliva had remained in my throat. I reached for the doorbell--finger extended--but briefly paused for a few seconds, giving one last thought to whether I was doing the right thing.

I just had to know.

I wasn't doing the right thing. I was insane! This was a repeat of 1989, with me thinking things are going to magically work out between us. We'd have a classic Hallmark moment, and a Greek chorus would sing a song about us. Except Greek choruses normally accompanied tragedies. The more I thought about it, the more terrified I got.

Again, I just had to know.

And I pushed the doorbell. I should have walked away, gone to one of the seven thousand Irish pubs that I had passed on my drive in and laughed off my stupidity over a pint of bitter. But then a sense of peace came over me as the chime rang out, because I realized I literally had nothing to lose. The deed was done. Now, I would wait and see the results.

I heard footsteps approaching the front door. As they became louder, my anxiousness started to reappear. The door opened and after fifteen long years I was once again face to face with Casey Martin. She looked exactly the same as she had fifteen years ago, with a few exceptions. Her golden hair now had subtle hints of gray weaved throughout, and her beautiful, forest green eyes were now framed with distinguished age lines. Her body had not let go at all and was still tight where it should be and round at the good parts. She was a marvel to behold. When her brain finally caught up to the rest of her, the expression on her face was one of shock and bewilderment. She stood there looking at me as if she had been the one to have just seen a ghost.

"Chad?" she asked. "What are you doing here?"

"I was just *three thousand miles away* from your neighborhood and I thought that I'd stop by and say hi."

"How...how did you find me?"

"Would you believe that I hired an expensive private investigator who tracked you down by your phone records, tax returns, police reports, and by sifting through your garbage cans at night?"

She gave me a deliberate look. "No."

At least I told her the truth. It was up to her to decide if it was real or not. I had come too far to hide behind lies and deceit. For all intents and purposes, this was the final drive down the field with the clock running down, and my team was down by four points. What happened next would define the rest of my life going forward.

"Do you want to come in?" she offered.

I did. I did want to go in. I wanted to sit down and talk to this woman for hours on end. I had wanted that for years, dating back to our college days. I had put everything on the line for the opportunity to be standing there, at that moment, and all I wanted to do was to step into her house, sit down, and talk.

"Yes," I said. Casey started to move backwards opening the front door just enough for me to squeeze through to the entryway. I felt that by stepping through that doorway, I was throwing the Hail Mary pass to try and win the game. My life's definition lay on the other side of the door.

And I stepped through.

Once in the house, she led me to a sitting room and asked me if I would like something to drink. Looking around, I didn't see a wet bar, but did smell the unmistakable scent of freshly brewed coffee.

"If that's coffee I smell, that would be wonderful."

"It is," she said. "Have a seat and I'll be right back."

While she was getting my coffee, I had a quick timeout to assess what had happened, and how things were going. I was inside her house, sitting on her couch, so I chalked it up as a good thing. I had to remain patient, something I could never do when I was younger. I'd learned so much more now. Babies don't run marathons.

I looked around the room. There were pictures on the walls, mostly of Casey and her girlfriends. There was a portrait of her father that had to be recent, and the mountain of a man had been reduced to a tired, old facsimile of his former self. The man in the picture would not have intimidated me in the slightest. One thing I did notice was that there weren't any pictures of Casey with a man, or Casey with children. My hopes started to climb.

"You like it black, right?" she asked as she sat a cup and saucer down on the table in front of me.

"As night," I replied. "Thank you."

She took a seat on a chair to my left. Her body language screamed that this was quickly becoming uncomfortable for her.

"So, how've you been?" we asked each other, almost in unison. We shared a laugh.

"You first," I said.

"It's a long story," she replied.

I couldn't wait to hear it, I had plenty of time.

"I don't even know where to start," she said.

"Start with you leaving the Deer Park hospital fifteen years ago," I said. She looked at me as if I had just stabbed her. "Look, Casey, that was a bad time. The worst time of my life. I was a much different person then. It took me years to get my head straight, and to get my priorities straight, and only then was I able to finally move on.

"I hope you don't think what you did or said to me that night was wrong, because it wasn't. You were right. About everything. I just wanted to come by, chat for a bit, find out how your life turned out, then I will fly back to California. It is as simple as that."

She looked at me as if registering each word I had said. She took a sip of her coffee and then set it down next to mine.

"Fair enough," she said.

We started talking about generalities. The description of her life read like a bio sheet in the front of a *PLAYBILL* magazine that you get when you attend a touring version of a Broadway play. After Miami College, she went on to Indiana State and got her masters in education. She had been teaching at a local university for the past 25 years and had recently taken a sabbatical, with the hope of possibly researching a paper on twentieth century perceptions of seventeenth century English Literature.

She had married in 1991, to a fellow teacher, but it ended in divorce five years later. She explained how she had rushed into it, and while they both had the best of intentions, they just weren't compatible as a couple.

I kept asking questions, about her career, about her not having kids, about everything. I wanted to know everything about her, where she had been and where she was going. After all this time, I just wanted her to keep talking. She was finally relaxed, and we were able to laugh more and we each told stories and reminisced.

We talked about Julie, before and after the accident. I told her how proud I was of Jenny, even though she and I had trouble connecting because she still struggled with the loss of her mom and somewhat blamed me. I explained to Casey how I felt; that I was Jenny's father, and even if she hated me, I still loved her more than anything on this planet. It was cathartic to talk about it, to be honest. I used to write this all out in letters and send it, but this was much better. This was the conversation I'd been waiting to have for years.

After the third cup of coffee had been poured, Casey finally asked the question that had been looming since I first rang the doorbell.

"Chad, why are you here?" she asked. "What are you looking to accomplish? What do you really want from me?" It was a question that I knew was coming, yet even after all this time, I didn't have an answer for her.

I chuckled and shrugged my shoulders. "Casey, for the past thirty years, I have been thinking about you, and trying to forgive myself for what I did to you. You were more than a high school flame. You were my best friend, my confidant, and when I lost you--when I screwed this up--I didn't just lose a girlfriend. I lost everything.

"I went off, and I found a new love, and a new life, but I always missed my friend. I always missed you. Julie was my world, and Jenny is everything to me, but losing a best friend is irreplaceable.

"Life dealt me a crappy hand," I continued. "I lost my best friend, I lost my wife, and I lost my daughter. I'm here because I decided I had nothing else left to lose. You brought out a part of me that I am desperate to find again. I needed to talk to you. I'm not looking for love. I don't need a girlfriend. I need my friend again. That's why I'm here."

She looked at me and asked me a question that I wasn't expecting. "Why me?"

"What do you mean? I don't understand?"

She sat back in her chair. "I mean, why me? What was it about me that made you so dedicated for all these years? I mean, It's flattering and all, but why me? I wasn't the best looking, or smartest girl you've ever dated, I mean, your wife was a medical doctor for crissakes! I can't compete with that. And you still look great. You probably have your pick of women to date, especially out in sunny California. But instead, you're here, talking to me about your life, your feelings and emotions.

"I'm just an adjunct English professor at a small liberal arts college who dumped you in college, who is losing the battle of age and weight, and who has ignored you for over 30 years. I just want to know why?"

I hadn't thought about that, about how it had affected her all these years later, and while I could have gone on for hours, I just smiled and gave her a simple response.

"What can I say, you made a helluva impact on me!"

She leaned forward, held my gaze, and then lowered her head and burst out laughing. I started laughing, too.

"Chad Breckenridge, you are indeed a crazy man."

I nodded in agreement, "Yes I am." Finally, I had to ask, "Did you receive my letters?"

She hesitated briefly. "I did. My dad would send me boxes full of them every month. I have to admit, I admired your persistence."

That was it? She admired my persistence?

"And…" I inquired.

"And…" she replied. "Well, your writing certainly got better over the years."

I laughed, I guess it was the teacher in her, grading my letters like term papers. "Well that's good to know. If you read them, why didn't you respond? I mean, I checked the mailbox every day for the better part of 15 years, waiting for anything, a post card, a letter, *anything* to let me know you still existed. You were my friend. There were times I was desperate to hear from you, when I was having trouble in my marriage, having a crisis of conscious, not knowing what was happening in my life. I needed you to respond and you didn't. Why?"

"I did it for you, Chad."

I was stunned. "I…I don't understand."

"Look, you poured your heart out to me," she explained. "But if I had sent you letters back, then I would have taken you away from your wife and family. We were adults, not grade school pen pals. Like you, I had a life of my own, and as much as I still thought about you, and as much as I allowed myself on occasion to think about what would happen if I did return the letters, I wasn't going to contribute to you wrecking your relationship with Julie like you did with me."

I remembered her words to me in the hospital. *I was your wife's Staci.*

Before I could respond, she continued. "Chad, I loved you. I loved your carefree attitude, your taste for life, your live-for-the-moment enthusiasm and when I was with you, you made me feel like I was the only girl in the world. But I reached a point where I thought you treated every girl like that, and rightly so. I felt that you only continued to pursue me because I was the one that got away. You loved the chase. Since Chad Breckinridge didn't get his way, he tried oh so hard to get it back.

"I still feel that way, I guess…"

"You shouldn't feel that way, Casey," I said. "You were the only girl in the world for me. I was immature, yes. I was stupid, even more so. I wish I had Marty's logic to go with my impulsiveness, and I wouldn't have dated anyone else. I was a world-class jerk.

"I…I can't explain why I did what I did 30 years ago, other than to tell you that I loved you more than anything. And I am desperately sorry for all of the hurt and anguish I brought you. I never stopped caring for you. All this time, I've tried to lose those feelings, bury them, kick them to the curb, but they kept coming back. I wondered where you were and what you were doing. I wondered if you got married, and how I compared to him. Even when I stopped writing you, stopped sending you cards, I still always wished you a silent Happy Birthday and Merry Christmas.

"I loved Julie, and she meant the world to me. She gave me love when I had none, and I even screwed that up. We made the best of our lives, even though I was an asshole. She gave me space and understanding, and I squandered that.

"I miss her terribly everyday, but she's gone," I said. "And as much as I want to move forward with my life, doing so without coming here and laying it all on the line would seem pointless. Casey, I'm sorry for hurting you, and I'm sorry for not being a better person and boyfriend, and I'm trying to make it right."

I paused because I knew what I said next could be a defining moment in my life.

"Casey, if you tell me to leave, I will go back to the airport and fly back to California, and you'll never hear from me again. If that's what you want, the least I can do is honor your wishes. I couldn't do it 30 years ago, but I *am* a different man now, and I *will* honor it, if you request it."

She was quiet, as if thinking it over. To me it felt like a century had passed before she spoke again.

"Well, you've come this far, the least I can do is buy you lunch."

I smiled and breathed a huge sigh of relief. I wasn't ready for what would have happened if she had told me to leave.

"That sounds great."

Casey suggested a small quaint little seafood restaurant out by the harbor named, *Captain Jack's*. She said that if I didn't have fresh lobster while in New England, it was a wasted trip. There was no way I could tell her that just being in her presence prevented this from being a wasted trip.

I noticed as I walked her to the car that she moved a little slower than normal and that she favored her right leg a bit. I meant to ask her about it, but we were in our fifties, we all moved a little slower.

As we drove out to the restaurant, we talked all about her past. She told me that she had moved to Boston in the late 1980s to teach and loved it and decided to stay. She told me about the schools she taught in, and the students that still come by to see her. In fact, she laughed and admitted that when I rang her doorbell, she had expected it to be another one of her former students. It was obvious that she was well loved and respected. It didn't surprise me one bit.

After arriving at the restaurant and being seated, Casey started to open up about how hurt she was when she saw me with Staci at the sorority house all those years ago. I sat there patiently listening to her every word, filled with anger, hate and disgust for what I did to her. I felt like a piñata that was being beaten until all of the candy had fallen out and then beaten some more until it had become detached from the rope that held it suspended above the ground. I just listened and let her get out all of the pain that still remained. Occasionally, I would interject with; "I understand," and "I was completely thoughtless and selfish!"

The crazy thing was, it was heartfelt on a level that I hadn't experienced before. I always apologized for things, but this came from a place that was true. It hurt to hear it all, and I felt I had to say something.

Once Casey had been able to release all of the anger that she had pushed down inside her all these years, she started to shows signs of her inner healing. She finally took a deep breath and casually wiped a few tears from her face.

"Well, I wasn't prepared to do this in public, but I sure feel better having told you how much you hurt me. I didn't realize how much anger I had held within me all these years and how it affected me. You *are* an asshole."

"I know," I said. "I figured it out a few years ago. Unfortunately, there aren't support groups for assholes. There is no Assholes Anonymous. All I can do is apologize, and hope and pray that you can forgive me, and let me show you the new 98% asshole-less Chad." That got a hearty laugh from her.

"Casey, I am an asshole, but I came here to say I'm sorry," I said. "My actions that night with Staci have haunted me for years, even throughout my marriage. I was immature and didn't know what a true relationship was. My life was lived in the moment without regard to anyone else's life around me, including yours. I was stupid, but know that I was in love with you. Real love. I think I loved you ever since seeing you up in the bleachers of the gymnasium that day in high school. And even though I was married, and I loved my wife with every ounce of my being, my feelings for you, on some level, never went away.

"I offer no excuses but only seek your forgiveness."

She leaned over the table toward me and I did the same, not knowing what to expect. She looked me square in the eye and asked me a question that floored me.

"Did you ever cheat on Julie?"

I sat back, not expecting the question. "I…I don't understand."

"Chad, did you ever cheat on Julie?" she repeated. "Yes or no. Don't lie, I can tell if you are."

"No. Never."

"Not once."

"No."

"What if I had wanted you to?" she asked. "What if I wrote you back asking for you to cheat on Julie with me?"

I was stunned. I never even thought of the possibility that I would ever have to choose. It made me realize how foolish I had been, to put her *and* Julie in that situation. Somehow, I knew the answer.

"I would have said 'no,'" I said. And I meant it.

She smiled warmly. "I actually believe you, " she said. "Then you're forgiven, Chad Breckenridge."

At this point, we both relaxed and we continued catching up and telling each other about our lives over the past thirty years. Drinks were brought to the table, followed by a clam chowder that literally melted my soul. We continued talking throughout the entrees. I took Casey's recommendation, well, more of a demand, and had the lobster. She ordered swordfish. We talked about high school, and college, and we revisited my time as a cross dresser. We moved on to dessert, where we shared a piece of pie and I wanted to know all about her ex-husband. She told me his name was Padrig Flannigan, and he was native to Boston, if I hadn't guessed by the name (I hadn't). She didn't say much except that he taught school with her, and had a zest for life that drew him to her. I smiled a little knowing that I hadn't been the only one who had attracted her like that.

She said as soon as they got married things changed. He had been a writer who taught to supplement his income. Unfortunately, he was more interested in *living* like Hemingway than *writing* like Hemingway. He drank every night, and when he was drinking, the relationship became abusive. Verbally, more so than physically.

"Physically, I could have handled," she said. "I would have kicked his ass. Dad taught me how to handle myself. But the verbal abuse..." she paused. "It's hard to come back when the person you think you love tells you that you are worthless everyday." Her voice trailed off.

I grabbed her hand. "You don't have to say anything else. I'm so sorry."

She smiled weakly. "No, I should have known. I was...was trying to fill a void, I guess."

"You are not worthless," I said. "You never have been, and you never will be. To me, you are priceless."

"Thank you," she said. It was then that I noticed how exhausted she looked. Here I was trying to fit in thirty years of catching up in a single day.

"Hey," I said cheerfully, trying to brighten the mood. "I don't even have a hotel yet. Why don't I drop you off at your place, then go get checked in someplace and then we can go have a late dinner and continue our conversation and talk about more pleasant memories."

Casey nodded her head, "That sounds good. I haven't been feeling 100% lately, so maybe some rest will help."

I drove her back to her house, and walked her to the door. After a morning and afternoon of soul-crunching life story sharing, I wasn't sure how to say goodbye. Were we at the handshake stage, or the hug stage? And if it was the hug stage, was it the old friend hug, or the hug of lovers? And I didn't even want to start thinking about the kiss. I decided to just let it flow naturally and see what happened. As we came to her door, I leaned in and gave her a kiss on the forehead, partly out of respect for the time that we had shared in our lives, and partly to make sure I didn't catch whatever she had.

"See you at seven?"

"Sure."

I got back in my car and drove to a hotel in town and I checked into my room. I was emotionally exhausted. I lay down on the bed and just reflected on the past fifteen years leading up to the time Casey and I just had at lunch. It was a cleansing of the souls. Too many questions were filling my mind, too many "what ifs." This chemistry, this strange sensation of being fully connected to another person, was still there with Casey and me. I felt something similar with Julie, not more or less, but different. I knew I had never stopped loving Casey, and now life had finally seen to it that we could come back together. I didn't want to overthink it, and definitely didn't want to jinx it. Either way, I suddenly couldn't wait for seven o'clock to come. I fell into a restful nap knowing that a few miles away, Casey Martin was doing the same.

I woke a couple of hours later and grabbed a quick shower and shave and got dressed. I was ready to go, but still had about two hours before I was to pick her up. The time difference was playing havoc on me.

I walked aimlessly around my hotel for about an hour just thinking, not knowing how I was going to handle this going forward. I had reconnected with her, which was my number one goal, but had no plans for the next step. I felt that deep connection to Casey that I had felt in school, and I knew then that I wanted to pursue this to the fullest. I didn't know what this would do to my improving, but still strained, relationship with my Jenny. I knew that if she wanted to see her father happy, she would approve. Just like old times, I had rushed into this without a plan. It had worked so far, but the new and improved Chad would have a plan in place. So I spent the rest of my time that afternoon making plans.

At six-thirty, I pulled up in front of her house, got out of my car and quickly raced up the sidewalk to her porch and rang the doorbell with the enthusiasm of an eighteen year-old. I was giddy. It was ridiculous.

After a couple minutes, I heard footsteps heading towards the front door, but then they stopped. The door didn't open. Then I heard a few more steps and slowly the front door opened to a six-inch crack. Casey stood there looking at me and it was obvious that she really had the flu.

Of all the times, I thought.

She wasn't dressed, and I wasn't sure what to do because she didn't back away from the door so that I could enter the house.

"Hi," Casey said softly. Something was definitely wrong but what could have happened since lunch?

"Casey, is something wrong?" I asked. "You look like hell."

"Thanks," she said. "I just have this...flu I can't shake. I thought it was just a cold, but it got worse as the day went on. I hate to cancel dinner tonight, but I'm so tired and not up for conversation. I'm going to the doctor tomorrow and will get some medication, so why don't we do this tomorrow? Will you still be in town?"

Truth is, I had no idea how long I was going to stay. My years of time with my law firm gave me the status and freedom that allowed me to come and go as I pleased.

"I'm in town for a while," I said. "Do you want me to take you to the doctor?"

She shook her head. "No, that's fine. I'll just be there for a few minutes anyway, nothing to worry about. I should have taken care of myself, but you know these modern flu bugs, it seems like you can't fully shake them. I'll be alright."

I gently grabbed her hand, and once again kissed her forehead and backed away.

"I'm staying at the Hampton on I-93," I said. My room number is 242 if you want to call me. I'll get in touch with you tomorrow afternoon and make sure you're okay. And if you're up to it, we'll do dinner."

Casey nodded her head. "Sounds good." She offered me a smile and then the door shut. I heard the locks latch and I walked back to my car wondering what I was going to do with the rest of my night.

The next day, I called into the office and spoke with my secretary, Danielle, who had been with me for just over six years and was someone I trusted fully. She was slightly older than my daughter, and although she had a family of her own, had acted as much as a friend as an employee. She had always asked me to holiday dinners, and I had always politely declined. I shared with her the reason I had gone to Boston, and before I left the office, she gave me a hug and wished me luck.

I told Danielle I was staying in Boston for a few days, and that I could get some work done from here. She asked how everything was going, and I joked that I had waited fifteen years for this, and that I'd picked the one week that Casey was sick. We both laughed, and then she gave me my messages. I got off the phone and returned a few calls, asking my clients to give me a few days to get back to them, as I was out of town visiting a sick friend.

With business out of the way, I sat at the desk in my room and thought about my family. I wondered how proud my father would have been to see me as a successful attorney. My brother Alex lived in Denver and had become a sports writer for the Denver Post. We exchanged holiday and birthday cards and talked on the phone every six months or so. Ever since mom and dad passed, Alex and I hadn't kept in touch as much as we should have. Maybe it was time to change that. This trip to Boston had become a full-fledged journey down memory lane. It was time to right all wrongs. Another new Chad was being born, whether I liked it or not.

Around five, I called Casey at home to check in and make sure she was feeling okay. As soon as she picked up the phone, I knew something was wrong.

"Hey, gorgeous," I said. "How're you feeling?"

Her voice sounded distant. "Chad, I...um. I'm feeling a bit better, but not quite up for dinner. I'm sorry."

I tried to be as enthusiastic as possible. "Hey, that's okay," I said. "No problem at all. We'll try again for tomorrow night. I want you to be back to 100%. I'm not going anywhere."

There was a long pause on her end. "I'm not sure," she said. "But I guess we can try then."

I found that strange. "Okay then, same time tomorrow night?"

Casey hung up the phone without saying goodbye. It didn't make sense. Now I didn't know what was going on. I walked and paced the room and my mind played out every possible scenario, most of them bad. One thing I knew for certain, I was going over to her house the next night regardless of what she said.

At seven the next night, I pulled up in front of her house and took a deep breath. Whatever magic had been there two days ago was slipping away and I had to fix it.

I knocked on the door, and like before, there was hesitancy to her answering. And like before, she opened it with the intent of sending me away.

I tried to be cheerful by playing it off like I wasn't noticing her erratic behavior.

"Hey Casey," I said, smiling. "Hope you're feeling better. I did some research on some great Boston seafood places, and I can't wait to take you to this one right on the water."

She looked down and took a deep breath.

"No Chad, I can't go," she said. "Look, It's been wonderful to reconnect with you, and I hope that you were able to find some closure, but to think we can pick things up where they left off after all these years is foolish."

"Casey, I don't--"

She interrupted "Chad, you got what you wanted, my forgiveness and my admission that I still had feelings for you. And I hope that gives you some comfort. But now it's time to go on with our lives and make the best of what we have left."

"I want to make the best of what we have left with you," I stammered.

"But I don't," she shot back. "Don't make this harder than what it is already. If you love and respect me as you claim, you'll respect my decision and leave me alone."

I was stunned and speechless. I took a step back, looked around searching for the right words to say, hoping that she would smile and tell me that she was kidding.

She didn't.

Instead, she looked me in the eyes and said softly, "Please, Chad?"

"Okay." It was all I could say. She closed the door and then the porch light went off. I stood there in the dark wondering what had just happened.

I slowly made my way off the porch and down the stairs to my car. For a moment, I stopped and turned back as if there might be a chance that she had second thoughts, that she would be standing on the porch, ready to call me back.

She wasn't.

I sat in the car for a moment trying to wrap my head around everything. I was confused and heartbroken and at a loss on what to do and how to proceed. After a few minutes, I started the car and pulled away from the curb. I thought that maybe I had seen her silhouette peeking out of the bay window of her front room as I drove away, but it could have just been wishful thinking. I made my way back to the hotel and immediately proceeded to check out. I drove directly to the airport and took the next flight home.

Tony Bennett once sang that he left his heart in San Francisco. I'd left mine in Woburn, Massachusetts.

Chapter 26

I arrived back in southern California only to find myself mystified and confused as to what had happened. Emotionally, I had gone from the top of the world to the lowly bowels of hell in just two days. And I had a cross-country flight to go over everything that had happened. Something just wasn't right with Casey. Her 180-degree turnaround left so many more questions than answers. I'd spent years interviewing witnesses and taking depositions and I knew when someone was hiding something, and she was definitely hiding something. I wanted to honor her wishes, and in so doing, honor my promise that if she rejected me, I would never try to contact her ever again, but the more thought I put into it, the more I realized that maybe what she needed wasn't to be left alone, but for someone to show how much they cared.

I was that someone.

That was when I decided that I was going to find out what was going on, and find out why she rejected me when all seemed to be going so well.

Over the next couple of weeks I tried calling her a few times, and I sent her e-mails, but as usual I didn't receive any response. I replayed the events of the trip over and over in my mind, and my gut instinct was telling me that something had happened. We had talked, we'd had lunch, we'd caught up on our lives, and then she got sick and removed herself from the equation. I mean, it was just the flu! I could have acted as her nurse and brought her back to health. Why did she send me away? After a month of unreturned phone calls, and unanswered emails, I had to try something new.

I decided that I had to return to Boston to see her again and once and for all find out what had happened. She may hate me for the intrusion, but I was back to betting all-in, because there was nothing left for me to lose. Once again, I made myself the promise that if she rejected me I was done with her forever. I even wrote the promise down and gave it to Danielle for safekeeping. Whatever the outcome, this was it.

Two days later I arrived back in Boston. After departing the airport, I made my way through dense afternoon traffic and arrived at Casey's house at just after six in the evening. With fierce determination, I got out of my car and walked up to Casey's front door. I rang the doorbell with authority, no hesitation this time. I didn't hear anything inside. Again and again, I rang the doorbell without any response. I would have called her first, to let her know I was coming, but she wasn't taking my calls. This was an all or nothing trip, and as I stood there on her porch, I feared it was going to be all for nothing.

I tried to peek through the stained glass in the front door to see if I could see anything or anybody inside, but only saw shadows. I walked around to the side of the house and found a side entry. I jostled the door but it was locked. I walked all around the house until I reached a large window in the back. I looked inside and it appeared dark and vacant. Had she moved? It had only been a month. She hadn't mentioned anything of the sort during our chat and there was no way she could have organized a move that quick.

As I walked back around the front corner of the house, I noticed her neighbor standing at the door, watching me. I offered a wave and walked over to the house.

"Excuse me, my name is Chad Breckenridge, I'm an old high school friend of Casey. Did she move?" This woman didn't know me from Adam, but my professional appearance and age would have told her that I wasn't out to rob that place.

"She still lives there," the old woman offered. "But I haven't seen her this week. She's had so many visitors. I tried to go over there a couple of times myself after she got back from the hospital." Her thick Boston accent made all of her "Rs" sound like long "As."

"Hospital?" I asked. "Is she okay?"

"I can't answer that," the woman said. "She's been in and out for the last few weeks. She might be there now."

"Which hospital?" I asked. "It's important that I talk to her."

"She was at Caritas Carney Hospital over in Dorchester," the woman said. "But that was the first few times."

"A few times!?!" I asked, getting frantic. *What the hell was wrong with her?*

"She's been sick awhile, sweetie," the woman said matter-of-factly.

"Can you tell me how to get to that hospital?" I asked.

"Sure thing," the woman said and disappeared into her home. She returned a minute later with a sheet of stationary with directions written down on it.

I took the paper from the woman and thanked her. I got back into the rental car and headed immediately over to the hospital.

Had this flu been worse than I thought? I pondered that question on the drive, thinking back to the way Casey had looked the last time I had seen her. I remembered her slight limp to her walk, and how she got so tired as the day went on. And the times I saw her after that lunch, she had just looked worn out. Maybe it had just been the flu, and it had developed into pneumonia. Julie used to tell me that could happen if I didn't take it easy when I got sick. Could my visit have pushed Casey over the limit? I had too many questions, and asking myself was getting me nowhere. I couldn't get to Dorchester quick enough. Since I wasn't even sure she was in this particular hospital, I parked in the patient load and drop off lot in case I had to get back into the car for a trip to another facility. Wherever she was in this state, I was going to find her.

I got out of my car and started walking at a brisk pace toward the main entrance to the hospital. Upon reaching the front information desk, I asked the elderly lady behind the counter if a Casey Martin was a registered patient there. The woman perused the computer's patient intake list and after a moment confirmed it.

"Yes sir," she said. "She's on six north, room 607." She then stood up and pointed down the hall, as if she had done this countless times before. "Go down the hall, following the green strip on the floor. The green strip will lead you to the elevators. Take them to the sixth floor and then head right." She was still giving me directions as I thanked her and started to walk away. I reached the elevator bay and found four doors. I assumed that all of them went to the sixth floor so I kept pushing the up arrow until one of the doors opened. Frantically, I entered the elevator and pushed the glowing "6" button. Before the doors shut, a hand appeared and the doors slid open again. Four people got on the elevator. The doors started to slid shut when I heard someone call out to "hold the doors."

C'mon, people, there are four elevators here!

Finally, the doors shut without any further interruption and then, as luck would have it, each person on the elevator with me needed to get off on each floor between one and six. I was losing my mind with each passing second. When the doors started to open on the sixth floor, I jumped through them turning right as directed. I was in such a hurry, I missed the sign that said: 6N - ONCOLOGY.

I reached the nurses station where I asked in which direction room 607 was. The nurse pointed down the hall without even looking up from her charting. As I slowly walked down the hall I started looking around at the various patient rooms and felt the moroseness of this floor. There didn't seem to be a lot of joy here.

As I approached room 607, I saw a doctor walk out of her room. He wore a white coat over regular slacks and a button up shirt, which told me he was more than just the attending physician.

"Excuse me, doctor?" I asked.

The doctor turned and looked at me. "What can I do for you?"

"Is this Casey Martin's room? Is she okay? What is wrong with her?" The questions kept coming and I must have looked like a complete loon.

"And you are?" he asked.

SHIT! SHIT! SHIT! SHIT!

"I'm...her husband," I said before my brain could talk me out of it. "Pad...er...Patrick O'Flaherty." That wasn't right. His name was...something else. I was screwing this up. I expected security to show up any second to escort me from the premises.

"I wasn't aware Ms. Martin was married," the doctor said suspiciously.

"We're separated," I explained. "Five years now. I took the dogs and moved to California, she stayed here. We've just never got the official divorce." The lies just kept coming, chambering themselves one after another. If this kept up, I would have come up with the exact scenario when I had proposed and song that we had danced to at our wedding.

"Your accent seems to be recovering, Mr. O...umm..."

"O'Flannigan." *That was it*!

The doctor gave me an incredulous look. All hell was about to break loose and I just had to know what was going on. I looked him square in the eyes and I opened my heart up.

"Look, sir," I said. "I love my wife with all of my heart and I always have. She tends to keep things from me to protect me, but her sister called and told me what was going on, and I caught the first flight out here. I just need to know that she is okay."

He knew I wasn't who I said I was. He probably knew that Casey didn't have a sister. He could have easily picked up the phone and possibly even had me arrested. Instead, he looked towards her room, and then back at me. "I'm sorry Mr. O'Flannigan, but I'm not allowed to discuss the specifics of her condition."

"I'm an attorney," I blurted out, as if that could help me here.

"...then you know why I can't talk about her condition, right?"

I looked down and caught a glimpse of his nametag, Doctor Mason, and noticed the word *oncologist* below it. Then I quickly looked around the area. This was no ordinary hospital floor. And I saw the sign on the wall. Oncology. Julie had taught me enough to know what that meant.

"Cancer?"

"Mr. O'Fla--"

"My wife was a doctor," I said. "In California. I know...I know what's going on. Is she awake? Can I see her?"

"Well," the doctor began. "Visiting hours are over soon. But seeing as you're her husband, I can make an exception." I looked at him, and he looked at me, and an unspoken understanding was passed between us.

"Thank you," I said. He stepped out of the doorway to let me pass. He then leaned in close to me.

"Whoever you are, if she asks you to leave, you leave. If you create any problems at all, I will have security here faster than you can come up with a new name. Are we clear?"

"Yeah, and thanks." I held out my hand and he took it. I stepped into the room before he could change his mind.

The room was lit only by a wall light above her bed and by the myriad machines that beeped, buzzed and whirred at her bedside. Casey was lying asleep. There were tubes going in and out of her and her face, once round and full of life had shrunk down to thin and pale. She was wearing a scarf on top of her head, and I guessed that her beautiful blond hair was gone. Despite all of that, she looked peaceful and beautiful, and my heart yearned for her to wake up so we could talk again.

I pulled a chair up next to the bed and waited. A few minutes later, a nurse came in to check on Casey. I wasn't sure if I'd be allowed to stay, but the nurse looked at me and smiled.

"Dr. Mason wanted to make sure I got you set up for the evening if you were staying, Mr. O'Flannigan."

"Thank you, but I don't think--"

"I went to school with your brother," the nurse said, her Boston accent obliterating the *R*'s at the end of every word. "Aren't you John O'Flannigan's little brother?"

"No, I don't think--"

"But I know you," the nurse reasoned. "Your family--"

"I didn't grow up here," I said. "I'm from the southern Indiana O'Flannigans." The lies just kept coming.

"Well, you can stay as long as you'd like. I'm sure your wife would like it if she woke up to a familiar face."

"Thank you."

The nurse finished her duties and stepped out of the room and Casey and I were alone. I sat and watched her breathe, her chest rising and falling with each breath. I wished so much that I could do something for her. Her actions the last month or so suddenly made sense. I felt ashamed for being mad at her for blowing me off, and I still felt mad, because she didn't let me help her. She had decided to lie to me and go through this alone. I could not--would not allow that. Not now, not ever. I was going to stay here and I was going to be at her side every step of the way.

The nurse came in once every hour, and I finally accepted a pillow and blankets. I was also given a makeshift cot to sleep on next to the wall, but I stayed in the chair. I wanted my face to be the one that Casey saw when she first woke up. I drifted off to sleep, serenaded by the beeps of the machinery that filled the room.

The next morning, I woke up and stood and stretched. It was just after six. Casey was still asleep, but as I sat back down, she stirred and opened her eyes. Her beautiful green eyes still looked the same. I smiled and my heart was alive with warmth. Casey saw me and then blinked a few times to make sure she was awake.

"Chad?" she asked. "I...I don't understand. What're you--"

"I was craving some of that amazing clam chowder," I said. "So I flew out here and stopped by your place. Your neighbor said that you were here. Besides, you know me, when have I ever taken 'No' for an answer?"

Tears welled up in her eyes. "I'm sorry, I'm so sorry. I didn't want you to know. I didn't want you to see me like this."

I grabbed her hand. "Hey, I understand, I just wish you would have told me."

"Chad," she said. "I'm dying."

"Not today," I assured her.

That got a smile out of her. Her hand gently squeezed mine.

"It came so quick," she said. "I'm stage four. It's bad. They're discharging me tomorrow and signed me up for hospice care."

"Casey, I'm sorry."

She started crying. "I wanted to tell you, but I didn't want you to go through losing someone else. Not after Julie. I thought maybe if I just froze you out, you'd stay away."

I squeezed her hand. "Hey, it's okay. I understand. I want to spend as much time with you as possible, as much as you'll let me. Who's going to take care of you when you go home?"

"I...I don't know," she said. "I don't have any family here. Dad's back in Indiana, and he's not in the best of health himself. Hospice will visit, but I guess I'll be back here soon." She looked around the room and loneliness swept over her face.

At that point, I knew what I was going to do. There was no way in hell that I was going to let the love of my life go through this alone.

"I'll stay with you," I said. "I'll stay here in Boston and take care of you. I promise you that you won't have to come back to this place."

"Chad, you can't," she protested. "I can't ask you to do that."

"You didn't ask," I said. "Casey, I want to do this. I want to take care of you like you've deserved to be taken care of your entire life."

"But what about your work? What about your daughter? You just can't stop you life for me."

"I want you to be my life," I said. "I've always wanted you to be my life. And besides, I've earned the right to take a vacation from work, and Jenny's in school. I'll be fine."

I leaned over and gave her a gentle kiss on the lips.

"This is what I want," I said. "Give me this?"

She nodded and I took her hand in mine. Whatever life had left to throw at us, we would handle it together.

When the nurse brought in her meal, I excused myself and went to the lobby to call Danielle and tell her my change of plans. I told her I was taking a 3-month leave of absence, and while I would tie up any loose ends from Boston, that I would not take on any new clients. She was equal parts happy and sad for me. I thanked her for her help and told her I'd be in touch.

After I hung up, I took a deep breath and called Jenny. I wasn't sure how she would take this. I hadn't even told her I was trying to date again, and now here I was 3,000 miles away with a woman I had loved for most of my life. This was not going to be easy.

"Hello?"

"Hi sweetheart."

"Hey, Dad," she said. "I'm on my way to class and don't have a lot of ti--"

"Honey, I need for you to do me a favor."

She paused. "If I can, what's up?"

I took a deep breath. "I'm in Boston, taking care of a friend. I need you to go check on the house occasionally, and send me some clothes and my mail to the address I'm going to e-mail to you."

"Wait, what do you mean a friend?"

I remained calm. "I'm in Boston. I'm taking care of an old friend."

The next words were spoken as each word was hitting a nail. "Is it that girl?"

"What girl?"

"The one that Mom used to be concerned about. Your high school girlfriend?"

Of course Julie would have told our nine-year-old daughter about Casey. It was her style to justify everything that she did in life, and Casey was the reason that Julie had come to Indiana with me. Not to be with me during a good time in my life, or to meet my old school chums. It was always about Casey. And she had told this to Jenny.

Suddenly, everything made sense. Jenny's reaction, and her distance to me these past fifteen years. She must have seen Casey as "another woman," and she must have thought that I had been cheating on her mother.

"Yes, her name is Casey, and that 'girl,' as you refer to her, is dying."

There was silence. "I'm sorry."

I regained my composure.

"Sweetheart, I'm sorry," I said. "I'm so sorry. I miss your mom every day, and I loved her with every ounce of my soul. But she is gone. It was a terrible accident, and don't think for one second that I don't wish it was me that died, or that she and I had died together. But that isn't what happened, okay. I was left behind. And I have tried to be the best father I can for you, even when you wouldn't even give me the time of day."

"It's been fifteen years, and at some point, you have to quit hating me. It was an accident. And I will always love and be proud of my little girl, but right now, I need to take care of Casey for as long as she has left. I want your support, I need your help, but I'm doing this either way."

There was another pause on her end. I thought for a second that the call had dropped. "I'll do what I can," she said finally. "Is there anyone here you want me to call? What about work?"

"Thanks, but no," I said. "She's on something called a "palliative care route" now, I'm just here to keep her comfortable and keep her at home for as long as she has left."

There was yet another long pause and then Jenny spoke again. I could hear the apathy and the anger removed from her voice. I think then, and right then, she finally got it. She finally understood that Casey was on, what we called in 'Nam, "short time."

"I'll take care of things here and make sure you get clothes and supplies. I love you, Dad, and...I never hated you."

"I love you too, princess," I said, my heart lifting at the words. "And thank you."

I pressed the END button on my phone and walked into a nearby restroom. I climbed into an empty stall and broke down crying. I was in there for at least twenty minutes.

The next couple of days I prepared myself for the coming weeks-- and hopefully months, or better yet YEARS--that lie ahead. I met the hospice staff and learned what my role would be, I helped get Casey home and comfortable, and got myself settled in as well. Her room had been gutted of her bed and furniture and had been replaced with a hospital bed, wheelchair and equipment to help her cope over the time she had left. The sickness had begun its takeover of her life. Gone were her warm, colorful, beautiful things, replaced by the cold, steel and sterile apparatus that would ease her into death. This made her sad and I did my best to keep her in good cheer.

At the end of the third day, there was a routine of people coming and going; friends, neighbors, former students and various people with the hospice agency. I became used to people in the house during the day, and barely noticed when new people walked in. I was, for all intents and purposes, her caretaker.

One day, as I was sitting there with Casey reading to her the *Globe* story on Pedro Martinez's chance at the Cy Young, I heard someone come in the room. I figured it was another nurse or friend, so I didn't bother to turn around. I just kept reading. Then I felt a hand on my shoulder and a gentle squeeze. I turned around to see Jenny standing there with a couple of suitcases and bags.

"Hi Daddy," she said. It was the first time she had called me daddy in fifteen years.

I smiled and stood from my chair. "You didn't have to hand-deliver them." I enveloped her within my arms. I could never have put a price on how much her being there meant to me at that moment. "But I'm glad you did."

Jenny hugged me back. She had not hugged me like this in so long that I didn't want it to end.

"Can't trust the post office," she said. "You know that. I had a couple days off and thought I'd come see my father." We held the embrace and then she whispered in my ear. "Oh, Daddy, I'm so sorry. I did blame you for Mom and I couldn't allow myself to forgive you. I thought that if I did, I would forget mom."

"Oh, Princess," I whispered back. "I've never loved you any less. We all had things to work through. I'm sorry I failed you as a father."

She laughed. "You failed me? Oh God, no. I failed you as a daughter. I just…I miss Mom so much and I didn't want you to replace her."

I pulled back and looked at her, "Oh, Sweetheart, no one will ever replace your mother. Ever."

Jenny looked around me and saw Casey looking at us, watching this long overdue exchange with tears in her eyes.

"Hi, I'm Jenny Breckenridge," Jenny announced with a slight wave and a smile.

Casey smiled back. "It is a great pleasure, Jenny," she said. "I feel like I know you so well already. Your father has told me so much about you. Hell, he doesn't stop talking about you"

Jenny appeared embarrassed. "Really? Because I haven't been the best daughter to him. And I guess I owe you an apology as well."

Casey shook her head. "No apology necessary."

"I'm staying for a few days," Jenny said. "I'd like to...get to know you guys. Both of you." She took my hand. "Again, I'm so sorry, Daddy."

"You can stay here," Casey offered. "There is a spare room in the back. And who knows, maybe you can use my situation for extra credit or something."

Jennifer did in fact stay at the house, and spent a lot of time asking Casey about the cancer and the processes. I could see the future doctor emerge within Jenny as she spoke about treatments and care. I watched them blossom into friends during those two days together. They talked about everything, and Casey learned all about Julie. As the brief visit went on, I marveled in the fact that my daughter was here with me, and was overjoyed in how she handled Casey. Julie would have been so proud of her daughter. I know I was.

For the next two months, I took over as primary care for Casey. I realized that this was the first time in my life that my "live for the moment" attitude could work for someone else. For most of my life, I saw other people, not as human beings, but as a way to reach my own goals, or as things to fill whatever temporary void I was feeling. Marty had preached that to me enough times growing up, and now, only as Casey lay dying in front of me, did I see what he was talking about all those years. And for the first time in my life, I didn't care about me; I was fully devoted to taking care of another person. And I loved the feeling.

On her good days, when her strength and vitality were strong, I would take her for walks around the nearby park, or we'd jump in the car and go sightseeing. Even in her condition, she would still guide me around Boston, telling me stories about certain monuments, or buildings. We even took in a Red Sox game. There was a ton of history to learn in that city, and learning about the past seemed to prolong our future.

One day, I even drove her out to the country and we rode in a hot air balloon. Casey was thrilled and kept grabbing my arm in excitement as the balloon lifted off the ground. We both realized that most of our lives were spent running, unable to slow down long enough to touch, breath in, or see the nature around us. As we slowly flew over the countryside, we saw farmers tending to their harvests, and the trees beginning to turn, the beautiful colors of fall starting to peek out of the green. We noticed the ever so slight movement of the clouds; watching them form into different shapes as they crossed the sky. Nature was coming alive before our very eyes and there was beauty in everything. We soon found ourselves drifting over a lake where we saw people in sailboats. I smiled at the memory, and Casey caught my eye and laughed to herself.

"I remember. You were trying to impress me with your sailing knowledge and about killed us both. I did love the fact that you wanted to impress me."

"If we tried today, I'd probably succeed. I haven't been sailing since."

She looked down at the lake, then back at me.

"Even though you were out of your element, I felt safe and trusted you," she said. Then I lost that feeling of trust and being safe. That was the biggest problem between us, Chad. I lost that ability to understand what trust and feeling safe was like." She took my hand in hers and pulled me to her. "Today, right here, I know what that's like again." I didn't reply, we just held each other for the rest of the ride.

On the days that she was too weak to get out of bed, we would watch movies or baseball games together, or just talk. Jenny called me every couple of days to check in. I was happy that she had taken an interest in Casey. In fact, it meant the world to me.

The hospice nurse would come by a couple days a week, and when we stayed in, we always seemed to have visitors, but most of the time, it was just the two of us. And I used every opportunity to tell her that I loved her, and even when she was embarrassed that I had to care for her, I simply replied that there was no place else I'd rather be.

One night, as I was preparing dinner for us, and told her that fall was approaching, and that the leaves had all turned and were dropping. I suggested to her that the next time she felt strong, that we should go jump in the in the leaves like we used to do. She was quite a bit weaker by this point, and we both knew we wouldn't be jumping in the leaves. She told me, with a deep sadness in her voice, "I don't know how many tomorrows I have left."

"Every tomorrow will be ours," I replied.

One beautiful Tuesday afternoon, I decided to take Casey for a ride to a special place that I had planned. Her physical body was ravaged at that point, and even getting out of bed had been difficult for her. She was starting to surrender. I saw it in the way she looked at things, at me. I wasn't ready for her to throw in the towel. I had hoped that the trip would awaken good memories of the past, and that in turn would trigger a craving for living a while longer.

I drove us to the park that we had used to come to when she was first released from the hospital. Back when she could walk, and talk and laugh without fits of wrenching pain wrecking her body. As I parked the car, Casey slowly surveyed the area and without a word, looked over at me and started to cry. I took her hand in mine.

"This is going to be a special day," I said. "This is our day; our time." I got out of the car and went around to the trunk and removed her wheelchair and oxygen tank. Then I slowly helped her out of the car and into the chair. I pushed Casey over to a heavily wooded area and began gathering leaves into a pile. I heard a low weak voice call out.

"What're you doing, you crazy old man?"

I turned to her and smiled.

"We're jumping into a pile of leaves." Casey shook her head in bemusement.

"Chad Breckenridge, you are something else." I then saw Casey reach her arm down, trying to help me. I walked over to her and took the few leaves she had gathered and put them on the top of the pile. I then pushed her to an area that was about twenty feet from the pile that I had created.

"I'm going to count to three and then we'll run and jump, together. Got it?" Casey, all but exhausted, looked at me.

"You count to two and I'll say three," she offered.

"Okay then."

"One, two and--"

"Three!"

I pretended to run real fast but was actually pushing her at a leisurely pace. Casey raised both hands in the air, as if on a carnival ride and I could hear her laughter. I brought the wheelchair to a stop and disconnected her oxygen tank. She looked at me, and I saw those beautiful green eyes flickering with life. I picked her up out of the chair and while holding her body tight into mine, we both fell into the leaves. We laughed together as we held each other close. The crackle of dead leaves, and the smell of fall enhanced the feelings that had encroached over us both. We lay together for a few minutes in silence, listening only to the sound of birds chirping, and leaves rustling.

"Forever Today," she said, and then turned to me. "Remember that?"

I had not heard those words in a long time. That was another time, another place. It could be argued that it had been another Chad and another Casey. So many things had changed from that wonderful fall day back in 1972. A lifetime of ups and downs, wins and sorrows had taken both of us for a wild ride, and now, at the very end, now I had finally found what I had always been looking for.

"I do, " I said. Casey had always been what I had been looking for. "I love you. I have always loved you and will for all time."

"I love you too," she said. "When I'm gone, please remember this time and this place. I'll always be with you and will wait for you on the other side." We didn't say anything else to each other then. We remained in that pile of leaves for a few minutes longer and let the world revolve around us. I looked down and saw that Casey had fallen asleep in my arms and continued to sleep even as I put her back into the wheelchair and took her back to the car. I slowly and gently put her into the passenger side and returned the wheelchair and oxygen tank to the trunk. I got in and started the car, but before I pulled away, I took one last glance at the pile of leaves that we had built. Then I slowly drove her home and put her to bed. She woke briefly as I laid her down and pulled her blankets over her. Her eyes were half open but she offered me a slight smile before going back to sleep. I knew it was time and that she did really love me.

Over the next few days, I sat by her side, holding her hand ever so often, reassuring her I was there. The hospice nurse from the hospital frequented the house, making sure Casey was free of pain and continued to monitor her vital signs.

On Friday evening Casey opened her eyes and looked at me and smiled weakly.

"You're still here?" she whispered. I grabbed her hand tightly and locked our fingers together.

"If I haven't given up on you after all this time, I'm pretty sure I'm in for the long haul," I smiled. "Hey, guess what? The Red Sox won the World Series."

"No way," she said as she smiled. "I guess that I can die now, huh?"

"I'd much rather you didn't," I said. "I'd get bored."

She chuckled at that. "You should get some rest." That was just like her, thinking of others in her time of need.

"I'm not going anywhere, love," I said. "I'll be right here."

She tried to grip my hand, but it was too weak, but she turned her head to me.

"I know," she said. "You always were a little thick-headed."

"You made me this way," I said, and then tears started to race down my cheeks. "I love you, Casey Martin, and I'll cherish these last few months forever."

In the slightest whisper, she said, "I love you, too," and she fell asleep.

An hour later, Casey took a deep breath, slowly exhaled, and then passed. She was gone. At that very moment, my will to live disappeared, and I wanted nothing more than to join her. I felt exhausted and without emotion. I tried to cry and feel the sense of this moment and yet somehow I was at peace. I remained at her side until the ambulance came to take her body.

After she left, I found myself wandering the various rooms of the house, just staring off as if I was in a fog. I stopped and looked at the pictures on the wall and ran my hands over some of the tables and furniture as if hoping to grab Casey's essence from each piece. Slowly, reality started to set in. I didn't know what to do or where to go. My life, my entire reason for being had just been loaded into the back of an ambulance and been taken away. I was alone. More alone than I ever thought possible.

"Mr. Breckinridge?" Carol, the hospice nurse, called to me.

I turned to her, figuring there was additional paperwork to fill out, or something else trivial that needed to be done. "Yes."

Carol was holding a plain white envelope in her hand. "Um, Casey wanted me to give this to you after she passed. She was very insistent that I wait until now to give it to you."

She handed me the envelope and I stared at it intently. It, like the objects in her house, carried Casey's essence. Just holding it made me feel better.

"I have no idea what's in it," Carol said. "A will, perhaps?"

"No," I replied. "We took care of that a couple of months ago."

It was a beautiful ceremony. As per her wishes, I had personally escorted her body back home, which was something I never got to do with my wife. Many people from Deer Park made an appearance to say their goodbyes. Most were friends from high school; others were old college friends and sorority sisters. Her dad was now well into his eighties and showed every bit of his age. He was no longer this beast of a man that had terrified me to my core back in high school. He thanked me over and over for everything that I had done for her in the end. I thanked him for letting me date his daughter all those years ago. We shared a laugh about that and then I excused myself as I noticed that he was starting to cry. A man like that deals with his emotions in his own way.

As I sat there on a folding chair, lost in my own thoughts and grief, the fall afternoon air grew chill as the sun was starting its descent to the horizon. The crowd of friends and family had dispersed and the pastor had come by to shake my hand and offer me his condolences. I sat there staring at her open grave, and the pile of dirt that would soon cover her forever. The trees that surrounded me started to move back and forth more rapidly as the wind moved through the branches. I started to weep. This would be the last time I would ever be this close to Casey Martin, the woman I loved, had always loved. I started to wipe away the tears when I suddenly felt a hand gently placed on my right shoulder.

"Whenever you're ready, buddy," Marty said. He'd flown up for the funeral, both as my support, and because I'm sure he had loved her too. The three of us had spent a lot of time together, and Marty used to say that she was like his sister. He had always been a good man.

"I just need a few more minutes," I said.

Rising slowly to my feet I turned to walk up the hill behind her grave. On the other side of the hill was Lake Whitney. I stopped and turned back and Marty nodded to me, and then he took my seat.

I turned back toward the hill and to the lake, kissed my left hand and then placed it on the headstone that had already been placed. The words cut into the polished limestone read:

Here Lies
Casey Michelle Martin
1951-2004
Forever Today

Then I walked up and over the hill and kept going.

NOW

So all that's left for me to do is to open this envelope and to read Casey's final words. I've gone over every possible scenario, every possible thing that she could say to me. I am dumbfounded that after thirty-six years of not returning any of my letters, she writes one on her deathbed. It's too much to comprehend.

It's time.

My hand is shaking as I finally tear the end of the envelope, careful not to rip the paper inside. I pull the letter out, and open it carefully. I close my eyes, take a deep breath, and then open my eyes to see Casey's final words to me:

Dear Chad,

Our life together has always been...complicated. From the very beginning, it always seemed that you and I just couldn't match up. School, the war, college, life, and now death. Everything kept getting in the way, and we never truly got to experience each other as much as we both wanted to. But now, if you are reading this, I'm gone. We both knew it was coming. But know that I love you now as I write this, and know that I have loved you for most of my life. I don't think I ever stopped loving you. You were a jerk, yes, but still I cared for you, even against my better judgment. I wish that I could explain it better, but I can't. So, the only thing I can do is show you how I've felt for all of these years. Please, go to my dad's house in Indiana. In my old bedroom, in the back of the closet you will find something that was very important to me. Something that I cherished day in and day out for most of my life. Something that kept me going, even when you weren't a part of my life. Then, once you see this, hopefully you will understand that I was always in love with you. Always.

Thank you for loving me back, and being there for me in my darkest hours. Your love alone kept me going these last few months, and I am grateful that I got to spend that extra time with you. Thank you, Chad.

I love you.
Forever...Always

My right hand quivers while holding the note and I spring to my feet. The wood of the dock creaks in protest as I run back and up the hill.

"Marty get in the car now," I scream. Marty sees my face and he doesn't question. "We have to go to Casey's house."

"In Boston?" he asks.

"No, her dad's place," I say. "You remember where it is?" He does. He was the one who told me how to get there all those years before. "Doesn't matter, I'm driving." I'm running now. Marty follows. I'm in the car with the door shut before Marty can even get his door open. The engine starts and we speed off.

"What's at Casey's house?" Marty asks.

"I don't know yet but we're going to find out!"

I'm not sure how long it takes us to get across town to Casey's house, but it felt like an eternity. As we turn down her street I immediately slow the car down to a speed that would challenge a slow moving tortoise. My hands grip the steering wheel and my knuckles go white. I start to breathe a little faster and I find myself holding each breath a little longer than usual. I'm nervous! Fear is engulfing my entire body. What am I afraid of?

I bring the car to a complete stop. I can't drive any farther. What's wrong with me? What's going on here? After a couple of minutes, I inhale a big breath of fresh fall air and then exhale pushing all the air inside my lungs out. I then push ever so slightly on the gas pedal, moving the car forward until I reach her dad's driveway.

Again, I find myself sitting motionless.

"Can we get out now or is this part of the surprise?" Marty asks.

"No, let's go," I say.

We both exit the car and I walk up the driveway to the front door, just as I had done countless times before. I hold the note firmly in my right hand, like it is a sword and I am going to slay a dragon. As I approach the front door, her dad appears and opens it.

"I kinda knew you'd come by soon," he says. I don't question. I enter the home. As my eyes adjust to the light, Casey's dad beckons me to follow him and I do. I proceed toward Casey's old bedroom. Mr. Martin opens the door for me.

"She sent them here a few months ago," he says. "I didn't know why then, but it makes sense now." I nod to him and step into her room. I go to her closet and open the door. I see two large boxes. "Chad Breckinridge" is written on the side of each in Sharpie marker. I pull both boxes out of the closet and drag them to the foot of her bed. They are moderate in weight and I'm puzzled at what they hold.

"I'll leave you be," Mr. Martin says. "C'mon, Marty, lemme show you my baseball card collection. Casey always said you liked the Reds." With that, he takes Marty and they both head back toward the living room.

I sit on Casey's bed and pull one of the boxes closer to me and peel back the lid to see what is inside. As I open the first box, I cannot believe what I am seeing. My eyes just stare at the contents for what seems like ten minutes. The box is full of letters. By the look at some of the envelopes, some of the letters appear to be from a very long time ago. The envelopes have faded, turning from what was white into a yellow milkish color. I reach for one of the letters on top and notice that it is addressed to me. Then I pull several more letters from the box and again notice that they are all addressed to me. I then push my right hand and arm deep into the box, pushing letters to the side until I pull yet another envelope out of the box. This one is also addressed to me in Vietnam. They are boxes full of letters! Letter written but never sent. All these years I thought that she didn't care enough to ever write me back, and all this time, she had been.

My emotions immediately get the best of me. Tears start to run down my cheeks uncontrollably. For the better part of four hours I sit at the edge of the bed and read the letters. Some of them date back to when we were in high school. She had written back every time I wrote. Her letters are filled with words like:

I miss you.
I love you.
I need you.
and most importantly, *I forgive you.*

I sit there and read them. Mr. Martin shuts the bedroom door and leaves me be. That night I fall asleep in Casey's bed holding a letter that reads:

My dearest Chad,

My life has been empty without you. I have never loved anyone more than you. I admit I was so angry for what you did to me, but through the hurt and pain I carried for several years, I learned to forgive.

In your own way, you love me unconditionally and you never ask for anything in return. It was from you that I learned that I am an important and valued person and a woman. It was you that made me whole.

But now your letters have stopped, and I fear that I have finally lost you forever. Know that I will treasure what we had for the rest of my life. Maybe one day soon, we will run into each other, and I can finally tell you all of this. But until then, my love for you remains locked inside me.

I hope you are living a happy, joyful life, and that you still think of me once in a while!

All my Love

Forever Today!!

 Casey

THE END

Made in the USA
San Bernardino, CA
09 March 2015